WILLIAM TREVOR IN PENGUIN

Fiction
The Old Boys
The Boarding-House
The Love Department
Mrs Eckdorff in O'Neill's Hotel
Elizabeth Alone
The Children of Dynmouth
Other People's Worlds
Fools of Fortune
The Silence in the Garden
Two Lives
Felicia's Journey

Short Stories
Collected Stories
Ireland: Selected Stories
Outside Ireland: Selected Stories

Autobiography
Excursions in the Real World

WILLIAM TREVOR

ELIZABETH
ALONE

PENGUIN BOOKS

PENGUIN BOOKS

Published by the Penguin Group
Penguin Books Ltd, 27 Wrights Lane, London W8 5TZ, England
Penguin Books USA Inc., 375 Hudson Street, New York, New York 10014, USA
Penguin Books Australia Ltd, Ringwood, Victoria, Australia
Penguin Books Canada Ltd, 10 Alcorn Avenue, Toronto, Ontario, Canada M4V 3B2
Penguin Books (NZ) Ltd, 182–190 Wairau Road, Auckland 10, New Zealand

Penguin Books Ltd, Registered Offices: Harmondsworth, Middlesex, England

First published by The Bodley Head Ltd 1973
Published in Penguin Books 1988
5 7 9 10 8 6 4

Copyright © William Trevor, 1973
All rights reserved

Printed in England by Clays Ltd, St Ives plc
Filmset in Linotron 202 Palatino

To Jane

1

At forty-one, Elizabeth Aidallbery had a way of dwelling on her past, and when memories were doubtful there were photographs to help her. At two she was anonymous on a tartan rug. At five she was freckled, thin-legged and laughing in a striped dress. At ten she was sunburnt beneath a tree, her pale hair in plaits, standing with Henry in the garden where her own children played now. There was a wedding photograph, an image that revealed the faded blueness of her eyes because it was in colour.

At forty-one, when she examined herself in the mahogany-framed looking-glass in her bedroom, the faded blueness had not altered and there was a beauty still in the thin, fragile-seeming face. The lines that gathered at the edges of her mouth were hardly noticeable in certain lights, the strands of grey that invaded her pale hair appeared to do so with discretion. There was a nervy look about the eyes, the lips were almost always slightly parted: a twitchy kind of face, she considered it herself. Smooth hair enclosed it like a helmet, calming it down.

The past she examined at forty-one was full of other people. There was her mother first of all, and her father, who had died. There were friends: Henry who once had been her greatest friend, and at school Di Troughton and Evie Faste, and Isabel Everest and Jean Friar and Tricia Hatchett and Betty Kemp. There were other friends later on, at Mr Feuchtwanger's art school, and later still, when she'd become a wife and mother. There was her husband, and Daphne's husband. There was Daphne, whom she'd caused to have a nervous break-down.

The past was full of changes and moods, of regrets that were still regrets, and resolutions. At seven, aware that her parents were not content in marriage, she had determined to marry happily herself. She had even then visualized a husband, who increased in elegance and charm as the years went on. Looking back at forty-one, she established that as the beginning of her romantic nature. At twelve, she had been unable to weep at her father's funeral and unable, also, to prevent herself from thinking that the house would be nicer now. Looking back, she established that as the beginning of the guilt which had since coloured her life.

Yet she'd felt guilt in her father's lifetime, too. He'd shuffled about the house, a grey, pernickety figure, exuding disapproval. He spread it like a fog about him, damply cold. He had grown like that, her mother said; he'd once been different. Grey clothes, Elizabeth remembered now, grey hair, spectacles hanging on a grey ribbon, a grey untidy tie. She remembered him in armchairs, and coming out of the room he called his study. She remembered him cleaning his shoes, polishing dark brown leather with brushes and a cloth. He blew his nose in a particular way, he pursed his lips, he watched her eating food. Wearily, he closed his eyes over school reports from Miss Henderson's and Miss Gamble's Kindergarten. 'Obstreperous,' he slowly said. 'It says here you're obstreperous, Elizabeth.'

She remembered entering the room he called his study. There was an index finger that pointed at her knuckles and asked her what they were called, and then asked her what they were for. She left the room and stood outside the door she'd closed. She knocked on a panel with the knuckles he'd drawn her attention to, and he told her to come in, saying that was better. She remembered making him a birth-day cake, seed-cake because it was the cake he liked.

Dwelling now on her past, with its friends and incidents and the beginnings of this and that, Elizabeth could make little sense of her life as so far it had been. She saw mistakes mainly, made by herself. She saw her life as something that was scattered untidily about, with-out a pattern, without rhyme or reason. She often wondered if other people, examining their lives in middle age, would have preferred, as she did, to see something tidier and with more purpose. At school Miss Middlesmith had said she had a talent for drawing flowers, and later Mr Feuchtwanger had said that her talent was developing nicely. Petals and pedicels, anther and filament, *Sedum album*, *Primula veris*: she hadn't drawn a flower for twelve years.

'Aidallbery,' her mother had said. 'What an odd name!' In Fiesole, in the Pensione Bencistà, he was in the hall one night, tall and hand-somely dressed, in a brown checked suit. He sat alone at dinner. 'What glorious weather!' he said some other time. He had a face like an eagle's face. He had a beautiful voice. 'What luck to meet you, Mrs Orpen!' he said, addressing her mother.

Her mother chatted, talking about books and episodes in books, and real people. He liked listening to her mother, it showed in his face. Years afterwards he said you could be in a room for hour after hour with her mother and not be bored. Yet her mother had been against the marriage. 'Yes, I did see through that charm,' her mother casually said.

She was nineteen, he was thirteen years older, but in the Pensione Bencistà he seemed ageless, and age didn't matter. In London, while still at school, she and Di Troughton and Evie Faste had gone out with a boy called Eric Cross and another called Neville Trim. They'd gone to the pictures, and Eric Cross or Neville Trim had slipped an arm along the seat she was sitting in. Eric Cross had spots on his neck and his chin, Neville Trim had an impediment in his speech. There were other boys, without spots or impediments, who didn't know what to say. There were older ones, working in estate agents' or architects' offices, or qualified already as accountants. There were students at Mr Feuchtwanger's art school, one called Bishop who was rather nice, another called Adamson, who'd said he'd like to marry her. There was Henry, whom she'd lost touch with but who'd then appeared again, outside the Gas Showrooms in Putney High Street one Thursday afternoon. He'd asked her if she'd like to go to the cinema, but she hadn't been able to because she was doing something else. 'Just thought I'd look in,' Henry said another time, arriving at the house one evening. They went for a walk and he put his arm around her and asked her to marry him. 'Dear Henry,' she said. 'No.'

In the Pensione Bencistà they sat after dinner, over coffee, in the larger sitting-room. He wasn't at all like Henry, or Eric Cross or Neville Trim. He talked about Egypt and Persia and Peru, and tribes he'd studied, and genealogy and psychiatry. 'The Achaemenians,' he said, 'extended this empire of theirs from what was called the Sind Valley to beyond the Nile. And from the Oxus to the Danube.' He showed her what he meant by drawing a map on a page of a slim, leather-bound note-book.

In London he took her to *Dido and Aeneas*, and to Wimbledon to see Louise Brough playing. He played tennis with her himself and taught her a thing or two. He was always hailing taxis and sitting in them beside her, faintly smiling, staring straight ahead of him. Timidly she took his arm when they walked along streets, and he said he was proud to be seen with her. He brought her to tea in Gunter's because she was curious about it. He brought her to tea in the Ritz because she was curious about that, too. 'The older man,' Di Troughton said. Evie Faste giggled. It all seemed a joke, a lovely

9

38 - 3 years ago

confection of a joke, she and an older man playing tennis and drinking chilled white wine afterwards. Then it all became real, more serious and even better, because she knew he was going to marry her,
because he'd asked her and she hadn't for a split second hesitated.

Yet when the moment arrived she didn't like sharing a bed with
him. This came as a shock to her and caused her painfully to assume
that she wouldn't have liked sharing a bed with any man. Some
women were like that, you read about them in newspapers: they
didn't like what the divorce courts called the physical side of marriage. On their honeymoon – among ancient ruins in Crete – she
didn't tell him, thinking it would be unfair to do so. She was upset
by the fact, and somehow ashamed. She didn't tell him, in fact, for
nineteen years.

It was sensible that her husband should come and live in her
mother's house. He took over the garden and worked quite happily
there, cutting the grass in summer, and growing raspberries, and
camellias and dahlias, her mother's favourite flowers. In the household he took quite naturally her father's place. In time, even, their
eldest daughter's untidiness enraged him, as Elizabeth's untidiness
had enraged her father. The noise of his two younger daughters
displeased him also. He couldn't work, he complained in
unemotional fury, coming out of the room that her father had called
his study: no man in the world could work with noise like that going
on.

She felt again a feeling of disapproval, and in the flat they'd made
for her at the top of the house her mother was soothing, as she'd
been in the past. It was incredible, but it did seem true, that beneath
the elegant exterior this man was very like her father. A psychiatrist
from whom she secretly sought help suggested that through her
choice of husband she had sought to exorcize her feelings of guilt
about her father. She didn't believe it and said so, causing the
psychiatrist patiently to smile. 'In that case, Mrs Aidallbery,' he suggested in his calm voice, 'would you consider it possible that you are
attempting to punish your father by punishing the man you married?'
The psychiatrist, whose name was Mr Apple, had been recom-
mended by Di Troughton, now Mrs Acheson. Elizabeth didn't understand him and wondered if Di Troughton, given to playing jokes as
a child, was playing another one. She was her mother's daughter,
she said to Mr Apple: love was cruel to women like her mother and
herself. But Mr Apple replied that that was rubbish. She paid him
and did not return. It seemed too easy an answer that a psychiatrist

10

should attempt to sort a marriage out with talk of guilt and punishment.

What troubled Elizabeth most was that she felt her husband had developed a disappointed way of looking at her. And when the subject of the children's noise or untidiness came up she felt he considered that she, more than the children, was responsible for the children's shortcomings. In retrospect, it seemed to her that becoming a husband had changed him a little, and becoming a father had changed him greatly. Often she felt that he regarded her as a fourth child in the house, a feeling accentuated by the fact that there were many activities which she engaged in with the children and which he did not. Understandably, he seemed too clever for all that; he was far cleverer than she was, his mind worked at twice the speed. Once she borrowed his car-keys without asking him, and accidentally dropped them down a drain in the road. The incident depressed him and caused him repeatedly to sigh. 'But how could you drop them down a drain?' he asked, shaking his head in disbelief. 'How could you possibly manage to?'

He'd suggested that she should read books about the Achaemenians and reports on the integration of the central African tribes that interested him. Dutifully she did so, but when she once suggested that he might like to glance through *Wives and Daughters*, which he'd never read, he said he didn't think it would much involve him. This was a disappointment for Elizabeth. Her mother had a way of speaking about fictional characters as if they were real: Mr Dubbley, Daisy Mutlar, Perugia Gaukrodger, Mr Edgeworth, General Conyers, Miss Keene, Major Ending, Lady Glenmire, Mr Woodhouse, and quite a few others. Elizabeth had become used to this kind of chatter, which had been there ever since the days she and Di Troughton had first come across the girls of the Chalet School and the girls of the Abbey School, and Angela Brazil's girls with their slim black legs, and Wendy and Jinx, and not-so-simple Sophie, and Lettice Leaf the greenest girl in school. Later on, she and her mother and Di Troughton used to talk endlessly about the slow wits of Captain Hastings and Henry Holt's *Murder in Mayfair*, and *The Crimson Circle* by Edgar Wallace, and Inspector Alleyn and Albert Campion and Arsène Lupin. Di Troughton used to lie on the floor, laughing and laughing over *The Lunatic at Large* and *The Lunatic Still at Large*. 'Lunatic?' he'd said when she told him that. 'No, I don't think I recall books about a lunatic.'

In the early days of her marriage Elizabeth had come to recognize the virtues of reports on African tribal integration, but now, at forty-one, she felt all that had been a pretence on her part. Everything had been a pretence, lying in bed with him, the endless coming up to scratch, the listening to a voice she'd once thought beautiful and then no longer did, the bearing of children because it was the thing to do, apologizing for noise and untidiness, apologizing when keys fell down the drain.

'You're desiccated,' she'd shouted at him, weeping when she said she wanted a divorce. He was fifty-one then, tall and upright, still with his eagle's face, not taking her out to tea any more. He stood quite still when she told him that she wanted a divorce, then he turned his back and looked through the french windows into the garden. 'I just want a divorce,' she said, knowing as she said it that it was more than that. It was more than loving someone else and wanting to have another marriage: she resented with a bitter passion the years she'd wasted with a man who'd married her because she was beautiful and young, so that she might listen and he could feel proud. The years were like useless leaves, dead now, yielding no memories that she wanted. There should be more than three children to show for nineteen years of a marriage, she cried with violence in her voice. And when he interrupted her, icily pointing out that she was endeavouring to justify her dirty weekends with grand but meaningless talk, she shouted at him again that he was desiccated. 'Maybe,' he said. 'Yet you haven't done badly out of me.'

He should have married a studious, tweeded woman who was older, actually, than he was, who wore studious glasses and did not often smile, who wore hats and brown coats and could talk about the Elamite script. He'd have been happy with such a woman, travelling importantly to examine Pasargadae. In a cold university somewhere he'd have been happy with her, with terracotta figures of a dead civilization for children, pieces of pots, bricks with signs on them. She couldn't help her bitterness and, looking back, she only blamed herself. Of her own free will she had once rejoiced in him. Of her own free will she had rejoiced when each of her three children had been born, delighting in them more than she'd ever delighted in drawing petals and pedicels. But after nineteen years of marriage she was now divorced, and her eldest daughter, over whose birth she had rejoiced most of all, appeared to regard her as a person not worth having a conversation with.

In Elizabeth's less cheery moments the disappointments and the untidiness of her life, and the guilt that had begun the day of her father's funeral, had a way of combining and of lowering her spirits further. Increasingly in middle age she found that combination hard to bear and felt, because of it, alone. She knew it was a silly feeling, because she wasn't in the least alone. She had friends. Her mother was still alive. She had, in Mrs Orvitski, a devoted daily help, and in her childhood companion, Henry, a devoted admirer. She had children, even if one of them now rarely spoke to her. It was absurd to feel alone when other people really were alone: people in bed-sitting-rooms, the elderly and the unhappy, people you read about, who had nowhere to go on Christmas Day. Her life wasn't in the least like that.

When Dr Love told Elizabeth that in his opinion she should undergo a hysterectomy, and when his recommendation was confirmed by Mr Alstrop-Smith, Elizabeth did not regard the news as momentous. She did not consider that this operation was, or would become, a landmark in her life, like her father's death, or her marriage, or her divorce. Her womb, at forty-one, might well not be up to its purpose, she considered instead: its removal was probably neither here nor there. But as the day of this operation approached, Elizabeth found herself more intensely involved with her past, as though she privately regretted this final surrender to middle age, or as though in some subconscious way she was more apprehensive about the operation than she admitted to herself. Whatever it was, the past that she had come so much to dwell upon seemed now to possess her. The guilt that flavoured it mocked her, and her errors of judgement took on larger dimensions. The damage she believed she'd inflicted on other people hurt her more, the patternless quality of the whole oppressed her. She would have listened to any comforting voice or to any explanation, but at the time there happened to be neither.

On the morning of her admission to hospital Elizabeth was reflected in her mahogany-framed looking-glass while she packed: a thin woman in a grey flannel dress. Outside the house, in cool February sunshine, her daughters waited for her: Jennifer eleven and Alice eight, Joanna seventeen. The man who'd been her husband was asleep in Aberdeen, where he now lived. The man who'd briefly been her lover, whose presence in her life had upset her marriage, was reading the magazine section of the *Sunday Times* in a house less than a mile away. In Meridian Close, not far away either, her childhood companion, Henry, shaved himself. In a home for the aged, the Sunset Home in Richmond, her mother ate toast and grapefruit marmalade.

Elizabeth packed a small white suitcase, watched by Mrs Orvitski, who stood in the open doorway, leaning against the door-frame. Laid out on the bed were a pair of blue slippers and an ivory-backed hairbrush with a comb that matched it, and a blue waterproof bag that contained her toothbrush and a new face-flannel and a nail-brush, and some paperbacked novels. In the white suitcase were four nightdresses and a dressing-gown. Folding a fifth nightdress, one with a pattern of rosebuds on it, Elizabeth said: 'It's terribly good of you, Mrs Orvitski. It really is.'

She'd said it already several times that morning, but saw no harm in making the statement again. She smiled at Mrs Orvitski.

'So what is good?' Mrs Orvitski said. 'So what is good to look after three lovely children?'

Vaguely, Elizabeth shook her head. There was a faint stiffness in the fingers of her right hand, as if the hand hadn't quite woken up yet. A middle-aged stiffness, or so she called it. Often when she woke in the morning she had twinges of rheumatism or some related complaint. She didn't quite know what the complaint was, but knew at least that the twinges hadn't been there when she was twenty-five or thirty, or even thirty-five. Sometimes she had trouble with her back and went to an osteopath, a Mr Lee, who had manipulated her mother also. She put off getting reading-glasses, although she knew she needed them.

'You not worry, heh?' Mrs Orvitski said.

She smiled again and shook her head. Dr Love had said that the one thing he insisted on was that she wasn't to go into hospital just to lie worrying about her children. 'Put them out of your mind, Mrs Aidallbery. Promise me that now.' She'd promised, knowing that she'd worry slightly anyway, even though Mrs Orvitski was being so helpful, arranging for her husband, Leopold, to cope on his own while she herself coped with the Aidallbery children. Mrs Orvitski was to occupy one of the spare rooms for the duration of Elizabeth's absence: it would be, she had repeatedly promised, as though Elizabeth had never left the house.

'Is good to worry?' Mrs Orvitski said now, still leaning against the door-frame. 'Is good for you?'

'I won't worry, Mrs Orvitski. I only hope your poor husband'll be all right on his own.'

'I leave Leopold chlodnik,' Mrs Orvitski said. 'Leopold is a good man.'

'It's very understanding of Mr Orvitski.'

'He is a good man,' Mrs Orvitski said again.

Elizabeth closed and fastened the white suitcase. She took a scarf and a grey tweed coat from her wardrobe and put them on. She glanced at herself in the looking-glass and saw that her make-up wasn't smeared and her hair was still tidy. She picked up her handbag from the dressing-table. She had everything she needed except writing-paper and envelopes, which were in her bureau downstairs. Mrs Orvitski moved towards the bed. She seized the suitcase and in spite of Elizabeth's protests insisted on carrying it.

'You know chlodnik, Mrs Aidallbery? Beetroots, hard eggs, fishes? Chlodnik soup?'

Descending the stairs behind Mrs Orvitski, Elizabeth said she had never had chlodnik soup.

'I make chlodnik when you are back again,' Mrs Orvitski promised.

The house was in a south-western suburb of London, a large, detached, three-storey house with back windows that overlooked the Thames. It was the house that Elizabeth had lived in all her life, her father's until he died in 1945, becoming then her mother's whose property it still, strictly speaking, was. It was a Victorian house, built of dark, almost black brick. The hall door and the woodwork of the windows, the drain-pipes and guttering, were white, as they had always been in Elizabeth's memory. In front of the house, in an expanse of shrubbery that lay between it and the quiet suburban road that ran by it, was an eucalyptus tree. At the back, a long, narrow garden sloped down towards the river. There were apple trees in the garden, and a lawn with two rose-beds in it and herbaceous borders next to wooden fencing. At the bottom of the garden Elizabeth and Henry had hidden among the raspberry canes, waiting to creep up on the man who used to come to weed the flower-beds and to cut the grass, a Mr Giltrap. Raspberry canes still grew there.

'I won't be a moment,' Elizabeth said in the hall.

The room which had always been called the drawing-room by Elizabeth's mother had once been two rooms, one at the back of the house, one at the front: Elizabeth's father had had the wall knocked down. It was an impressive room now, seeming only a little narrow for its length, and even in that reflecting quite pleasantly the proportions of the garden on to which its french windows opened. Nothing had changed much in this room during Elizabeth's lifetime. The wallpaper was similar to the wallpaper she first remembered being there, a dark pattern of flowers, brown and bronze and yellow, formal in its effect. The rugs on the polished natural-wood floor were

15

brownish too, with red in them, and black. The covers on the arm-chairs and the sofa were as they'd always been, striped in two shades of blue, the same material as the curtains. Neither she nor her mother had ever wanted to make changes, nor had her husband when he'd come to live in the house.

In this room she'd said to her mother that she wanted to marry. In this same room she'd asked for her divorce. She'd had her last conversation with Joanna here, and here, too, she'd argued fruitlessly against her mother's plan to accept a place in the Sunset Home. The present state of her guilt had to do with all these matters, with not knowing before her children were born that her marriage was not successful, with her brief abandonment of Joanna because she'd put the man she'd fallen in love with before anyone else, with her inability to persuade her mother to remain in a house that meant so much to her. Her mother had insisted on going because Elizabeth had three children to look after and should not, so her mother said, be required to worry over an ageing parent. If the marriage had continued it might somehow have been different.

Elizabeth collected writing-paper and envelopes from her bureau and returned to the hall. Mrs Orvitski had opened the hall door. The car had come, Alice shouted, rushing into the hall. 'Minicab,' a man in a black leather coat announced.

The man tried to take the white suitcase from Mrs Orvitski, but Mrs Orvitski wouldn't let him. Mrs Orvitski was to accompany Elizabeth and the two younger girls in the minicab so that she could afterwards see them safely back to the house. They'd begged to go to the hospital, and although it meant another bother for Mrs Orvitski, Mrs Orvitski had said she didn't mind.

'Why's Mrs Orvitski got to come?' Alice demanded now, and Elizabeth explained. 'We could easily come back by ourselves,' Alice said loudly, looking distastefully at Mrs Orvitski. 'That man'd look after us,' she said, pointing at the minicab driver.

'Don't be silly, Alice,' Jennifer said.

'Rain about,' the minicab driver remarked, leading the way to his car.

Silent on the pavement, dissociating herself from the house and the shrubbery and the eucalyptus tree, stood Joanna, with her friend Samuel. She was wearing beads, and a faded purple dress she'd bought at a jumble sale. Samuel was in frayed jeans and a blue tee-shirt with the words *Jesus Loves Me* on it, in orange letters that approximately matched the colour of his waist-length hair. Samuel

16

and Joanna didn't look at Elizabeth or greet her. Instead, they stared through wire-rimmed spectacles at the man who was to drive the minicab, surveying him as though he intrigued them. Neither of them required the assistance of spectacles for this observation: the glass within the wire rims was not optical. The spectacles were a part of their dress, worn at the instigation of a woman called Mrs Geraldine Tabor-Ellis, at whose instigation, also, they had taught themselves to converse in deaf-and-dumb language. While still regarding the minicab driver, Samuel now made a motion with his fingers, to which Joanna replied. Soundlessly, Samuel laughed, showing long teeth that always reminded Elizabeth of fangs. Samuel frightened Elizabeth.

When Joanna was five, she'd said she'd never get married because she always wanted to be Elizabeth's friend. 'Oh but, Jo, you can still be my friend,' Elizabeth had said, but Joanna had argued that it wouldn't be the same. It was at that time, during the years before the other two were born, that they had become fond of one another, and the two other births had made no difference to that. When she was pregnant with Jennifer she walked with Joanna by the Thames, both of them wondering if the baby would be a boy or a girl. They made rag-dolls and prepared a cot. When Jennifer was born, Joanna, at six, used to cradle her in her arms, and when Alice had come, three years later, Joanna had known what to do from the start. It was the same relationship that Elizabeth had had with her own mother, with things taken for granted.

'Well, goodbye,' she said to Joanna, and Joanna smiled fixedly at her, without speaking. Joanna usually broke her silence only to say that she couldn't stand her school much longer. At first she'd wanted to leave and go to a technical college, but then she'd become friendly with Samuel, who was at the same school and whose idea was that they should both join Mrs Geraldine Tabor-Ellis in her commune in Somerset. In the months Elizabeth had known him this ambition was the only information he'd shared with her. In silence they'd both smiled at her the afternoon she'd foolishly walked into Joanna's room without knocking and found them in bed together. On that occasion she'd felt herself to be in the wrong for not respecting their privacy and had afterwards tried to say so: listening to her, they'd only smiled again. 'Joanna and I would really like to go to Mrs Tabor-Ellis's place,' Samuel said later, over cups of tea in the kitchen. 'It really makes sense to us, Elizabeth.' He said it as though nothing else in the world made sense to them, and in fact he meant this. 'One of these days we'll just have to take off, Elizabeth,' he said with his smile, and she knew she hadn't been forgiven for walking into her daughter's room without knocking. Mrs Geraldine Tabor-Ellis had written a book which Samuel said everyone should read, but when Elizabeth tried to do so she couldn't make sense of it. On the back of the jacket Mrs Tabor-Ellis was shown to be a floppy woman in brightly coloured clothes, elephantine and elderly, with flowers sewn on to the knees of her tangerine jeans. Mrs Tabor-Ellis believed in the spirits of stones and in the spirits of children and infant animals, in human touch and feel. In her commune in Somerset she kept goats.

Outside her house, Elizabeth wanted to kiss Joanna, but she knew she mustn't.

'We may have to take off this week, Elizabeth,' Samuel said, smiling with his long teeth.

She felt he hated her because she was wearing a grey tweed coat and had make-up on her face and shoes on her feet. He'd once stubbed a cigarette out on the surface of a mahogany table, and when she'd protested he'd shaken his head at her, smiling again. She often had the irrational feeling that all the deaf-and-dumb language and the wire-rimmed spectacles and the silences and the smiling had been developed for her benefit alone. Samuel had that kind of effect on her.

'You mustn't do anything like that until I come out of hospital,' she said to Joanna. 'You really mustn't, Joanna.'

Still smiling, Joanna sighed.

'Please now, Joanna.'

'Oh, of course I won't.'

'We may have to, Elizabeth,' Samuel said. Again he laughed, soundlessly, as if he'd made a joke.

'Try not to be out too late at night,' she said to Joanna with simulated briskness, returning Joanna's smile. 'Try not to,' she said.

She sat in the back of the minicab with Jennifer and Alice, and Mrs Orvitski sat beside the driver. No need to worry, Mrs Orvitski said.

2

In London that morning, 11 February 1973, other women prepared themselves for hospital, among them Sylvie Clapper and Miss Samson. In a room in Shepherd's Bush Sylvie Clapper put two night-dresses and washing things in a Victor Value carrier-bag and dropped on top of them a number of packets of cigarettes, Embassy Kings. At Number Nine, Balaclava Avenue, Miss Samson added a Bible and a Prayer Book to her hospital requirements.

'I'll miss you,' Sylvie Clapper's boyfriend, Declan, assured her, while in Balaclava Avenue Miss Samson's friends said they would naturally pray for her. 'That the pain is as little as God allows,' the Reverend Rawes added, in case Miss Samson might misunderstand the nature of their prayers. But Miss Samson only smiled. She was in His hands, she pointed out; an operation was a tiny thing, a bubble of vapour. She had her happiness, she explained; everywhere she looked she saw messages of hope.

One of the Tonsell brothers carried her suitcase, Carol Pidsley and Mrs Delve were ready to accompany her in the car they'd hired from Timms' Garage. The Reverend Rawes, who'd been an inmate at Number Nine since his retirement thirteen years ago, shook hands with her. The little Welsh girl and Arthur, whom Miss Samson had taken out of a home for the backward to do the rough work at Number Nine, said she must get well soon. The little Welsh girl was trying to hide her weeping, and Miss Samson touched her arm and said again that the operation she was to undergo was only a little thing.

'I'll be lost without you,' Declan said in Shepherd's Bush. He nodded, emphasizing the words, wishing Sylvie would say he shouldn't bother to go to the hospital with her. Hospitals gave him the creeps.

'You'll not be lost,' Sylvie said, laughing.

She had a shrivelled look, as if in need of food. Her eyes were heavy with make-up and constantly blinked. Her hair, naturally dark, was the colour of brass. Her teeth were false, noticeably so in a harsh light or when she smiled carelessly.

19

'We'd better go,' she said.

He followed her down the stairs, staring at the shoulder-blades that moved sharply beneath her blouse. She was twenty-five, he two years older, a hatchet-faced man with greased black hair combed straight back from a widow's peak. He was small and thin, with darting eyes. In childhood he had been likened to a ferret.

'You be good now,' she said chirpily, not turning to look at him. 'You be a good old Declan now.'

He laughed and said of course he would. With the girl he loved incarcerated in a hospital, there'd be no temptation to be anything else.

In Cheltenham Street, in the hospital towards which these women moved, life continued in its routine way. In the entrance hall the dark eyes of Lady Augusta Haptree gazed sternly from a greenish background, dead as doornails within a gilt frame. In their glass-paned cubbyhole the daytime porters, Pengelly and Frowen, talked about an item Pengelly had heard on the wireless, about a woman who had persuaded her bank to issue a cheque book to her cat. In the hospital's boiler-room old George Trigol, who had been employed in the hospital all his working life, checked the temperature gauges of his furnaces and made a mental note to keep an eye on No. 4, which in his opinion was groggy. In the wards the Sunday-morning cleaners had been and gone, beds had been made, some patients had been washed. In the Olivia Hassals Ward a woman called Mrs Proctor had died in the night: there was that to be disposed of. Earlier that morning there'd been an emergency admission: a woman whom the hospital had previously confined for some months because her pregnancy for twins was not straightforward had begun her labour pains in a house in Paddington, to which she had been permitted to return for what Mr Azu called psychological reasons. The houseman who received her back at ten minutes to five said afterwards, over coffee in the staff canteen, that Mr Azu had made a mistake. No matter how tedious life had been in the hospital for this pregnant woman and no matter how often she'd wept in frustration, she shouldn't ever have been permitted to break the programme which Mr Azu had originally laid down for her. She lost her twins at half past six and wept more bitterly than ever she'd wept in the frustration of waiting. It stood to reason, the houseman confidently said.

The hospital had been built in 1841 by the Haptree family, who

20

had made their money out of tea. Distressed by the conditions under which the women of London's less prosperous classes bore their children and by illnesses and complications that were too often ignored, Lady Augusta Haptree had surrounded herself with a number of women who shared her charity and her zeal. Then, having founded the hospital, she turned her attention, and theirs, to its humane organization. The less prosperous women who occupied its wards were visited by Lady Augusta herself and by Lady Olivia Hassals and Mrs Faith Rowan and Mrs Marie Atkins, among many others. They came with small gifts and flowers, a few with tracts, or novels designed to lift the mind. Apart from specialists and doctors, it was a woman's world and had remained so for more than a hundred and thirty years, although it was no longer, except for complicated cases, a maternity home. 'Lady Augusta Haptree's Hospital For Women' had been its title once, and this was still officially so. But people now more often called it the Cheltenham Street Women's Hospital.

The cream tiles decreed by Lady Augusta for the corridors were still a feature, and here and there, in unimportant rooms, a stained-glass window depicting a scene from the Old Testament was a reminder of the past. Otherwise, waves of fresh enthusiasm, long after the death of Lady Augusta, had brought the hospital up to date. Unaltered structurally and presenting from without the same brick façade, only weathered to a uniform brown, in detail the hospital was a modern place: the zeal of Lady Augusta had turned, quite naturally, into zealous medicine. Pictures hung against the cream tiles now, prints of Van Gogh and Renoir. Cheerfulness was the thing.

On this Sunday, as on other days, the women of the hospital walked through its corridors like cautious automatons, pale-lipped, in dressing-gowns. Those who'd recently been stitched had been urged to find their feet again, though gradually at first. In the gynaecological wards recovery was a compromise, as Mr Alstrop-Smith was never tired of pointing out. There was the urgency to be better and the protests of an injured body: between the two impulses lay a satisfactory speed for a return to normality.

Outside the hospital, in quiet Cheltenham Street, another woman walked, as slowly almost as the patients within. In spectacles and red trousers, and a red plastic mackintosh, she paraded up and down, a familiar sight. *Liberation Now!* a banner attached to a sweeping-brush handle said. From early morning until dusk, every day of the week, this woman walked by the black wrought-iron railings in front of the weathered brick façade, past the steps that led up to the hospital's glass swing-doors, to and fro past the wrought-iron gates of the hospital's side entrance. She handed out no leaflets, nor had she ever bothered a patient or a member of the hospital staff. No one knew why she had chosen a women's hospital to make her protest in front of, or to what end she walked with her banner, or if the liberation the banner urged was liberation specifically for women, though this was generally supposed to be so. Dr Mary Malcolmson had once attempted to hold the woman in conversation, but the woman had only said she was doing what must be done. Dr Pennance, a houseman, said that in his opinion the woman was touched in the head.

New patients often asked about her because it was something to say, and were told in reply that nothing was known about her. She was within her rights to walk up and down, and unless she caused a nuisance she couldn't be asked to cease. The hospital's two matrons didn't take to the presence of the woman, feeling there was something untidy about it. Both of them had personally asked her to go away, but the woman had said that she was doing what must be done. 'A sign of the times,' new patients occasionally remarked, and it was sometimes agreed that no doubt the woman was this.

In the Marie Atkins Ward, sitting up in bed with her spectacles on, her pink angora bed-jacket covering the nylon of her nightdress, Lily Drucker read a book that Sister O'Keeffe sometimes lent patients who were likely to be in the hospital for a long time. It was the autobiography of Lady Augusta Haptree, written fifteen years before her death in 1886. It was not a book that Lily found it easy to concentrate her attention on, but she persevered because Sister O'Keeffe had a way of asking questions. It was said in the hospital that Sister O'Keeffe knew every page of Lady Augusta's autobiography off by heart.

I determined that it should not be, Lily read. *I determined that women who were treated no better than water-rats should in sickness at least be offered the privileges of common humanity. There were brought before my husband two men from the Shoreditch neighbourhood who had beaten with chair-legs the wife of one of them because she would not sell the clothes her mother had left her. In the hospital to which this woman was brought nothing was done for her. Nurses refused to undress her, believing her to be a street-walker. She was unable to undress herself and died on the third*

22

day of her confinement, the wounds beneath her clothes having taken in poison. That the hospital should bear a share of guilt equal to that for which the two men were imprisoned I have no doubt. Yet a hospital can be judged only by the law of God.

Lily let the heavy volume slip from her hands. She was small; the hands that now lay on the open pages of Lady Augusta's autobiography were small; her small face was made to seem even smaller beneath the weight of her black-rimmed reading spectacles. Brown hair hung loosely to her shoulders, and behind a tenseness that rarely, these days, left her she was pretty in her tiny way, olive-skinned, with brown eyes and a slight, straight nose. Her lips she'd once hoped would grow full and generous, but in fact they had remained as neat and as small as everything else about her. Sitting up in bed, she might have been a child: she was thirty-three.

For nine weeks Lily Drucker had been in the Cheltenham Street Women's Hospital, moved about from ward to ward, fitting in because she wasn't an urgent case: she was trying to have a baby. 'As for you, Mrs Drucker,' Mr Alstrop-Smith had said, 'I'm *quite* determined about you.' Her baby would be born was what he was determined about, as also were Mr Azu and the hospital's registrar, Mr Greer, and Dr Mary Malcolmson, and the matrons. Mrs Drucker would stay where she was for her remaining seven weeks in order to prevent another miscarriage. Naturally, after so many miscarriages, she felt she had no option.

For nine weeks Lily Drucker had watched the drama of the hospital and its more mundane organization, the coming and going of women in their hundreds, young and old, black and white. Some passed her by, others she came to know well: Mrs Fleming, in for a Fothergill Repair at sixty-two, who'd believed she wouldn't survive it but in fact who'd sailed through everything, as right as rain. And Angela, from Jamaica, who ate peaches all the time, who'd had frightening complications after a routine operation, the clearing of her Fallopian tubes. And Valerie from Virginia Water who talked about her garden, and Miss Downe, a schoolteacher, and Maudie Tulipino, who worked in a branch of Oakeshotts, and poor Agnes Rodesteer, whose mother had died the day after she'd had her hysterectomy.

Day into night and night becoming day, Lily read and talked and listened to the chatter of disc jockeys on her radio; often, because she was given to tears, she cried. She'd been in the Marie

23

Atkins Ward for three weeks, in a corner, near one of the ward's two windows. She liked the ward because it was the smallest in the hospital, with only four beds. But even so she'd rather have been at home, in her flat with Kenneth, which was the only home of that kind she'd ever really known. Abandoned as a baby because of her illegitimacy, she'd spent her childhood in the care of people who weren't her parents, in St Clare's Home for London's Girls, in Higham's Park. She was used to institutions.

The Marie Atkins Ward was one of the wards where women recovered, as they did in the much larger St Agnes Ward and St Susanna Ward and several others. Before their operations and for a day or two afterwards they lay in the Faith Rowan Ward, or the St Beatrice or the St Ida. The subsequent change of scene, associated as it was with recuperation, was assumed to be beneficial, but the more practical consideration was that beds in the operation wards could be prepared for the next admissions. The recovery wards tended to fill up, the operation ones usually had beds to spare. Cheltenham House, in Eastbourne, was the hospital's convalescent home. Patients were keenly urged in its direction.

On this Sunday morning the Marie Atkins Ward was empty except for Lily Drucker. The other three beds, with fresh white sheets and pillow-cases, were nobody's beds until the new women came. There was a waiting meaninglessness about them: existing only for human occupation, they reflected now no real human connection, like seats unoccupied in a cinema, or houses without furniture. White-painted cupboards by each bed, metal-frame chairs with canvas seats, and the large table beneath the windows were as clinical and unowned as these empty beds. The table's surface, of fawn Formica flecked with white, bore no stains of the meals that had been eaten from it by women recovering, nor the marks of knives and forks carelessly thrown down, nor the imprint of sun or passing time. But cheerfulness broke through, as in the hospital's corridors: there were two pictures on the pale cream walls, one of the ducks in St James's Park, the other of tulips in a bowl. On rails around each bed cheerful curtains, in restful shades of pink, were drawn back now and framed each bed-head. Beneath the rolled blue blinds February sunlight spread over the floor's linoleum, fawn flecked with white to match the table-top.

The evening before, after Mrs Griffin and Mrs Farmer and Mrs Klis had left the Marie Atkins Ward, the night sister, Sister Kolulu, had wondered about moving Lily into the St Agnes Ward and had given Lily a choice. Lily had asked to stay in the Marie Atkins. 'You'll be alone till after Monday's ops,' Sister Kolulu had pointed out. Lily didn't mind. She liked the little ward, she said.

But that morning, when Sister O'Keeffe had come on duty, she hadn't been pleased. While she'd chatted with Lily in her usual way, Lily could see her thinking that being alone in a ward wasn't good for anyone, especially for Lily. 'We're a bit on the full side in the St Beatrice, Mrs Drucker,' she said an hour later. 'We're going to pop a few admissions in with you until tomorrow morning. The same three that'll be back again after their ops.'

Lily sighed after Sister O'Keeffe had smiled and gone. She hadn't meant them to shunt patients around just because she'd said she'd rather stay in the little ward. 'She'll go all mopey on her own,' she imagined Sister O'Keeffe saying. They were always keeping her spirits up, as if they'd decided that that was her prescribed treatment. The beds that were waiting for the admissions in the St Beatrice Ward would have to be wheeled along the corridor, out of the way, to one of the recovery wards. Tomorrow morning the three beds in the Marie Atkins Ward, with the new women in them, would have to be wheeled into the St Beatrice Ward so that the women could be prepared for their operations in the correct environment. 'No trouble at all, dear,' Sister O'Keeffe had said. 'Give us something to do.' Sister O'Keeffe broke regulations on purpose, Lily had once overheard Nurse Wibberley saying in the middle of the night, just to keep everyone on their toes. In a medicine room Nurse Hampshire and Nurse Summerbee were probably cursing their heads off.

'That's Mrs Drucker,' Nurse Hampshire said now, coming into the ward with a grey-haired woman whose age Lily guessed to be sixty or thereabouts. Lily smiled and the woman smiled back.

'Miss Samson,' Nurse Hampshire said, twanging out the information in brittle Australian accents.

'Look, I'm sorry,' Lily said. 'I'm sorry I asked to stay here, Nurse. I didn't mean –'

'Everyone likes the Marie Atkins,' Nurse Hampshire said, smiling and seeming not to mind at all. 'I like it myself.'

There was something the matter with the grey-haired woman's face, a birthmark that was swollen as well as crimson, misshaping the features and affecting her left eye, which did not seem real. When the woman held out her hand, Lily felt herself shivering. But Miss Samson smiled and to Lily's horrified surprise referred to her affliction, saying she'd always had it and with God's help had learnt to live with it. 'It's not so terrible,' she murmured, but Lily, shaking the proffered hand, felt that it was terrible enough for any woman, an ugliness like that.

Quite suddenly, Henry was there. While Mrs Orvitski was pushing herself out of the minicab and Alice and Jennifer were arguing about figure-skating, Henry drew up in his old, broken Zephyr and shouted to Elizabeth along twenty yards of pavement that he'd come to see her safely in. He'd called at the house, he said, but there'd been no one there. He'd promised he'd drive her, he reminded her: he'd said he'd come at half past ten.

Elizabeth heard the children giggling and felt embarrassed to have Henry there, blocking the way of a woman with a banner, stared at by Mrs Orvitski, who never knew what to make of him. Henry had grown into a heavy, dog-like man with an elaborately freckled face and reddish hair, with large hands that were elaborately freckled also. He was dressed this morning, as usually he was, in a golfing jacket, unironed flannel trousers, and a red-and-blue shirt of the style favoured by Canadian lumberjacks. In middle age he spent a lot of his time brewing home-made beer and endeavouring to cultivate mushrooms for profit. He and Elizabeth were in the same boat, Henry regularly claimed, a statement that was true in a way because he had been married and was now alone, his wife having removed herself and their child to her parents' flat. For the last few months, once a week or so, he had been taking Elizabeth out to dinner, to a restaurant in the Fulham Road called the Gay Tureen.

It was sometimes hard to believe that Henry had been different, or that the boy who'd been her friend in 1938 could possibly be related to this large man. Red-haired and slim, always running, making her jump over a stick stretched across two others in the garden, he'd been about the nicest person she could think of in 1938, with the exception of her mother. In the garage attached to his parents' house he dressed up as a clown, saying he intended to become a real clown one day. He mimed a variety of parts for her, putting on different sets of his mother's old clothes. Sometimes he invited her to join him, and they made up a plot together and acted it without an audience. On the tow-path of the river they used to creep up on people, men and girls cuddling usually. They loved creeping up on people, best of all on Mr Giltrap when he

26

came to cut her parents' grass and do the weeding. Whenever she looked back on her childhood, she couldn't imagine what it would have been like without Henry. They were exactly the same age, both born beneath the sign of Gemini, within hours of one another.

Their friendship was interrupted by the War, when Elizabeth's school was evacuated to Gloucestershire and Henry was sent to a preparatory school in Essex called Anstey Grange. It was here that he met D'arcy and Carstairs, the sons of two doctors who were in partnership in Kingston Hill. A trio was formed that was to last for the remainder of Henry's schooldays and which, when the War was over and since Kingston Hill was not far away, became a feature of holidays also. D'arcy and Carstairs and Henry roamed the local golf-courses, stealing the balls when they were hit into the rough. They smoked surreptitious cigarettes in a shed that still existed, at the bottom of Carstairs's garden. They cycled all over the south-western suburbs, ringing their bells and shouting. They attended the Putney and Kingston cinemas, irrespective of what was showing. At a party given by Henry's mother Carstairs once exploded a balloon just behind Elizabeth's head, and on another occasion D'arcy put his hand up her skirt while they were both hiding in a cupboard, playing Sardines. At Anstey Grange and later at Radley, D'arcy and Carstairs were intent on following their father's footsteps into the world of medicine. Henry, his ambitions to become a clown forgotten, planned to enter his own father's wine business.

But for Henry as an adult everything seemed to go wrong. There was, for a start, an unexpected loss of family money: at the beginning of his career in the wine business, the firm went bankrupt. His parents sold their house and moved into a flat in a block in the Upper Richmond Road. Hurriedly, Henry's mother contacted a relative in a firm that manufactured women's clothing with a view to seeking employment for Henry, but after a six months' trial period the management of the firm came to the same conclusion as Henry, that he wasn't cut out for a career in women's clothing. His father, who once had been cheerful, died of depression in the flat in the Upper Richmond Road, and within three months of his death Henry's mother died also. Henry in the meantime had found a position in the car-tyre division of a rubber company. It was while he was employed there that he married, and after that there were other jobs: selling advertising space, cruises, investment plans, the *Encyclopædia Britannica*, a new exhaust system to the motor trade, and bathroom showers to hotels. He had a job with coin-in-the-slot machines now, a vending-machine operator he was called.

Henry's house in Meridian Close, a suburban compound begun in February 1962 and completed in November 1962, was one of nine dwellings arranged in a semicircle around a central area of concrete and small trees. The houses were of a uniform design, built in two storeys but conveying a bungaloid effect. There were gardens at the front and at the back of each, those at the front being unfenced so that they tended to run into one another, a deliberate intention of the architect in his wish to create illusions of space. Henry had acquired his house in Meridian Close when he'd married, in 1963, not purchasing it outright since he was not in a position to do so, but borrowing a mortgage deposit from his father-in-law and agreeing to make mortgage repayments to the Abbey National Building Society at the rate of thirty-seven pounds a month.

When Henry had first driven Elizabeth into Meridian Close she'd been immediately struck by the fact that one of the nine dwellings was different from the rest. The wood-work and pebble-dash finish of Henry's house required a coat of paint, its windows were grimy. Weeds grew between the paving stones of the garden strip in front of it, and in the small rectangular area of soil that the strip contained an ash tree gloomily sprouted. The other houses had roses growing in front of them: each pebble-dash façade gleamed with house-holder's pride.

Within Henry's house, in the uncarpeted hall, were cartons containing packets of biscuits and crisps, and coffee, chocolate and milk, and varieties of powdered soup. Henry explained that they were the materials with which he regularly filled his vending-machines. There were also packets of Nutty Pops, which he told her were nuts and caramel-coated maize, a new and popular line. In a cupboard beneath the stairs he showed her plastic sacks full of fibre and organic matter, in which he attempted to grow his mushrooms. His home-brewing kit was in the bathroom.

The house smelt of the beer and the organic matter, and everywhere rubbish had accumulated: leaflets and circulars among the cartons in the hall, stacks of empty cartons in other rooms, small pieces of furniture that were damaged and could no longer be used, piles of magazines. The telephone and the telephone director-ies were on a step of the stairs. The back garden was a jungle.

28

There was a feeling in the house of everything coming apart at once, not just a marriage, but all the possessions that hire-purchase had obtained to set the marriage up. Henry himself, accident-prone and luckless in adult life, had the same kind of built-in obsolescence about him. He drank too much of his home-brew beer, and too much beer and gin in the King of England. Late at night he had a way of bringing men home from the King of England to try his home-brew, and his wife had objected to that as much as to the cartons and the disintegrating house. It was just a habit, he'd tried to explain to Elizabeth. You got talking to people and it seemed natural when the pub closed to say come on to your place. But Elizabeth could imagine that it hadn't seemed like that to his wife. She imagined men explaining to his wife why Henry, now shamefaced and flushed, hadn't returned when he'd said he would, in time for a meal five hours ago. She imagined such men remaining in the house and often being there in the morning, asleep in the sitting-room, exhaling the fumes of Henry's home-brew. A vending-machine that should have been filled with Nutty Pops and biscuits would have been forgotten: someone would telephone at half-past eight. Once, Henry said, a man who'd spent the night in the sitting-room had a heart attack and an ambulance had to be sent for. Elizabeth could imagine his wife having to deal with that because of Henry's hangover, and making the best of the cartons and other late-night guests and of Henry's conviction, fired by a newspaper advertisement, that he could make thirty pounds a week growing mushrooms under the stairs. She hadn't known his wife, but now and again she'd seen her with their child on Barnes Common, a slight figure always in the same navy-blue coat. In the end, apparently, she'd just packed and gone.

Outside the hospital, Henry was unaware of Elizabeth's embarrassment or the children's giggling or Mrs Orvitski's reluctance to release the suitcase, which he wished to carry. He kept pawing at Mrs Orvitski's gloved hand, but her grip remained firm.

'You really shouldn't have bothered, Henry,' Elizabeth murmured as all together they trooped up the steps to the hospital.

'I said I'd drive you,' he repeated, taking her arm, his voice a little aggrieved. 'I'd have liked to, you know.'

She said she'd forgotten, and was sorry. She hadn't forgotten: two nights ago in the Gay Tureen he'd made her promise to let him drive her to the hospital, assuring her that the Zephyr was in tip-top shape these days. She'd ordered the minicab because she'd no way of knowing just how tip-top the Zephyr's current shape was. More than once they'd left the Gay Tureen late at night to find a puncture in one of the Zephyr's tyres, or trouble with the carburettor, or the battery so flat that nothing worked at all. Henry would then attempt a repair, banging about for up to an hour sometimes, while she huddled in a doorway or in the vehicle itself. It was the return of Henry to her house after these occasions that had caused Mrs Orvitski, who was usually baby-sitting, not to know what to make of him on account of his dirty and dishevelled condition. Once he had driven Mrs Orvitski home and had had to change a wheel on the way, an incident that Mrs Orvitski regularly referred to.

His shoulder struck a nurse as they crossed the hospital's entrance hall, but he didn't appear to notice. 'Why wouldn't she let me carry the case?' he asked on the way upstairs, and Elizabeth, not wishing to have a conversation about Mrs Orvitski while Mrs Orvitski was still within earshot, said that he must have more to do on a Sunday morning than seeing people into hospital.

Henry shook his head. He had a brew going, he said, which he hoped would be ready by lunchtime, and he wanted to re-set the plugs of the Zephyr, but apart from that he'd nothing whatsoever to do. On the way back he'd look in at the King of England for an hour. He'd re-set the plugs after he'd had something to eat, a Fray Bentos steak-and-kidney pie probably.

Outside the Marie Atkins Ward, Nurse Hampshire took the suitcase from Mrs Orvitski and led Elizabeth away. 'Is Mummy coming back?' Alice whispered, and Mrs Orvitski explained that in the ward Elizabeth would change into a nightdress and put her clothes into the suitcase. Henry nodded, smilingly confirming this. She herself, Mrs Orvitski said, would take the clothes and return with them a day or two before Elizabeth's release. 'Or I might,' Henry said. 'Save you the trouble, Mrs Orvitski.'

On the long wooden seat a tall girl and a woman sat. The woman had a countrywoman's air about her, red-cheeked and plump, the girl was shyly awkward. They were Mrs Delve and Carol Pidsley from Number Nine, Balaclava Avenue, the friends of Miss Samson. Mrs Delve whispered, saying the hospital seemed an excellent place. Carol Pidsley nodded.

'Well, here we are,' Miss Samson said, emerging from the Marie Atkins Ward and handing her suitcase to Mrs Delve. 'Seems awfully nice, you know.'

Carol Pidsley and Mrs Delve bade Miss Samson goodbye, repeating that in their prayers in Balaclava Avenue she'd naturally be remembered.

Elizabeth returned, a yellow dressing-gown over the nightdress with the rosebuds on it. 'Goodbye, Mummy,' Jennifer said, and Elizabeth kissed her two younger children and told them to be good with Mrs Orvitski. She reminded them to feed and give water to their hamsters. 'Thanks for coming, Henry,' she said. 'And thank you, too, Mrs Orvitski.'

The children clung to her, wanting to have a last-minute conversation, but frightened of raising their voices in the silent corridor. 'I think you'd better go,' she said, and Mrs Orvitski seized the suitcase as Henry was about to. The children still lingered, whispering to her, saying they wished it didn't have to be Mrs Orvitski who was to look after them, saying they loved her.

'I can't bear it,' Jennifer murmured as they went downstairs.

'Cutting her,' whispered Alice.

Mrs Orvitski was silent. She didn't like the man, arriving like that in dirty clothes, taking Mrs Aidallbery's arm and wanting to carry the suitcase. What on earth did a man like that think he was up to? 'I'll have to jack you up, old girl,' he'd said the night he'd given her a lift and she'd thought at first, having never heard the expression before, that he was going to put his hands on her. She'd gripped her handbag, preparing herself to strike him on the side of the head as soon as he started anything. She'd tried to open the door of the car but there was something the matter with the catch, and before she could make any sense of it he'd got out of the car himself. A moment later she'd felt herself being raised in the air and he was shouting at her that it wouldn't take a jiffy.

They crossed the entrance hall, the children leading the way. They passed through the glass swing-doors and descended the steps to the pavement. 'Well, now,' Henry said jollily, colliding with the woman with the banner, 'who's for a Coca-Cola? Or Nutty Pops?' He had some Nutty Pops in the car, he said, but the children ran to the minicab, pretending they hadn't heard him, and when he smiled at Mrs Orvitski and said that Coca-Cola and Nutty Pops might cheer things up she didn't reply, either. The minicab drove away, and he stood for a moment outside the brown façade of the hospital. He was thinking of nothing in particular, not of Elizabeth Aidallbery, or the reluctance of her children to drink Coca-Cola and eat Nutty Pops, or of the hostility of Mrs Orvitski. His mind was empty as he walked towards his battered Zephyr, until suddenly he thought of the Fray Bentos pie that in two hours' time he would take from a cupboard and place in the oven, setting the oven at Regulo 8. He saw quite clearly the blue-and-red tin that contained the pie, and his own hands taking the tin from the cupboard and using a familiar tin-opener on it. Every Sunday since his wife had left him he'd opened a Fray Bentos steak-and-kidney pie at fifteen minutes past two, after the King of England had closed.

3

Lily watched them. The one called Mrs Aidallbery looked as though she could do with a rest. Like the others, she'd smiled at Lily when Nurse Hampshire had introduced her, but in her time in hospital Lily had discovered that new patients were often uneasy behind their smiles. Not frightened of the operations that were to come, but concerned in different ways about the people they left behind. Only the older woman among the three new ones, the Miss Samson, seemed to cover nothing up with her smile.

In the bed next to the door, on Lily's far right, Miss Samson already lay. Next to her, between her and Lily, was the one called Sylvie Clapper, who had just finished arranging make-up bottles in her cupboard. Across the ward, on her own a bit because there wasn't a bed on either side of her, Mrs Aidallbery tidied away things, too. They were all three in for hysterectomies.

'Are you allowed smoking?' Sylvie Clapper asked.

She said they didn't like you to smoke in the wards, that they'd rather you did it in the corridor. 'Although there's no particular rule,' she said.

'I told them I didn't want to come in at all, but they reckon I'm a mess inside. Like an army's marched through me, one bloke said.'

Lily smiled. 'You'll be all right,' she said.

'Nice way to put it, though, an army going through you.' Sylvie Clapper laughed. There was a bright cockiness about her eyes as if nothing upset her for long. She said: 'I'm not married or nothing. Did you see that fella? My boyfriend? Declan he's called. Irish.'

Lily shook her head.

'He's taking me up to Liverpool afterwards. He has uncles there. We'll maybe settle in Liverpool.'

Lily said that after a hysterectomy it was meant to be a good idea to have a holiday, or to go for a while to the hospital's convalescent home in Eastbourne. Sylvie Clapper nodded without paying much attention. She said: 'I work in a Woolworth's, down in the basement. Paints, cleaning stuff. Quite nice, really. What are you in for, Lily?'

'I can't have a baby.'

Sylvie said she'd wanted to have a baby, too, but never would now, not after the operation. 'Declan says it doesn't make no difference. Not to worry, Declan says.'

'He sounds nice.'

'Declan's fantastic.' She moved towards the corridor with her cigarettes and matches in her left hand.

'You get a bit low, I dare say,' Miss Samson said.

Lily said you couldn't complain. It was only the boredom. She hoped they'd let her out soon.

Miss Samson shook her head. It was better to be safe than sorry, she suggested. Time passed, no matter what the circumstances. There was one thing no one could do in spite of all the advances these days, and that was to interfere with the passing of God's time.

'No. No one can do that.'

'I'm the manageress of a boarding-house,' Miss Samson said. 'Church folk, the inmates I call them. Nine, Balaclava Avenue.'

Lily smiled.

'S.W.17. I've been there since 1931. We've always been Church folk at Number Nine. Ever since Mr Ibbs's day.'

'I see.'

'I came to work there in the kitchen. I've no education, you know. Before Mr Ibbs died he asked me if I'd take on as manageress, and then in his will we found he'd left me the house.'

Miss Samson smiled, Lily nodded. She found it difficult when speaking to Miss Samson not to stare at the birthmark on her face. It was difficult to know where to look otherwise in case Miss Samson should think she was averting her eyes.

'And for Private Foot serving in Belfast,' a voice said in Elizabeth's ear, 'with all the love in the world from his Mum and Dad, sisters Joan and Angela, girl-friend Lesley, all of Essington Street, Newcastle; and for Mr and Mrs Parrish and Hilda, of Rodway Road, Tottenham, London, from their son Ted, in Germany; and for all the boys of Unit –'

She turned it off. There'd been a girl at school who'd repeatedly tried to get a record played on Forces' Favourites, as the programme had been called then: Irene Baddley, with bad breath and shoulders like a man's. People were always leaving *Picture Post* or *Illustrated* on her desk, open at one of the Colgate advertisements, which told of personal tragedy due to halitosis, but Irene Baddley had never taken the hint.

34

In the minicab they'd be arguing now, and Mrs Orvitski, unaware of their mood, would be attempting to hug them. Joanna and Samuel would be with their friends, all of them conversing in deaf-and-dumb language in a shed they went to, a place they rented on Sundays from some French onion-men. They listened to pop music on a transistor there, and cooked brown rice on a primus, and lay about on sacks. They smoked, Elizabeth suspected, cannabis. She closed her eyes, imagining the onion-men's shed being invaded by the police and Joanna being taken into custody, a development Mrs Orvitski certainly wouldn't be able to cope with. For a brief moment she saw an image of Henry standing in a police station talking to a desk-sergeant, trying to explain that he was a friend of the family, asking if he might be allowed to see Joanna.

'Settling in, Mrs Aidallbery?' a voice said. 'Finding your feet, are you? I'm Sister O'Keeffe.'

She was a woman of fifty-one, from Kinsale in Co. Cork, of medium height, plumply made, with a round plain face and blue eyes that reflected sometimes her devotion to the work she had chosen. 'You'll have your little op tomorrow,' she said, bustling from bed to bed. 'How're you getting on with it?' she asked Lily Drucker, nodding her head at Lady Augusta's autobiography. 'How d'you you do, Miss Samson?'

They'd met Nurse Hampshire and Nurse Summerbee, she said; later on they'd meet Sister Pearson and Nurse Aylard and Nurse Emamooden and Nurse Wibberley and the night sisters, Sister Kolulu and Sister Swaine. 'We're a happy little ship on the first floor,' she said.

An elderly Indian woman in a green overall wheeled a trolley into the ward. Sister O'Keeffe moved away. 'I'm Sister O'Keeffe,' she said to Sylvie Clapper at the door. 'Take it easy today, dear.'

'I was having a smoke,' Sylvie said.

'Coffin nails,' said Sister O'Keeffe.

The Indian woman placed lunchtime cutlery on the fawn-topped table. She winked at Lily, which was something she often did when she came round with her trolley. Her face was wrinkled and bony, the dark skin loose and touched with faint pock-marks. 'You're not in the dumps, Mrs Drucker?' she inquired, eyeing Lily with sharp, searching pupils. Lily shook her head. They liked her to get up for meals, but whenever she could she had a meal in bed. They liked her to get up repeatedly during the day, to go for walks to the other wards. But the more she got up the more her back ached, as it had ached during her other pregnancies. They were afraid of thrombosis if she lay too much in bed, another woman had told her, but Lily wasn't afraid of thrombosis, she was afraid of making a mess of it again. 'Nice little toddle,' Sister O'Keeffe would breezily say, even though Lily had told her that she felt a strain whenever she went for a nice little toddle. She felt a strain even when she walked to the lavatory, or got out of bed to sit at the fawn-topped table. If no one was about, the elderly Indian woman slipped her meals on to her bed-table.

'Don't seem too bad,' Sylvie Clapper said. 'Efficient, by the looks of things.'

'And kind,' Miss Samson said. 'You feel it in your bones.'

But Sylvie Clapper said she wasn't so sure about that. She'd had an altercation with a nurse while she'd been having her smoke in the corridor. 'Told me to mind where I dropped the ash. Black as your boot, she was.'

Miss Samson talked about her boarding-house. She described the present inmates, and said she'd never had a happier bunch. The Reverend Rawes, retired for thirteen years but still called upon at the nearby St Matthew's, was small and quite wizened, really – like a sharp little blackbird, Miss Samson often thought. Mrs Delve was younger, of course, widowed and pleasantly chatty, in charge of the kitchen while Miss Samson was indisposed. The Tonsell brothers, Edward and Robert, were younger still, somewhere in their early thirties, dark-jowled and dark-haired, the joint proprietors of a printing-press that took on work of a religious nature. The Tonsell brothers were lunchtime lay-preachers and were regularly to be seen addressing a small crowd outside St Matthew's, or in some other public place where their presence did not interfere with traffic or pedestrians. They were sombre men, of a serious nature. Carol Pidsley was twenty-nine, a tall girl, Miss Samson said, and did not add that Carol Pidsley was very tall. Nor did she say that Carol Pidsley suffered a little from acne and was unhappy because of this; nor that she was unhappy because she greatly disliked the appearance of her legs, considering them to be like tree-trunks. Carol Pidsley worked in a stationer's shop where the manager, a Mr Blacker, was hard on her. This fact Miss Samson did reveal, assessing it to be information that Carol Pidsley would not mind being passed on. She spoke of the little Welsh girl who was employed in the kitchen of Number Nine Balaclava Avenue, and Arthur who did the rough work, who was backward but you'd hardly know it.

She described the house, the sitting-room with its cosy-stove, the dining-room with a cosy-stove also and six chairs around the table, and how on Sunday mornings they all went together, Arthur and the little Welsh girl as well, to St Matthew's. In the hall there was a small embroidery, flowers in *petit point*, neatly framed in passe-partout. *Welcome to Happiness*, it said. Mr Ibbs had placed it on the wall long before her time; it could have hung there for fifty years for all she knew. Someone had said to her when she first came to work in the kitchen of Number Nine that Mr Ibbs himself had embroidered the flowers and the message, but she had never believed that, preferring to think that if Mr Ibbs had had a hand in the embroidery it had only to do with the application of the passe-partout. Mr Ibbs's old walking-stick still stood in the umbrella-stand, a stick that he'd once told her had belonged to his great-grandfather.

In the evenings at Number Nine Miss Samson said that she often spoke to the other inmates about Mr Ibbs, since none of them had known him. 'Live out each day as though it be your last,' he used regularly to intone in the kitchen, and on his own last day he had had a happy time, walking all afternoon with his yellow labrador, Thomas. Towards the end of his life he had enjoyed more than anything these walks in the suburbs of S.W.17, past other boarding-houses, and shops and stucco villas. He died with his dog's head resting on his chest. 'The happiest man I ever knew,' Miss Samson said.

Over the years Miss Samson had brought this gaunt man to life for the new inmates of Number Nine, and now she did so in the Marie Atkins Ward: a man in slippers and an old tweed suit, with strands of grey hair brushed this way and that, and pebbly spectacles. It was Mr Ibbs who had decreed that Church people only should occupy Number Nine. Often at St Matthew's he had read the lesson, and Miss Samson described this: his resonant voice, the meaning he gave to every single word, the way he walked from his pew to the lectern. She went on to describe other aspects of Number Nine: the garden where they sat in summer, the black elephants on the sitting-room mantelpiece, the cosiness on a winter's evening when everyone was in. Each morning of his life the Reverend Rawes called in to see if the old woman in Number Ten was all right. Mrs Delve and Carol Pidsley collected for the Church of England's Children's Society. The Tonsell brothers were sidesmen at St Matthew's.

'Well, there's something very nice,' Miss Samson said. 'Something we've noticed, Mrs Delve and I. The last three Sundays Edward Tonsell has always walked to church with Carol.'

There was something else that was nice. The inmates were insisting that she should take a little holiday after the operation. Bexhill-on-Sea they prescribed, seven days of rest and good sea air, a gift from them. It had come as a lovely surprise, she said, this gesture of friendship from the inmates.

The elderly Indian woman wheeled her trolley into the ward again, with covered plates of roast beef and potatoes and peas. Miss Samson got up and put on her dressing-gown, and she and Sylvie Clapper and Elizabeth ate the meal from the fawn-topped table. Lily had hers in bed.

'You going on a holiday after, Elizabeth?' Sylvie asked, and Elizabeth said that by the time the operation was over she imagined Mrs Orvitski would have had enough of her children.

'What age are they, Elizabeth?' Sylvie asked.

Elizabeth told her, and Miss Samson said Elizabeth had been fortunate. Sylvie repeated that her boyfriend, Declan, was going to take her to Liverpool when she'd had the operation. She talked about Declan in much the same way as Miss Samson had talked about Nine Balaclava Avenue. 'I was with another girl and he came up to both of us – Sharon Timpson it was, she worked in Cuff's at the time. "Can I have this dance?" he said to her and she said no, she wasn't dancing, so he asked me and I said no, too. "Declan's the name," he said, and I said I'd never heard a name like that before and he told me it was Irish. He came from Enniscorthy, he said, and he asked me if I'd ever been there. I said I'd never heard of it. That's how I met Declan,' said Sylvie.

After the roast beef there was jelly with fruit in it, and the women at the table idled over this, none of them much caring for it.

'It's interesting your friend working in Cuff's,' Miss Samson said. 'I often buy things in Cuff's. We had new curtains for the sitting-room windows about eighteen months ago. I got all the material at Cuff's.'

'Sharon's in the Woolworth's now, the counter beside me, electrical stuff.' Sylvie smiled at Miss Samson. 'We danced a few times that night,' she said, 'and then he said could he see me again some time, and we agreed to meet the following evening in a pub called the George on Hammersmith Broadway. You've probably seen it, Miss Samson? Next to Lloyds Bank.'

Miss Samson shook her head.

'It has the Cruskeen Bawn Lounge,' Sylvie said, 'all done out with Irish road signs. It's an Irish pub. Declan likes it.'

Miss Samson nodded. She had never had an intimate connection with a man; no man had ever proposed marriage to her. It was not her role in the world to attract the attentions or desires of men, Miss Samson had told herself since the age of thirteen. Had that been her role, God would not have permitted the accident at her birth and the ugliness she had ever since carried on her face. Yet at the centre of her life there was the generosity of a man: the kindness of Mr Ibbs, who had taken her into Number Nine, even though others might have argued that her deformity would put paying guests off. Mr Ibbs, dead since 1958, was the man who existed most brightly in Miss Samson's imagination and was honoured for his goodness and his wisdom, sharing precious glory with Christ her Lord.

Lily Drucker listened while the others talked, occasionally saying something herself but more often lying quietly, not wishing to draw attention to the fact that she was having a meal in bed when she wasn't meant to. Jane they wanted to call it if it was a girl and Andrew if it was a boy. Lily said the names over to herself, trying to imagine a child in her arms, a live creature she could fuss over. But even as she thought of this, the image fell from her mind beneath the pressure of a more immediate prospect. On Sunday afternoons Kenneth did not visit her alone. His parents accompanied him, which was something she had learnt to dread and which she had always to prepare herself for.

'No, actually I'm divorced,' she heard the one called Mrs Aidallbery say, answering another of Sylvie Clapper's questions.

4

Henry drank in the King of England with his friends D'arcy and Carstairs. It had become something of a tradition that they met in the King of England on Saturdays and Sundays at lunchtime, in continuing celebration of the friendship that had begun at their preparatory school, Anstey Grange. Yet it was a celebration that increasingly disturbed Henry, emphasizing as it did – and more harshly as the years went by – the difference between his circumstances and those of his two friends.

Henry's occupation as a vending-machine operator was a self-employed one, but it was none the less dominated by a man called Rammage, who occupied a prefabricated office in Fulham. Henry did not own the machines he operated, nor did Rammage. The machines were owned by New-Way Vending Limited, an organization that extended its operation throughout London. New-Way Vending Limited rented its machines to schools and colleges, launderettes, swimming-baths, garages, offices, and other concerns where a profit might be made by the New-Way operators. Henry kept the machines filled with the necessary commodities, was responsible for their smooth running, and in return received all the money the machines earned. Rammage's role was to oversee the smooth operation, to supply New-Way engineers when the machines broke down, and to deal with complaints about operators. Henry had met Rammage only once, four years ago when he'd first become an operator, but had since spoken to him almost daily on the telephone. Rammage's voice was slow and nasal and was often rendered unintelligible due to the fact that he invariably spoke with a cigarette in his mouth. The voice matched a physical presence which Henry had little difficulty in recalling: Rammage was a stained middle-aged man in a suit with cigarette ash on it, a weighty man for whom it was an effort to stand up. On the occasion when Henry had met him he had repeatedly placed a straightened-out paperclip in one or other of his ears and removed a quantity of wax, which he then rolled about on the chipboard surface of his desk. 'Always call a customer "sir",' he'd said on that occasion. 'Do not re-regulate New-Way machines to give weak drinks.' From time to time during the subsequent four years Rammage would pause in the middle of a telephone conversation to repeat these commands. 'I sacked a man last week,' he once said, 'for getting bolshie with a garage attendant. Just watch all that kind of thing.' Once Rammage had telephoned Henry to say that the head-mistress of a secondary modern school had put in a complaint about Henry's appearance, questioning the fact that Henry should be handling food. 'I'd watch that if I were you,' Rammage had said. 'Clean yourself up, mate.'

Since his schooldays such men had haunted Henry. In the women's clothing business there had been a Mr Wauk and in the tyre division of the rubber company a Mr Dibbins, and in the bathroom showers business a Mr Rinsal. There'd been Z. Jacob Nirenstein and T. J. B. Antler and a man called Posit, known as R.J. Such men had differed considerably in appearance but had otherwise much in common, in particular a cold, dead gaze. They hadn't laughed when Henry laughed. They hadn't been jolly men.

As he drank with his friends in the King of England, Henry couldn't help reflecting on the small injustices of fate that had driven him over the years into the company of such men as Mr Rinsal, T. J. B. Antler and Rammage, while D'arcy and Carstairs had so agreeably thrived. Some years ago they had taken over their fathers' joint practice on Kingston Hill. They were now well-to-do and respected, their marriages were secure, one of D'arcy's boys was currently at Anstey Grange and would go on to Radley. Yet when they'd been at Anstey Grange themselves, under Bodger Harrison, the story had been different. 'Carstairs's a common criminal,' the Bodger had once announced to a classroom of boys and had then read out a piece of work which Carstairs, without an effort at disguise, had copied from a boy called Pinmack-Jones. It was, in fact, Pinmack-Jones's front teeth that D'arcy knocked out later that term in a piece of rowdyism in the dormitory. 'I don't know what you imagine Pinmack-Jones is in this school for,' Bodger Harrison had said, 'but it is hardly to be put to uses such as these. I have not expelled D'arcy, but I can assure you the thought has been foremost in my mind. Pinmack-Jones will be inconvenienced with dental trappings for the rest of his life.'

That Sunday morning D'arcy and Carstairs were dressed in their usual suburban weekend wear, D'arcy in a pair of navy-blue Levis and a navy-blue fisherman's jersey, Carstairs in maroon Levis and a maroon windcheater. They were big men, like Henry, and pinkcomplexioned, known for their charm and their easy, extrovert manners. D'arcy laughed a lot and had a way, when excited, of grasping people's elbows. Carstairs was quieter. At Anstey Grange, in Bodger Harrison's 4B, they'd all three sat together in the second row from the back. 'Are soles fish, sir?' D'arcy had asked the new young English and Divinity master, and the man had said yes, one kind of soles were. 'Oh, my God, you're a scream, sir!' D'arcy had cried, amid a tumult of desk-thumping and laughter.

D'arcy was now a keen supporter of the nearby Rosslyn Park Rugby Football Club, and would regularly succeed in persuading the other two to spend a Saturday afternoon cheering on the Park from the touchlines. Sundays were different: at two o'clock, when the King of England closed, the three men would promptly part until the following weekend, D'arcy returning to his wife and children, Carstairs to his, and Henry to his house in Meridian Close.

Since his wife had left him, Sunday afternoon was a time Henry found difficult to sustain. On Sunday afternoons he had access to his son, Timus, now aged five, and increasingly this proved to be a frustrating and unsatisfactory experience. Four times in the last two months his ex-wife had telephoned him on a Sunday morning to say that Timus claimed not to be feeling well. His ex-wife lived in Willesden now and Henry had the rather long journey across London to collect and return Timus, which he'd often thought was an advantage because it used up the time nicely. But apparently Timus didn't like the journey and had complained to his mother that there was a smell of petrol in the Zephyr, which made him feel sick. Other people had mentioned a smell of petrol too, but Henry couldn't smell anything himself.

'Well,' Carstairs said while D'arcy was ordering further pints of beer, 'you tucked her in?'

Henry nodded. He had tucked Elizabeth in, he said. And then, feeling suddenly rather depressed, he explained about the misunderstanding there'd been: how he'd arrived at her house to find nobody there and had caught up the minicab as it was stopping outside the hospital, how Mrs Orvitski wouldn't let him carry the suitcase.

'What's all this?' D'arcy demanded, returning with the beer. 'You don't look at all well, you know,' he said to Henry.

'Henry's been seeing that Elizabeth into hospital,' Carstairs said. 'Or trying to.'

'Really puffy, you look,' D'arcy said. 'You drink too much, Henry.'

'Yes,' Henry said, a reply that caused his friends to glance at one

42

another. D'arcy said Henry's liver was probably the size of a football. Carstairs advised Henry to undergo a thorough examination.

'Yes,' Henry said again. He wasn't listening. He was remembering, a long time ago, eating magenta-coloured ice-cream that Elizabeth's mother had made, and Elizabeth laughing, with teeth missing. It was an afternoon, they were in the garden. There were striped deck-chairs, red and blue, and green and orange. Elizabeth's mother was reading to them. They lay on the grass, kicking at one another's feet. *'The tray,'* Elizabeth's mother said, *'was placed safely on a little table beside the bed, and Katy sat watching Cousin Helen eat her supper with a warm, loving feeling at her heart.'* He didn't know why on earth he'd remembered that single sentence, since he'd forgotten so much else. Absurd, to remember a sentence like that.

D'arcy laughed. Carstairs was telling a story about an elderly patient who'd died during the week because of some inefficiency on the part of a district nurse. He'd had a letter from the elderly patient's son blaming him for the mishap and announcing that steps would be taken. D'arcy said he knew of a district nurse who'd been giving an old fellow in East Sheen the wrong injections for four years, and Carstairs told a story that Henry had heard before, about a district nurse who'd once attempted to get him to treat her dog.

'I had this woman on Tuesday,' D'arcy said with his face close to Henry's. 'A new patient called Mrs Horsewell said she wanted a heart transplant on the National Health. "But there's nothing wrong with your heart," I said to her. D'you know what she told me, Henry?'

Henry shook his head. The pink flesh on D'arcy's face shook as he prepared himself for laughter. He seized Henry's right elbow.

'She said she'd been to see a Madame Norma, a fortune-teller.'

D'arcy began to laugh, making a familiar cawing sound. Enthusiastically, he worked Henry's elbow up and down. Carstairs had evidently heard the story before: the pink flesh on his face shook too, and suddenly he broke into a loud giggle, drowning what D'arcy was saying. As far as Henry could make out, the juxtaposition of spades and hearts in the pattern that Madame Norma estimated to be Mrs Horsewell's fortune had convinced Madame Norma that Mrs Horse-well should see a doctor and make the request she had made.

'Ha, ha, ha,' giggled Carstairs, rocking his large body back and forth.

'I swear to God,' D'arcy said, still working Henry's elbow. ' "I think I should have a transplant, Doctor," she said, as if she was asking to have a wart taken off.'

'I never touch warts, actually,' Carstairs said.

'God, no.'

They spoke of other cases that had cropped up during the week. They referred to an elderly Dr Sweeting, a colleague of theirs in Kingston, who was apparently addled in his mind, and to an anaesthetist who was a drunk.

'Who's in charge of Elizabeth?' D'arcy asked Henry.

'A man called Alstrop-Smith.'

'God almighty,' Carstairs murmured, and D'arcy said that Alstrop-Smith should have been struck off in 1947.

They went on talking about the man who was going to operate on Elizabeth, lengthening the case against him until it seemed to Henry that Elizabeth stood little chance of survival. But he knew the talk was exaggerated, because almost every week in the King of England, on the Saturday or the Sunday, he listened while medical fantasies were elaborately spun: in this particular way his friends relaxed after a week of being serious and successful. There was a time, he remembered, the same term that Pinmack-Jones had been subjected to their attentions, when Bodger Harrison had questioned him closely about his choice of companions. 'You are yourself neither furtive nor violent,' the Bodger had pointed out. 'We have faith in you. You are on the Credit side, you will go far. Yet you consort with useless persons. You are constantly in the company of D'arcy and Carstairs nowadays.' When he was at Radley he'd once gone back to Anstey Grange. He'd had tea with Bodger Harrison – chicken-paste sandwiches, as always – and over it the Bodger had asked him about D'arcy and Carstairs. He'd replied that he thought they were settling down, but the Bodger shook his head and said that in his opinion D'arcy and Carstairs would never settle down. 'They'll disappear into the gutters of Soho,' he said, and then reminded Henry that Carstairs had covered the palms of his hands with information for a geography test, that D'arcy had cut a desk with a saw. 'You have a better brain than either of them,' the Bodger had said with a schoolmaster's finality. 'And a better character.' At Anstey Grange he had been Captain of the 1st XI and Captain of the Hockey XI, and Bodger Harrison's Head Boy. Even at Radley he'd been quite successful.

'Did you see Andy Ripley yesterday?' D'arcy asked, referring to a Rosslyn Park rugby player who had represented England in an international match.

44

Henry said he hadn't.

'That last Irish try was over the deadball line. Damn ridiculous, you know.'

'They'd have won anyway,' Carstairs said. 'That McGann's a great little kicker.'

'I never saw an English side play as badly. Except for Andy.'

Carstairs agreed with that opinion. Henry said:

'Did I ever tell you I went back to see the Bodger once?'

'Bodger Harrison? He's been dead for donkey's years.'

'Praise be to God,' Carstairs said.

'It was when I was at Radley. 1947.'

'He was affected in the head, that man,' D'arcy said.

Carstairs giggled. They began to talk about Bodger Harrison, recalling anecdotes about him, how he used to eat pieces off his moustache, and the time Wiltshire Minor took his false teeth out of a glass by his bedside and dropped them into a saucepan of porridge that was cooking overnight on the Aga. They laughed uproariously, D'arcy making his cawing sound. Henry had wanted to say, laughing a bit over it too, that he'd had the usual chicken-paste sandwiches with the old headmaster and then, without using the Bodger's actual words, to imply the Bodger's opinion that Henry would eventually do well in the world. He didn't know why he wanted to talk about that, except that he often did nowadays.

The laughter and D'arcy's cawing continued, and Henry knew it would be impossible to return to the subject he wished to return to. He joined in their laughter when D'arcy recalled the time he and Wiltshire Minor had poured a bottle of Syrup of Figs over the Bodger's steamed pudding. But even as he laughed, his mind filled with resolutions and plans. They came quite easily to his mind, as though they'd been just outside it somewhere: he wanted to start again, even at forty-one.

He would, to begin with, tidy up his house. He'd noticed it as he was leaving that morning: old cartons everywhere, two stair-rods loose because the screws had come out of the brackets that held them, the curtain-rail in the sitting-room sagging badly beneath the weight of the curtains. It was remarkable how easily a house got into a state without a woman about, or with a woman who didn't care. 'Just look at the condition of the place,' she'd said to him a fortnight before she left him, as though he'd been responsible. She'd led him to Timus's room and made him stand in the doorway. There was a bed and a cupboard, and a bedspread tacked up over the window, nothing else.

She said that for years she'd been asking him to do something about it. He tried to explain that it was a question of finding time, but she hadn't listened. Instead she said something about the King of England, which was irrelevant, and about the mushrooms he was growing in order to supplement their income, and his home-brewing apparatus.

While Elizabeth was in hospital he'd knock the whole place into shape. He'd burn the cartons, he'd fix the stair-rods and the sitting-room curtains, he'd tackle the garden, probably borrow a lawnmower from the woman next door. He'd have the whole place sparkling, and the first night she was well again they'd have a drink or two in the sitting-room before going on to the Gay Tureen for dinner. He'd say quietly that he'd like her to come to the house with her children whenever she felt ready. He'd show her the upstairs rooms, one for Jennifer and Alice, one for Joanna, one for themselves. She might argue that it would be easier if he came to her house, but he would quietly resist that, implying that he had his pride.

Henry nodded to himself, and took a mouthful of beer. That afternoon, after he'd fetched Timus, he'd telephone Jennifer and Alice and ask them if they'd like to come over and play. It would be nice for Timus, and nice for them because they'd probably be feeling a bit lonely. He'd see if he could get the television going, and they could watch the Sunday afternoon film if they wanted to.

As he stood with his friends, hearing their laughter but not listening to their chat, he saw a future that was different from any past there had been since the afternoon he and Elizabeth had eaten magenta-coloured ice-cream. One summer, in a heatwave, his parents had taken her with them on holiday, to Budleigh Salterton, where there wasn't any sand. His father, red-cheeked and jolly, showed them how to fish with a line for mackerel. Across the warm shingle they crept up on a clergyman, who was angry and waved a stick at them, and they ran away, laughing, pretending to be terrified. In a shop that sold buckets and spades they bought a bar of Crunchie. They sat on the shingle, watching the sea coming in, telling stories in turn.

'Come on,' Carstairs said, drawing Henry's attention to their three empty tankards.

Not far from the King of England, the man with whom Elizabeth had had a love affair talked about Value Added Tax. Five adults were in the room with him, two other couples and his wife Daphne, whom

46

he'd once promised Elizabeth he'd leave. The people in the room drank sherry, and gin mixed with vermouth or tonic water, and whisky. In the garden their children played.

He did not know, as he drank and spoke of taxation, that a woman he'd once loved had that morning been admitted to a hospital in a routine way, for a gynaecological operation. But once, in passing, he thought of her because it had been in this room, on a Sunday-morning occasion exactly similar to this one, that their brief love affair had begun. The love affair had brought about the end of her marriage because she'd been unable to keep up the deception: when she'd telephoned him one night at midnight to tell him she'd failed in that way, he'd felt an icy sweat on his stomach because instinctively he'd known that what was happening wasn't what he wanted. A month after they'd parted he'd had a letter from her and they'd met and had lunch in the Casa Peppino in Frith Street. 'I thought we might meet,' she'd said in the Casa Peppino, 'if it's possible. From time to time.' And in reply he'd found he had to tell her that it would be better if they didn't. It had been a difficult occasion.

The woman who was still his wife laughed in a corner of the room, and her laughter drew his attention, for he found the talk of Value Added Tax tedious. Daphne had suffered, but they had pulled the pieces together. Even now, after all that time had passed, it was good to hear her laugh.

'It's going to hit launderettes,' the man beside him said.

'Yes, of course,' he agreed, glad now to fall back into the tedium. Memories were no good, not memories of that kind anyway.

'Darling,' Daphne said, crossing the room to him, 'we've all got empty glasses.'

He put his arm around her shoulders. It was a gesture he often found himself making now, ever since he'd been cited in the divorce case, a gesture to show that they were friends again, to show that Daphne had forgiven him.

In the Sunset Home in Richmond Elizabeth's mother, Mrs Orpen, read *Bleak House*. Two days ago she'd become eighty-two. She'd been forty when to her own and everyone else's surprise she'd been told she was pregnant. It had been the first and only time in a marriage that had eventually lasted twenty-one years. It was a long time ago now, too long ago to think about.

She sat in a wicker chair, in a conservatory that caught the morning

47

sun. Beside her, in another chair, a woman, older than she was, read a Sunday newspaper.

'Extraordinary things they write about,' this other woman said.

Mrs Orpen didn't hear. Her lower lip, swollen a little and marked with the blotches of old age, was pushed out in concentration as her eyes tried to steady the print in front of them. *Mr Skimpole*, she read, *was as agreeable at breakfast as he had been overnight. There was honey on the table, and it led him into a discourse about Bees.*

'Extraordinary, the things you read,' the other woman more loudly said.

Mrs Orpen nodded slightly, as though unwilling to expend energy on a more definite gesture.

'Listen to this,' the other woman said, and in a slow voice read aloud, about a man who ate shoe polish in order to induce hallucinations.

Mrs Orpen said she didn't understand any of it.

'Hallucinations. Like dreams, they are. You take stuff these days.'

The newspaper dropped on to the tiled floor of the conservatory and the woman began to talk about a jackdaw that her husband had once trained, hoping that it would maybe talk. 'Snapper,' she said. 'He called it Snapper.'

Mrs Orpen nodded. Often you didn't get a moment's peace to read a book. She'd read *Bleak House* before, of course. In a way it was her favourite book and in a way she much preferred *The Mill on the Floss*. The woman was talking again, but she couldn't hear what she was saying. She went on nodding, pretending to hear, not wishing the woman to raise her voice. She couldn't remember the woman's name.

Elizabeth was alone, she suddenly thought, having not thought it for a day or two. History had repeated itself. Elizabeth had been foolish. You made your bed, you had to lie on it. *It was not necessary for the Bee to make such a merit of his tastes*, she read, her eyes urgent on the print, not wishing to go on thinking about Elizabeth being foolish. But the woman in the chair beside her had raised her voice again, still talking about the jackdaw called Snapper. Her husband had trained it to sit on his shoulder while he walked about the house. He used to shave, she said, with the jackdaw in attendance.

'Yes,' Mrs Orpen said.

She remembered him standing there in his brown check suit, in the hall of the Pensione Bencistà, saying his name was Aidallbery. She remembered him alone at his table in the dining-room, and Elizabeth looking across at him in a schoolgirlish kind of way. She should

48

have taken her away at once. She should have pretended she had stomach pains and had to return to London. Too easy, being wise after the event.

A gong sounded and both women obediently rose, each of them gripping the cane arms of her chair and then gradually straightening.

'He hunted everywhere,' the other old woman said. 'In the shed, behind his bonfire stuff, all over the house. He cried, you know, when Snapper went.'

They moved together through a sitting-room with bright chintz covers on its armchairs, where other elderly people were moving also. There was a smell of gravy and brussels sprouts.

'Funny,' the other woman said, 'he never found the body. I miss him, you know,' she said suddenly, poking her way cautiously across the carpet.

Mrs Orpen nodded again. She didn't miss her own husband, which was true. And Elizabeth, of course, didn't miss hers. It would be nice if Elizabeth married again, a different kind of person, someone whose handwriting wasn't all screwed up. Dry as a document, he'd turned out to be.

In the dining-room the old women found their places and carefully seated themselves. You always had faith in marriage even after it had let you down. You tried again if you could, she'd have tried again herself. No one really wanted to be alone.

'For what we're about to receive,' it was the turn of a thin old woman, Miss Fine, to say, for it was a tradition that the residents themselves said grace. 'The Lord make us thankful,' Miss Fine said.

Maids came round with plates of pork and vegetables, and the gravy for which the present cook in the Sunset Home was famous.

The telephone rang just after Mrs Orvitski had finished washing up the lunch dishes. 'Ah now,' said Mrs Orvitski, but before she'd finished drying her hands on a tea-towel the ringing ceased. 'Hullo,' she heard Jennifer saying.

Mrs Orvitski left the kitchen and stood in the sitting-room doorway. Alice was lying on the floor reading *Terry the Girl Guide*. 'Yes, this is Jennifer,' Jennifer was saying on the telephone.

'Heh?' Mrs Orvitski inquired. 'Who is this?'

'No, thanks,' Jennifer said. 'No, definitely not, thanks.' She replaced the receiver and giggled.

'Heh?' Mrs Orvitski inquired again. 'Who was there?'

'A heavy breather,' Jennifer said. 'A sexually perverted man.'

'My God!' cried Mrs Orvitski shrilly.

'He wanted me to meet him.'

'Never to answer the telephone,' cried Mrs Orvitski. 'Never neither of you to answer.'

'Actually, he sounded a nice bloke,' Jennifer said.

'Oh my God!' cried Mrs Orvitski again. She spoke for a moment shrilly, issuing threats in the direction of the telephone, agitatedly waving the tea-towel at it. Jennifer sat down on the sofa and pretended she couldn't stop laughing. She rolled about on the sofa, stuffing a cushion into her mouth. Alice began to giggle. 'Silly old twit,' she said, but Mrs Orvitski didn't hear her.

'The telephone rings,' Mrs Orvitski said, 'you wait like two good girls till Mrs Orvitski answer it.' She nodded repeatedly, to give emphasis to this command. Still nodding, she returned to the kitchen.

'Actually,' Jennifer said, 'it was Henry. On about some creature called Timus.'

'A dog?'

'Actually, I think it was a human person. He wanted us to go and play.'

'Ha, ha, ha.'

'He said he had packets of Nutty Pops. He's a most peculiar bloke, that Henry.'

'He's touched in his brainbox if you ask me,' Alice said.

In the onion-men's shed Joanna and Samuel sat with their friends, listening to rock music on a transistor radio. A number of their friends wore the same kind of wire-rimmed spectacles as they did, and leaned against one another as they were now doing. Some of them conversed with one another in deaf-and-dumb language.

Listening to the music, Joanna imagined a jet plane rising from a runway, leaving behind it a pale twilight of London in February. And leaving behind, also, tube trains full of tired people, men in suits and women wearing winter coats, and a school that was unpleasant in every way. She imagined sleeping on the jet plane, reclining on it as it gathered speed, running free with it through the night sky. She had read a story of such an adventure, of two people flying into fantasy, of a sudden suspension of unsatisfactory reality. In the story the land where the jet plane came down had exotic vegetation and the animals were tame. The foxes and the badgers, birds, weasels, voles and other undergrowth animals were not afraid and did not attack. Peacocks and buzzard-hawks were companions in small, brightly hued forests, or on the lawns that stretched around mansions. Coniferous trees were of a luxuriant shade of green that became black against the night sky and turned bluish in early morning mists. Through forests and mansions, the adventure that had begun on an aeroplane continued. Winged creatures that were not birds led the way through the exotic land, to people who were not quite people and yet more beautifully were. In the landscape and the vegetation there was beauty everywhere.

It was a story that Mrs Geraldine Tabor-Ellis had composed and it was contained in the paperbacked volume that contained, as well, the elements of Mrs Tabor-Ellis's philosophy. Mrs Tabor-Ellis did not believe in the commitment that one human being was often called upon to make to another, since such commitments were shackles, and shackles in Mrs Tabor-Ellis's view were life-destroying. They were more life-destroying in relation to the human spirit than to the body, for one might remain physically shackled for a lifetime and still know freedom: a prison cell could be less damaging than the imprisoned life-force. Shackles were strangling the contemporary Western world, Mrs Tabor-Ellis had written, as the ivy strangles the mulberry tree. Shackles were perfidious and often latent. *Shackles* was the title of Mrs Tabor-Ellis's paperbacked volume, price 40 pence, published by the Open Door Press, 42 Athoy Road, N.W.1., printed in Reading.

Samuel had written to Mrs Tabor-Ellis, inquiring if there was room in her commune for two more interested parties. Mrs Tabor-Ellis had said there was, explaining how the commune was run and explaining about the goats which were reared, and the wheat which Mrs Tabor-Ellis was attempting to grow, and the mead she made. For a long time Joanna and Samuel had talked about joining the commune, but their talk had been vague until Samuel received the reply to his letter from Mrs Tabor-Ellis. Now he was all for joining immediately, since neither of them saw any point in the unpleasant school or in the laughy, crinkly-haired headmaster whose only concern appeared to be that cannabis should not be smoked in the lavatories. They hated the laughy headmaster and would not speak to him. They hated the staff who bent over backwards, trying to understand their hatred. They hated the sponginess of the place, the way it never answered back, like a shop or a post office would answer back if you attempted to rob it. At the end of term you got on a stage and did psycho-drama, and people played guitars and other people sang. The laughy headmaster said it was marvellous when it wasn't marvellous.

Joanna wasn't quite as certain about the commune as Samuel was, but she felt that anything would be better than the school and the house where she lived, and Mrs Orvitski, and her mother. For months she'd been upset after her mother had turned her back on her, her mother who'd been so very warm and so very kind to her, who'd made up so much for what she'd always taken to be her father's dislike of her. Samuel was warm and kind to her now, which was something her mother wouldn't understand in a million years.

In the onion-men's shed she leaned her back against Samuel's shoulder, sitting cross-legged on a sack. The music and the silent conversation continued. Cigarettes smouldered and kept going out.

In Somerset Mrs Tabor-Ellis sat at the kitchen table in her farmhouse, glad for once that all her young people had gone down to the river. She felt a little unwell, but knew that if she sat in silence, staring at the timber surface of the table, she would quite soon feel much better. The timber surface of the table was always a help on the mornings after she'd slightly overdone it. It was the friendliest table she'd ever actually known, pleasantly marked with rings from the mugs of young people, and with other homely stains of this and that. Mrs Tabor-Ellis, in her floppy patchwork dressing-gown, her grey hair loose on her shoulders, closed her eyes and in spite of her small indisposition felt at peace.

In Aberdeen Aidallbery walked slowly through the February sunshine, taking pleasure from its faint warmth on his face. In Union Terrace he passed the Caledonian Hotel, but did not take a particular interest in it. Years later, looking back on the few minutes it took him, that Sunday, to walk past the Caledonian Hotel, he marvelled that he could so casually have done so, that some instinct did not warn him that the hotel was soon to be no ordinary place for him.

5

Earlier that day, before the other women had arrived, they'd mani-
cured Lily's fingernails, and the night before they'd washed her hair.
Just before her visitors were due she tidied herself, putting on new
lipstick and powdering her face. She was wearing a blue bed-jacket
when they came, an angora jacket like the pink one she'd been wearing that morning, but one which she valued more.

They came together into the ward, having been waiting on the seat
in the corridor until it was time. Two at a time by a bedside the
rule was, but it was relaxed on Sundays, and on weekdays when a
patient's children came. Up to four you could have by your bedside
then.

Kenneth was wearing his dark Harris tweed jacket and one of the
plain blue Marks and Spencer's shirts she'd bought him, and a tie
with anchors on it, and dark gabardine trousers. One of the side-
pieces of his spectacles had been repaired with Sellotape. She'd asked
him about it last night; he'd said it had just snapped.

'You're looking well, Lily,' his mother said. 'Really well. Isn't she,
Kenneth?'

He bent to kiss her. He'd brought her some nightdresses which
he'd washed and ironed, and some apples. 'Yes, you're looking well,'
he said. He spoke in a subdued voice, as he always did in the presence
of his mother.

Mrs Drucker was a large-bosomed, tall woman, almost as tall as
Mr Drucker and Kenneth. But Kenneth was thin and his parents were
both well covered.

'Hullo, Lily,' Mr Drucker said. He was a tailor by profession and
his wife a dressmaker. His grey hair was cut close to the scalp of his
head, his face was usually without expression. Mrs Drucker, on the
other hand, grew her hair long and kept it in a tidy bun at the back
of her head; her face, in which teeth and eyes featured prominently,
constantly reflected surprise, distaste and incredulity.

'I feel well,' Lily said, smiling at Kenneth because she knew he
worried about her. Once, when his parents weren't there, she'd wept

53

all through his visit. She'd asked him to pull the curtains around her bed, which he'd hated doing because it drew attention. He'd done his best to comfort her, but on that particular evening she hadn't even wanted to be comforted. As soon as he'd gone she'd written to him, apologizing.

They settled themselves around her bed, on three of the metal-frame chairs. Kenneth sat closest to her, the dark tweed of his jacket seeming sombre against the pink bed-curtains. Beside him, his chair pulled well back, Mr Drucker gazed at the picture of the tulips. On the other side of the bed, Mrs Drucker was almost as close to her as Kenneth was.

'It's Kenneth that doesn't look so good,' Mrs Drucker said. 'Skin and bone he's gone to. Chalk-white if you look at him.'

Nobody replied. Mrs Drucker went on talking. She spoke of the small terraced house in which she and her husband lived and plied their trade, Mr Drucker in shirtsleeves and waistcoat, a tape measure around his neck, she in various flowered dresses that she'd made herself, talking through a mouthful of pins. Two Singer sewing-machines rattled in the terraced house, customers came and went: women to see Mrs Drucker, men to see her husband. Mrs Drucker talked about whipcord trousers that her husband was making for Mr Greabe, and how cavalry twill for Mr Caperdown hadn't come yet, and how she'd twice gone to Mrs Taggart's house during the week to give Mrs Taggart fittings, that being the arrangement she had with this particular customer. 'Her sister *will* make curries,' Mrs Drucker said. 'Really nasty smell in that house.'

Lily nodded. Curries did smell strongly, she said.

'No bowels could stand it, stuff with a stench like that. "Whatever's that smell?" I said, thinking maybe something was in the drainage. "Curries," Mrs Taggart said. "Cut the stomach out of you." "Put them down the toilet, that's what I'd do," I said. Well, I mean, Lily, your heart goes out to the old soul, seventy-two last December. I mean, she couldn't have the bowels for it, no elderly person could. Wasn't I right to say it, Lily?'

'Yes, of course, Mrs Drucker.' She asked Kenneth if he was still managing all right, if he was having proper meals.

'Any time Kenneth can come over to us,' Mrs Drucker said. 'Any time, I said to Kenneth. Any time, any meal he likes. Bed and break-fast, supper at night, whatever he fancies.'

'I'm managing all right,' Kenneth said.

She smiled at him, trying to smile privately, but Mrs Drucker noticed and winked at her husband. Upright on his chair, one hand on either knee, Mr Drucker remained impassive.

'Better off, really, if Kenneth'd move in. I say that to Kenneth, Lily, only he doesn't take a pick of notice of me, never has. He's lost a good stone since you came in here, Lily. Thin as a penny he's gone.'

Kenneth shook his head. He said, murmuring, that he hadn't lost any weight.

'I said it to your dad, Kenneth. I said it last night, didn't I, Dad? A good stone, you can see it in his face. Thin as a penny, poor Kenneth's gone.'

Kenneth shook his head again. He said: 'What did Mr Alstrop-Smith say, Lily?'

'Same as ever. They all say the same. Lie there, get up for meals, go for walks down the corridor –'

'I was telling Mrs Taggart. She said she never heard anything like it, lying up in a hospital. She was a nurse, you know, Mrs Taggart was. Charing Cross Hospital. Worst thing you could do in a case like that, apparently. Woman Mrs Taggart knew dropped stone dead –'

'I think they know what they're doing,' Kenneth said.

She'd met him seven years ago in the East Hill public library, where he still worked. He picked up a book she'd dropped, *Dr Bradley Remembers*, and then he said he'd seen her in the library before. He'd seemed about to say something else, but he hadn't. 'Would you like to have a cup of tea?' he said the next time, coming up behind her as she was leaving the building. He was finished for the day, he said: if she liked, they could have a cup of tea in the Geranium Café. He was wearing a grey overcoat and a woollen scarf and gloves; he gave the impression of a person who suffered from the cold. She hesitated over his invitation to tea in the Geranium Café, wondering if she should accept it and in the end deciding that no harm could befall her with a library employee in a café. He was awkward as they crossed the street together and nervous in the café, hardly speaking at all. She liked him better than the men in the Eagle Star Insurance Company, where she worked, men who'd try something on in a corridor, like Mr Hopegood, who would have retired by now, who was always groping at your hips with his hard, bunched-up hands, or Ally Glazier who modelled himself on the Duke of Edinburgh and pretended he wasn't the one who left messages on the girls' typewriters, saying what he'd like to do.

'It took me a year to pluck up the courage,' Kenneth told her later. 'I was always looking out for you.' He said he'd fallen in love with her the first time he'd ever seen her, even before he knew what her voice was like, or her face, because she was walking away from him at the time. She found that hard to believe, but he insisted that it was true, that he had fallen in love with her back. He loved her tininess, he'd said then, her tiny face, and her hands and her feet. He loved everything about her.

'Is Binks all right?' she asked, referring to a cat.

He nodded, as he always did when she asked the question.

'Can't ever be good for the creature,' Mrs Drucker said, 'alone on its own all day. Can't see why Kenneth doesn't bring it over to Dad and me, Lily.'

'It's nice for Kenneth to come home to. It's company when –'

'Nice to come home to a cat! Whatever will our Lily say next, Kenneth!'

His mother kissed her cheek, laughing excitedly. There was malice, Lily believed, hidden beneath that display of affection: Mrs Drucker hated her. Every Sunday afternoon as she lay there she imagined she could feel Mrs Drucker hating her: typical, Mrs Drucker thought, not to be able to have a baby, typical of the kind of girl she was. Mrs Drucker had said the marriage was the worst idea she'd ever heard of, and Mr Drucker had told his son that he didn't think it was a good idea, either. 'We've nothing against illegitimacy as such,' Mrs Drucker had assured Kenneth. 'But that girl has unfortunate blood in her, Kenneth, which your dad and I will never be capable of forgetting.' Kenneth hadn't told Lily that, but Mrs Drucker had, saying she thought Lily ought to know that this conversation had taken place. It would be better for Lily to know, Mrs Drucker had said, and better for her to marry someone of her own kind. 'It's in kindness to you, dear,' Mrs Drucker had said, taking Lily's hand and smiling at her with her large, prominent teeth.

The first time she'd met his parents had been a Sunday afternoon, when she'd been invited to tea in their house. It was a house that all his life, Kenneth said, had oppressed him. In the sitting-room there were heavy net curtains on the single window, and a mantelpiece laden with ornaments, and chintz covers on the tightly stuffed arm-chairs. There were bamboo tables with further ornaments on them, large china animals, dogs and cattle and cats. There was a hearth-rug in maroon and blue and black, which Mrs Drucker claimed was worth a fortune, being Egyptian, but which Kenneth told Lily afterwards had a label stapled on to the wrong side stating that the rug had been

56

manufactured at an address in Edgware and was thirty-five per cent wool.

There'd been bread and butter, and loganberry jam, and chocolate digestive biscuits and a jam-roll. Mrs Drucker had complained about the jam-roll, saying she didn't consider it fit to be eaten and blaming her husband for having accepted it from a shopkeeper whom she mentioned by name, a Mr Dodd, who'd palm off anything on you. Mr Drucker didn't say anything, about the jam-roll or anything else. He smeared loganberry jam on to his bread and butter and sat impassive in his chair. Mrs Drucker spoke of a Mr Cove, a man who came to clean their windows, whom she used to give tea to until the day he finished off a whole plate of figrolls. She spoke of someone else, a Mrs Strachan, who was a customer of hers, who had put on two stone in a month because she'd developed a fancy for McVitie's fruit-cake. 'Don't you like loganberry, dear?' she said when Lily refused the jam, and when Lily said she didn't like loganberry jam there was a silence.

In St Clare's Home for London's Girls Lily had often wondered what it would be like to live in a house with a mother and father. She felt embarrassed when Kenneth's parents objected to the marriage and there was no objection from anyone on her side. She had lodgings at the time with a Mrs Malprits, but Mrs Malprits said it was an excellent idea, marrying a chap who had a good job in a library. Sister Eugenie at St Clare's said the same, and so did everyone else who'd known her at St Clare's. Because there was no objection from anyone on her side she felt that the Druckers were probably right. Any illegitimate girl was lucky to be marrying into a respectable family, Kenneth was getting the worst of the bargain.

'The new thing now is, Lily, Dad wants to do up the bathroom.'

Lily listened while she was told about this. The bathroom needed doing, Mr Drucker said, speaking for the first time since he'd greeted her. Top to bottom, Mrs Drucker explained, walls, woodwork, skirting, ceiling and the two surrounds. Kenneth sat hunched in his chair. As always in the ward, his mother's voice was loud.

Elizabeth read, Miss Samson dozed. Sylvie, hearing all that was said around Lily's bed, thought about her own parents, whom she no longer saw. Lily had told her that she had been brought up in a home and Sylvie wondered about that. There'd been girls at school who'd come from Church of England homes or from the Methodist place in Wandsworth. Just like anyone else they'd been, you didn't even feel sorry for them. Sylvie's parents were not like the Druckers. They didn't have the Druckers' respectable air, nor were they unfriendly to one another, as the Druckers appeared to be.

Sylvie had last seen them in 1965 when she'd been seventeen. As far as she knew, they were still living on the high-rise estate where she'd been brought up. Declan thought it strange to lose touch with your parents, especially since your parents lived in the same city. Declan was devoted to his mother and his sister, who lived in Enniscorthy, and spoke with affection of his two uncles, one a priest, in Liverpool. But Sylvie had never been aware of much devotion within her own family. Her parents were an easy-going couple, her father employed in the loading bay of a firm that manufactured cakes, her mother making as much as she could as a cleaner in various private houses. When she was a small girl, Sylvie remembered men coming to the flat and asking to see a scooter she'd been given for Christmas, and her father saying that the scooter must have fallen off a lorry because he'd found it in the middle of a street one night. On another occasion men had come to the flat looking for jewellery that had disappeared out of one of the houses where her mother worked. Her mother hadn't minded in the least: she'd given the men a cup of tea and let them search the flat without a warrant. Sylvie's brother, Nickie, and a gang he belonged to used to chase homosexuals on Wimbledon Common, near Tibbet's Corner, where the homosexuals went to pick up friends. Sylvie's parents used to laugh when Nickie told how they'd chased some man, throwing pieces of paling and stones at him. 'Filthy bastards,' Sylvie's father would pronounce, and her mother would remark that she knew for a fact that the police didn't bother with Tibbet's Corner any more, now that the gangs were there to chase the men off. 'Keep Britain Tidy,' her mother used to say, laughing at the humour of it all. Every evening after they'd had their tea Sylvie's parents went down to the Black Horse, except on Tuesdays and Fridays, when Sylvie's mother played bingo and her father played billiards or went to the greyhound stadium.

When he was fifteen Sylvie's brother was taken into a Borstal for breaking and entering, and Sylvie's parents were greatly upset. 'The best years of Nickie's life,' her mother sadly declared, unable to eat and not up to putting in an appearance at the Black Horse. 'I'll take the bloody skin off him,' her father threatened. But a month or so later her parents looked on the bright side. A gang of youths from the high-rise estate were heavily sentenced for battering a homosexual to death on Wimbledon Common: Nickie, had he been at liberty, would almost certainly have been involved. There was always a silver lining, Sylvie's mother said.

Her parents didn't mind when Sylvie went. At first she used to go back and see them, but often they weren't in when they'd said they'd be, so in the end she just stopped going. She once noticed Nickie in a dance-hall but he pretended not to see her. Some time later she heard he'd been sent to prison for two years.

She told Declan all about it, the high-rise estate and the scooter and everything else. They lay in Declan's single bed and she told him, and he told her: about his boyhood in Enniscorthy, how he used to buy buns in Murphy-Flood's bakery and hold the woman in conversation so that she'd forget he hadn't paid for them. He told her the names of the Christian Brothers who'd taught him, Brother Finnigan and Brother O'Brien, and Brother Lynch who tore Kevin Driscoll's ear so that it had to have a stitch. He told her about the time Jack Doyle and Movita put on a show in the Atheneum and how Jack Doyle kissed the women in the front row of the audience, and how he chased a honeymoon couple up Vinegar Hill at half past two in the morning. There was another man who'd come across a number of wooden crates in the hall of a hotel one night. He opened the crates and released five hundred day-old chicks just for the fun of it. Declan was full of stories like that, the time he and other boys removed two seats from Enniscorthy's cinema, the way he and other boys used to slip into people's gardens for apples. In the single bed he sometimes talked all night long, about people she tried to visualize and a town that was all hills. He'd bring her there one day, he promised. He'd show her Murphy-Flood's shop and Vinegar Hill, and Bennett's Hotel where Jack Doyle and Movita had stayed. There was a castle covered in Virginia creeper and a square with a tree in the middle of it, where the Post Office and the Bank of Ireland were. His father had one time tried for the porter's job in the Bank of Ireland, but he had not been successful. 'He wasn't trustworthy with money,' Declan said, laughing the way he always laughed when he mentioned his father, a man who had come to live quite easily in Sylvie's imagination, grey-haired and stern and drunken, long since dead. When Declan got going the words would pour out of him like a waterfall, and he often said that when he was with her he never wanted to stop, he wanted to tell her every single item he could think of. In her whole life no one had made her laugh the way that Declan could. They'd be sitting in the Cruskeen Bawn Lounge and he'd see his countryman, Mr Maloney, coming towards them. 'Will you look at

59

the cut of him in the overcoat?' he'd say, and she wouldn't be able to stop giggling, although Declan always kept a straight face. 'The hard man,' Mr Maloney would say, easing his weight on to a chair beside Declan's, and he'd turn to her and ask her if she was keeping fit. Mr Maloney always called Declan the hard man and inquired if she was keeping fit. It made her giggle to hear him because Declan was always doing imitations of him. 'Will you lend me that overcoat?' Declan said in a bar in Shepherd's Bush one night, to a man who was wearing a long black overcoat just like Mr Maloney's. 'You look like De Valera in that,' someone remarked when Declan put it on, but everyone else said he looked just like Mr Maloney. 'The hard man,' Declan said, ponderously sitting down on a chair. 'Are you keeping fit?'

The other boyfriends that Sylvie had had didn't seem to her to be at all like Declan: Danny Grimes on the estate, and Raymond Bonford who'd been much older, and Harry Sweet and Edmund Laper and Tippy Kenzie, and a lot of others. Before she'd met Declan she'd lived with a long-haired man called Brian Stronach in the flat his wife had just walked out of, in Notting Hill Gate; and before that she'd been with another man who'd once been married, a Ted Roper. In 1967 she'd been engaged to a man called Ossie Savage, who said he was a psychotherapist. She hadn't been in love with Ossie Savage any more than she'd been in love with Ted Roper, but she'd felt at the time that she couldn't go on living with this man and that, or falling in love so much that it hurt, like she'd fallen in love with Raymond Bonford and Tippy Kenzie. Raymond Bonford unfortunately had a wife, and Tippy Kenzie didn't want to marry anyone. He couldn't love a woman, Tippy Kenzie said, but at the same time he wanted to have sexual relations with as many women as he possibly could, in particular various film stars. Ossie Savage turned out not to be a psychotherapist at all but to be engaged in the blue films business. 'It's a kind of therapy,' he'd tried to persuade her, but although she liked him she felt she couldn't rear children on money made out of blue films. For her children she wanted a healthy upbringing, not like what she'd known herself, with her toys being questioned by detectives.

Yet when she'd first met Declan she'd assumed that she'd be able to have children, and had Declan said he was in the blue films business she'd have had his children and brought them up, and it wouldn't have mattered. If Declan had said he was married already she'd have taken a chance with bigamy. With her arms around him in the bed in Shepherd's Bush, she knew she loved him more than she'd ever loved Raymond Bonford and Tippy Kenzie, which was saying something. And he wasn't twenty years older, like Raymond Bonford, or peculiar about film stars like Tippy Kenzie. He would last her a lifetime, and all the time he'd go on making jokes. No one was fun like Declan was.

It was only after she'd known him for some months that she suspected he had the same tendencies as her parents and her brother. It was all in the past, Declan assured her, but she knew that until he settled down to regular employment the past would not be entirely finished with. London was no good to him, he'd often said himself, because it was full of trouble, which no matter how hard you tried to avoid it would catch you in the end. He'd written to his two uncles in Liverpool and had been assured, by return of post, that suitable work could very easily be found for him. The uncle who wasn't a priest was a hall-porter in a hotel, the Star of the Sea in Renvyl Street. He lived with his wife in a bungalow on a brand-new estate, and since another seventy-five of these bungalows were to be completed by the autumn, Declan's other uncle had offered to lend him the deposit on one. In the meanwhile, Declan and Sylvie were welcome to stay for as long as they wished in the bungalow occupied by the married uncle. It surprised Sylvie that the two uncles should be so good to Declan, but Declan said it was a family thing. They were like that because they wanted to give him every chance to live a decent life and not bring unhappiness on their sister, who was his mother. On another occasion, when he'd drunk a quantity of Guinness, he laughingly said it was because they thought he'd end up in Wormwood Scrubs and cause his mother to drop dead over the shock of it.

Sylvie couldn't quite see what life in Liverpool was going to be like. She'd never been there, but one of the girls in Woolworth's had told her that it was a black-looking city. That was true enough, Declan agreed, but it applied only to the central areas. On the outskirts, where the bungalows were, it was bright and sunny. It was a fantastic town, Declan said, held by many to be the centre of the world's culture. Anything that London had, Declan assured her, Liverpool could beat.

She didn't mind leaving London, especially since she felt that Declan needed the protection of his uncles. Between them all they'd be able to steady him down, which was what he, as much as she and his family, desired. 'There's a fine head for business on Declan's shoulders', the man called Mr Maloney had more than once said.

Sylvie opened the autobiography of Lady Augusta Haptree, which

61

Lily had lent her. *I am angered sometimes,* she read, *by the exploitation of women, not in the factories, of which we nowadays hear much, but in the homes which they themselves have helped to make. And I am angered by women's folly in encouraging that exploitation and by accepting without protest the status of mindless creatures.*

'I thought a nice green,' Mrs Drucker said. 'Green for a bathroom's that smart. Oh, the new colours are lovely, Lily. Some of those greens and blues, I don't know how they do it.'

'I'll not put on green,' Mr Drucker said quietly, staring at Lily's bed-jacket.

'Dad says there's damp, Lily, but then of course all bathrooms have damp, stands to reason. I mean, how could you have a bathroom, Lily, that didn't get wet? I mean, a bathroom gets wet, as such it's bound to.'

'I'll not put on green,' Mr Drucker said again, turning his head, addressing his son.

Kenneth nodded. He'd been to the cinema the night before, he told Lily. One of the girls had been asked to leave the library: he'd forgotten to tell her that. It hadn't been much good, the film.

'I said it to Mrs Taggart,' Mrs Drucker said. 'Condensation, rivulets down the walls; as such, there's bound to be a bit of damp. No good looking for trouble, I said, no good adding trouble on. As it is, he shouldn't be doing it at all. Kill him, doing work like that at sixty-two, up and down ladders with the complaints he has. You could be talking to the wall, Lily.'

'There's a piece of skirting needs replacing,' Mr Drucker said, still addressing Kenneth. 'Rotted up with damp where the water's been splashing over the side.'

Kenneth nodded again.

'It's not large, of course,' Mrs Drucker said. 'I'm not saying for a moment it's a large bathroom, Lily. Well, you've seen it yourself. All I'm saying to him is that it's doing something you're not used to that counts, stretching and straining, standing on a chair. There's that man, Mrs Skinner's brother, got something from doing a painting job. He was breathing it in, Lily. Laid up for nearly a month, Mrs Skinner said. They put these chemicals in it nowadays, you know, fly-killers most of the time. Stands to reason it can't be good for a man of sixty-two. I mean, he's had his medical troubles, Lily.'

'I wouldn't put green on a bathroom wall if I was paid money for it,' Mr Drucker said. He stood up and extended his right hand towards Lily. When she'd shaken it he left the ward.

'What d'you think, Kenneth?' Mrs Drucker said.

'About what?'

'Dad doing out the bathroom.'

'Well, he doesn't want to do it green.'

'I wish you'd come over and do it out for us, Ken. it's no job for a man of sixty-two, the weight he is up there on a chair. I wish you'd come over evenings, dear.'

'I come to see Lily in the evenings.'

'After, dear. No reason why you can't come on after. I'll have a nice good supper for you. Always likes his supper, Lily, ever since a baby. Dad's in the sulks, Kenneth, better go and see to him. He gets into the sulks these days, Lily, no reason at all. Have a nice little word with him, Kenneth.'

'He's sitting in the corridor,' Kenneth said. 'He's perfectly all right.'

'Well, I think that's hard!' Mrs Drucker cried shrilly. 'Poor man sitting in a corridor! You only have the one father, you know, Kenneth.'

Kenneth sighed. He rose from his chair slowly and shambled off with his head down.

'Well, I did think that was hard, Lily,' Mrs Drucker said. 'I really did, you know.' She began to talk about the bathroom again. She said she'd take it as a personal favour if Lily encouraged Kenneth to come over in the evenings and do the painting. He would have in the past, she said, before he was married. He'd do anything like that, you only had to ask. 'Dad's really not fit for it,' she said. 'Poor Dad's not well, you know.'

Kenneth had once said he wondered if his mother was entirely sane, but Lily had no such doubts. Mrs Drucker was eminently sane. She was devoted to achieving her own way, and every word she spoke and every action she took were designed to help her in this ambition. The bathroom would be painted green by Kenneth; no power on earth could prevent that from happening now. And while Kenneth was painting the bathroom and eating the food she'd prepared for him, Mrs Drucker would seek to destroy the marriage that her only child had so foolishly engaged upon. That for once she had been successfully defied, and on so large an issue, was a fact that Mrs Drucker could not accept. Even now, though her son had been married six years, she saw no reason to admit defeat.

Tea was brought around by the Indian woman and Mrs Drucker

asked if she might have a cup. She had a cake, she said, and took a paper bag from her shopping-bag. The Indian woman went away to get an extra cup.

'They don't really like visitors to ask for tea,' Lily whispered.

But Mrs Drucker said they wouldn't bring her a cup of tea if they didn't like doing so, it stood to reason. 'Of course they don't mind,' she said. 'The nursing profession's marvellous.' She took a knife from her shopping-bag and cut the cake. She'd bought it in Coombes's, she said. 'Thanks, Nurse,' she said to the Indian woman, who was now supplying her with tea.

Lily ate a piece of the cake, and Mrs Drucker suggested that some should be offered to the other patients in the ward. She began to cut further slices.

'Oh no, don't bother,' Lily whispered, not wishing Mrs Drucker to engage the other women in conversation as she had, on previous occasions, engaged their predecessors.

'Ah, it's selfish not to, Lily,' Mrs Drucker said, crossing the ward to Elizabeth Aidallbery's bed.

In the corridor Kenneth sat on the seat with his father, neither of them speaking. He stayed for a while and then returned to the ward, trying to get a smile on to his face as he approached Lily's bed. His mother was still handing round cake. He said:

'Don't worry, Lily.'

'I wish I was at home.'

'I know. It won't be long.'

'I feel like crying.'

Mrs Drucker's voice had become shrill again, telling Elizabeth Aidallbery that Mrs Taggart said she'd never heard of a pregnant woman being kept in hospital like an invalid.

'Don't cry,' he said. 'Don't cry, Lily.'

'I don't know why you put up with me.'

'Oh, love.'

She looked at him, remembering him in the Geranium Café that day. She hadn't thought much of him. She'd wondered why she was sitting there with a clerk from a public library who didn't seem to have anything to say. 'I'd like an éclair,' she'd said, and the waitress had said that the Geranium didn't do éclairs. There were meringues if she wanted them, white or pink. 'My name's Kenneth Drucker,' he'd said. He began to talk to her hesitatingly. He asked her where she lived and if she'd lived there long. He'd often seen her in the library, he said.

He wasn't at all the kind of person she'd ever thought she'd marry, delicate-looking, with glasses. In her childhood in St Clare's, when she was eleven and twelve and thirteen, she'd thought about marriage and men. She'd giggled with other girls over boys they'd seen, delivery boys who came on bicycles to St Clare's, or boys who lived near by, who were sometimes on the look-out when girls of St Clare's went for a walk in a crocodile. In private, after seeing a film called *A Place in the Sun*, she imagined Montgomery Clift taking off her clothes, the tips of his fingers sending shocks of electricity through her. But she'd come to love Kenneth more than she could ever have come to love Montgomery Clift: she knew that for a fact, she felt it. The first night of their marriage she'd felt the shocks of electricity surging through her body, better than the shocks she'd imagined with Montgomery Clift.

'Oh Kenneth,' she whispered.

'Don't worry, Lily,' he said, stroking the back of her hand. 'Please don't worry, dear.'

'D'you still love me, Kenneth? You'd tell me if you stopped, wouldn't you, Kenneth? Even though I'm in hospital you'd tell me, wouldn't you?'

'Of course I love you, Lily.'

'I can't think why you do.'

He smiled at her, holding her hand. She asked about the library, about the girl who'd been made to leave. He told her, and then about a man the police had finally run down, who'd been writing obscenities in the margins of books. 'We thought he'd be some lonely old fellow,' Kenneth said, 'but actually he's quite young. A chap called Glazier.'

'Glazier? Not Ally Glazier, Kenneth?'

'Who's Ally Glazier?'

'You know. I told you. He used to write messages on our type-writers. No one could sell motor insurance like Ally Glazier, they said, but they had to sack him in the end.'

'Good heavens!'

'Poor Ally Glazier.'

They looked at one another, sharing the astonishment that a man who'd once misbehaved in the Eagle Star Insurance Company should turn out to be the same one who'd been misbehaving with library books. They smiled at one another, giggling happily, as though they were on their own. He leaned towards her and kissed her, squeezing her hand.

Across the ward, she could hear Elizabeth Aidallbery saying that the cake was lovely and Mrs Drucker telling her she'd bought it herself, in Coombes's, which was the best for cakes.

'My son's her husband,' Mrs Drucker said to Sylvie Clapper, giving her some cake. She began to talk about when Kenneth had been born and how there'd been no difficulties with the birth. Easiest birth she'd ever known, the midwife had said. Lily had lost four, no one knew what was going to happen next. 'Lily's so small,' she said, lowering her voice, but Lily could still hear her. She always said that to the women in the ward, even though Lily had told her that Mr Alstrop-Smith said size had nothing whatsoever to do with it. 'Bound to make a difference,' her mother-in-law explained to Sylvie Clapper. 'Stands to reason.'

A bell rang, an indication that the visitors in the wards should prepare to leave.

'Used to be a Mrs Ridge in that bed last,' Lily's mother-in-law informed Miss Samson, and Miss Samson smiled and thanked her for the piece of cake.

Lily gave Kenneth a plastic carrier with a nightdress in it. Kenneth kissed her again.

'Don't worry,' he whispered. 'I couldn't ever not love you, Lily.'

'Goodbye then, Lily,' his mother said.

'Goodbye, Mrs Drucker.' She wanted to cry again because he was going and they'd said so little to one another, because all it had been was the usual Sunday-afternoon horridness, whispering surreptitiously, with only Ally Glazier to cheer them up.

'Bye-bye,' Mrs Drucker said to the elderly Indian woman, who had come into the ward to collect the tea-cups. 'Bye-bye,' she said, smiling at all the beds.

Lily closed her eyes to stifle the tears she couldn't prevent any more. She could hear his mother's voice in the corridor. It would continue on the stairs and in the hall, and on the street outside and on the bus, chattering about the curries Mrs Taggart's sister had taken to making and about the bathroom and about Lily herself. 'Unfortunate blood,' Mrs Drucker would say, lowering her voice on the bus, and Kenneth would sigh, not wanting to have an argument about his wife's blood on a bus. She remembered his eyes when he'd said that he could never not love her. They were grey, not like either of his parents' eyes. His eyes were the same as they'd always been when he'd talked to her about love; not in all the six years of their marriage, not through all her miscarriages and the perpetual efforts of her

66

mother-in-law, had they changed. For a moment, even while still imagining the Druckers on the bus, she believed that this time her baby would be born. She would feed it at her small breasts. She would love it with the mother's love she'd never known herself, with a different kind of love from the love Mrs Drucker gave her son.

In the bus Mrs Drucker talked, but Kenneth didn't listen to her. The child would not be born, he thought.

By five o'clock that evening the women in the Marie Atkins Ward, with the exception of Miss Samson, were known to one another by their Christian names. Elizabeth and Sylvie Clapper sat on the two edges of Lily's bed. Miss Samson turned over the pages of Lady Augusta's autobiography, looking at the illustrations. Kenneth's mother wasn't easy, Lily said, and Elizabeth said mothers often weren't; her eldest daughter thought she was difficult. She'd been lucky herself in her relationship with her mother; she hadn't liked her father.

'There was a bloke called Danny Grimes,' Sylvie said. 'My dad went after him with a dog-chain. He was famous on the estate, Danny Grimes was. For getting you pregnant.

'Like Mr Hopegood,' Lily said, 'in the Eagle Star. Couldn't leave you for a second.'

'I worked in a different Woolworth's once,' Sylvie said. 'There was a bloke like that, a supervisor he was, married with four kids. Wandering Hands we called him.'

Lily told about Ally Glazier, how he'd written dirty messages and left them on the girls' typewriters and was now, apparently, up to his tricks with library books. She flushed, thinking of the things he'd written. *98% of girls masturbate*, a note had once said. *How about that, Lil? I'd really like to do you, Lil.*

'I think I'll just fill up my diary,' Miss Samson murmured, returning the autobiography to Lily's bed-table. Earlier she'd told Sylvie Clapper a bit more about her boarding-house, but she'd seen from the expression on the girl's face that she considered it odd that people should live in the manner she described, with prayers in the sitting-room every evening before bedtime. 'We're Church folk,' she'd said more than once, trying to get the feel of Number Nine into the girl's mind. The girl said her boyfriend was a Catholic but that she herself had only once been to a service in a church, when she'd gone with him to Brompton Oratory to see what it was like. The other girl, Mrs Drucker, had been brought up in a Church atmosphere, in an orphanage Miss Samson had heard of, in Higham's Park. Mrs Aidallbery had been married in a church and often took her two younger children to All Saints in Barnes.

Around Miss Samson as she settled herself comfortably with her diary, the conversation of the three other women drifted, being general for a while and then splintering into fragments, touching upon the men who occupied a place in the other women's lives. Elizabeth spoke of how she'd felt when she'd first been divorced, after nineteen years. Lily told about how Kenneth said he'd fallen in love with her back. She laughed, saying she'd never believed it. Sylvie talked about Declan.

Nurse Hampshire came into the ward and said good night to them because she was about to go off duty. 'What a pretty young thing!' Miss Samson remarked after she'd gone, and Lily said she was one of the nicest nurses in the hospital. Sister O'Keeffe was nice too, but there was a night nurse, Nurse Wibberley, who wasn't popular.

'I'm going down the corridor,' Sylvie said. 'Honestly, I could do with a drink.'

She collected her cigarettes and cigarette-lighter from the cupboard by her bed. There'd been a women in the St Ida Ward once, Lily said, who'd brought in bottles of gin with her. Sister O'Keeffe had been furious.

Elizabeth returned to her bed. Lily read. *Few women are as fortunate in their marriages as I was*, Lady Augusta had written. *He was a man of little charm, for he did not hold its possession to be a virtue. He did not laugh much, not being blessed with a feeling for the humorous. Yet he was kind in every way to all God's creatures, to me and to our children. His character was strong, his nature loyal. I believe in my seventieth year that no woman can expect more of a man. My husband did not ever love me.*

In the corridor Sylvie Clapper smoked with a woman called Mrs Thring. 'Complications,' Mrs Thring said. 'They've opened me four times. You never know what they'll find, you know.' A home-help had moved into her flat, she said, but her children played the woman up and Mr Thring hadn't realized what was happening. 'They put cornflakes in her bed, some bloody nonsense like that. You lie here worrying in case they set the place on fire. She walked out, of course, after a week. God knows what kind of a shambles it is. He's a well-meaning man, but he can't get control of them.' She wasn't married herself, Sylvie said, but she was planning to be soon after she'd had the hysterectomy. They wouldn't be able to have children, of course.

'A blessing in disguise,' said Mrs Thring. 'If I was you I wouldn't touch any of it. If I was starting again I'd be a single woman.'

In the colour supplement of a Sunday newspaper Elizabeth read a recipe for tripe Lyonnaise. You cut a pound of tripe into domino-sized strips, you rinsed it and drained it. You sliced half a pound of onions and cooked them in two ounces of butter until they were golden. You served the dish with plenty of parsley and lemon juice. She'd never tasted tripe and she rather thought she didn't want to. *Tripes à la mode de Caen* was the best known of all tripe recipes, she read.

She pushed the colour supplement away. Outside, there were small islands of blue in a grey sky. The eyes of Lady Augusta Haptree were pinpricks across the ward, on the cover of her autobiography, which Lily was reading again. On the plain walls the pictures of the tulips and the ducks were more colourful than she'd noticed before. Sylvie Clapper's wash-bag, new and shiny, daisies on a green ground, was on her bed. Miss Samson wrote intently.

It was pleasant not to think at all, but in a hospital bed that wasn't easy. Nor was it easy to control your thoughts in any way. You couldn't run away from something you didn't like by getting up and doing something else, or suddenly going out for a walk. You couldn't make a cup of coffee. She closed her eyes and memories flashed, like pictures on a screen. Her father looked away. Her mother put a hat on. In her grey school uniform with a yellow blouse, she stared from her bedroom window at barges on the Thames. She watched rain falling on loads of coal.

Miss Digg came to the house to give her piano lessons, spindly Miss Digg who always wore colours that didn't suit her, who took trouble and was nice. At Christmas Miss Digg gave her flowers she had pressed, on her birthday a flat box of Callard & Bowser's toffees. 'You're a Gemini, you know,' Miss Digg had said, the first person to tell her that. 'Worst sign of the lot,' Di Troughton said, years later.

She walked along the towpath with Di Troughton and Evie Faste, and a dog she and her mother had. The dog, a mongrel terrier called Ned, was later killed by a car that didn't stop. She wept and her mother said they'd get another, but she said she didn't want another. From Barnes you could walk by the river all the way to Putney and a bit beyond. Once on the towpath Henry found a pound and years later, almost on the same spot, a man offered Di Troughton a bar of chocolate. By the railings of Harrods Depository she and Evie Faste found a woman who'd fainted. You could see the Boat Race from the windows of the house, and other races, races between London banks, the Midland and Lloyds and the National Provincial. Pleasure boats passed by in summer, carrying crowds of people who sometimes waved. Fog clung to the water in November.

'Of course have them to tea,' he'd said. 'Of course.' On three different Sundays they came, soon after the honeymoon: spindly Miss Digg, and Mr Feuchtwanger, and Miss Middlesmith, who'd first of all made her draw flowers. She wanted him to meet them because she'd always liked them very much. Mr Feuchtwanger was tall and thin, metallic-looking, like a Giacometti man. Miss Middlesmith was fat, with a face like a moon. There were silences when each of them came to tea.

'A cure for quinsy,' Mr Feuchtwanger said, '*Ajuga reptans*, often called the purple bugle. Remember *Ajuga reptans*, Elizabeth?' Mr Feuchtwanger was always ringing off the names of flowers because he liked the sound of them. Meadow clary and mother of thyme, *Valeriana officinalis*, *Atropa belladonna*, larkspur and wood anemone, cuckoo bread, whinberry, stonecrop. Just to think of them made Mr Feuchtwanger happy. You'd go mad, he used to tell her, if you lost your faith in happiness.

Mr Feuchtwanger and Miss Middlesmith and Miss Digg were special people in her life. Her mother was special, too, and Henry had been. Di Troughton and Evie Faste had been more special than other friends. Mr Feuchtwanger had drooped about the place, bent like wire at the shoulders, rarely smiling and yet constantly cheered by the happiness he spoke of. Miss Middlesmith was a happy person also, but more obviously showed it. Miss Digg was kind. Miss Digg had once lent forty pounds to her charwoman and even when the charwoman hadn't returned it had lent her another ten. Di Troughton and Evie Faste considered Miss Digg foolish to have done that, but they nevertheless shared Elizabeth's affection for her. Di Troughton and Evie Faste were special because they were funny, because they giggled at things that Elizabeth was more serious about. 'Life's not a party, you know,' a grim-faced teacher of mathematics had once informed them, but Di Troughton and Evie Faste, wives and mothers now, still considered that it was.

'Heavens, I thought he'd never stop!' her husband had laughingly said after Mr Feuchtwanger had been to tea. 'What a tedious old man!'

Perhaps he was, and perhaps Miss Middlesmith was greedy about cake and perhaps Miss Digg was as he said, pathetic. It didn't matter, and even now she didn't want to remember his condemnations of people who were special to her and who did no harm. A few months after making his statement about Mr Feuchtwanger he revealed that he thought Di Troughton immensely silly; and Evie Faste, he said, had polygamous eyes. On Henry he passed no opinion, her mother he liked. Daphne, ironically enough, he rather liked also. But then Daphne had never been special, except in another sense.

She tried to close her mind, but could not now. Against all her will she thought of Daphne: Daphne weeping and then horribly screaming at her, tears marking dark patches on a lime-green dress. It hadn't been fair on Daphne because Daphne suffered anyway, asthmatic in the summer months, too delicate to be savaged so, too vulnerable in other ways.

Beneath the bedclothes she twisted her fingers together, again trying not to think. Dr Love had said she'd feel better when she'd had the hysterectomy, more able to push her way through everyday worries. It was silly to get so worked up about Joanna: there were thousands, maybe millions, of girls just like her. You saw them everywhere in their hippy clothes, with that fashionably vacant look in their eyes, and the smile. After all, she'd been a problem herself when she was only a few years older than Joanna, saying she wanted to marry a man she didn't properly know.

They would forget to feed their hamsters. The hamsters would die of dehydration and lack of nourishment. They would weep miserably and bury the hamsters in the garden. She forced herself to think of that since it was impossible to think of nothing. She saw, on the dresser in the kitchen, the packets of hamster food, the picture of a hamster on them. *Kim* the food was called, white letters on red: *Gerbil, Hamster, and Mouse Food*. In the two blue cages the hamsters didn't run around on their wheels, or climb about the wire bars. They were underneath the hay, hibernating or dead.

In the morning she'd write Jennifer a note, reminding her that every day the hamsters must be given Kim, and hay, and water, asking her to prop the note up on the dresser so that they'd both see it and not forget.

She turned her radio on. '*Blockbuster* still there at Number One!' a male voice shrilled at her. She turned it off again. *The rich, traditional craftsmanship of Florence*, she read in the colour supplement. *Value £40 – yours for £17.95, post free.*

Through green and gold images of coffee-tables and trays, another image forced its way. She closed the colour supplement. The face of

71

the man who'd been her lover smiled slightly at her. He poured her Tio Pepe, straw-coloured, into a glass with a stem. Other people were in the room, standing around having Sunday-morning drinks. He gazed at her piercingly, only yards away from Daphne, who was wearing, that day too, her lime-green dress. 'You have beautiful eyes,' he said, carelessly and loudly in the crowded room.

A week later, when she brought Jennifer and Alice to Mr Brook's Ducklings Class at the swimming-baths, he was there with his own two daughters, although it was Daphne who usually brought them. Mr Brook was a bronzed man in blue trousers and a vest, whose hair was yellow because he used a sun-ray lamp. He drilled the small children in his Ducklings Class sternly, ordering them to find the bottom of the pool and wave their feet in the air, threatening them with expulsion from his class if they didn't take part in all activities. Afterwards, while their children drank hot chocolate in the foyer of the swimming-baths, they talked about Mr Brook because it was a natural thing to do. 'Come back and have a drink,' he said. In the sitting-room he put his arms around her and kissed her.

She tried to push these memories away, but again could not. Endlessly it seemed, again and again, they had lunch in the Casa Peppino. They walked on the towpath because it was a convenient place, watching the crews from Lloyds and the Midland. Men constructed boats in the riverside workshops at Putney; there was a smell of timber and paint, and the noise of saws, and whistling. A bearded coach rode a bicycle along the towpath, shouting at schoolboys through a megaphone. Crews stood by their boats and lifted them with a sudden jerk from the water. They strolled through sunshine, middle-aged and hand in hand, illicitly in love.

She lied quite easily, not even averting her eyes: she was going to Oxford to help Evie out over the weekend. Evie was ill, recovering from glandular fever, Evie Gibbings she was now. 'Oh, *darling*, how exciting!' Evie said on the telephone.

She saw herself, a naked body entwined with his beneath sheets and blankets, her own pale hair on a pillow: in Room Eleven of the Foxley Hotel, Bishop's Stortford, A A appointed. 'I love you, Elizabeth,' he whispered. 'Oh, how I love you, darling.'

Slightly he'd run to fat. His fair hair was thinner than it once had been. But the eyes that had piercingly gazed at hers that first Sunday morning hadn't aged. They were a deeper blue than hers, like looking into a summer-blue sea it was. In the Foxley Hotel, Bishop's Stortford, he was warm and generous and laughing and nice, and in room eleven everything was different. For nineteen years she had assumed that the physical side of marriage was something she didn't care for, yet it seemed now that in another marriage this wouldn't have been so. 'I love you, too,' she said, and added, as he had, that she'd never loved anyone in this same way.

Harrods Depository was beautiful. 'My God, it's all ridiculous,' she said, whispering and clinging on to him. She was no longer sunburnt with plaits, or at school in a grey uniform, varnishing her fingernails at weekends. She was a brisk mother in a flannel suit, with a body changed by childbirth, and grey in her hair. It was all ridiculous, the lunches at the Casa Peppino, and the Foxley Hotel, A A appointed, the sunshine by the Thames. He kissed her and said it was the nicest thing that had ever happened to either of them.

But it wasn't nice. It wasn't nice when she took her children to tea, when Daphne smiled and laughed and said her wretched asthma was pulling her down again. It wasn't nice when Daphne's tears fell on to her lime-green dress.

Again she turned the pages of the colour supplement. She read about a party given in Paris by a German millionaire. Guests were invited to attend dressed as vampires and other horror figures. They came with bats pinned into their hair and knives sticking out of their backs, with fangs, and ketchup on their faces. Elsewhere, she read that the Morris Marina 1.8 estate car had 58.4 cubic feet of load space.

But Daphne's face was still there, more alive than the faces with ketchup on them, more real than the red Morris Marina. It would always be there, Elizabeth thought, in the gallery of faces that would always be there, also: the face of the man she'd married, and Joanna's face, and her father's, her mother's blurred with age. She turned her radio on and tried to listen to music.

Naturally, Miss Samson wrote, *I miss Number Nine, but everyone here seems very nice. Little Mrs Drucker is waiting for the gift of a child*, *the other two are in for ops.* She paused, and then added: *Thy rod and Thy staff. Strength groweth from Affliction*. Like the welcome in the hall, in coloured wools and framed beneath glass in passe-partout, the words appeared on the first-floor landing of Number Nine: *Strength groweth from Affliction*. They were the personal words of Mr Ibbs, or so at least many of the inmates over the years had believed, others insisting that the Bible contained this statement and others again arguing that it was a phrase of the late Sir Winston Churchill. *Only God's love matters*, Miss Samson wrote, and blotted the words with green blotting paper and closed her diary.

6

Still in the Victor Value carrier-bag, the clothes of Sylvie Clapper had been placed by Declan in the wardrobe of the room they'd shared in Shepherd's Bush. Yellow distemper flaked on the walls of this room, revealing blue distemper underneath it. In a corner near the window there was a sink, and beside it, on a white wash stand, a gas ring, saucepans and a kettle. A yellow net curtain drooped across the lower half of the window; on the window sill in front of it were detergent, sugar, tea, an instant Chinese meal in a packet, Vim, Brillo Pads, a bottle of Camp Coffee and a small bottle of Power's Irish Whiskey.

The single bed had an iron bedstead and was covered with a blue checked bedspread. Beside it, on a white table, stood a lamp with a frilled shade that matched the blue in the bedspread, and an ashtray with the words *A Double Diamond Works Wonders* on it. Sylvie and Declan ate their meals from this table, Sylvie sitting on the edge of the bed and Declan on the room's single chair.

Entering the room now, Declan poured into a cup what whiskey remained in the Power's bottle, added a quantity of water to it and placed the cup on the table beside the frilled lamp. He removed the jacket of his blue serge suit, stretched himself out on the bed, and closed his eyes. Declan did not think about Sylvie Clapper, but instead about the man who had once declared to Sylvie Clapper that Declan had a good business head on his shoulders: Mr Maloney. From time to time as he lay there considering in his mind the face and personality of Mr Maloney, he opened his eyes and reached out his right hand for the cup of whiskey and water. The face of Mr Maloney was red and large, his personality devious. He was a man of advanced middle age and considerable weight, unmarried, and originally from the town of Clonmel in Co. Tipperary. In the Cruskeen Bawn Lounge of the George public house in Hammersmith he was a regular presence, never seen there without a black hat on his head and his extensive black belted overcoat. He was obliging to his fellow-countrymen in that, at times of exigency, he would advance them small sums of money against security, at a rate that

74

depended on the extent of the loan and the degree of the debtor's distress. As security, he accepted only transistor radios of reputable manufacture, or portable typewriters. Two months ago, having been ordered by a court to make a payment of twenty pounds for an offence he had committed, Declan had lodged with Mr Maloney two Olivetti typewriters that he'd found in a filing-cabinet in a branch of J. Moxon & Co., Turf Accountants, where he'd worked for a day, laying linoleum. Against the security of these typewriters, Mr Maloney had lent him the twenty pounds, on the understanding that Declan would pay back twenty-seven, and in the ordinary course of events Declan would have been happy enough with the situation. Over a drink in the Cruskeen Bawn, he'd have explained to Mr Maloney that it would suit him better to let the typewriters go rather than endeavour to repay the debt, and Mr Maloney would have shaken his hand and said there were no hard feelings on either side, a statement for which he was well known. Unfortunately, Mr Maloney now claimed that the typewriters had never been in working order and had, in fact, various parts missing from them. Declan did not believe this. What had happened, he estimated, was that Mr Maloney had removed the parts himself in the hope that Declan, having repaid the loan, would tell him to throw the machines away. Mr Maloney would then replace the parts and sell the machines.

What worried Declan was that a week ago Mr Maloney had given him seven days in which to raise the twenty-seven pounds. They'd had a companionable drink together in the Cruskeen Bawn Lounge, over which Mr Maloney had explained that unless the money was forthcoming within the allotted time he would naturally have to resort to proceedings for its recovery, since the typewriters were useless. He was a businessman, he reminded Declan, as well as a friend to his exigent fellow-countrymen; as a businessman, he had a living to make. He pursed his lips as he spoke, making a sucking noise that those who knew him were familiar with. He was thinking of Toner Coglan, Declan could tell from the look in his eye, and he wished it to be known to Declan that he was thinking of Toner Coglan. Six months ago Mr Maloney had entered Toner Coglan's lodgings and had removed clothing and other goods in lieu of the three pounds that Toner Coglan owed him. In Declan's case the clothing and other goods would have fallen far short of the outstanding twenty-seven pounds, but there were other ways in which Mr Maloney had been known to initiate proceedings against a debtor. He might even hint that the Hammersmith police would be interested

75

in the two typewriters, which he had received in good faith as security for a loan and which were, as stated on Declan's IOU, Declan's property.

Declan reached for the whiskey. He sipped a little and let it remain warmly in his mouth, under his tongue. He was no longer employed as a layer of floor-coverings: for some weeks now he'd been in receipt of National Assistance. He and Sylvie had been in the habit of pooling their resources, and what worried Declan almost as much as the difficulty with Mr Maloney was the fact that without Sylvie's contribution it was going to be hard to make ends meet. He closed his eyes and at the same time released the whiskey from beneath his tongue. There was nothing he'd have liked better than that he and Sylvie should set up a little bungalow on the estate in Liverpool. The only difficulty about it was that when his uncle who was in the priesthood had offered to lend him the money for a deposit, he'd replied to the letter saying there was something more pressing where money was concerned and that was twenty-seven pounds he owed, through no fault of his own, to a man from Clonmel called Maloney. His uncle had sent a cheque by return of post, but when Declan cashed it he found it difficult to hand over the money to Mr Maloney and instead spent the afternoon at Hackney dog-track. As a result, he was left in a position of owing Mr Maloney and his uncle twenty-seven pounds each. A few weeks later his uncle had written to him to remind him of this debt, and since Declan hadn't replied he felt it would be difficult at the moment to bring up the matter of the deposit on the bungalow.

Declan was roused from these melancholy considerations by a knock on the door. He didn't answer, and when he saw the door beginning to move he pretended to be asleep.

'Hey,' a voice said, and he opened his eyes and saw his West Indian landlady, a Mrs Vendericks, standing by the bed.

'Ah, come in, Mrs Vendericks,' he invited in a sleepy voice. He yawned, stretching himself and propping himself up on the bed. 'I was in the middle of a dream,' he said. 'I was standing in a fieldful of hens.'

Mrs Vendericks said that for two weeks she hadn't received any rent. She was a stout woman, dressed now in a shade of electric pink.

'Rent?' repeated Declan in the same sleepy voice. He spoke slowly, yawning again in order to give himself time to think. 'Aren't dreams extraordinary, Mrs Vendericks? Would you credit it –'

'Two weeks is owing.'

'Surely to God, I paid it? God, I was certain I paid the old thing –'

'There is proof of no payment in your rental book.'

'Oh, I'll take your word, Mrs Vendericks. I wouldn't doubt you for a second. I'll settle it first thing in the morning, Mrs Vendericks. As soon as the banks open their safes you'll have every penny that's owing.'

Mrs Vendericks began to say something, but he continued to speak, not wishing to hear what she had to say.

'It's due to an oversight on my own part, all the fuss with Miss Clapper going to hospital. Isn't it shocking, Miss Clapper gone in for an operation? God, it's a terrible thing, the poor girl –'

'I've told you, mister: this is a room for one person only.'

'Ah, of course it is. Isn't it a grand little room, Mrs Vendericks?'

'Extra coming and going with another person, extra use of toilet paper –'

'I know what you mean, Mrs Vendericks, and I'll be in to you in the morning with the rent. That's a lovely dress you're wearing. Is it new, Mrs Vendericks? "That's a charming outfit she has on," I said to myself when I opened my eyes. I'd have remarked on it at the time only I'd just come out of the dream I was having, hens in a field, a most extraordinary thing, to tell you the truth.'

Mrs Vendericks said that if the rent wasn't paid by half past nine tomorrow morning she would seize the room. She said that if Sylvie Clapper returned to the room a double rent would be due. She went away, closing the door behind her.

He had no money in a bank. What money he possessed was on his person, eight pounds and forty-three pence. This sum would have covered the rent that was due to Mrs Vendericks and would even, briefly, have quietened Mr Maloney. But Declan had no wish to part with any of it. He rose from the bed, filled the kettle with water and lit the gas. 'Soldier boys are we,' he sang softly, beneath his breath, rinsing tea-leaves out of a small brown teapot. He wondered how she was getting on, if she was settling in OK. A hospital was a terrible place to be. If there was one place in the entire world he couldn't stand it was a hospital. There was a smell that got right into your stomach, the smell of the stuff they used to wash the floors, or their instruments, or the patients – God knows what they washed with it. When he'd been standing waiting for her in the corridor that morning he'd thought he was going to bring up the entire breakfast he'd eaten.

He heated the brown teapot and then knocked four teaspoons of tea into it. It was terrible not having the wherewithal the whole time, trying to make plans for a marriage and then having a black woman demanding every penny you had for a room that wasn't fit for fleas. And a character like Maloney pressing the charges, exploiting you to the hilt. No better than prostitutes most of those black females were, dressed up in a colour like that on a Sunday. Maloney was no better than a criminal, worse for all anyone knew. What you needed was to be rid of people like that, fifty-four pounds to settle the two debts and a bit more for the rent that was owing. Then up to Liverpool to get the deposit fixed up for the bungalow. With a hundred pounds in his pocket, he could square the lot of them and have a bob or two left to take Sylvie on a little holiday when she came out from the operation. They could spend a weekend in Blackpool or maybe go up to Scotland, which he'd heard was a great place. He poured tea into the cup he'd drunk the whiskey out of. He added sugar and milk, still thinking about money. At seven p.m. the Cruskeen Bawn would open its doors for the Sunday-evening trade. Maloney would be there in the hat and the long overcoat, on his hands the pair of black gloves that he always wore on a Sunday. It had happened in the past that if you bought him a few drinks he'd come up with a plan of how you could achieve the means of repaying his own debt. 'Sure, aren't we all in it together?' was a favourite sentiment of Mr Maloney's.

Henry eased the Zephyr through unusually heavy Sunday traffic in Tottenham Court Road. 'Must be something on,' he remarked to his son, Timus. 'Or perhaps there's been an accident.'

His son did not reply. He sat bleakly in the back of the car with the window open because of the petrol fumes. He'd spent the afternoon kicking an old Ant and Bee book over the bare boards of a room that once, so he was told, had been his nursery, but which he did not remember as such. He'd eaten four packets of Nutty Pops, even though he didn't like them, and had spent a long time in the lavatory, sitting on the floor with the door locked, looking at the linoleum. His father had said he knew some girls who would like to come to play, but they hadn't wanted to. His father had tried to make the television work, but unfortunately hadn't been able to.

'Funny day, Sunday,' Henry said, speeding up a little when the traffic thinned. 'Funny in London, I mean, with everything different, all the shops closed.'

He inclined his head to catch his son's response to this, but Timus did not speak. It would all be different, Henry thought again. It took years to straighten yourself out after a family business went bankrupt and then a marriage that didn't work. Naturally it took years. 'When I grow up,' he remembered saying to his mother and father, 'I'm going to marry Elizabeth Orpen.' They'd laughed, seeming delighted that he'd said such a thing. They'd both been fond of Elizabeth.

A week ago he'd heard of an opening in a frozen foods firm. The money was better than the money he received as a vending-machine operator, and he'd be supplied with a car. Tomorrow, Henry decided, he'd see about the opening, and with a bit of luck when he next saw Elizabeth he'd be presenting himself in an entirely new light. He'd resist going to visit her in hospital immediately. He'd wait until mid-week, Wednesday probably, until he'd sorted a few things out. He'd walk into the hospital ward in a new suit, with flowers and fruit. He'd sit down beside her and explain.

'I saw a friend into hospital this morning,' he said as the Zephyr gathered speed in Chalk Farm, and then he whistled for a few moments. 'Not a bad time of year to be in hospital, I dare say. Better than August, for instance.' Again he inclined his head for his son's response, but the silence in the back of the car continued.

Henry sighed quietly and did not speak again. Timus got out of the Zephyr in Willesden and Henry caught a glimpse of his ex-wife at the window of her parents' flat, which was on the first floor of a large mock-Tudor block. He waved and she waved back. She had gone back to work at the time of the divorce and was now, according to Timus, secretary to a managing director. It had been necessary for her to go back to work because Henry had not been able to supply her with much money. She'd said he should have sold the house in Meridian Close, but somehow he hadn't cared for the idea of moving into a bed-sitting-room and she'd been sympathetic about that.

He drove slowly back through London, thinking about his ex-wife without emotion. It was all dead, that part of his life, except for Timus once a week. When he saw her at the window of the flat or on the steps of the mock-Tudor building he felt neither bitterness nor regret. She'd told him once, a year before the divorce, that she thought she was going mad, that the very sight of him made her feel uneasy in the head. He'd been amazed to hear her saying that.

He drove to the King of England and parked the Zephyr just around the corner, in Appian Road. As he entered the saloon bar, familiar faces smiled at him. People asked him how he was, others nodded at him. He could have joined any group he cared to, but tonight he preferred to drink alone. No one disturbed him, for it was known in the King of England that of late he occasionally liked to have an evening on his own. He sat on a barstool watching Felicity, the barmaid, filling glasses with beer. On the bar in front of him he built three stacks of coins, five-, two- and one-penny pieces that he'd collected out of his machines. He always had a large quantity of small-denomination coins on his person. His wife had complained about the effect they'd had on his clothes, and about being given her house-keeping allowance in this form. It was all money, he'd tried to explain, but she hadn't seemed to see it.

The thing was, he loved Elizabeth. He'd loved her for a long time, ever since they were children, as far as he could see. He'd asked her to marry him that night he'd taken her for a walk, but she'd said no and he shouldn't have taken no for an answer. She'd married some-one else and he'd married someone else, and nothing had been right since.

As he sat alone in the King of England, he had a brief vision of her, not as she'd been as a child, but as she was now, in a blue dress she sometimes wore, with her children in his garden. Timus was there too, on a visit, and he himself was strolling into the garden from the kitchen, having just arrived in Meridian Close in a blue-and-white car. 'There's Daddy now,' Elizabeth said.

He kissed the top of her head and sat down beside her. They talked about holidays. He wanted to take all of them, he said, Timus as well, to Dinard in Brittany. 'Dinard!' Jennifer and Alice cried, clapping their hands together, and Joanna said she'd always wanted to go to Dinard. 'Oh, it'll be lovely,' Timus said in his earnest way. 'Lovely,' Elizabeth repeated.

In the garden they all had tea, with cress sandwiches and coffee-cake. In the garden there was a smell of newly-cut grass. A red setter he'd bought came bounding out of the house. 'After tea,' Alice said, 'let's all play Monopoly.'

In another public house, the Rose and Thorn, not far from the Chel-tenham Street Hospital, Nurse Hampshire drank pale lemonade shandy with Dr Pennance, the houseman who believed that the woman who paraded with the banner was touched in the head. Dr Pennance promised that if Nurse Hampshire was pregnant he would see her through. He would arrange everything, he promised, and pay whatever expenses there were.

'Sorry,' Nurse Hampshire said, for she'd been complaining. 'Pig of a day.'

Dr Pennance put his arm around her waist and squeezed it. Through her dress he could feel the elastic that kept her tights in place. He caressed it gently, running the tips of his fingers beneath it. He'd had a pig of a day himself, he said. A patient had carried on like blue murder in the Olivia Hassals Ward, upset because of the death there the night before. Grim-lipped and silent, Sister Hobson had been inclined to blame him, implying some weakness on his part. 'And poor old Mrs Studdard doesn't help matters,' he said, 'hanging on for dear life.' The patient who'd been difficult, an elderly woman called Mrs Mars, had repeatedly taken off her nightdress. He didn't know how to handle that kind of thing, Sister Hobson's eyes had accused; of course they'd take their nightdresses off, of course they'd carry on if you sympathized too much, women of that age, in that state. 'I hate that bloody ward,' he said, and Nurse Hampshire agreed. No one liked the Olivia Hassals Ward, where old women died.

Dr Pennance removed his fingers from the elastic of Nurse Hampshire's tights and took their empty glasses to the bar. As he did so, a girl in a navy-blue suit, with a headscarf, entered the lounge of another public house, a mile or so across London: the Cruskeen Bawn Lounge in Hammersmith.

'Mary Tracy,' Mr Maloney said. 'I was telling Declan about you. Are you keeping fit, Mary?'

'I'm great, Mr Maloney.'

'Charmed to meet you, Mary,' Declan said mechanically, shaking the girl's hand.

'From Tralee,' said Mr Maloney. 'In London a week. The Rose of Tralee,' he said, and laughed. 'Will you wet your whistle, Mary? Bring us a big John Jameson,' he called out to the barman, his voice authoritative in the crowded lounge.

Mr Maloney had just been told that Declan's financial prospects were in no way improved. Declan had talked about sources in Liverpool that, if the worst came to the worst, would not let him down, but Mr Maloney took the information with a pinch of salt. In the end it was always the same with debtors like Declan. In the end you had to offer aid of another kind so that the loan might be repaid with full, accumulated interest, and if that didn't work you had to employ any methods you could think of. Aware that Sylvie Clapper was in a hospital, Mr Maloney now offered aid in the person of Mary Tracy, who had not come from Tralee empty-handed. There was no reason at all, Mr Maloney considered, why at the end of this Sunday evening

81

Declan and Mary Tracy should not be close companions and why Mary Tracy shouldn't offer temporary assistance to Declan, placing him in a position to hand Mr Maloney twenty-seven pounds the following morning, which he had stated a week ago he would do without fail.

'I was asking Declan,' Mr Maloney said, 'if he'd maybe assist you to find work.'

The barman placed a glass of whiskey on the table. Mr Maloney made no move to pay for it, nor did the girl from Tralee. 'Forty-two pence,' the barman said.

Declan placed one of his eight remaining pound-notes in the barman's hand. The girl smiled at him, revealing teeth in need of attention. She had eyes like a pig's, he said to himself.

'Declan has influence with Lipton's,' Mr Maloney said.

'Lipton's?'

'It's a grocer's shop, Mary. Branches everywhere. Great gas altogether, tip-top remuneration.' As he spoke, Mr Maloney nudged Declan with his knee, indicating that he should make a statement about his influence with Lipton's. 'Wasn't it a bacon counter you were telling me about, Declan? Could you sell bacon, Mary?'

Declan gave an embarrassed laugh. The girl doubtfully shook her head. She didn't think she was qualified to sell bacon, she said; she'd been employed in a brush factory in Tralee.

'Or a hotel,' suggested Mr Maloney. 'Wasn't there a hotel you were talking about, Declan? In the Goldhawk Road, was it? The Goldhawk Hotel, wasn't it?'

'I have a brother a hall-porter up in Liverpool, the Morning Star Hotel –'

'Ah, sure, what use's Liverpool, Declan? Didn't you tell me you had connections with a big place in the Goldhawk Road?'

'I'd like hotel work,' the girl said.

'Oh, it's great gas certainly, a hotel. And wasn't there another crowd you were in with, Declan, making soup somewhere?'

Declan made a noise that could have been negative or affirmative. He noticed that Mr Maloney's glass was almost empty. 'Well, good night so,' he said, beginning to rise.

'Stay where you are,' Mr Maloney commanded, grasping Declan's leg with his left hand. 'Get us three more drinks and then I'll leave you to fix Mary up. All I mean, Mary, is if he couldn't get you into a hotel he'd fix you into the soup business. Was it tinning the soup,

Declan, or sticking on labels? Eighteen a week, Mary, entirely unskilled.'

Declan approached the bar with the three glasses. According to what Mr Maloney had told him, the girl from Tralee had seventy pounds in notes. Mr Maloney was great at that, keeping well within the letter of the law, letting someone else do the dirty work. It was scandalous exacting interest at thirty-five per cent; it was scandalous telling lies, saying a person had influence in a hotel and in Lipton's. He could have broken a glass in Mr Maloney's red face, the way he'd nudged him under the table and held him back by the leg when he'd wanted to go home. 'Have you security, Declan?' Mr Maloney had said to him the evening he'd asked him for a loan of twenty pounds. 'Transistors, typewriters, anything like that?' In his need he had unfortunately mentioned the two typewriters he'd noticed in the betting-shop when he was laying linoleum with another man. 'Will you be back there again?' Mr Maloney had asked, interested at once, and he'd said he'd be back there the following day. Mr Maloney said there was no problem whatsoever in that case, but unfortunately that did not prove so because it was as a result of removing the typewriters from the betting-shop that Declan had been declared redundant by the floor-coverings firm. No accusations had been made against him because nothing could easily be proved, but Declan often had a suspicion that he was being observed by plain-clothes policemen. He had said as much to Mr Maloney, and Mr Maloney had replied that since Declan had done nothing wrong he had nothing whatsoever to be afraid of. When Declan began to remind him of the source of the typewriters Mr Maloney said he didn't want to hear stuff like that. 'I misunderstood you entirely,' he said. 'I thought they were payment for laying down the linoleum.' If he'd come by the typewriters dishonestly, Mr Maloney advised him to confess the matter to a priest.

'I think I knew your father,' Mr Maloney was saying to the girl when Declan returned with the drinks. 'I think we played hurley together.'

'Jeez, I never knew he played hurley,' the girl said, and Declan laughed sourly. Mr Maloney had made an art of finding females like this, in London only a week. He was forever watching and hanging around, smelling people out like a dog would smell a rabbit. 'Excuse me,' he'd said to Declan a few months ago, 'you're not the brother of Paddy Burke?' And when Declan had said he wasn't, Mr Maloney had bought him the only drink he'd ever bought him and asked him his name and where he came from. 'Well, isn't it the small world?' Mr Maloney had said. 'I think I played hurley with your father.'

'The hard man,' Mr Maloney said now, receiving the whiskey and consuming it rapidly. 'He's great gas when he gets going, Mary. You'll be tied up in stitches laughing at him.' He stood up and saluted them with the open palm of his hand. 'I'll leave the pair of you. God accompany you, Mary.'

'Is he a military man?' the girl asked after he'd gone, and Declan said that no matter what else Mr Maloney was he had never been enrolled in an army.

'Can you really get me work?' she asked, smiling at Declan with her darkened teeth. She took cigarettes from her handbag and offered him one. He took it. He wanted to hear himself saying that the man who'd just left them was the biggest confidence trickster at present operating in London, that no word of truth had ever been permitted to pass out of his mouth, that the best thing she could do would be to walk out of the Cruskeen Bawn Lounge and find work at a labour exchange the following morning. He wanted to hear himself saying that he was unable to find work for himself, never mind anyone else, that he owed rent to a West Indian woman, that plain-clothes men were observing him. 'My girl-friend's in a hospital,' he wanted to hear himself saying, 'having her womb taken out,' He owed Sylvie money, too, a total of fourteen pounds seventy-five. 'There's no girl like you,' he'd said to Sylvie the night before, whispering to her in the single bed.

'Can you, Declan? Can you get me work?'

He smiled and wagged his head at her. Beneath the table the calf of his left leg moved close to hers. He pressed and she pressed back.

Kenneth Drucker watched a television programme with the cat, Binks, on his knees. A woman with black hair was putting on lipstick. She pouted into a mirror and then stood up. It was a film about waterfront gangsters, the same film that Mrs Orvitski was watching in Elizabeth's sitting-room. 'Hi, baby,' a gangster said, kissing the woman without taking his hat off.

In the room they shared above the sitting-room Jennifer and Alice were asleep, and as she watched one gangster striking another on the back of the neck Mrs Orvitski heard the front door closing and guessed that Joanna had returned. She rose at once and turned down the sound of the television. 'Heh?' she called out, opening the sitting-room door. She waited for Joanna to reach the first-floor landing and then she spoke again, telling her to sit down in the kitchen, where there was food prepared for her. Joanna smiled and did not reply, brushing by Mrs Orvitski to go to her room.

Shaking her head, Mrs Orvitski sat down again in the sitting-room. A large white dog appeared on the television screen, standing mournfully between two labelled tins. *Dulux Is A Home's Best Friend*, a printed message pronounced.

'What's that mean?' an old woman asked Elizabeth's mother in the Sunset Home in Richmond, and Mrs Orpen was about to say that it was an advertisement for paint when someone else said that the commodity called Dulux was dog food.

'I'd like a dog like that,' Daphne said, but the man with whom Elizabeth Aidallbery had been unfaithful shook his head and pronounced the breed unsuitable for a London suburb. 'Oh, I don't know,' Daphne murmured, as the waterfront gangsters returned to the screen.

'Thank heaven for that,' Mrs Drucker remarked in the Druckers' terraced house, pouring out tea for her husband and herself. 'Can't stand those ads,' she said, which was what she liked to say when a batch of advertisements came to an end. 'Dare say Kenneth'll use Dulux for the bathroom,' she said.

Stirring his tea, Mr Drucker did not reply. On the television screen the woman with the black hair fired a series of bullets into a gangster's stomach.

In Somerset Mrs Geraldine Tabor-Ellis felt better than she'd felt that morning. Euphoria possessed her as she moved among the young people of her commune, as she smiled and touched and reflected.

In an upstairs room a girl from Nottingham played a harp. In the kitchen there was a meal of brown rice and nuts and chopped fresh cabbage, which the young people had prepared and which would be taken when they felt the need of it.

Mrs Tabor-Ellis moved her hands and her fingers, conversing with those who had chosen to make a home with her. In similar fashion they replied, saying that the goats had been milked and fed and were now safe for the night.

In Aberdeen Aidallbery made notes on a subject that was of academic interest to him. He sat alone in his room in the University, with three bars of an electric fire going because the night was chilly. He was absorbed in his task, and content to be so.

Not far away, in a bedroom of the Caledonian Hotel, an American woman called Mrs Vincent stood naked. Her body gave an impression of strength, with fleshy haunches and wide shoulders, and breasts that were proportionally generous yet did not sag. The hair on her body was black, that on her head grey. She had a handsome face, with determination in the lower half of it, and eyes that were candid and expressive.

Aidallbery was as yet unaware of Mrs Vincent's existence. Her name had been mentioned to him but he had forgotten that, having not been much interested in what someone was saying about a woman from Boston who was to be at a University dinner-party. But she, having listened with greater care, knew who he was and was aware that they were to meet. 'Aidallbery,' she'd said. 'What an interesting name!'

'We'll take a taxi,' Declan said, but when the taxi arrived at the address where the girl from Tralee was staying he rooted through all his pockets and said it was an extraordinary thing, he'd spent all his money except for one and a half pence. Hearing this, the taxi-driver blasphemed, but the girl opened her handbag and handed him a pound note. 'I'll pay you that back,' Declan promised.

In her room he took off her navy-blue suit, and then her jumper and a blouse and her underclothes. 'Am I drunk?' she asked him, swaying in front of him. She laughed and said he had hard hands. 'Jeez, I'm drunk as a blinking lord,' she said, and laughed again.

He got her into the bed and then got in himself. He turned the light out because he always preferred going about this kind of activity in the darkness. The seventy pounds would be in one of the drawers of her dressing-table, hidden under a few clothes, or maybe under newspaper or old wallpaper that would be there as a lining in the drawer. 'Will you marry me?' he said to the girl, thinking the suggestion might give her pleasure. 'God, you're great,' she said in reply.

She was bigger than Sylvie. She had large, cold legs, and folds of flesh on her shoulders. There'd never be another girl like Sylvie, he thought as he fondled the girl's stomach. Sylvie was as cheerful as a chaffinch, always seeing the bright side, always saying it didn't matter. When he'd first brought her to the room in Shepherd's Bush he'd thought that maybe she'd object to the place, but she hadn't at all. She'd made a cake in a saucepan, cooking it over the gas-ring like she'd read in an evening paper. Bed-sitting-room catering it was called.

The girl fell asleep, and he lay beside her, with a cramp in his right foot. She murmured something in her sleep, something about buying nails, and then she turned on her side, breathing more heavily. He'd spent a pound and seventeen pence getting whiskey into her.

It took him almost five minutes to ease himself out of the bed and another five to get into his clothes. If she woke he'd say he had to go to the lavatory. There was a faint orange light in the room, coming from a street-lamp. Her clothes, scattered on the floor where he'd thrown them, had an orange tinge to them. In the dressing-table mirror he saw he had an orange tinge himself.

His fingers found the notes where he'd expected to find them, at the bottom of a drawer, beneath the newspaper that lined it. He slipped them into his pocket and quietly left the room.

In Meridian Close Henry began to clear up the rubbish in his house. In the sitting-room he filled the large empty cartons that had contained packets of powdered drinks and biscuits and Nutty Pops. He put smaller cartons into them, and egg containers, broken ornaments and toys and old baskets, pieces of wallpaper, old newspapers and magazines and copies of the *Radio Times*, and the circulars that had accumulated in the hall.

He found a blue cardboard suitcase on top of the wardrobe in his bedroom, its fastenings rusted and broken, its metal handle attached in only one place. He opened it and discovered that it contained a hat and a skirt that belonged to his ex-wife, and the letters he had written to her before they'd married, when her parents had taken her to Austria for six months in the hope that she'd meet someone else. *Dearest darling*, he read.

He found a brush and a dustpan, and swept out the room that had been his son's nursery. The wallpaper was torn where the child had pulled at it from his cot, posters illustrating fairy tales were fixed to the walls with drawing-pins. He removed the posters and resolved to patch up the wallpaper.

Extraordinary, saying Bodger Harrison was affected in the head. He'd been a bit odd in many ways, the way he expressed himself in particular, but no one could call him mental. Sour grapes on D'arcy's part; strange, not to have forgiven an old, dead headmaster after all these years. 'You're on the Credit side,' he remembered the Bodger saying again. It was a funny way to put it, but you could see what he'd meant. Nowadays D'arcy and Carstairs considered him to be very much on the Debit side, you could see it in their faces sometimes. He remembered once, a couple of months ago, he'd gone to a party given by D'arcy and his wife, an occasion when Peggy D'arcy had behaved most extraordinarily to him, as though she'd forgotten that he was a man. He'd arrived a bit early for the party, as he sometimes did. 'My God, there's someone here already,' he'd heard her calling out in agitation when he rang the bell. 'It'll only be Henry,' D'arcy had soothingly replied, opening the door as he spoke. Peggy D'arcy was in her underclothes, with her hair wound round white plastic rollers. D'arcy emptied nuts from a large red-and-blue tin into a number of bowls, and then went away to change. 'I'd read your *Evening Standard*,' Peggy D'arcy suggested. 'Nobody'll be here for ages.' She removed the plastic rollers from her hair and dried it at the electric fire, crouched on the floor in her underclothes. It didn't embarrass her in the least to have him in the room with her, he might have been another woman or a blind person. She didn't think she'd made enough paella, she said, wriggling in front of the electric fire. The underclothes were coffee-coloured, with small bunches of purple flowers on them. Her legs and arms were naked, her stomach was naked, and almost all her back was. When she went upstairs and came down again in a brown dress and green-and-gold Indian sandals, he went on imagining the coffee-coloured garments clinging to her, warmly scented by her body. He'd been offended by the episode, including D'arcy's saying: 'It'll only be Henry,' when he'd rung the bell. He'd almost mentioned it to D'arcy later on in the King of England, but he'd decided that it would be better not to. He'd never been able to look at Peggy D'arcy since without imagining the coffee-coloured underclothes, and feeling put out that she hadn't minded his being in the room with her.

Henry worked all night. He repaired as best he could some broken pieces of furniture. He put up a curtain-rail in the room that had been Timus's, and replaced the screws that were missing from the sagging curtain-rail in the sitting-room. He screwed the two loose stair-rod brackets into position.

He carried from the sitting-room the cardboard cartons he had already filled, and dumped them at the bottom of the garden. In his bedroom he found further clothes belonging to his ex-wife, a fur tippet that had been nibbled by mice and two blouses that he couldn't remember ever having seen before, a green satin evening dress which she'd had when he married her, and which years later she'd cut a piece out of in order to make clothes for one of Timus's teddy bears. He threw them all on to the heap at the bottom of the garden, with the blue suitcase and clothes of his own he didn't want, tweed jackets and pullovers that were too ragged and stained with oil to be of use to anyone. He found more letters: answers from firms to which he'd applied for jobs, and angry threats from a hire-purchase organization called the United Dominions Trust, and from the North Thames Gas Board, the London Electricity Board, the Abbey National Building Society and the General Accident Insurance Company. He found the letters that his ex-wife had written to him. *Dearest darling*, they said too. He found their wedding photographs, still in the red folder in which, years ago, they'd arrived, a fortnight after the wedding itself. She was there with her father, standing on the path that led to the church. They were together: entering a hired car, cutting wedding cake, holding up glasses of champagne. With the letters and the threatening communications, he threw them all on to the heap in the garden.

He cleared the mushroom fibre from the cupboard under the stairs and threw it on one of the flower-beds in the garden. There was an unpleasant smell in the cupboard, which he reckoned had come from the manure he'd had to use with the mushroom fibre. He propped the door open and made a mental note to wash the place out with disinfectant. It occurred to him then that when the cupboard was clean and smelling all right he could move his home-brew apparatus into it from the bathroom. He could easily rig up a light, trailing a flex from the plug in the hall. It had never been very convenient really, making beer in the bathroom.

He carried another load to the heap at the bottom of the garden, the dew on the long grass damping his legs through his trousers. Tomorrow he'd start on the garden itself, and when everything was in order he'd have a bonfire. He might even try and paint the wood-work of the windows, and the drain-pipes and the guttering, and the front and back doors. No reason why he shouldn't. He could borrow a ladder, and if the weather remained fine it might all be quite pleasant. He smiled, standing in the garden, looking at his brightly-lit house. Then he entered it and climbed the stairs to the bathroom. He poured himself some beer and drank it.

7

After breakfast, Miss Samson, Sylvie Clapper and Elizabeth were wheeled in their beds from the Marie Atkins Ward to the St Beatrice Ward. 'Bye,' Lily said, smiling at each of them in turn. 'Pray for us, Lily,' Sylvie Clapper said.

The St Beatrice was like an enormous edition of the Marie Atkins. It had the same pink curtains around each bed and the same blue blinds on its five windows, and the same fawn linoleum and white cupboards. On the pale-cream walls the pictures were larger: pictures of fruit, bunches of flowers, a landscape with a ruin, and four scenes of eighteenth-century London markets. There were twenty-eight beds in the St Beatrice, and a lot of bustle and talking, and nurses whom the women who'd been in the Marie Atkins Ward hadn't seen before. There were metal-frame chairs all the way down the middle of the ward, and two Formica-topped tables, much larger than the one in the Marie Atkins.

With the women of the St Beatrice Ward, Miss Samson, Sylvie Clapper and Elizabeth were prepared for their operations. And in other wards other women about to undergo hysterectomies, or a D and C or a Repair, were prepared also. Junior nurses drew the screens around the women's beds and made up lather and shaved away the growth of hair that made gynaecological surgery difficult. Night-dresses were exchanged for operation gowns. Preliminary injections were given.

In the St Agnes and the St Susanna and the Olivia Hassals Wards Mr Azu and Mr Greer made their Monday-morning rounds. Mr Rolle, who wasn't due on Mondays, had come in specially, to keep an eye on a tricky case that had worried him over the weekend. Mr Azu, in the Olivia Hassals, told Sister Hobson to change the treatment he'd prescribed for Mrs Hannay. 'Feeling better, Mrs Thring?' Mr Greer enquired in the St Agnes Ward, and Mrs Thring said she was feeling anything but better. She mentioned her children and her husband to Mr Greer, and the home-help who'd walked out because the children had put cornflakes in her bed. She hadn't slept a wink, she said, with the worry of it. But Sister Hobson, out of Mrs Thring's hearing, said that the night sister's notes stated that Mrs Thring had slept for ten hours.

Mr Alstrop-Smith drank coffee with Dr Mary Malcolmson and Dr Pennance. Dr Mary chatted, smiling brightly, wintry sunlight glinting on her pink-rimmed glasses. Dr Pennance nodded and made replies, Mr Alstrop-Smith was silent.

'You'll be all right on your owny-oh?' Sister O'Keeffe said in the Marie Atkins Ward. 'Thumbs up now, Mrs Drucker?'

Lily smiled and said she'd be quite all right. She was reading a book by Daphne du Maurier instead of Lady Augusta's autobiography because she felt like a change.

'*The House on the Strand*,' Sister O'Keeffe said, glancing at the title. 'Good, is it?'

Lily said it was.

Through the smell of ether that had offended Declan, prone women were silently wheeled. Anaesthetists made preparations in the theatres. Instruments were checked, gutta-percha and plastic twine placed ready for the final stages.

Outside the hospital the woman with the banner walked. A car she hadn't noticed in the street before was parked in a position usually occupied by another car: some morning shopper forced away from the more convenient parking places. A Mother's Pride bread-van drew up and the driver shouted good morning to her. He thought it was going to rain, he said, reversing the van through the wrought-iron gates of the hospital's side entrance.

A traffic warden walked slowly in Cheltenham Street, noting down car numbers. Another van drew up, double-parking outside the row of hospital cars. A woman in a green uniform hurried from it with flowers in cellophane, leaving the engine running. Two nurses, known by sight to the woman with the banner, entered the hospital, in a hurry also. 'Rain about,' the traffic warden remarked, and the woman said people seemed to think so. Her banner was getting tatty, the traffic warden thought.

With delicacy, Mr Alstrop-Smith cut the flesh of Elizabeth Aidallbery. He had a way, when operating, of endeavouring to recall the details of journeys he had made, recalling in particular the times of trains. His memory was good; for twenty years he had employed it in this manner, not as an aid to concentration but in order to calm certain tendencies of his imagination when human bodies lay at his mercy.

91

As a gynaecologist, Mr Alstrop-Smith always performed his own operations. As a surgeon, his skill was rarely in question. But at heart, if he permitted it, he was squeamish.

He cut again, the scalpel sliding through tissue with assured control. His eyes were steady. Behind the mask, his lips were tightly clamped together. His mind traversed familiar ground.

You left Victoria at nine thirty in the morning, you were in Paris Nord at five twenty-five. You left Paris Lyon at six twenty-two, you were in Rome at nine fifty-five the following morning: the Palatino, via Modane and Turin, a beautiful train. You left Victoria at three thirty, you were in Sežana at nine nineteen the following night, and in Skopje at four seventeen the next afternoon, and in Istanbul at ten past nine the morning after that. In the large, empty bar of the Pera Palas you could sit for ever, a stranger among the Turks, drinking White Horse whisky. In Cairo your clothes stuck to you, in Athens it could be windy in October. In Segesta, if it was cold, the station-master would turn on an electric fire, a stout, kind station-master, not at all obliged to heat up a waiting traveller. It was a family concern, the railway-station at Segesta: the station-master's grandchildren ran about, his son wrote out the ticket if you left your luggage, his daughter grew flowers. The fare was eight hundred lire from Palermo to Segesta, six hundred from Palermo to Cefalù, nine hundred from Agrigento to Enna. From Erice you could walk all the way to Trapani; among pine trees down the mountainside, a lone Englishman with a suitcase.

He stitched. He hated stitching. One day it would be a thing of the past. Funny, in twenty years not to have come to terms with stitching flesh. He nodded, and received the scissors.

You had to bring food with you on the Orient Express, but on the Mediolanum you didn't have to bother. The Mediolanum was all first class: Innsbruck five twenty-eight, Verona eight fifty-seven. In Innsbruck there was a dentist, Olaf Wiedemann, who didn't hurt. In Berlin a man fell down on the street and needed a doctor. The railway-station at Brigue was pleasant; you could live in the station at Rome, Mussolini's magnificence. At half-past eight in the morning good-time girls sat drinking coffee in the Rome *Termini*, smiling at travellers. In the buffet at Basel the food was very good.

A man had lived for years on Italian trains, moving about, never leaving a railway-station. Florence depart ten minutes past midnight, arrive Bologna one twenty-four. Milan depart ten minutes past midnight, arrive Venice-Mestre four twelve. Venice, Santa Lucia, depart thirty-four minutes past midnight, arrive Milan four minutes past five. Rome depart fifty minutes past midnight, arrive Reggio di Calabria eight minutes past eleven. Naples depart twenty-three minutes past midnight, arrive Taranto fifty-seven minutes past six. Rome eleven twenty. Copenhagen six forty-five two mornings later. Rome eight thirty-two, Munich five minutes past ten the following morning. In Bulgaria you could lie in your sleeper watching cobs of corn being harvested. In Yugoslavia oxen moved slowly in brown fields. In Czechoslovakia people waved at you, in Hungary people stared, in Russia they tried to buy your clothes. In Moscow you could sit alone, drinking vodka in your hotel room. It seemed they expected you to.

Mr Alstrop-Smith also found it advantageous to recall the details of his journeys while making an examination, and sometimes while making his rounds of the wards. He had perfected this dividing of his mind over the years, and because of it was known professionally as a man with a distant manner. On a famous occasion a woman in the St Agnes Ward had, without any warning, shouted hysterically at him. 'You're a humbug,' she'd shouted as he entered the ward with half a dozen students. She'd remarked on his grey striped trousers and the rose he always wore in the left buttonhole of his jacket. 'Like a bloody tailor's dummy,' the woman had shouted at him. He'd failed her, she'd noisily protested. He'd performed the operation incorrectly; she was stitched up tight as a drum, he'd ruined her sex life. None of the students tittered, nurses were aghast. Mr Alstrop-Smith had sat on the edge of her bed, a thing he never did with patients. He explained that it always felt a little tight at first, like any piece of stitching. She would be quite all right, she would be better than before. The woman, a Mrs McVeagh, a Scots woman, had wept and said she was sorry. 'I am sorry too,' he'd said in his distant manner. 'I am sorry you were upset, Mrs McVeagh.' And then, with the slow tread that caused some to liken him to an emperor and others to a god, he had preceded his students on their journey through the ward. The incident had hurt him, but he had not let it show.

Mr Alstrop-Smith's rubber gloves were removed from his hands. The instruments that had entered the innermost anatomy of Elizabeth Aidallbery were sterilized for use within the anatomy of Sylvie Clapper. Nurses tidied the body of Elizabeth Aidallbery, and then wheeled it away. Mr Alstrop-Smith's mask was removed.

Beneath his tapering nose there was a small moustache that matched the leadlike grey of his hair. In his ante-room, beyond the

93

possive √.

inner sanctum of the operating theatre, he relaxed, staring through glass as the theatre was again prepared. Empty now of remembered time-tables, his mind attempted to register the ordinary facts of his life, but this he prevented it from doing. His mind fogged and became blank, which was something else he had, over the years, taught it to do and which heightened the effect of a distant manner. He was aware of the opinion of others, of students and patients, colleagues, nurses, and other hospital staff, and he was aware that the opinion was correct: the professional expertise that his calling demanded had to a small extent devoured his own humanity. It was the price you paid. You couldn't weep when you found cancer, you couldn't do anything except stitch it all up again. And you walked through the wards like an emperor because you couldn't dare to seem less. Every summer you took a train somewhere, and every spring and every autumn.

The theatre was ready, another woman lay there. The theatre sister glanced up at him. He nodded and moved.

8

She was aware of numbed, slight pain, and of sleepiness, and of being lost. There were beds, and windows with dark blue blinds pulled down a little, and flowers in vases, and a picture of a ruin. There was a pillow under her head, she was in bed herself. 'Mummy,' she heard her own voice say. 'Mrs Aidallbery,' someone else said.

She walked across the landing, and in the hall below the grandfather clock softly chimed. There was a smell of polish, the landing was dim and cool. Beneath her bare feet the rugs were soft. Through the gloom she could make out the carved mahogany of the banisters, spirals and curlicues. 'I love this house,' she said.

Miss Digg was waiting for her, the music open on the piano. There were roses in a bowl and a smell of roses in the room. She played the Bach, the Minuet in G. 'You've practised,' Miss Digg said. 'I can tell you've practised, Elizabeth.' She went on playing. The notes came easily and she couldn't understand it because she hadn't practised at all. 'That's really very good,' Miss Digg said.

The french windows were open, outside it was sunny. Miss Digg set the metronome going with her long fingers. Miss Digg didn't know she was playing the piano in her sleep, which was why it was so easy; you didn't have to practise if you could play in your sleep. Miss Digg didn't know she should be in bed because she'd just had an operation. No wonder it hurt her, no wonder she couldn't wake up; no one should play a piano just after an operation.

A nurse in blue and white was holding her wrist, speaking to her. Curtains were near her, not drawn but hanging close by her, pink curtains. Paper rattled, someone was reading a newspaper: a man in a black suit, with polished black shoes, a man in the Pensione Bencistà, sitting on an upright chair, reading *Le Monde*. Men came, in black also, to take away her father. They kept their voices down, easing the coffin into the house and out again, on their shoulders. 'Here it is,' Joanna said, and when she opened the package that Joanna gave her she found it was a cup and saucer. 'You said you'd like a cup and saucer,' Joanna said. 'Just for yourself.'

Joanna's periods were beginning. 'Not once a *month*? Oh Mummy, not all this once a month?' Joanna came out in little pimples, around her mouth. Her face was paler than it had ever been. 'He says I look terrible,' Joanna said, speaking of her father. 'He thinks I'm awful.'

Joanna said she flushed all over her face and neck whenever anyone spoke to her. The palms of her hands sweated. In a chemistry lesson she dropped a retort with mercury in it. People noticed her on the street, she said, thinking she was ugly. She dreaded every fourth week when, sure as clockwork, it would come. 'You're not ugly, dear,' Elizabeth in a hurry said, with other things to think about.

The man who was reading *Le Monde* said she must not accept the cup and saucer because the cup and saucer were dangerous to use. 'We're doing our best,' the man said, 'to get to the root of this.'

He represented the police, he said: the girl was trafficking in drugs, no use pretending. The onion-men were French, he was French himself. 'Ten years I've been on this case,' he said. 'Cannabis resin under the skin of onions. That girl's hooked.'

He wasn't a French policeman, he was Mr Feuchtwanger. 'You don't get snakes,' Mr Feuchtwanger said, 'where the rest-harrow grows. *Ononis spinosa*, of the *papilionaceae* family.' He examined the *Ononis spinosa* she'd drawn. He bent his thin face over her cartridge paper. The calyx should have five teeth, he pointed out; the stipules weren't quite right. 'Still I admire your pupil's work, Miss Middlesmith,' Mr Feuchtwanger admitted. 'Pity she never went on with it,' Miss Middlesmith said.

Samuel laughed without making a noise, showing his long teeth. 'He's a Jesus freak,' Miss Middlesmith said. 'Jesus freak,' said Mr Feuchtwanger.

'I'm likeable really, Elizabeth,' Samuel said. 'Joanna and me have a whale of a time.'

'I'm sorry, Elizabeth,' Daphne said. 'I'm sorry I had a silly breakdown.' The tears fell down, on to the lime-green dress. Elizabeth tried to explain. She was hot and agitated, and she knew that her body and her mind had become separated. She could see herself standing, trying to explain to Daphne, and she knew that her mind was in a corner of the room. She wept, unable to say the words she wanted to say, unable to say any words.

'Obstreperous,' her father said. 'Dropping keys down a drain.'

'Oh please,' she cried.

'Hullo, Mrs Aidallbery,' someone said. 'You've had your operation.'

Red clover was beautiful if you drew it well. *Trifolium pratense.*
Meadow clover it was called: ten stamens, the lower nine fused, the
upper one free. 'The petioles of the basal leaves are long,' she said,
and Miss Middlesmith nodded her large moon face. Elizabeth smiled.

She walked with Henry, with sandwiches, when the tide was out.
They climbed up the cliffs and lay on the grass, among gorse bushes.
Bees buzzed about them, pausing sometimes on flowers. It was very
hot. They lay on their backs, watching a skylark, pretending it was a
vulture, pretending they were in the desert, tied down to wooden
pegs. Later they pretended they'd run away and walked for hours
along narrow, dusty roads. They asked a woman in a dog-cart. She
said they were five miles from Budleigh Salterton.

'You'll be all right,' Nurse Hampshire said. 'Doze if you want to.'

There was a piano in the St Beatrice Ward and Miss Digg was there,
sitting by a table with roses on it. 'You'd be much better off doing
your practising,' Miss Digg said, 'instead of taking other women's
husbands off on dirty weekends. Sex, sex, sex, Elizabeth: you should
be ashamed of yourself.'

But when Elizabeth tried to cross the floor of the ward to do her
practising she felt pain again, and knew she couldn't make the journey. 'Mrs Aidallbery!' shouted Sister O'Keeffe, her face crimson, her
eyes glaring and unpleasant. 'Mrs Aidallbery, are you out of your
mind?' But Mr Alstrop-Smith said pianos were a new thing in all the
London hospitals, being tried out now for the first time. 'We're most
obliged to you, Mrs Aidallbery,' he said, taking her by the arm and
leading her down the aisle of the church. She ran from the ward, but
she couldn't run properly because her labour pains had started. 'Miss
Digg's dying,' she tried to call out, but she couldn't form the words
properly because of the drugs they'd given her. 'That woman's
dying,' she whispered to her father, but her father said it didn't
matter. 'Get back to your bed at once, Elizabeth,' Sister O'Keeffe
screamed at her. 'For heaven's sake, Elizabeth!' her mother said.
'You'll lose your child.' But the child was in her arms: her child had
Miss Samson's birthmark all over its face. 'Because you let it be born,'
Miss Digg said. 'Because you didn't walk away from him.' Mr Feuchtwanger said that that was correct. If you could see a person who'd
been savaged by heroin you wouldn't bring a girl like Joanna into the
world; what on earth was the point of it? 'There,' said Mr Alstrop-
Smith, handing the baby back to her, 'we've cleared the nastiness
away.' 'Savaged,' Mr Feuchtwanger said. 'you can't clear that away.'

In the Foxley Hotel she asked for the key to Room Eleven. 'Your husband's in the bar,' the receptionist said and she said no, her husband was at home, with her three children. 'I'm having a dirty weekend,' she said. Mr Brook in his vest and blue trousers, laughed and said he'd come without his Ducklings Class because he wanted a dirty weekend himself. He went a lot to Harrods Depository, he said. 'I found a pound there,' Henry said in the King of England, and all around him the drinkers applauded. Henry balanced a pint of beer on his chin, and balanced on the rim of the beer mug a sweeping-brush. People said they'd never seen anything like it. 'Whatever are you doing,' her mother cried, 'with a man like that in the Foxley Hotel? Are you mad, Elizabeth?' She shook her head; she wasn't mad, she explained. She'd had her happiness, she said; in that house and that garden she'd had all the happiness that was allowed to a person. She should have realized that, they should have told her instead of letting her drink chilled white wine with a man who was thirteen years older than her, instead of letting the children be born, and sending her off to the Foxley Hotel. Look at her now, with Joanna hating her and Henry doing tricks with a sweeping-brush.

'Oh, for heaven's sake!' cried Miss Digg, her spindly body twitching with exasperation, her hands gripping the rail at the end of Elizabeth's bed. 'For heaven's sake, you're lucky, Elizabeth.'

'Think of Miss Samson,' her mother said. 'Think of your face all twisted and marked like that. Who'd have taken you then to the Foxley Hotel, or on a honeymoon in Crete, or anywhere else?'

'Think of Sylvie Clapper,' Miss Middlesmith said, 'beginning her marriage with a hysterectomy. And Lily Drucker with four miscarriages and Kenneth's mother.'

'Would you like that, Elizabeth,' Mr Feuchtwanger asked, 'a mother-in-law gawking at you with prominent eyes, and a father-in-law who doesn't say a word, and a husband terrified by both of them?'

'What's it like for Lily Drucker?' Miss Digg asked. 'What's it like for poor Miss Samson, and Sylvie Clapper with her boyfriend out of work?'

'You do go on so, Elizabeth,' Miss Middlesmith said, 'always about yourself. You put your mother in a home, you know.'

He was there with his eagle face. It was entirely true, he said. She'd been a terrible wife, like a nun in the bed they'd shared, unable to keep the children quiet, failing Joanna, failing him. She'd been stupidly romantic about him, and then about another woman's husband. The time would come when she'd fail Jennifer and Alice too.

What use was drawing flowers, for heaven's sake? What use were ridiculous people like Miss Middlesmith and Mr Feuchtwanger and Miss Digg, who turned against you when you were in hospital? Laughable, inviting them to tea.

But Henry came into the ward and said it wasn't laughable in the least. He'd known Elizabeth all his life, he said. Her mother had insisted on the Sunset Home, it was Daphne's husband who should feel guilty, Joanna would come round. Elizabeth made mistakes, he said; everyone made mistakes. 'Stop this talk at once,' Henry ordered, and her mother and Miss Digg and Miss Middlesmith and Mr Feuchtwanger all smiled at her warmly, and explained that they'd only been joking. 'You're the best wife a man ever had,' her husband said. 'Of course wives have to pretend. You did your best darling.' Everyone laughed in the ward then, Miss Samson and Sylvie Clapper and Lily Drucker and Elizabeth herself. They were all happy enough, they said, really and truly. 'Welcome to happiness,' Miss Samson said.

Sylvie

In the yard behind the Masons' Arms Sylvie waited, pressed back against a whitewashed wall, hidden by stacked-up crates of empty bottles. Men came into the yard to urinate. Her father was there, using words he wouldn't have permitted himself to use in their home. 'Hullo, Sylvie,' Danny Grimes said.

The dream became confused then because it wasn't Danny Grimes she was with but a man called Benny Wainway, a man who owned a grocer's shop. 'Oh, Christ above!' he cried out. His fingers gripped the flesh of her back. He laughed and quivered, obscenities poured from his lips, she thought he was having a heart attack. He took false teeth from his mouth and placed them on the edge of a crate. She tried to run away from him, but he was always able to get her into a corner of the yard: when she tried to scream, she couldn't. He was wearing a hat and his white grocer's coat, he had a bayonet from the end of a rifle. Her father and Danny Grimes were watching. It would teach her a lesson, they said. 'Leave that girl alone,' a man shouted out and she saw that it was Declan's friend, Mr Maloney. 'Get her into an ambulance,' Mr Maloney said, 'and I'll stitch her up.' He had a doctor's bag in his hand and a stethoscope hanging from his arm. He was a qualified doctor, he told her, and when she looked at him more closely she saw that he wasn't Mr Maloney but a doctor she'd gone to a few years ago for an abortion. 'She's my patient under the National Health,' Benny Wainway said. 'She came into the shop

99

saying she was up the spout. I was fixing her up.' The ambulance came and they laid her down on a bed in it. They sat on the other bed, her father and Danny Grimes, Benny Wainway and the man she'd thought was Mr Maloney. Declan was there too. They were all playing cards.

Miss Samson dreamed that she was in the kitchen of Number Nine. Robert and Edward Tonsell were washing potatoes at the sink, and the little Welsh girl was taking knives and forks from a drawer of the dresser, counting them out for the dining-room table. Through the kitchen window she could see that the coal-shed door was open; she could hear Arthur shovelling coke for the two cosy-stoves. It was a Saturday evening. Robert and Edward Tonsell had been preaching that morning at quiet street junctions in S.W.17. Their sombre faces were intent as they washed the potatoes and told of the people who had paused to listen to them. A man had come by, they said, and had shown them the impression of the stigmata on his hands and feet. He had sat on the edge of the pavement and had taken off his shoes and socks, and people had crowded round to see the nail-marks. 'There was no mistaking,' Edward Tonsell said.

'Did you tell the Reverend Rawes?' Miss Samson cried in her dream. 'And the man? Where is the man now, Edward?'

'We thought to tell you first, Miss Samson,' Robert Tonsell replied. 'Naturally,' his brother added.

They all came to the kitchen then, the Reverend Rawes, Mrs Delve and Carol Pidsley. Arthur came in from the yard with his hoppers full of coke.

'Tell them,' she cried, urging the Tonsell brothers on. Calmly they continued to wash the potatoes. She ordered the little Welsh girl to stop taking the knives and forks out of the dresser drawer, to listen to what was being said. 'Do you understand, Arthur?' she cried. 'A man with the marks of Our Lord crucified. Where they nailed Him to the Cross.'

The Tonsell brothers repeated what they had said already. The man was upstairs, they said, asleep in Mr Ibbs's old room.

'Has he come here?' she cried. 'Has he come to Number Nine?'

The Tonsell brothers, still washing potatoes, nodded silently.

'Bless this day,' said the Reverend Rawes.

'A man with the stigmata,' Mrs Delve said to Carol Pidsley.

'I have never seen the stigmata,' Carol Pidsley replied.

A tall, upright man in a muffler and an overcoat entered the kitchen, and Miss Samson saw that it was Mr Ibbs, risen apparently from the dead. The others still did not know him, for they had not known him in life. To them he was still a miraculous stranger, a man who'd taken off his shoes and socks on the public street in order to show the Tonsell brothers his stigmata.

'Miss Samson,' he said, and to the amazement of the people in the kitchen, an amazement she could see in their eyes and their faces, he put his arms around her shoulders and drew her near to him. He kissed the bad part of her face, beneath her eye.

'This is Mr Ibbs,' she said, 'of whom I have spoken.'

'Thou good and faithful servant,' said Mr Ibbs.

'Have you risen, sir?' Robert Tonsell inquired, and Mr Ibbs said yes, he had that morning risen from the dead. The little Welsh girl cried out that she was frightened, but the Reverend Rawes and others said there was nothing to be frightened of. Carol Pidsley comforted the little Welsh girl, and then Mr Ibbs went round everyone, shaking hands, Mrs Delve's plump hand and the Reverend Rawes's small one, and Arthur's and Carol Pidsley's and the little Welsh girl's. He did not shake the hands of the Tonsell brothers because, he said, he had done that already.

'I have returned to Number Nine,' Mr Ibbs said, 'to be with the inmates for an hour or so. You are happy here? The folk are happy, Miss Samson?'

She said they were and asked if there were any complaints. Only Mrs Delve spoke then, saying the breakfasts were sometimes on the cold side.

'I have placed myself upon His Cross,' Mr Ibbs said. 'I have received the holy stigmata that I may pass them on to you.

In the dining-room, when they sat down to brawn and cooked ham, with potatoes and salad, Mr Ibbs did not take off his muffler and overcoat. She asked if he felt cold, but he said he didn't. They had tinned apricots afterwards, with custard, and *petit beurre* biscuits.

'I knew by an interior light that I must die,' Mr Ibbs said, 'and as soon as I knew I made arrangements for Miss Samson to take over Number Nine. "Pass down my precious stigmata to the inmates," He said. "To all except Miss Samson, who received them at birth. Let it be a miraculous thing," He said, "that you have returned with my holy marks to Nine Balaclava Avenue, Mr Ibbs. Let it be a sign of my love for my people." '

Mr Ibbs rose then and left the room. They sat in silence, awaiting his return.

101

'I think he's in the toilet,' Edward Tonsell said, but Mr Ibbs was not in the toilet when they looked, nor was he anywhere in Number Nine. She wept, for he had not said goodbye. He had come mysteriously and had gone without a word.

'I think it was a dream I had,' she said, but the others assured her that it was more than a dream. They showed her their hands, which were marked with crimson nail-wounds. The Reverend Rawes took off his shoes and socks and pointed at the crimson marks repeated on his feet.

'We must telephone the *Daily Express*,' Edward Tonsell said, but only his brother agreed with him in this suggestion.

'It's what Mr Ibbs wished,' Robert Tonsell explained, and he quoted Mr Ibbs, who had spoken the words of Jesus Christ: ' "Let it be known as a miraculous thing that you have returned with my holy marks to Nine Balaclava Avenue. Let it be a sign of my love for my people." '

But Mrs Delve and Carol Pidsley said it would be blasphemous to telephone the words of Jesus Christ to the *Daily Express*, and the Reverend Rawes agreed. Miss Samson, still flustered by the visitation, didn't know what to think.

'I forbid you,' Mrs Delve said loudly to the Tonsell brothers, in a way that was quite unlike her. 'It is a private matter for this house.'

'No one leaves this room,' the Reverend Rawes said, moving to the door and standing with his back to it.

'I've never cared for you,' Carol Pidsley said to the Tonsell brothers, 'if you want to know.' Her acned face was red with anger, her eyes flashed dangerously.

'We found him,' Robert Tonsell said, his face flushed also. 'He came to us on the street.'

'People have a right,' his brother began, but Mrs Delve interrupted him by shrieking wildly that if he telephoned the *Daily Express* she would hammer his brains out.

'Yes,' Carol Pidsley said. 'Yes.'

Miss Samson wept. No one ever had spoken such words in Number Nine. In all her years, since she'd worked first of all in the kitchen, no one had used such language, or shouted. There'd been Church folk always in Number Nine.

'You're a Communist,' Edward Tonsell said to Mrs Delve.

'The way you leave the lavatory,' shouted Mrs Delve, rushing at Edward Tonsell and pulling at his clothes. 'You're filthy dirty.'

'It's Robert actually,' Edward Tonsell said, 'who leaves the toilet like that.'

'Don't call it a toilet,' screamed Mrs Delve.

All over Number Nine then there was shouting and anger, and Mr Ibbs came back and laughed. It was all a nonsense, he said: he'd been out to look, there was no God anywhere. Tell that to the *Daily Express*, he said.

It was horrible in Number Nine. Hell had come, the Reverend Rawes said, with his back still against the door of the sitting-room.

'Since we're speaking the truth,' Mrs Delve said to Miss Samson, 'the food is inedible.'

'You're preposterous,' Edward Tonsell shouted at Carol Pidsley. 'You should be ashamed of yourself, trying to get men.'

'The Ramblers' Club,' his brother said. 'She belongs to that.'

'Rambling after men,' Edward Tonsell said.

'Another thing,' Mrs Delve said to Miss Samson, 'we don't like being served by a half-wit.'

'Arthur's not,' she cried, tears pouring on her cheeks. 'Mr Ibbs always took in people. Poor Arthur can't help his affliction.'

'That Welsh girl,' the Reverend Rawes said, 'never washes her hands.'

She cried out again, with further tears coming: she'd trained the little Welsh girl to wash her hands. Always after the toilet, always before touching food.

'Don't call it a toilet,' screamed Mrs Delve.

'Oh, please,' she cried.

'You put people off,' Mrs Delve said, 'looking like that.'

She closed her eyes and put her hands to her face, covering it. She could never open her eyes again, she promised herself, she would never take her hands away. 'We are in darkness,' she heard the voice of the Reverend Rawes saying and there was a crashing sound and she knew that the Tonsell brothers had broken the framed embroidery in the hall. 'Welcome to happiness,' the voice of Robert Tonsell said, and he and his brother laughed. 'I would like to die,' said the voice of poor Carol Pidsley, who had suffered miserably, being called preposterous. The Tonsell brothers laughed again, and then the others laughed too, Mrs Delve and the Reverend Rawes and the little Welsh girl and Arthur. She could hear their laughter, but could not see them because her hands still covered her face. She heard the laughter of Mr Ibbs, and her own weeping, and the weeping of poor Carol Pidsley. 'God help us all,' cried Carol Pidsley. 'I have looked,

He is not there,' replied Mr Ibbs. 'He's a big fat confidence trick, organized by the *Daily Express*.'

In her dream she felt herself thinking that Carol Pidsley had no right. What right on earth had Carol Pidsley to think she could get married to Edward Tonsell? She didn't even like Edward Tonsell, or his brother; she'd just said so.

'Acne,' she screamed at Carol Pidsley. 'And legs like tree-trunks. You're seven feet tall,' she screamed at Carol Pidsley, 'and awkward with it. Your hair's terrible.'

Carol Pidsley ceased to weep and laughed instead. 'You're jealous, Miss Samson,' she said. 'You're jealous of me and Edward Tonsell.'

'You're marrying a man you don't even like,' Miss Samson screamed. 'You'd marry anyone, in the Ramblers' Club or any-where else.'

'I am extremely beautiful,' Carol Pidsley said. 'If you look at your-self in a mirror, Miss Samson, you will see that I am extremely beauti-ful.'

Miss Samson wept. 'It isn't fair,' she cried. 'I wanted to marry Mr Ibbs.'

Mr Ibbs laughed. 'No God would have done it to ·you,' he said. 'What's the point of a God turning you out like that? Or Arthur? Or Carol Pidsley? I climbed up trees and there was still no sign of Him. I climbed up telegraph poles.'

The laughter came in waves, so loud she could scarcely bear it. It hurt her. It was a disease she was suffering from, someone told her.

'It's quite all right, Miss Samson,' another voice said. 'You've had your operation, dear; you're waking up.'

'Our Father,' she murmured, 'which art in heaven.'

'Yes, dear,' the other voice soothingly said.

'We'll adopt,' Declan said. 'We'll give a home to a little stray.'

Suddenly she was wide awake. He'd been sitting there, on the chair by her bed, and for a moment she couldn't make out whether he'd really been there or whether she'd been dreaming it. The ward seemed strange after her dreams. The outlines of the other beds and of the cupboards and the long row of metal-frame chairs were sharply defined, the colours had a fresh look about them.

'Well, there you are,' said Sister O'Keeffe, smiling down at her, seeming fresh and sharply defined herself.

'Was Declan here?'

'You had a little dream about Declan, dear. Is Declan your boy-friend?'

'I dreamt he was sitting here.'

'You'll have a few little dreams,' Sister O'Keeffe said. 'Tell Declan I was asking for him. What part of Ireland does he come from?'

'Enniscorthy. There's a place called Vinegar Hill. Halfway up Vinegar Hill he comes from.'

'I'm from Kinsale myself. If Declan's in another little dream tell him Sister O'Keeffe was asking for him. Aren't the Irish everywhere? tell him.'

She slept. In the Cruskeen Bawn Lounge she sat with Declan and Sister O'Keeffe, waiting for Mr Maloney. 'I'm going to marry Maloney,' Sister O'Keeffe said.

While Sister O'Keeffe was saying that in Sylvie's dream Sylvie's clothes, still in the Victor Value carrier-bag, were found by Mrs Vendericks in the corner of Declan's wardrobe.

One by one, Mrs Vendericks took the articles from the bag: high-heeled shoes in suede that was dyed a shade of lilac, a short imitation-leather skirt, tights, underclothes, a sleeveless imitation-leather jacket and a lilac blouse. She returned the articles to the bag and placed the bag on the bed. Other clothes of Sylvie's were in the room. Mrs Vendericks examined them and put them, with shoes and odds and ends, in a cardboard box she'd brought upstairs for that purpose.

The room contained little else that attracted Mrs Vendericks. On the windowsill the bottle of Camp Coffee remained, with the Vim and the Brillo Pads. Declan, who had come quietly in the night, had taken everything else away, his own clothes, all edible food, the sheets from the bed, and the curtain that had hung in the front of the window. On the bedside table, kept in place by the frilled bedside lamp, was a note. *I will pay up the outstanding rental*, Mrs Vendericks read. *Don't worry about that. Miss Clapper's clothes are in a bag in the wardrobe. She's in the Cheltenham Street Hospital at this moment and will be requiring the clothes on her release. If anyone who is going that way could drop the bag in to her it would be an act of charity for a girl who's had a severe operation. Otherwise she will have no clothes to come out in. I will be fixing the rental very shortly. Thank you. Declan Quigley.*

Mrs Vendericks added the Camp Coffee, the Vim and the Brillo Pads to the contents of the bag, and made her way downstairs. You could trust the Irish the way you could trust a bouncing little snake. They'd be all smiles and talk in your kitchen, all jokes and carry-on, and then they'd turn round and walk away with your curtaining. They'd leave you owing two weeks' rent and then they'd ask you to take clothes into a hospital. Mrs Vendericks put on her coat and fixed a scarf about her head. Leaving the Camp Coffee, the Vim and the Brillo Pads on her kitchen table, she set out into Shepherd's Bush with the carrier-bag and the cardboard box full of Sylvie Clapper's belongings. She received a pound and seventy pence for them from a Mr Kusum in Tombs Street.

Henry was busy. The attendant at the swimming-baths where Mr Brook still held his weekly Ducklings Class telephoned him and said he couldn't get tea out of the hot-drinks machine. Yesterday, he said, there'd been complaints about the coffee. People had been on about it all afternoon, saying it tasted of oil.

Henry drove round to the swimming-baths and poked at the faulty machine with a screwdriver. 'It's bloody ridiculous,' the attendant complained. 'Nothing but trouble, these New-Way machines are.'

'I'm afraid we'll have to call in our engineers, sir,' Henry said, having failed to locate any trouble that could be causing the coffee to taste of oil and preventing the machine from issuing tea in any form.

'Engineers?' repeated the swimming-baths attendant unpleasantly. 'And what d'you think you are, may I ask?'

Henry explained that he was merely the machines' operator: his job was to keep the hot-drinks machines filled with powdered tea, coffee, chocolate, and soup, to supply crisps, biscuits and Nutty Pops for the snacks machines, and soft drinks for the soft-drinks machines. As well as which, he explained, he was qualified to attend to minor running repairs.

'They're bloody useless, the whole damn lot of them,' the swimming-baths attendant said furiously. 'It's no better than a bloody con trick.'

'Be that as it may, sir,' Henry replied quietly, screwing a metal plate back into place, 'I fear you'll have to wait for the engineers.'

He telephoned Rammage and asked him to send round an engineer. 'Can't you fix it yourself?' Rammage crossly demanded in his laboured, nasal voice. 'New-Way engineers aren't two a penny, you know.'

'I've tried. It's something fundamental.'

'Oh, Jesus bloody Christ.' He spoke as if the effort brought death a little closer. Henry imagined the cigarette ash scattered over his clothes, and the closed eyes and the leathery yellowness of Rammage's upper lip. He told the swimming-baths attendant that two New-Way engineers would be with him within an hour.

'Approximately an hour,' he said, aware that it would be ten days or a fortnight before the engineers arrived. He gave the man Rammage's telephone number and told him to ring it if he had any further difficulty.

'Difficulty?' the man shouted at him. 'Don't you think I've had enough bloody difficulty?' He continued to swear and to threaten, saying you could rely on nobody these days. In a fury he banged the side of the defective machine with his fist, shouting that he had a dog's life, claiming the country hadn't been governed properly since the War.

Henry drove away, wondering why he hadn't attempted to leave the vending-machine business years ago. He stopped at a telephone-box and telephoned the frozen foods firm about the opening he'd heard of. He spoke to the secretary of a man called Bastable, and at half past four, in a suit and a clean shirt and his Radley tie, he presented himself for an interview.

The man called Bastable was fifteen or so years younger than Henry, but was nevertheless a member of the firm's board of directors. After ten minutes he said that Henry was definitely the kind of material the frozen foods firm was looking for.

'Our fish division's brand new,' Mr Bastable said, adding that the firm's fish division would be where Henry would find himself.

'Ask Mr Ring to step in,' Mr Bastable said with sharp abruptness into a mushroom-coloured phone, and a minute later an even younger man urgently entered the office.

Henry was impressed by the two men's vigour and by the fact that both of them were very different from the stained, ash-covered Rammage behind his chipboard desk, and different, too, from Mr Rinsal, T.J.B. Antler and Z. Jacob Nirenstein. 'We're building things up,' Mr Bastable said. 'We're all in it together.' It was a pioneering job that was needed, he added: the brand-name of the frozen fish was wholly unknown in the territory which the firm was hoping to open up. He looked sharply at Mr Ring and Mr Ring said sharply that that was correct.

'Your task,' continued Mr Bastable, 'is simple. To get our packets into the deep freezers of supermarkets against heavy existing competition.'

'Or to put it bluntly,' said Mr Ring, 'to get our competitors' packets out and ours in. We would, of course, give you what help we could.'

107

They all three chatted agreeably for a minute or two longer, and then Mr Bastable shook Henry's hand and repeated that he was definitely the kind of material the firm was looking for. Mr Ring said that that was correct.

Henry agreed to return to the firm's offices in two days' time, on Wednesday, for further, more detailed briefing on the work. He shook hands with Mr Ring, who told him that before he left the firm's premises on Wednesday he could collect an almost-new Vauxhall Viva from the firm's garage.

'If you could start in on the territory on Monday,' Mr Bastable said, 'it'd suit us nicely.' And Mr Ring suggested that he might like to spend the few days before that driving around the territory in the firm's Viva, familiarizing himself.

'You should know a territory like the back of your hand.' Mr Ring said, 'before you attempt to sell anything. As you're aware, of course.'

'Yes, well, I'll do that certainly.'

'Get the feel of the supermarkets,' Mr Bastable said. 'Parking facilities, one-way streets, type of shopper, type of outlet. Anything and everything.'

'Correct,' said Mr Ring.

After the interview Henry drove straight to the King of England. He arrived just as it was opening, and telephoned Rammage to say he wouldn't be able to operate the machines after Wednesday. Rammage said he couldn't do that since it was necessary to give New-Way Vending Limited at least a month's notice. But Henry pointed out that at the moment of employment Rammage had stressed that New-Way Vending Limited could dismiss an operator without any notice at all, and had implied that this arrangement was mutual on both sides. He heard Rammage sighing, muttering through his cigarette. A moment later, in the familiar dying voice, he pressed Henry to continue until New-Way Vending Limited could find someone else, even if it meant giving his customers a reduced service. For four years, week after week, Rammage had let him down: not sending engineers when he said he would, blaming him to his customers when something went wrong, blaming him to New-Way Vending Limited. 'They're doing their nuts about you,' Rammage had once told him, when the reason for a machine being out of action for a month had been entirely due to Rammage's inability to get his engineers to look at it. Listening to Rammage pressing him to go on operating the machines until a replacement was found, Henry remembered

108

all this. He said in reply that he was on to a far better job, with two live-wires called Bastable and Ring, who were out to make a fortune. He said he intended to make a fortune himself, even if he was starting at forty-one. 'Just give them a minimal service,' Rammage urged, as though he hadn't heard. 'Any old pretence at all will do. Week or ten days at the most, Henry.' Affected by euphoria and a feeling of goodwill, Henry agreed to do the best he could, although what he had meant to do was to laugh and tell Rammage to go to hell. In the public bar he bought drinks for two old-age pensioners and a man who was delivering bottles of lager.

In the sitting-room of Nine Balaclava Avenue the Reverend Rawes and Mrs Delve discussed the holiday they planned for Miss Samson. An aunt of Carol Pidsley's had stayed at the Seaview Hotel in Bexhill and had said that it was excellent.

'The difficulty is,' Mrs Delve remarked over a pot of tea and macaroons she'd made herself, 'we don't know when Miss S'll be ready for a room. We'll have to book, of course, to be sure of something nice.'

The Reverend Rawes, who found the macaroons hard to bite, slipped the remains of his into his pocket, hoping he would not forget it was there.

'There might be news tonight,' he said, 'when we ring the Sister. Some indication perhaps.'

'A nice front room,' Mrs Delve said. 'A real treat for her.'

9

Alone in the Marie Atkins Ward, Lily Drucker had shepherd's pie and tapioca for lunch, and tea with two biscuits at three o'clock. On both occasions she was caught consuming the food in bed by Sister O'Keeffe, who scolded her playfully the first time and severely the second, accusing her of being uncooperative. Lily cried. She mentioned her backache again, and Sister O'Keeffe said she was being silly. If she didn't get a little exercise every day the backache would become worse. 'Cheer up now, Mrs Drucker. What's the use of being in hospital if you don't help yourself along?'

'Yes,' Lily said.

She'd be sitting in her garden this summer, Sister O'Keeffe promised, with the baby on her lap. She'd be out walking with a pram, delighted with herself. 'How far've you got?' she asked, and when Lily said page 191 Sister O'Keeffe said wasn't it great the way Lady Augusta kept her spirits up, even when she'd run through every penny of her husband's money?

Lily slept a little and then Nurse Emamooden came in and had a chat with her. Nurse Emamooden told her that her ambition was to go round the world. It wasn't difficult, she said, a nurse could get work anywhere. She'd been all over the place already, Africa, New Zealand, America. She liked Cheltenham Street Hospital, she said. It was a really homely place.

'Yes,' Lily said.

After Nurse Emamooden had gone away she felt a bit low again. She went to the lavatory, hoping she'd meet Sister O'Keeffe so that she could be seen to be cooperating, walking about. But Sister O'Keeffe wasn't in the corridors.

Lily washed, spending a long time over that, hoping to cheer herself up. On the way back she met Mrs Thring, having a smoke. She was going to walk out, Mrs Thring said, unless they came to some conclusion within the next few days. She'd never felt better, she said, but they insisted that she wasn't right yet. 'It's doing you no good, either,' she said. 'I'd walk out tomorrow if I was you. Rings under your eyes you have, love.'

In bed, quietly behind her spectacles, with the book propped up, Lily cried a little. She thought maybe she should walk out. How could she stand it, another six or seven, maybe eight, weeks? Twice or three times again the Marie Atkins Ward would fill up with recovering women. Mrs Thring would go home. Others would come, and after a few days they'd feel they'd been there for ever. 'Can't think how you stick it,' they'd say, meeting her in the corridors.

She felt better after her cry. She dried up her tears with a tissue and wiped her spectacles. It was the Indian woman's evening off. Another woman, known to her as Doris, who'd once described to her an operation she'd had for varicose veins, brought her fish and stewed apples at six o'clock. When she'd eaten it she went to the lavatory again. She washed again and brushed her hair and put on fresh lipstick. Kenneth would come at seven.

In the hospital it was another routine Monday evening. In the medicine room opposite the Marie Atkins Ward, Nurse Hampshire and Nurse Summerbee drank cups of tea. Higher up in the building, in a primrose-papered office, one of the hospital's two matrons, Miss Endicott, drank tea also, with sugar-coated biscuits. Sister O'Keeffe, in a small room near the Olivia Hassals Ward, poured water from an electric kettle on to Ribena in the bottom of a plastic mug. In the staff canteen Dr Pennance and another houseman, Dr Talkler, ate sardines on toast. 'There's a chap in Lincolnshire,' Dr Talkler said, 'looking for a third in a partnership. I'm seriously considering it.'

'Odd, the whole thing,' Nurse Summerbee said, referring to a rumour at present current in the hospital about Mr Azu's wife.

'She drinks, I heard,' Nurse Hampshire said, but Nurse Summerbee denied that, saying that the oddness about the consultant's wife had nothing to do with drink.

'She came here once,' Nurse Hampshire said. 'I remember her sitting in the hall, waiting for him. Beautiful.'

'Actually that wasn't his wife,' Nurse Summerbee said, 'according to Aylard.'

Nurse Aylard entered the medicine room as her name was spoken, early for night duty. She didn't know how true it was, that the beautiful woman who'd waited for Mr Azu was not his wife. She'd heard it in the Rose and Thorn.

In her small room Sister O'Keeffe told Sister Kolulu that the day had been ordinary. The wards for which she and Sister Kolulu, Sister Hobson and Sister Brown were responsible had suffered no emergencies. Women were still sleeping after their operations. Other women were almost ready to go home, some had experienced slight setbacks. There was still indecision about how to treat Mrs Thring. 'Mrs Drucker's on the mopey side,' Sister O'Keeffe said. 'Poor little scrap, it's lonely for her.'

The telephone rang. 'I'm inquiring about Miss Samson,' a man's voice said, adding that his name was Rawes. 'We were just wondering how she was.'

'Miss Samson's had her operation, Mr Rawes,' Sister O'Keeffe said. 'Everything went perfectly well. She's still asleep, in fact.' She listened while the Reverend Rawes inquired if there was any way of knowing when Miss Samson would be released, but Sister O'Keeffe said it was early days yet. She listened again while the Reverend Rawes said that some of the people from Miss Samson's boarding-house would come and see her tomorrow evening. 'That'll be quite all right,' she said. 'Two at a time by the bedside. Good night, Mr Rawes.'

Sister Kolulu suggested that Sister O'Keeffe should go to the pictures, mentioning a film that was showing in an Odeon not far away. But Sister O'Keeffe was doubtful. 'I'll maybe take it easy,' she said, not specifying what she meant by this, but seeing herself as she spoke, sitting in front of her electric fire, eating two poached eggs and reading *Folly Bridge*, which she was currently enjoying. She could be in bed by ten, in time for *The World Tonight* on Radio 4, and later on *A Book at Bedtime*.

In the hospital laundry, women and girls ceased their task of sorting out sheets and pillowslips and surgical masks. In the kitchen the chef, Mr McIntyre, prepared porridge for the next day's breakfast. In the boiler-room old George Trigol stoked his furnaces and afterwards made himself tea. In their glass-paned cubbyhole in the hall the daytime porters, Pengelly and Frowen, talked about the pay rise that hospital ancillary workers had been hoping for but which, due to the national economy policy, they had just been told they would not receive. Tired after a strenuous day, Mr Greer sighed as he closed his registry door behind him.

From the window of her primrose office Miss Endicott gazed down at the woman who walked with a banner. She sighed at this reminder of disorder, wishing the woman would agree to talk it over with her, whatever it was that troubled her. She'd really feel happy, she

112

reflected, if she looked out one day and found that the woman was no longer there. It was strange how things like that could upset you.

Lily, having been feeling more cheerful, was low again when Kenneth came. His presence reminded her of her mother-in-law, of her mother-in-law talking while he painted her bathroom for her. 'No wonder she's mingy, with blood like that,' Mrs Drucker would say. 'No wonder she can't have a baby like a proper person.' And Kenneth, for the sake of peace, wouldn't argue.

'She's turned me into a nerve-case, Kenneth. Ever since that day you brought me back to tea with them I've felt nerves all over me. I get jittery every time I think of her.'

'You're not a nerve-case, Lily.'

'Of course I am. I'm a nerve-case that can't relax properly. My babies don't want to be born.'

'Oh, Lily –'

'You shouldn't ever have married me, Kenneth.'

'But Lily, I love you.'

'I wish she'd leave me alone. I wish she didn't come on Sundays.'

'I'm sorry, Lily. I tried to tell her. I tried to say –'

'I'm coming out tomorrow. I'm looking terrible, a woman was saying. How could I be anything else, lying here like this?'

'You can't come out tomorrow, Lily. You mustn't even think of such a thing. Please now –'

'The whole thing's driving me mad.' She began to cry. He tried not to sigh. He found a handkerchief for her, under her pillow.

'Roast meat and cups of tea, buttered toast, going for little toddles down a corridor – it couldn't be normal, a baby born under conditions like that. Even supposing it is born.' She whimpered, blowing her nose. 'Even supposing it isn't dead as a door nail already.'

'Oh, Lily, don't be silly.'

She shook her head. She wasn't being silly, she said; she was telling the truth. She talked about the first years of their marriage, before all the miscarriages, before his mother had taken strength from their misfortunes. He'd taken her away from her past, from the memories of St Clare's, and from her present too, from her gloomy lodgings with Mrs Malprits. She'd taken him from the oppression of his parents' house. Together they'd made everything different. People had looked at them on the street because they were always laughing. Whenever they met, they put their arms around one another and

113

didn't mind who saw. Boys whistled at them when they went on kissing.

'Nothing could touch us then,' she said. 'No one and nothing.'

'Lily –'

'We haven't the strength any more, not after the miscarriages. She'll win in the end.'

He didn't say anything. He didn't know what to say. Her face was red with bitterness and anger, in a moment she'd begin to cry again. He tried to take her hand, but she pulled it away from him. Hospitals were worse than prisons, she said. Nobody cared, although they pretended to all the time, with their hot drinks and their smiles, and putting people in with you to keep you company. It was all hypocrisy. You were just a number to them, a thing in a bed.

'They do their best, Lily.'

'I don't care what they do. I don't care if it's born or not.'

He gazed at her, astonished.

'It's all right for a man,' she said. 'A man can manage.'

He shook his head. He said a man couldn't manage. He couldn't manage himself, he was lonely without her, with only Binks and the television. Every evening he came into the cold flat and Binks pushed herself against his ankles, missing her too.

'You don't know what it's like.' She whispered, even though there was no one else in the ward. 'Brooding in here all day.'

'I do –'

'How could you?' She turned her head away from him. She said he'd better go. 'It'll be lovely, having babies,' she'd said before they were married. That first time in the Geranium Café she'd looked no more than a child herself, even though she'd been twenty-five. She could still buy children's clothes for herself because she was so small, dresses and skirts in C & A.

He stayed, sitting in silence, until the bell went. 'She hates me,' she said. 'She hates me because she thinks I'm not a proper person.'

'She doesn't hate you, Lily –'

'I wish you'd tell her to leave me alone.'

An hour and a half later Kenneth began the painting of his parents' bathroom. He stood on a step-ladder which he'd placed in the bath and washed the walls down. In overalls and an old pair of his father's slippers that his mother had insisted he should wear, he applied a coat of emulsion paint to the ceiling. 'Tea,' his mother called from the hall.

He didn't reply, although he knew that he would not be permitted to continue painting without having tea and biscuits, and whatever else his mother had prepared.

'Tea, Kenneth,' his mother called again.

When he didn't answer he heard the tray of tea things being placed on the hall table and various protesting sounds coming from his mother. She mounted the stairs. He couldn't see her from where he was but he knew that she was standing on the landing.

'Tea,' she said again.

On the way downstairs she said she'd heated up sausage-rolls. There was a jam-roll that she'd bought that afternoon, and Lincoln Creams, his favourites. He didn't know how, or when, she'd got it into her head that Lincoln Creams were his favourite biscuits. She'd been saying it for twenty-five years and once or twice he'd contradicted her, but then he'd let it go.

His father was in the sitting-room, watching a comedy show on the television. Mr Drucker didn't relax when he watched television but sat stiffly upright, intently listening and gazing. 'Oh, turn it off, Dad,' Mrs Drucker said, and turned it off herself. Mr Drucker continued in the same intent manner to observe the grey screen.

'Can't stand those advertisements,' Mrs Drucker said. 'Dad'll watch them for hours. He's got a real thing about the ads, I tell him. Take a sausage-roll, dear.'

He took one. She said he mustn't forget to feed the inner man. 'Can't stand that one for Mr Kipling's Cakes,' she said. ' "Exceedingly good cakes," ' she quoted from the advertisement. ' "Mr Kipling makes exceedingly good cakes." Can't stand that.'

He drank tea. She pushed a plate of sliced jam-roll at him. She went on speaking, about the difference between the television channels, and various advertisements which she particularly disliked. 'Can't stand that one for Stork,' she said. 'Couldn't eat Stork if you paid me.' There was one for a cough remedy that had someone like Lily in it, she said. 'Spluttering all over the place, and then she takes this stuff in a bottle.' She described the person who looked like Lily, a small person, she said, ill-looking because of the spluttering. 'The first day you brought Lily in here, Ken, I said to myself that girl's got TB.'

Mr Drucker rose and turned the television on again. He waited for the picture to appear and then returned to his chair.

'A lot of those children's homes are riddled with TB,' she said. 'Mrs Taggart nursed in one of them one time, forty per cent had TB in some shape or form. Mind you, that was in the thirties, Kenneth, when the

115

disease was a scourge. I said to Mrs Taggart about Lily and she said you do still get it in the homes. TB babies we used to call them. That's a child, Kenneth, that's born to a TB parent. I said to Mrs Taggart that maybe that was poor Lily's problem because TB babies don't grow properly. "Well, she's no more than a dwarf," I said to Mrs Taggart at the time, not meaning anything nasty, you know what I mean? "She's probably a TB baby," Mrs Taggart said. I said to Lily she should mention it to this Dr Alstrop she has, explain to the man that Mrs Taggart was a nurse. The thing is, some of these old nurses could buy and sell a man like Alstrop, no question of that at all. I mean, I don't know the man myself, but from what Lily says I often wonder if he knows what he's doing. I always remember that poor Sammy Bates who used to come to your dad for alterations when he put on weight. He went in to have a finger done, and before he could stop them they had the arm off at the shoulder. His mother never got over it, you know. Really odd in the head she went, poor old thing.'

She continued to speak. Kenneth ate a Lincoln Cream. Mr Drucker watched children throwing stones at a soldier in Belfast.

Kenneth was frightened of his mother, and as far as he could remember he always had been. His mother would say anything. All day long her words would smear over people in what appeared to be a casual, quite ordinary way. As a child, he'd felt them smearing over himself, reducing him to silence, as they had reduced his father. It would be no good saying to her in some reasonable kind of way that she upset Lily when she visited her on Sundays because his mother wouldn't listen, or she'd pretend not to understand. He'd often thought that the only thing his mother would understand would be if someone struck her on the face.

As a child, Kenneth had developed a private nature. Few conversations had taken place between him and his father, and his mother had been so interested in everything that happened to him in school, what teachers and other children said to him and what he said in reply, that he had learned at an early age to prevaricate. He didn't report incidents that had occurred: the time Tim Draper hit him, or the time he saw a man and a woman fighting in Beech Street, or trouble he got into at school. He learnt instead to answer his mother's questions with bland, untrue information that was specifically invented to elicit the minimum of comment.

In his parents' terraced house Kenneth had crept about, listening to the rattle of the sewing-machines and his mother's voice talking to the women she made clothes for, and the silence of his father, which was

116

audible also. When he was twelve he saw through his mother's slightly open door a woman called Mrs Uprichard taking off her skirt, and after that he often crept to his mother's door when a woman came for a fitting. He would crouch in the shadows of the landing, bent to the keyhole of the door, and catch glimpses of clothes being removed or replaced, peach-coloured petticoats, silk straps on the flesh of women's shoulders. 'Well, of course she's not a person you could care for,' his mother would say about some other woman, while he watched. At night, alone, he talked to himself.

Once in a cinema, when he was fifteen, a woman had leant her ankle against his and from that moment his private nature had developed new dimensions. He'd thought at first that what happened was accidental, but then he felt a pressure, and the woman put a coat over their legs. In the darkness he never saw her face.

Afterwards, when he returned to his parents' house, he washed his hands very thoroughly, plastering them with soap, because they smelt of the woman. As he sat in the sitting-room, he was aware of shame and yet could not prevent himself, in his parents' presence, from surreptitiously recalling each detail of the incident. In bed he had recalled the details again, but not with the same secret pleasure.

'More jam-roll?' his mother said. 'Really good it is, fresh at Coombes's this morning, Kenneth. Really good, those sausage-rolls, I thought. We had terrible ones the day before yesterday. Dad got them in Evans's, all mildew they were.'

When she talked, he still had a habit of recalling the woman he'd watched being fitted and the woman in the cinema, and other women. A couple of years after the episode in the cinema he'd found himself one night hanging about the streets that prostitutes frequented, looking at them. He returned on another occasion and a woman spoke to him, asking him if he was looking for business. She was a woman with a round, fat face. 'Business?' she said in an oozing voice, cocking her head enticingly. He hurried by her, but later he imagined going to a room with her and watching her while she took off her clothes. He imagined a stout body to match the stoutness of her face. When she'd spoken to him he'd smelt the powder she was wearing; she'd put a hand on his arm.

He returned to look for this woman one night, and found her not far from where she'd been before, parading dismally along the street. A car stopped in front of her. She moved without much interest towards it. She shook her head in answer to some proposal; the car slowly drew away from her. A man without an overcoat, a bald man with glasses, advanced on her. While Kenneth watched from a doorway, they got into a taxi.

In the bathroom he began on the walls, covering them thickly with a green paint his father had refused to use. His mother came and sat on a chair in the doorway, saying she'd be company for him.

'Are you using Dulux?' she asked. 'I said to Dad you'd probably use Dulux; he was watching that ad with the dog in it. He's watching a play at the moment. I tell him he doesn't understand it but he doesn't take a pick of notice. He's great for his age, of course, don't you think he is, Kenneth? Still on a full day's work; well, he'll never retire, I say.'

She went on talking. He applied the green paint, recalling how he used to slip out of his parents' house at night, and the sense of adventure as he quietly crept away from it, and the pound notes in his pocket in case he should have the courage to get into a taxi with a woman himself. 'Looking for company?' the same stout-faced woman said, cocking her head as she'd cocked it before. Her hair was black, bushing around her head. 'Three?' she said. 'Three pounds, darling?'

When she spoke, he wanted to go away. He was afraid of the woman, like he was afraid of his mother. He was afraid of her smile and her oozing voice, and a nervous look she had in her eyes, as though very abruptly her mood might become aggressive. She mentioned her feet, saying they were sore because she'd been walking about since half past nine. 'Bloody plain-clothes,' she said 'all over the bloody place.' She took his arm. 'I reckoned you'd be all right,' she said, and he knew that all he had to do was to say he was sorry, that he'd made a mistake. Or to say he'd remembered that he hadn't got three pounds on him. Or simply to walk away. He could feel the softness of her large breast against the arm she was holding. She pressed his arm into the softness, as if sensing the uneasiness in his mind. Her fingers tightened, digging into him. As they paused on the edge of the pavement, looking for the orange light of a taxi, she leaned against him and he could feel one of her knees.

Even getting into the taxi, he thought he could still run away. There was a moment, with his hand on the door, when he might have banged it after her and turned away as quickly as he could. Instead he sat beside her. She took her shoes off and leaned back. Her black coat was open, showing a red and yellow dress, tight on her large breasts and her stomach. Her knees were wide and thick. She was almost sixty, he imagined.

'Been out at a party?' she said. 'Drinking?' Her lips were shiny with lipstick, thick blubbery lips that caused a sensation in his stomach

118

when he imagined his own lips against them. The red and yellow dress was cut low, revealing the beginning of a slit between the two mounds of her breasts. 'Amie the name is,' she said.

In her room one bar of an electric fire was burning when they entered; a dim light came from a bedside lamp. The double bed was covered with a crimson quilt that matched the crimson of the drawn curtains. On the wall above the bed there was a coloured poster of a naked girl in a haybarn, with a pitchfork stuck into the hay, between her legs. There was another poster of two girls standing naked with saddles in their hands.

The woman asked him for the money, and when he gave it to her she said they could do something special for another three. 'Amie'll go through the cards for you, darling,' she urged, but he shook his head. She sniffed and said it was a pity. Tetchily she asked him for something for the maid, and when he handed her some coins she said they weren't enough. He gave her more.

He watched while she threw her coat on to a chair and kicked her shoes off and undid the zip at the side of her dress. She crossed to a wash-basin in the corner of the room and ran a little water into a tooth-glass. She opened a tube of Alka-Seltzer and dropped two of the tablets into the glass, shaking the glass to make them dissolve. She'd had a stomach upset the weekend before last and hadn't been feeling chipper since. 'Some goose a friend had,' she said.

He listened while she told him, standing in her stockinged feet with the side of her dress undone, still shaking the glass of Alka-Seltzer. Four of them had shared in a goose to have on the Sunday for lunch. She mentioned two men by name and a woman called Honor. The same four people, she said, had bought a turkey at Christmas. 'We had it in Honor's place. Potatoes, brussels, all the trimmings.' In the dim light of her room she looked older than she'd looked when he'd first noticed her on the street, older even than she'd seemed in the taxi. There were varicose veins in her legs, her neck was bloated and red.

'There was definitely something the matter with it,' she said. 'The four of us queuing for the loo.' Honor had bought the goose the Thursday before, but when they looked at Honor's fridge they found it wasn't freezing up properly. 'Four days I was off, diarrhoea, vomiting, the lot.' She continued to juggle the glass of Alka-Seltzer. She still had stomach pains, she said, a lot of wind coming up. The doctor had given her a bottle for the diarrhoea, but it wasn't any good. She drank the Alka-Seltzer and ran more water into the glass, which she drank also.

119

Then she lifted the red and yellow dress over her head. 'I used to be in the Ti-Hi Club. Know it, Ken? Strip joint, Green Street?'

She took a black petticoat off. She smiled at him. 'How about the other two quid, Ken? We'll have a really nice time, darling.' She wore stockings and suspenders. Her thighs were even larger than he'd imagined, her stomach was tightly contained by a black elastic roll-on. 'They're French knickers,' she said. 'I'll leave them on if you like, Ken.'

He thought she might call after him but she didn't. He stumbled through darkness, across a passage, down stairs. He fumbled at the latch of the hall door, and on the street he felt sick himself. He thought he would be sick, but in fact he wasn't.

'There's nothing like green for a bathroom,' his mother said. 'Really gorgeous that is. It's really nice, Dad,' she shouted down the stairs, even though the sitting-room door was closed and the television was on. She called on her husband to come up and see it, but he did not do so. 'Deaf as a post,' she said.

For many years, until he'd first met Lily, he had gone to the rooms of women he met on streets watching them while they took their clothes off and then going away, even though no other woman had ever disgusted him with talk of a stomach upset. He had never told Lily, or anyone else, nor had he ever, after his marriage, felt the desire to creep away from a house at night.

Kenneth took off the overalls his mother had insisted he should wear, and his father's old pair of slippers. He folded the overalls and put the slippers on top of them and handed them to her. He washed his hands, cleaning the paint from the paint-brush at the same time, mixing Polyclens with warm water in the washbasin. He took his spectacles off and washed his face.

'Would you like an Ovaltine, Kenneth?' she said. 'A nice cup before you go?'

He thanked her, shaking his head, but she didn't seem to hear or to notice because she made at once for the kitchen, saying she'd bring Lincoln Creams as well.

He waited in the sitting-room with his father, watching animals on the television screen. 'Oh shut that up,' his mother said, coming into the room with the Ovaltine.

She switched the television off herself. 'Really gorgeous that green is,' she said to her husband, and told Kenneth to sit down. He refused a Lincoln Cream, causing his mother to ask him if he was unwell. He said he was all right and took the biscuit because it was the simplest thing to do. He finished the cup of Ovaltine and stood up. He'd be round tomorrow, he promised, about the same time as tonight, after he'd visited Lily.

'You really should stay, Kenneth,' his mother said, but he pointed out that he had the cat to feed.

'Well, I do think you should bring poor Binks here. Don't you think so, Dad?'

Mr Drucker didn't reply.

In the hall Kenneth put on his brown gabardine overcoat and his woollen scarf and gloves. His mother stood watching him, and when he opened the hall door and said goodbye she went on watching him as he walked away from the house. 'Give Lily our best love,' she called after him. 'Don't tell her what we were saying earlier, offend the creature.'

He walked through orange-lit streets. People straggled by him, couples hurrying home, men on their own moving more leisurely, a man on a bicycle, pedalling hard. Men in cars crawled by the kerbs, glancing up side streets for girls. Four youths with a paint-spray wrote *QPR* on a post-box.

'Excuse me,' a man said, stopping in front of him.

The man was old, grey-faced with a grey hat. He smiled at Kenneth.

'Yes?' Kenneth said.

A smell of alcohol and tobacco smoke came from the man's clothes, the acrid smell of hand-made cigarettes. He put a hand on Kenneth's arm and smiled again. 'Hullo, dear,' he said.

Kenneth pushed by, repelled by the suggestion the words implied. With a sudden harshness, he was reminded of his own past, strangers approaching one another on a street or in a cinema, looking through a keyhole. In the cold night air and the artificial light it wasn't the same as recalling the past while his mother talked: except in the presence of his mother, he hated the thought of the woman with the Alka-Seltzer, and the faceless woman in the cinema, and the other women. He hated the thought of himself, no different from the grey-faced man, hanging about streets.

Two policemen strolled slowly towards him. Lights changed from red to green. A lorry with a load of steel bars released its air brakes. A police car signalled at a small grey van, ordering it to stop.

He turned into another street, a silent street with builders' signs hanging outside many of the small terraced houses, and builders' skips full of masonry and bricks and ripped-out timber, beams and doorframes. Most of the houses were dark, as though unoccupied. Some, partly demolished, were ruins in the moonlight.

He imagined Lily asleep in the ward, her head on one side, her small fingers grasping the sheet, as they sometimes did. 'I love you, Lily,' he whispered to himself. He felt unworthy of her; he felt he was deceiving her, not sharing his past with her.

In Cheltenham Street Lily slept, as Kenneth visualized her, and the hospital whispered with the small sounds of night. Women spoke in their sleep, or groaned a little. Night nurses rustled through the dark wards, or turned the pages of magazines or books on their night desks. Kettles came to the boil, paper bags rattled. Housemen slept, on call if anything went wrong. In quiet, night-time voices, nurses from Jamaica and Pakistan and British Honduras told each other what life was like at home, how it differed from life in London, in a nurses' home or sharing a flat. Patients were woken to be given medicine. Blood pressures were regularly taken if an instruction had been left, and pulses and temperatures if necessary. The matron's primrose office was still and dark. George Trigol's furnaces burnt at the rate he'd estimated.

In the hospital the women dreamed, as Elizabeth and Sylvie Clapper and Miss Samson had dreamed in spasms since their operations. Reality and fantasy drifted and coalesced, fears came and went, confusion was left behind. Alone in the Marie Atkins Ward, Lily dreamed that Kenneth, with a bag of peaches, did not come to see her but sat instead with Elizabeth Aidallbery. She watched while they laughed and talked, while Kenneth held the other woman's hand and kissed her lips from time to time. 'You're a nutcase,' Dr Pennance said, appearing abruptly by Lily's bed. 'You realize you should be at home, Mrs Drucker?'

In the St Beatrice Ward, as in other wards, the worlds of its occupants vividly existed and yet were private to each dreaming woman. The Tonsell brothers were there, washing potatoes again, with Mrs Delve and the Reverend Rawes. The man who'd been Elizabeth Aidallbery's husband turned his eagle face away from her. Declan said everything would be all right. 'You never loved me,' Joanna Aidallbery protested in one moment, and in another Mr Ibbs complained. 'Thy rod and thy staff,' Mr Ibbs said. 'All your days you have your beloved Saviour to believe in. All your days Christ died for you on the holy Cross and then suddenly you're dead and it's all rubbish.' Sylvie stretched her body on hot brown sand in a white swimsuit; Declan brought her a glass of vermouth, dressed as a chauffeur, a character in a television advertisement. Carol Pidsley said her hair had been replaced by better hair and her legs by better legs, and her face by the face of the Duchess of Kent. God in his mercy, Carol Pidsley said, but Miss Samson whispered that Mr Ibbs was right: she couldn't bear it sometimes, the way people looked at her afflicted face. If He was good, He wouldn't let it happen. She shouldn't ever have left Number Nine. 'Ha, ha, ha,' said Mr Ibbs.

Other people were there, the son of a woman called Mrs Knipe, a son she hadn't seen since the day he went off on the HMS *Vigour*. A Mr Gold was there, an assistant in a wallpaper shop, and a Jack Edmunds, high up in Selfridge's. And a Mrs Green, and a Valerie Raye, and a Mr Bush. Husbands and fathers were there, and children, and mothers, and relatives and friends, and people who were vague shadows from childhood. Animals entered the St Beatrice Ward, dogs and cats and coloured birds in cages. Fictional people came, from *Coronation Street* and *Waggoners' Walk*, from the *Morecambe and Wise Show* and *Dad's Army*. A nameless man, encountered in a zoo thirty-five years ago and since forgotten, enacted the main part in the fantasy of a Mrs Treen. Two beds away a horse whinnied, by the door a snake uncurled itself. Men in white aprons loaded a Pickford's van with furniture. The Euro-vision Song Contest took place.

Declan said he couldn't marry Sylvie because policemen had seen him taking a scooter off a lorry. Mr Ibbs was in the kitchen, laughing with his diary in his hand. Henry was in the Gay Tureen. It was his birthday, he said, nine candles on his cake.

Elizabeth awoke. The pain was there, and a kind of stiffness. She felt hot and pushed at the bedclothes, and then lay still. The blinds were drawn, there was moonlight at their edges. A faint light spread into the ward from the open door, and then petered away. She could make out the outlines of the other beds.

Her watch, on her bed-table, gave the time as half past two. She reached out for it and held it for a moment to her ear, wondered if it had stopped. She heard the tick. She wound it because she didn't want it to stop, because she hated not knowing the time. She slept and dreamed pleasantly, of her childhood again.

10

'Fighting the flab,' the disc jockey said. 'The thighs, the tummy and the waist. If you've a hoop handy, get ready to sit down on the floor with it.'

Sister O'Keeffe buttoned her uniform, surveyed herself in her bedroom mirror, and was satisfied. The night before she'd done what she'd planned, not going to the pictures as Sister Kolulu had suggested, but taking it easy, in bed by ten. As a result, she was ready for the day that lay ahead.

She felt refreshed and clean. In her mouth there was a taste of toothpaste, a faint peppermint tingle. She'd brushed her teeth after her tea and Shredded Wheat, which was what she had for breakfast every morning except on her days off, when she just had tea. Her bed was made, and the dishes she'd used at breakfast were washed up and stacked in her red plastic drainer. Living alone, she'd discovered it was a good idea to leave everything shipshape in the mornings so that her return later on wouldn't be depressing. Sometimes you came back with the feet walked off you, with just about the energy to boil an egg. You'd feel low as a kind of luxury, because you'd been bright all day.

'Casey would waltz with the strawberry blonde,' sang a woman on Sister O'Keeffe's radio, 'and the band played on.' In her kitchenette she quickly checked the contents of the refrigerator. *Butter*, she wrote on a scrap of paper. *Eggs, frozen haddock, peas*. She switched off the electric fire in her bed-sitting-room. 'Alice Faye,' said the voice of the disc jockey, and the voice was again referring to the fighting of the flab when she turned off her radio. Terry Wogan, she said to herself, Irish of course. Someone once told her he'd worked in a bank in Dun Laoghaire.

She went softly down the stairs, avoiding a step that creaked. Her bed-sitting-room and kitchenette were in a private house; she shared the bathroom and lavatory.

The United States had devalued the dollar, the morning papers said.

In the night, hopes of gas peace had been killed: the General and Municipal Workers' Union and the Transport Workers' Union would begin their campaign at midnight. The headmaster of a school that was famous for its royal pupils had been attacked while his butler was serving him dinner. A film star had had a miscarriage, a housewife had been awarded £21,510 damages because a surgeon's knife had in error pierced her spinal cord.

It was a cold morning. Snow was not falling in London, but in the North of England and the West Country there'd been snow and hail showers during the night. The BBC warned that roads were hazardous.

In London people hurried in overcoats. The man who'd taken Elizabeth to the Foxley Hotel in Bishop's Stortford hurried with them, anxious not to miss a bus. Joanna Aidallbery caught another bus. The woman who'd agreed to take Jennifer and Alice to school while Elizabeth was away, a Mrs Singwell, backed a red Hillman estate car out of her garage. 'Oh, keep your head down,' she ordered a Dalmatian, a dog called Salmon, who sat near the rear window. 'Oh, please to hurry,' cried Mrs Orvitski in the Aidallberys' house while Jennifer and Alice argued.

At Number Nine, Balaclava Avenue the inmates began their day in different ways. Mrs Delve turned rashers of bacon on a large frying-pan. Arthur and the little Welsh girl sat at the kitchen table, finishing their breakfast. In the dining-room the Tonsell brothers, their dark jowls closely shaven, waited for theirs, though not impatiently.

The Reverend Rawes returned to the house with the *Daily Telegraph*, having personally collected the newspaper, as he always did, so that the delivery charge might be avoided. 'Good morning,' Carol Pidsley said to him in the hall. He greeted her and reported that the morning was cold.

In the dining-room he stood with his back to the cosy-stove. 'I hope she had a comfy night,' Carol Pidsley murmured, and the Tonsell brothers nodded their heads. Breakfast was on the late side, Carol Pidsley was thinking, which was only to be expected in the circumstances, but the circumstances couldn't be explained to Mr Blacker. 'You're late, Miss Pidley,' he'd said on Thursday when she hadn't been late at all. He always called her Miss Pidley, although she'd repeatedly told him that it wasn't her name.

An army officer was accused of murdering his wife and marrying his mistress, the Reverend Rawes read in his *Daily Telegraph*. There were photographs of the army officer and of his mistress and his

125

wife. The Reverend Rawes examined them, considering the whole affair extraordinary. The officer said his wife was in Australia, he wasn't sure where.

Mrs Delve and the little Welsh girl came in, each carrying a tray. As the inmates ate their breakfast, they talked again about Miss Samson. They were all of them concerned about the room in the Seaview Hotel, Bexhill, about how best to arrange its booking since they didn't know when it was required for. 'Let's wait till tonight,' the Reverend Rawes said, but Mrs Delve looked worried. As she ate her bacon, she thought of Miss Samson tucked away in a room at the back, with no sea air and a view of other people's windows. The holiday would be a disaster, not at all what they'd planned. 'It'll be all right,' the Reverend Rawes assured her, smiling across the table. 'Don't worry, Mrs Delve.' The Tonsell brothers and Carol Pidsley nodded. It would be all right, they said.

The attendant at the swimming-baths telephoned for the eleventh time the number that Henry had given him the day before. He drummed his fingers on the coin-box. 'Come on, come on,' he irritatedly muttered, but the telephone on Rammage's chipboard desk remained unanswered at that early hour. 'Keep the arms horizontal,' urged Terry Wogan. 'If you haven't got a hoop, imagine one.' The baths attendant swore, banging the telephone down. 'Bloody Irish tramp,' he shouted at Terry Wogan.

In Aberdeen he shaved his eagle-like face, peering at it short-sightedly because he always took his glasses off when he shaved or washed. The devaluation of the dollar would make a difference in all kinds of ways, although in what ways and how precisely he did not know, not being an economist. He removed the blade from his safety razor and washed both razor and blade beneath the hot tap. He dried them and replaced the blade in the razor, for he estimated that there was one more shave in it. He placed the razor on a glass shelf in front of him, a little to the right. He washed the remains of lather from his face, dried his face on a towel, and put on his spectacles. He did not think about the woman who'd been his wife while he did any of this; he did not ever permit himself to think about her. Once a month he wrote three letters to their three children, but as the children grew older he found it difficult to think of anything to say to them. In time, he knew, he would cease to write altogether, for this monthly association was increasingly a painful business. He let the water out of the washbasin and rinsed away the mixture of soap and beard. He thought about Mrs Vincent.

In the Caledonian Hotel she did not look like the woman whom Elizabeth had seen as the wife her ex-husband should have married. As she breakfasted, Mrs Vincent wore neither tweeds nor studious glasses.

'Kippers, madam,' a waiter in the Caledonian Hotel said, placing that fish in front of her, while a second waiter hovered with toast and coffee.

'Why, how lovely!' said Mrs Vincent. She made a joke to the second waiter while he was placing the coffeepot on the table, to the effect that since the dollar had been devalued she doubted that she'd be able to pay her bill. The waiter obligingly laughed.

She ate her kippers, with *The Times* propped up in front of her, not reading it. She was thinking of the man who had sat beside her during dinner last night, and had afterwards driven her home. He was a lonely man, with eyes that were wounded, like an animal's, behind his spectacles. She'd liked his voice, and the precise way he'd driven his car, not dashing about like a mad thing the way men of that age often did in order to impress you with their youthfulness of heart. In the car she'd found herself telling him about her brief marriage and had been amazed to hear herself because she'd never talked about it to anyone before, let alone a stranger in Scotland. She'd had too much cherry brandy, she'd said to herself.

Mrs Vincent consumed her kippers, and said in her polite American way that they'd been delicious when the waiter came to collect her plate. She buttered toast, and added marmalade to it. She poured herself more coffee. She could feel for that man, she found herself suddenly thinking.

11

In the St Beatrice Ward Mr Alstrop-Smith stood at the bottom of Sylvie Clapper's bed, his students a little behind him. He handed his patient's temperature chart to the student nearest to him, who looked at it and passed it on. 'Well, Miss Clapper,' he said, 'how're you feeling?'

'Bit better,' Sylvie said. 'Bit weak, really.'

'You're bound to feel weak, Miss Clapper. You've a lot of mending to do, you know.' He smiled at her and informed her that she had nothing to worry about. There were no complications, he said.

The curtains were pulled around some of the women's beds as Mr Alstrop-Smith made his examination. He disappeared within them with Sister O'Keeffe, sometimes inviting his students, sometimes not. Nurse Hampshire was in attendance.

When the students remained outside the curtains they stood silently, not whispering or communicating in any way. The women watched them. There was respect for Mr Alstrop-Smith, one woman thought, the one who'd dreamed of the Pickford's van. Another woman thought that Mr Alstrop-Smith held himself too rigidly as he walked, and wondered if it could be good for him. The more she watched him, the more she thought it couldn't be. It surprised her that Mr Alstrop-Smith, being a medical man, held himself like that. The woman who'd dreamed of a man in a zoo thought Mr Alstrop-Smith attractive. 'We're very pleased with you,' he said.

Journeys came into his mind, the faces of people he didn't know, people on trains who spoke in languages he didn't understand. '*Vilket väder!*' a voice said. '*Ce vreme!*' said another. Nuns got in and out of railway carriages, old women carried suitcases that were too heavy, girls read *Marie-Claire*. At Hergiswil the air was icy fresh.

In low voices his patients talked to him, saying how they felt. 'Not much pain, I hope?' he murmured to Miss Samson, and Miss Samson replied that there wasn't more pain than she'd expected.

'We've a tip-top patient here,' Sister O'Keeffe jollily interjected. 'A pleasure for all of us.'

128

Nurse Hampshire pulled the curtains back. Mr Alstrop-Smith smiled.

'Gallivanting?' he said in the Marie Atkins Ward, finding Lily on her feet, looking for a pair of nail-scissors. He smiled and the students smiled. 'Not forgetting your daily dozen, eh, Mrs Drucker?'

She was a hospital joke, Lily said furiously to herself as she got into bed. All these women being cut up and stitched up and scraped and having their insides taken out, all this blood and pain, and there she was just lying about like a bloated cabbage. In the staff canteen they probably made bets about whether or not it would be all right this time. Seven to one against were probably the odds that Dr Pennance laid.

'Still enjoying it?' Mr Alstrop-Smith said, nodding at Lady Augusta's autobiography. He always said it when he didn't know what else to say to her. He asked her questions and examined her. He told her everything was all right.

'You could move two or three in, Sister,' he said. 'Company for Mrs Drucker.'

He smiled again at Lily and she smiled back at him, although she didn't want to. He never noticed, anyway, if you smiled or not, because he had a way of looking over your shoulder when he was addressing you, and unless he was actually examining you he didn't seem much interested. A woman who'd been in the hospital a long time once told her that she reckoned he was troubled in his mind, the way he constantly had that brooding look about him. He'd never married, women said. *The medical profession*, Lily remembered Lady Augusta putting it, *can easily get above itself. With doctors and with lawyers, there is that tendency*.

In the corridor, on the way to the St Agnes Ward, Mr Azu spoke to Mr Alstrop-Smith, murmuring that he was worried about a Miss Brecon in the Faith Rowan Ward, on whom he'd done a Fothergill Repair yesterday. He wondered if Mr Alstrop-Smith would take a look?

They went together, with Sister O'Keeffe, Nurse Hampshire, and the students. Nurse Summerbee was waiting in the Faith Rowan Ward. The curtains were drawn around Miss Brecon's bed.

'Never felt better,' Miss Brecon said, the most cheerful patient Mr Alstrop-Smith had seen that morning. She wasn't young. Her grey hair was long, falling on to her shoulders; he wondered how she wore it otherwise. He wished Mr Azu didn't look so anxious. You had to hide anxiety; the man should know that, for goodness' sake.

He examined Miss Brecon, and then Nurse Summerbee and Nurse Hampshire settled her back on her pillows and drew up the bed-clothes. He smiled at Miss Brecon. They'd think he was crazy if they knew about his trains, the Palatino, the Mediolanum. Yet the absurd was often helpful. Azu might make fewer errors if he ever discovered that.

In the corridor he took Mr Azu aside and said that it had nothing to do with him but it really was a mistake to look in the least bit anxious. Some carelessness somewhere had caused Miss Brecon to catch an infection. He told Mr Azu what, in his opinion, the precise nature of the infection was. Miss Brecon would begin to suffer pain and fever within an hour, or less. It would set her back, but she would be all right. 'Thank you,' Mr Azu said, and Mr Alstrop-Smith nodded.

God he thinks he is, Mrs Thring thought a moment later in St Agnes Ward.

Later that morning Miss Samson, Sylvie and Elizabeth were wheeled back to the Marie Atkins Ward, and other women in the St Beatrice Ward were wheeled to the St Agnes and the St Susanna Wards. 'Hullo, Lily,' Sylvie said, and the other two greeted her, too.

They looked different. Their eyes seemed further back in their heads. Their voices weren't loud. They lay still in their beds.

'I had strange dreams,' Miss Samson said.

Elizabeth said she'd had odd dreams too, that had seemed to go on for ever, all day long and far into the night. She'd woken up at two o'clock, she said, but afterwards she'd dreamed again. Sylvie said her dreams were unmentionable.

'It's the drugs,' Lily said, out of bed again, looking for her nail-scissors.

'I could hear myself moaning,' Sylvie said.

Miss Samson remembered with unpleasant vividness the coming again of Mr Ibbs to Number Nine and the turmoil that had ensued, and Mr Ibbs saying he had looked and found that God was not there. During the night, every time she'd woken up, she'd been frightened. She'd remembered Mr Ibbs with his diary in his hand and had remembered, too, how two days before she'd come into hospital she'd found in an old hat-box the diary Mr Ibbs had written for the year he died. She'd opened it, for he'd said that his diaries were not to be private. She'd read only three lines: from these, she knew, her

130

dream had come. She'd burnt the diary in the sitting-room cosy-stove.

'Dreams are funny,' Sylvie said.

'Mine were nightmares,' Miss Samson said. She spoke hoarsely, in a voice choked with uneasiness.

Lily read, the others didn't talk. They drifted into sleep and out of it again, not dreaming much any more except that now and again their waking thoughts turned into fantasies of a kind. Elizabeth wondered about Jennifer and Alice, imagining them at school. She wondered about Joanna, imagining her, too. Miss Samson thought of Mrs Delve preparing the supper, but the Mrs Delve she imagined somehow didn't seem to be the right one. Sylvie wondered if Declan had made the arrangements for going to Liverpool.

Chicken came at lunchtime, cold legs and wings, with salad. Elizabeth and Miss Samson didn't have any; Sylvie ate a little without much appetite. Lily got up and sat alone at the fawn-topped table.

'Oh, I do feel tired,' Miss Samson said. She tried to sit up. Her pillows were in a heap behind her. 'Now, that's not at all comfy,' Nurse Summerbee said, organizing the untidy bed.

In the afternoon, by three o'clock, they were all tired except Lily. Elizabeth's children seemed far away then, and the effort of worrying about them was too much for her. And Miss Samson couldn't easily find the strength to visualize Mrs Delve, and Sylvie didn't want to think about anyone who was not herself.

Nothing mattered except themselves. Their world was now a body in a bed, and sheets and pillows, and the endless vision of the Marie Atkins Ward instead of the St Beatrice. Their world was lying still, trying not to feel low, sleeping and waking, getting better. Outside there was watery sunshine, wind and a little rain. They didn't care what was outside.

12

Since the children were at school, Mrs Orvitski spent the afternoon at her own house, making her husband's bed and cooking him further chlodnik. Her husband, Leopold, in carpet slippers made of imitation tiger skin, complained that he couldn't manage on his own. Six months ago he had retired as a van driver and was now at home all the time. He'd burnt his hand on steam, he told Mrs Orvitski, trying to make a cup of tea.

Mrs Orvitski was sympathetic. He was a good man, she said, it was a pity he had burnt his hand. While the chlodnik was cooking on the stove, she opened a tin of apricot jam for him and then washed the dishes in the sink. He'd had cooked ham for breakfast, he said, because he couldn't find any bacon. She opened the refrigerator and pointed at the bacon. He was a good, patient man, she said; and it was all worth while because she was being paid four pounds a day by Mrs Aidallbery.

Mr Orvitski did not agree with that. It wasn't worth four pounds a day to him, he pointed out, to burn his hand on steam. The Aidallbery family were a nuisance.

'Leopold!'

Mr Orvitski read the *Daily Mirror*, chewing a mouthful of bread and jam while his wife told him what he already knew, that Mrs Aidallbery was in hospital. The Aidallbery children were lovely children, she said, Mrs Aidallbery was a lovely woman, the Aidallbery family weren't at all a nuisance. Mrs Aidallbery had a hard time, bringing up children on her own; she was a good, generous woman.

'You know what happened to that woman, Leopold? You know?'

A tragedy would occur, Mrs Orvitski said, while her husband read about another tragedy: about the army officer who was charged with murdering his wife. Mrs Aidallbery would marry again, Mrs Orvitski said, for the sake of company. 'Some slop,' Mrs Orvitski said. 'Some slop she marries.' Mrs Aidallbery would marry such a man because more suitable men were naturally already married, because there wasn't the choice at that age. Mrs Orvitski mentioned Henry, whom she'd mentioned before to her husband. He'd been there on Sunday, she reported, taking Mrs Aidallbery's arm at the hospital.

The accused, Mr Orvitski read, appeared in the dock wearing a brown jacket and cavalry twill trousers. Mr John Inskip Q.C. alleged, for the prosecution, that the statements the accused made were totally untrue.

'A lovely woman,' Mrs Orvitski said, 'ending up with a slop.'

Henry rang the bell of the house next to his, wishing to borrow a lawnmower. There was no reply.

'I think those people are out,' a woman with a shopping-basket on wheels called to him from the pavement opposite. She was a sharp-faced, middle-aged woman who lived in Meridian Close, too; he'd seen her about.

'You don't know who could lend me a lawnmower?' he asked her. She knew him well by sight, a man whom other people in the Close talked about, whose wife had left him, whose house and garden were a disgrace. 'Lawnmower?' she repeated, crossing the road.

'I'm tidying up the garden,' Henry explained.

The woman, whose name was Mrs Passes, did not like Henry. For some reason she didn't like his freckled face and the smile that was sometimes on it, and his large freckled hands. She shared with Mrs Orvitski a dislike of the clothes he wore, the lumberjack's shirt and the golfing jacket and the stained flannel trousers. Other men in Meridian Close did not wear such clothes, even at weekends; other men didn't let their houses fall into rack and ruin in a few years, nor did they allow weeds to grow to a height of six feet in their gardens. She had often observed Henry from the window of her own house, lying down under his motor-car or putting cartons into the boot, and had considered that he was an unsuitable person to occupy a house in the Close. She had remarked as much to her husband and to other householders, all of whom had agreed.

'Haven't you got a lawnmower?' Mrs Passes asked Henry. 'Most people possess lawnmowers these days.'

In reply, Henry said with a laugh that somehow he'd never got round to buying a lawnmower. He recalled, but did not share the recollection with Mrs Passes, that his wife had persuaded him to buy a washing-machine when Timus was born. The washing-machine had long since ceased to operate, but he was still paying monthly instalments to the United Dominions Trust hire-purchase organization.

It occurred to Mrs Passes that at the end of her garden, in a small shed, there was a lawnmower that had not been used for some time. Four years ago her husband, deciding that he could no longer push it, had purchased a new one. Mr Passes had asked the dustmen to take away the older model, but the dustmen had refused, pointing out that for objects which were not of a purely household nature special arrangements must be made with the council. When Mr Passes telephoned Wandsworth Borough Council, he was told that a special collection could be made at his house the following Friday morning at 11 a.m. for a nominal charge of one pound. Mr Passes had said that that was unsatisfactory, and the lawnmower had since remained in the garden shed.

'Yes,' Mrs Passes said, seeing an opportunity to get rid of the unwieldy machine. 'I can let you have a mower.'

'Well, that's most kind of you –'

'Mrs Passes the name is.'

They did not enter Mrs Passes' house, but went round the side of it and through a wooden gate in the wooden fence, into the garden. She left the shopping-basket on the grass. 'That's the new one,' she said, pointing at a green lawnmower in the corner of a small conservatory that had been built on to the back of the house. She led the way to the shed. 'Now, somewhere here,' she said, 'is the other thing.'

She began to pull out coils of hosing, and chicken wire and old garden sieves. Extraordinary, she thought, how he'd laughed over not having a lawnmower. Extraordinary how he just stood there, lighting a cigarette without asking her if she minded: dreadful kind of man he was. Her clothes were getting dirty, she said, he'd have to forage for himself.

Henry removed further chicken wire, a bucketful of cement which had become damp and had set solid, bamboo canes and flowerpots, a broken camp-bed, and a bicycle which Mrs Passes said her husband had ridden all through the war and for three years afterwards. 'That's the mower,' she said, pointing into the gloom.

With difficulty, Henry hauled it out on to the grass. Rust came off on his hands. The blades of the machine wouldn't go round, nor would its large, heavy rollers. 'You don't get mowers like that any more,' Mrs Passes said.

He put the other things back into the shed. It seemed odd to him that they'd gone to all this trouble to get at this particular lawnmower when there was a much better-looking one sitting in the conservatory.

'A drop of oil,' Mrs Passes said, remembering her husband with an oil-can, undoing nuts with a spanner and a hammer, swearing when he skinned his knuckles.

Henry tried to wipe the rust from his trousers and his golfing jacket, but it didn't come off easily. The machine was too heavy to carry. He tried to release the rollers but without success. He'd have to pull it behind him on the pavement, with everything jammed.

'It's very kind of you, Mrs Passes,' he said. 'I'll bring it back in the morning.'

But she said there was no need whatsoever to bring the lawnmower back.

'Oh, but I couldn't –'

'Let's say two pounds,' suggested Mrs Passes.

He stood looking at the lawnmower, smoking his cigarette. He began to phrase a statement in his mind to the effect that what he'd actually wanted was the loan of a lawnmower, but in the middle of this composition he tired of it. He took a quantity of coins out of the pocket of his golfing jacket and counted out two pounds' worth, at the same time reflecting that D'arcy would not have done that, nor would Carstairs. Without ever using the words, D'arcy would have smilingly told Mrs Passes to go to hell. He'd have implied that the lawnmower wasn't worth the oil you'd use on it, let alone two pounds. Carstairs would have pretended not to have two pounds in his pocket and would have successfully endeavoured never to pay her. And somehow, Henry felt, neither D'arcy nor Carstairs would have been led past the green lawnmower in the conservatory. D'arcy would have taken Mrs Passes by the elbow, all smiles and charm. Carstairs would have pretended that he thought this was the lawn-mower she meant. They'd have been in and out of the conservatory before she knew what was happening to her. Still, there was no point in being gloomy about it. He dragged the lawnmower through the side gate of his garden, whistling to keep his spirits up.

Still whistling, he removed long strings of grass from the axles of the machine, and loosened flakes of rust with the screwdriver he carried in his golfing jacket for investigating minor faults in vending-machines. As he did so, he idly wondered how much he'd get for the Zephyr. He was prepared to drop a few pounds for a quick sale so that he could buy some shirts and possibly another suit, and some kind of covering for the hall floor. If he waited, he reckoned it would fetch a hundred and fifty; he'd take a hundred and twenty-five. There were two men from Putney Square-Deal Motors who came into the

King of England every day at lunchtime and usually again in the evening. He often had a drink with them, and had once brought them back to Meridian Close to sample his beer. They'd be helpful, he imagined, and would probably offer more than a car dealer who didn't know him.

He oiled the lawnmower and then turned it upside down. He spun the blades and, less easily, the rollers. The blades needed sharpening, he noticed, but otherwise it really didn't seem a bad machine, and he began to think that maybe two pounds hadn't been excessive after all. That was the trouble with D'arcy and Carstairs: they were never prepared to spend a little time over a matter like that, getting something going by patiently poking at it, like he'd so often got the Zephyr going. It probably wouldn't even have occurred to them that someone quite near at hand might have a secondhand machine lying about; they'd probably have gone off and bought a new one somewhere. The first time he'd driven up to the King of England in the Zephyr they'd both said they were surprised he'd bought it.

Unlike the Zephyr, however, the Passes' lawnmower refused to perform the task for which it had been designed and built twenty-five years ago. This was not wholly the lawnmower's fault. The soil was sodden and the grass was thick and long. The blades succeeded in pulling some of it out by the roots, and long green strings again wound themselves round the axles, preventing them from turning. The man whose lawnmower Henry had tried to borrow in the first place looked over the garden fence and said that a scythe was necessary for the job Henry was attempting. 'One of those rotary things might do it,' the man said, 'when the ground's dried out.' It was unusual, he added, to attempt to cut grass in early February, or to cut grass at any time of the year with the kind of antiquated contraption that Henry had. He then spoke about weeds, saying that when weeds got going in a garden their seeds blew into other people's gardens, causing bad feeling. 'I often wondered if you were aware of that,' the man said, nodding at Henry and going away.

Henry abandoned the grass, resolving to make inquiries in the King of England about how to cut grass in February, when the ground was sodden. He turned his attention to the weeds, and for two and a half hours pulled up dandelion roots and convolvulus, nettles, ragwort, Scotch grass, chickweed, and docks. He dug them out of the soil with a fork, digging up peony tubers and iris tubers as well, and the remains of rose-bushes. He rooted up Michaelmas daisies that his ex-wife had planted, and chrysanthemums and aubretia. In the house he found the plastic sacks that the mushroom fibre had come in. He filled them with what he'd removed and threw them on to the heap at the bottom of the garden. He forked through the beds he'd cleared, and gathered up bay leaves that had been lying on the ground for some years, refusing to disintegrate. He found a number of empty yoghurt cartons, bottles, tins, and a coat that he must have left in the garden and forgotten about.

In the house the telephone rang. He tramped in to it, lighting a cigarette.

'They haven't arrived yet,' a cross voice said. 'This bloody thing's U.S. if you ask me. It's a damn sight worse since you went tampering with it –'

'Who haven't arrived? Who are you, for a start?'

'Your bloody New-Way engineers haven't arrived. I've telephoned this man Rammage twenty-one times. Is he mentally deficient or something? You can't understand a thing the bloody man says.'

'It's no good ringing me, sir, no use at all.' Henry was unable to keep the cheerfulness out of his voice. 'As a matter of fact, I'm giving up the vending-machines altogether. I'm going into the frozen foods field –'

'I don't care what bloody fields you're going into. They're your bloody machines, you're meant to operate them.'

'I'm sorry,' Henry said. 'I'm extremely sorry, sir, but the trouble with your drinks machine must be sorted out by Mr Rammage of New-Way Vending Limited.'

'You're the operator New-Way bloody Vending Limited gave me,' shouted the baths attendant. Henry could hear a repeated banging, which suggested that man was striking the side of the telephone's coin-box. 'I have all these kids yelling their bloody heads off because they can't get a hot chocolate. It's undrinkable anyway, the muck that comes out, at the best of times. The whole thing's a racket, as a man like you must –'

'The usual practice, sir, is to put a notice on a machine that's temporarily out of order. Get a piece of card, sir –'

'Will you stop calling me sir,' shouted the baths attendant, and banged down the receiver.

Henry smiled. None of it concerned him. It gave him pleasure to imagine the baths attendant shouting abuse at Rammage, and Rammage trying to calm him down without taking the cigarette out of his mouth, telling him that the trouble was all Henry's fault. The telephone rang again, and a woman at the Washthru Launderette

137

said that something was clogging her snacks machine. She had a feeling that a packet of crisps or Nutty Pops had somehow become torn and that the crisps or Pops had got into the works. Henry spoke softly and sympathetically. By the sound of it, he said, it was a job for the company's engineers. He gave her Rammage's number and said two New-Way engineers should be with her within an hour of ringing it. He didn't replace the receiver.

All that remained was the clearing of the front garden and the grass at the back, and one or two small jobs in the house, like the wallpaper in the room that had been Timus's and the washing out of the cupboard under the stairs. In fact, he'd wash the whole house through, he decided as he carried a carton to the front garden and began to throw weeds into it. He'd get rid of the smell of mildew that seemed to hover about the upstairs of the house, and thoroughly mop over the floor of the hall before putting down a rug or something.

The man next door came out of his house with his wife, and a sealyham on a lead. He pointed at the ash tree that grew in Henry's flowerbed. 'Needs to be lopped, you know.'

His wife said that when the tree was in leaf she had to have the light on in the hall at midday. She spoke with sourness in her voice, and Henry suddenly realized that an unsigned note which had been put through his letterbox protesting unpleasantly about the ash tree must have been written by this woman.

'I can't tell you how pleased we are,' the woman said, more agreeably, 'that you're doing something about all this at last.' She glanced at the Zephyr as she spoke, and Henry recalled a similar note stuck under one of the windscreen wipers stating that Meridian Close was not a scrapyard. 'I'm selling the car,' he said. 'I have a Viva due on Wednesday.'

The woman nodded approvingly. He could get a couple of rose bushes for the flowerbed, she suggested.

'The Putney Garden Centre,' the man advised, and as they moved off with the sealyham Henry agreed that he'd probably go along to the Garden Centre later in the week.

By half past five he'd cleared the front garden to his satisfaction. He found a saw in a coal-bunker at the back of the house and sawed off most of the ash tree. He carried the carton, now overflowing with weeds and trimmings from the tree, through the house to the bottom of the back garden. Spring or something like it seemed to freshen the evening air. A month ago it would have been pitch dark now.

The palms of his hands burned with nettle-stings, thorns had torn

138

his flesh, but his mood was buoyant. If he met Mrs Passes he would good-humouredly say that when he'd tried the lawnmower out it had proved incapable of cutting grass. He'd laugh and say it didn't matter, and if she offered to return the two pounds he'd refuse to accept it. He laughed, thinking of the woman next door writing notes. She probably wasn't a bad woman at all.

In his bathroom Henry lit a cigarette and filled a blue china mug with beer. He ran a bath, and drank while waiting for the water to rise. It was good to feel tired. He lit another cigarette and drew off another mugful of beer. He stepped into the bath and let the hot water soak into the aftermath of his labours.

They walked away from the wide sprawl of concrete buildings that were classrooms, laboratories for scientific subjects, laboratories for languages, assembly areas and performing areas, dining-rooms, changing-rooms, and lavatories.

They spoke in deaf-and-dumb language, or did not speak at all. Joanna believed that Samuel didn't love her as much as she loved him. She did not say so. They talked about Mrs Tabor-Ellis's commune.

They walked by high buildings, offices and insurance blocks, one occupied by an oil company, by banks that were now closed. Evening papers were on sale. *Sterling Floats On*, a headline said.

Samuel intended to join the commune whether Joanna accompanied him or not. Intuitively she felt that if that happened it would be the end of their relationship. She couldn't bear that. She couldn't even bear the thought of it. 'Love,' her fingers said.

'Peace,' Samuel replied.

Passers-by paused to watch them speaking in deaf-and-dumb language, their hands and fingers moving elegantly as they walked. 'Load of old cock,' a man selling newspapers conversationally remarked to a regular purchaser of the *Evening Standard*. 'Them two have tongues like anyone else.'

Samuel laughed his soundless laugh. He tossed his hair back. His fingers spoke obscenely, condemning the paper-seller to death.

They had tea together.

'And what about *your* marriage?' she said.

In the Caledonian Hotel they ate egg sandwiches and toast on which they might, if they wished, spread raspberry or greengage

139

jam. There were slices of Swiss roll and fruitcake, but they hadn't reached that stage yet.

'She was much younger,' he said. He wanted to leave it at that. He didn't want to try and explain something he didn't understand himself, anyway. She was much younger was what he'd thought ever since the day she told him she wanted a divorce: he'd accepted that as the reason why she'd had a love affair with another man. 'She was twenty when I married her,' he said. 'I was thirteen years older.'

Mrs Vincent ate toast with raspberry jam on it.

'I don't know why we're talking about marriages,' he said.

Twenty-four hours ago he hadn't even known what she looked like. He'd been unaware of her existence, even though other people had mentioned her arrival in Aberdeen.

'What happened?' she said.

'Happened?' He looked at her, alarmed. She smiled, touching the left corner of her mouth with a lace-edged handkerchief. She said:

'What happened to your wife?'

'Nothing happened to her. She looks after the children. She has money from her father, which she always had, and money from me. Naturally. Even though she was at fault.' He paused. 'She'll marry again.'

A silence fell between them. A waitress came and asked if they'd like more hot water. Mrs Vincent said they would. The waitress lifted the silver-plated water-jug and departed with it. Mrs Vincent smiled again. She said:

'I can imagine your wife. A very beautiful woman. Tall and efficient. The sort of woman other women like to have on committees.'

'Good heavens, no. Elizabeth's not in the least like that.'

He described her and Mrs Vincent nodded, visualizing then this fair-haired woman who had been, unfaithfully in the end, his wife.

'She never grew up, in a way,' he said. 'She was greatly attached to her mother. Well, I was attached to Mrs Orpen myself. Poor Elizabeth!' Shaking his head, he gave as a reason for saying it his belief that Elizabeth was the sort of person who could not easily be alone. 'I suppose that's the tragedy of women like Elizabeth.'

The waitress came with the hot water. Mrs Vincent thanked her. Then she said:

'So you really think your wife'll marry again?'

'Look, I'd really rather not talk about her. She's not my wife in any case –'

'And you? Will you marry again?'

Blood came into his face and remained there, two small spots high on his cheeks. He blew his nose to cover his confusion.

'I wonder you divorced her, in a way,' she said. 'I mean, she didn't really want you to in the end, did she?

He drank tea.

She smiled at him. She was thinking that he had the most beautiful voice she'd ever heard coming out of a man. He was an enigma sitting there, so precise in his black suit and precisely knotted tie. He had had three children by this woman who was thirteen years younger than him and yet you could tell that, because of what had happened, neither she nor those children meant much to him. That woman had never loved properly, she'd never discovered what there was in him to satisfy. She'd never explored him, Mrs Vincent thought, relishing that expression. 'I love your wounded eyes,' she wanted to say, but naturally did not. She was grateful at least to the woman for causing wounds like that, for wounds needed care and attention, and another woman's touch.

'I wonder you divorced her,' she repeated, prisingly.

'Pride, I suppose.' He paused and then he began to tell her everything, because all of a sudden he wanted to.

13

By evening they felt better. They had thin vegetable soup and plaice, and stewed apples and custard. They talked in the Marie Atkins Ward; only Miss Samson still seemed bewildered and far from herself.

As visiting time approached, Sylvie put on eye-shadow. She treated her lashes and her fingernails. She said she was feeling quite perky.

Mrs Delve and the Reverend Rawes came. They sat on the left-hand side of Miss Samson's bed, on two of the metal-frame chairs. Everything was all right, they told her, but she couldn't help remembering how in the dream the Reverend Rawes had stood with his back to the door of the sitting-room and had forbidden the Tonsell brothers to telephone the *Daily Express*, how Mrs Delve had referred to Arthur as a half-wit, how she'd shouted at her and she said she put people off.

'Now, when're they going to let you out?' Mrs Delve asked briskly. 'We're very anxious to know, dear.'

Miss Samson shook her head. The only time they'd mentioned the matter was when they'd asked her if she was booked into the convalescent home in Eastbourne. They let you out quicker if you were, she'd heard. She spoke in a whisper, finding it difficult to speak louder.

'Thing is, we want to make the booking in the Seaview.' Mrs Delve repeatedly blinked, which was a sign of anxiety with her.

Miss Samson shook her head again.

'Oh, dear!' Mrs Delve cried, and the Reverend Rawes hastily interjected that they'd had a nice piece of neck for supper. 'Everything's going really trim,' he said. 'No need to worry.' He added quietly, addressing Mrs Delve, that they'd sort the matter of the hotel out afterwards. Better to talk about something else, he suggested, and after a hesitation Mrs Delve accepted his judgement.

'Edward Tonsell's definitely taking an interest,' she said. 'Carol's a different person.'

Miss Samson nodded. She remembered Edward Tonsell's face in her dream, the way it had all been cruelly twisted, the dark jowl sinister in the sitting-room, the eyes glaring at Carol Pidsley. Carol Pidsley's face had been twisted, too.

'They were talking on the stairs tonight,' Mrs Delve said in whispering, confidential tones.

Miss Samson nodded again, managing to smile.

The Reverend Rawes remarked that it was hot in the ward and wondered that Miss Samson could stand it. It had been a cold day, he said. There'd been snow in the West Country and the North.

'She's really a different person,' Mrs Delve said. 'She was singing like a linnet this morning. I heard her in the bathroom.'

'Who's this?' the Reverend Rawes said.

'Carol Pidsley, Mr Rawes. She's been paid attentions by Edward Tonsell.' Mrs Delve was red in the face. For several months, she confessed to the clergyman, she and Miss Samson had been speculating about Carol Pidsley and the older of the Tonsell brothers. They had been certain that attentions were being paid; they had in fact been aware of them long before Carol Pidsley was.

'Well, I'm blessed,' said the Reverend Rawes. 'But are you sure of it? Has Carol said something?'

Mrs Delve laughed. It was far too soon for that, she said. Edward Tonsell was shy; well, both brothers were shy if it came to that. And Carol Pidsley certainly wasn't one to push things on. She'd once pushed things on a bit herself, Mrs Delve confessed, but then she was entirely different from poor Carol. She'd swap her nature for Carol's any day.

'We're perhaps tiring Miss Samson.' The Reverend Rawes interrupted Mrs Delve's flow, but Miss Samson shook her head.

'Oh, it'll be so nice at the Seaview!' Mrs Delve cried. 'A nice room at the front. We'll book it at once, dear, when we know where we stand. They say the Seaview's awfully good. Carol's aunt's our source on that. Comfy, and really tasty food.'

It would be lovely, Miss Samson said. It was awfully good of them.

'You're awfully good to us, you know,' the Reverend Rawes said.

'I'm not going to be difficult,' Lily had murmured to herself repeatedly that day. She'd said it aloud several times, alone in the lavatory, whispering it, drilling it into herself.

'I'm sorry I was cross last night,' she said as soon as he arrived.

His mother was right: he didn't look well, his face was white. 'How's Binks?' she asked.

He said the cat was all right.

'What's happened to Ally Glazier?' She smiled at him, far more cheerful than she'd been the night before.

He shook his head. He didn't know, he said. He tried to talk to her, thinking about his mother. He'd lain awake most of the night, thinking about his mother, and Lily, and the way he'd never told Lily the full truth, and the grey-faced man who'd approached him, repelling him and reminding him. That evening again his mother would sit in the bathroom doorway, saying that Lily was a TB wife, asking him what the matter was when he refused a Lincoln Cream. Why should he and Lily bring a child into the world so that his mother might afterwards terrify it? His mother had made him what he'd been – as though she'd wished him to get into taxis with women from the streets, as though she preferred it to having him normally married. His mother had forced his furtive privacy on him. His mother hated Lily, and Lily knew it. What Lily said about that was true, not nonsense.

'You painting the bathroom?' Lily asked.

Sylvie waited. 'Declan's late,' she called across the ward. 'You expecting someone, Elizabeth?'

She said she wasn't. She'd asked Mrs Orvitski not to bring Jennifer and Alice until the next evening, and wasn't very happy even about that because by the time they'd get home afterwards it would be long past their bedtime. If they didn't get their sleep they wouldn't get up in the mornings.

'Hullo,' Joanna said.

She was dressed as she had been when Elizabeth had said goodbye to her in front of the house on Sunday, in the faded purple dress she'd bought at a jumble sale, with beads and spectacles. Her long hair didn't look clean.

'Hullo, Joanna.'

She watched while her daughter crossed to the fawn-topped table and seized one of the metal-frame chairs. 'Hullo, Joanna,' Sylvie said. 'I've heard about you.'

'Mummy,' Joanna said, sitting down. 'I want to go to Geraldine Tabor-Ellis's place.'

Elizabeth smiled, retaining the smile with an effort. She felt an iciness inside her. 'I want to go with Samuel,' her daughter said.

144

'You mean, you want to leave school before you've done the rest of your A-levels –'

'A-levels are useless.'

'Yes, I know, but you need them if you want to get a job.'

'I don't want to get a job,' Joanna whispered. Her face had reddened slightly. 'What's the use of going on in the same awful old way?'

'What way, darling?'

Beneath her whispering, Joanna's voice collected emotion. She didn't want just to go on, she said again. She didn't want to get some kind of job and then to marry some awful person. 'Look at you,' she cried, still whispering. 'Look at you, spending half your life with a useless marriage and then having a thing with that awful man.' She spoke quickly, as though urgently wishing to be rid of the words. She looked away, at the Reverend Rawes sitting with his black-clad legs crossed.

Elizabeth said nothing. Then, feeling that her silence was disloyal, she said:

'He wasn't awful.'

'Of course he was awful. An awful middle-class man, trying to be young again. He didn't even have courage.'

'I don't think you should go to this commune place. There's your father to consider for a start –'

'I don't want to talk about him.'

'He's your father. You can't just go rushing off to communes, leaving school without your A-levels –'

'Oh, for heaven's sake, stop about A-levels!'

She'd never see her again, Elizabeth thought. Joanna would walk out of this ward and she'd never in her life see her again. You heard of things like that all the time now, there were programmes on television and articles in the colour supplements. The Yes Generation they were called. They started with cannabis and then they went on to LSD, they didn't care when they caught venereal disease, they lived on National Assistance, they got sick and died. Savaged by heroin, Mr Feuchtwanger in her dream had said.

'Listen,' Joanna said. 'I don't want to marry a dull stick like you did and have some useless affair with a fat man when I'm forty. I don't want to be stuck in a suburb with three children and a charwoman, and Henry slobbering round. I don't want any of it.'

There was another silence between them, and then Elizabeth said:

'When are you thinking of going to your commune?'

145

'Tomorrow.'

'Tomorrow.' Elizabeth repeated the word flatly, not turning it into a question, not registering shock on her face because she didn't feel up to that. 'Tomorrow,' she said again, nodding, remembering the day Joanna had been born, a wet day in August. It hadn't been an easy birth, and Joanna had been late anyway, almost a month late. When her labour pains started she'd had a premonition that something was going to go wrong, but nothing had, except that it had all taken a very long time. August 20th, 1955, St Bernard's Day.

'I wish you'd wait a bit,' she said. 'I wish you'd wait till the summer. After all, it's only a couple of months –'

'It's five months.'

'Yes, but even so –'

'I'm sick of it all. I'm sick of that awful school and that awful suburban house, and people sitting on Tube trains, and Barclay's Bank –'

'Barclay's Bank?'

'Oh, you know what I mean.'

Elizabeth shook her head, not knowing what her daughter meant by Barclay's Bank. She said:

'Please don't go tomorrow, dear, not while I'm still in here. I've had a hysterectomy, you know.'

Joanna looked away. She began to sniff, and Elizabeth wondered if she was crying, but she wasn't. There'd been a time when she might have cried because her mother had had an operation. Two or three years ago, before she'd felt herself let down.

'I'm sorry, Mummy, I should have asked you –'

'I'm all right. I'm getting better.'

'I should have brought you something. I'm sorry.'

'I don't need anything.'

'I'm sorry.'

'Actually, I need some clean nighties. D'you think you could take some home and ask Mrs Orvitski to wash them?'

'Yes, of course.'

'I think people may ring Mrs Orvitski up to find out if there's anything I need. Just clean nighties, tell her.'

'Yes.'

'Please don't go tomorrow, Jo. Please just think about it, for a day or two at least.'

'I've thought about it.'

'I know, but I'll be out in three weeks.'

'I'll take your nighties, Mummy.'

She found them and rolled them up. She'd take them as they were, she said, she didn't need the bag that Elizabeth offered. 'Goodbye,' she said, kissing Elizabeth.

'Goodbye, darling.'

Elizabeth watched her leaving the ward. The Reverend Rawes turned his head and smiled at her, but Joanna didn't notice, or else felt shy. She didn't look back when she reached the door, as visitors sometimes did.

'She's really pretty,' Sylvie said. 'That lovely hair.'

'The lovely hair needs washing.' Elizabeth tried to laugh but found she couldn't. She felt faintly sick, the feeling she'd had the day she'd gone into Joanna's room and found Samuel in bed with her. At the same time she couldn't help saying to herself that at least Joanna had broken her silence. It was a pathetic consolation, and she felt ashamed of it.

'I'm Mr Rawes,' a voice said. 'How d'you do, Mrs Aidallbery?'

He held his hand out. 'You're progressing satisfactorily, Mrs Aidallbery?' he said.

'I think so,' she said. 'Thank you.'

'Well, it's no weather to be outside. You're just as well off in your nice warm bed.'

'He smiled at her and crossed the ward. 'And you're Miss Clapper,' he said.

He talked to her for a while about the weather before returning to Miss Samson. Mrs Delve went then, so that he and Miss Samson might pray. But instead of joining in a prayer Miss Samson told about her dream.

'Our Father,' the Reverend Rawes began when he'd heard it all, 'which art in Heaven, hallowed be thy Name.'

Miss Samson repeated with him the familiar words in a voice without much strength or heart in it. She had a frightened kind of look, he thought when he opened his eyes again, which perhaps was due to the upset of the operation, and the pain.

'A wedding at Number Nine, eh?' he said cheerily. 'There's that to look forward to when you come back from the Seaview.'

'That'll be nice,' Miss Samson said quietly, remembering her jealousy of Carol Pidsley in her dream, and the violence that had come from her.

The bell went. Kenneth lingered with Lily for a minute or two, sorting out her nightdresses. The Reverend Rawes carried the chairs that he and Mrs Delve had been sitting on back to the fawn-topped table. Noticing that Joanna hadn't returned hers, he carried it back too. 'Thank you,' Elizabeth said.

'Declan's probably on nights,' Sylvie said. 'There'll probably be a letter.'

Surely not even Samuel would persuade her to go away when her mother was still in hospital?'

'Very nice-looking girl, Mrs Aidallbery,' Miss Samson said, speaking so quietly that Elizabeth scarcely heard her, nodding across the ward.

'Quite like you, Elizabeth,' Lily said.

Later that night Miss Samson tried to pray on her own. 'O dear sweet Jesus,' she whispered, but found it difficult to go on. She'd discovered the hat-box on top of the wardrobe that had been his, in the room that was now Robert Tonsell's. *H. R. Ibbs* it said on the fly-leaf of the diary: Horatio Rowland his names had been. She'd opened the diary at random. The last three lines, written a week before his death in royal-blue ink, had caused weakness in her legs, and sudden, wild palpitations in her body and her head. *I no longer doubt. I am certain now that God and all the rest of it is a myth we've made to keep us happy.* She'd sat on the edge of Robert Tonsell's bed, staring in amazement at the royal-blue words. In Number Nine she'd always said he'd been a happy man when he died, with the head of his dog, Thomas, resting on his chest. She'd seen him herself, lying in bed, with the dog as still as a statue, sensing what was to come. The words in the diary were absurd. In terms of the man who'd written them, they were without meaning. His mind had been affected, as he sensed himself what was about to come. He'd suffered from a touch of irrational senility, maybe. As the diary burned in the cosy-stove, she'd resolved to put it completely out of her mind, and in this resolution she had been successful. In the house she continued to be herself, convinced that he had died as he had lived. When she'd spoken to the Reverend Rawes about her dream, she hadn't mentioned the diary. She did not intend ever to do so, no matter what her dreams were.

For the imagination of man's heart is evil from his youth: that was a text that the Reverend Rawes had taken once when preaching in St Matthew's during the summer absence of the Reverend Last. She tried to think, but couldn't remember what the Reverend Rawes had said, or what form his sermon had taken. All she could recall was that she'd been apprehensive in St Matthew's that Sunday, worried about a joint of mutton that had smelt a bit. When she tried to remember what the Reverend Rawes had said about the text, her mind at once filled with a memory of herself in the kitchen of Number Nine, dabbing at the meat with Dettol before confining it in the oven. She'd specially sent the little Welsh girl on some errand and had told Arthur to get ready for church so that she could have the kitchen to herself. In the midst of that memory the voice of the Reverend Rawes was lost, and she was mocked instead by the unhappy association of a holy text from Genesis and her underhand action.

She heard again an echo of laughter from her dream, the ugly laughter that her imagination had evilly drawn from Mr Ibbs, who'd never hurt a fly. Yet she seemed now to know that she'd been wrong to assume senility and an affected mind. The royal-blue handwriting had been firm and clear. Mr Ibbs at the end of his life had not believed.

14

The car salesman from Putney Square-Deal Motors did not offer Henry a hundred and fifty pounds for the Zephyr, nor did they offer him a hundred and twenty-five. 'Fifteen quid, old chap,' the larger of the two men suggested, and the smaller man pursed his lips, implying generosity. Both men had sprawling RAF moustaches. The larger had wavy black hair, the smaller one was mainly bald, with notably wide shoulders. It was said in the King of England that they'd been wing-commanders in the war.

Henry at first rejected the offer of fifteen pounds for his car, but other people in the King of England said they doubted if he'd get as much on the open market. Felicity the barmaid, to whom Henry had once given a lift in the Zephyr, said she considered fifteen pounds extremely good value when you compared it with the thirty-five pounds that the men from Putney Square-Deal Motors had given Eddie Bevington, also a drinker in the King of England, for his much newer Morris Minor.

'You're not trading it in, Henry,' the larger of the two salesmen explained. 'That's the difficulty about this one. Now if you were asking me to get hold of a newish Austin for you, something like that –'

'There's a car with the job, a Viva.'

'That's the difficulty, old chap.'

'I thought it might perhaps fetch a hundred and twenty. Dropping a bit for a quick sale –'

'Oh, I'd hardly say a hundred and twenty, old chap.'

'I'd drop down to a hundred and ten, or even five. I just thought that maybe you'd know someone looking for a model like this. It's been pretty well looked after, you know. I've serviced it myself.'

'I don't think you'd get a hundred and five pounds for this one, Henry.'

In the end Henry accepted fifteen pounds. He'd had no idea that the car was worth so little, but Putney Square-Deal Motors had a good local reputation and the two men were known to everyone who regularly drank in the King of England. He didn't for a moment doubt that he'd received a fair price.

Henry remained in the company of the salesmen. He told them about his new job, and said that as far as he could see he was to be put in charge of a division, the fish division. He told them about Mr Bastable and Mr Ring and how impressed he'd been by their youthful vigour. It was the kind of opportunity he'd been chasing all his life, he said: the opening up of a new London territory, in which the brand-name of the fish he had to get into the deep freezers of super-markets was at present wholly unknown. He was an area sales executive, he said.

'A challenge,' the broad-shouldered salesman said, and his colleague laughed and said it sounded too challenging for him.

'I can't think why I went on with those wretched vending-machines,' Henry said. 'A load of trouble, those things are.' He told them about the swimming-baths attendant and the difficulties this man was having with Rammage. He laughed, and realized that he was laughing in just the same easy way that D'arcy and Carstairs laughed in the King of England when they came at weekends. It didn't matter a tuppenny damn that he'd received only fifteen pounds for his car.

The men talked about a boxing contest that was to take place the following night in Las Vegas. 'Seventeen to one against Bugner,' the bigger man said.

'Oh, look,' Henry said, 'have either of you any idea how I should chop down grass about four foot high?'

'You want a rotary job,' the broad-shouldered salesman said. 'Wait till the ground's dried out –'

'I want to do it now, actually, and I haven't got a rotary job. All I've got is a heavy lawnmower that a woman called Mrs Passes palmed off on me.' He laughed again, amused at that, amused at the memory of how unnecessarily upset he'd been.

'What you need's a bill-hook,' the bigger salesman said.

'The man next door said a scythe.'

'You'd cut your feet off with a scythe, Henry.'

'Bill-hook,' the broad-shouldered man said. 'Curved thing, like for cropping down a hedge. A bill-hook's what you need, Henry.

They talked about the forthcoming fight again, and the barmaid joined in. Ali had promised a knock-out in the seventh, she said.

'Same again,' ordered Henry. 'Have something yourself, Fel.'

He laughed because he felt like laughing. He put an arm on the

151

smaller salesman's shoulder and said he was going to get married again. 'Elizabeth,' he said. 'marvellous, marvellous girl.'

'Mrs Aidallbery?' the larger salesman said. 'Surely not, Henry?'

But Henry nodded emphatically. It would happen, he said with drunken earnestness: he and Elizabeth would marry because they were old friends and were both on their own.

'As a matter of fact,' he said, 'I've always loved her.'

They went for a walk, and then they returned to the Caledonian Hotel and had a sherry in the cocktail lounge.

'We could have dinner,' Mrs Vincent suggested, 'if you're not doing anything better.'

'I seem to be living here,' he said, laughing in the cocktail lounge. He wasn't a man who went in much for hotels, yet he rather liked this cocktail lounge, and the face of the barman who served them, and the low table they sat at. He liked the clothes of his companion and her unfussy grey hair and handsome, firm face.

Ever since that moment at tea, when he'd given his own pride as the reason for his divorce, he'd wanted to feel her sympathy. On their walk, he'd gone on telling her about his marriage, finding it easy to talk about for the first time since the divorce. Over sherry, because she wanted to know, he told her more.

'There's suffering in your face, you know,' she had remarked on their walk, pleasing him more than embarrassing him.

He'd explained to her then that their nineteen years of marriage had been for his wife Elizabeth nineteen years of failure. With precision, he recalled the circumstances of his wife's eventual unfaithfulness and her remark, when confessing her unfaithfulness to him, that she wished she'd been guilty of it years ago.

They had two more glasses of sherry. He asked for a menu. They chose and ordered. 'Nuits St Georges to go with all that,' he murmured lightly to the wine waiter. '1961.'

They moved to the dining-room and after a brief delay a waiter placed pâté in front of Mrs Vincent and celery soup in front of him. As they ate, he heard himself saying that his wife Elizabeth had never cared for the physical side of marriage with him. He was surprised to hear himself saying such a thing in a public dining-room, while a woman he scarcely knew smeared the chef's special pâté on toast: as surprised as she had been the night before, when she'd found herself talking about her own marriage. The physical side of marriage was something that his wife had discovered, he said, in a hotel in Bishop's Stortford, with someone else's husband.

'What a frightful woman she sounds!'

'Oh, no,' he said. 'Oh, no, no.'

The waiter brought the cutlets, with peas and carrots and two different kinds of potatoes. February in Aberdeen was pleasantly invigorating, Mrs Vincent said while the food was being dispensed and the Nuits St Georges poured.

What Elizabeth hadn't understood, he thought, was that you can't say you dislike the physical side of marriage with a man and ever expect anything to be the same again. You can't come blurting out with all that, raving on about an idyll with someone else, and when the idyll fails to materialize just say you're sorry. You can't kick away nineteen years and then say you hadn't intended to kick it away. 'Oh, isn't it all beautiful!' she'd said on their honeymoon in Crete, and nineteen years later she'd said she should have walked away from him then. She'd shouted at him with bitter passion, tears streaming from her eyes. She'd made him feel abnormal, she'd made him feel ashamed that children had been born.

'Well, silly then,' Mrs Vincent said, as the waiter moved away. 'At least admit you married a silly creature.'

He placed a forkful of food in his mouth and chewed it slowly, not looking at Mrs Vincent but regarding instead the cutlets and the carrots, with peas and potatoes, on his plate.

'Yes,' he said when his mouth was empty. 'Yes, she is a silly kind of person, I'm afraid.'

'She married above her, it seems. Let's hope when she does it again she'll find her level.'

Joanna packed a suitcase and laid it open on the floor, ready to receive her nightdress and her washing things in the morning. Somerset was only a few hours away; her mother had forgotten that. It wasn't as though you were taking off on a jet plane.

Slowly she took her clothes off, and put her nightdress on and got into bed. Her mother would never really understand because her mother was part of it all. Her mother believed in Tube trains and Barclay's Bank and the awful laughy headmaster and all the sponginess. And when you tried to explain to her she didn't know what you were talking about. As Samuel said, you couldn't just go on accepting. If you went on accepting you'd begin to die at eighteen, like her mother had, drawing flowers in an old man's art school.

153

It was grand to see, Mrs Orpen read in the Sunset Home, *how the wind awoke, and bent the trees, and drove the rain before it like a cloud of smoke.* Her eyes closed. The book slipped from her hands on to the bed-clothes, and then slipped to the floor. It was pleasant being old, she thought in a brief moment of wakefulness just before she slept. It was pleasant to read *Bleak House*, to murmur over the cook's good gravy, to move from room to room without responsibility. Lucky, she thought, to end like this. Lucky to be finished with all the rest.

'You may have a sleeping pill, you know,' Nurse Aylard said, and Elizabeth said yes, she might as well.

Miss Samson and Sylvie didn't have pills. If they wanted them later they might have them, Nurse Aylard said. Lily wasn't ever offered one.

Miss Samson was afraid to sleep in case she had the dream about Mr Ibbs again, Sylvie wanted to go on convincing herself that it was a natural development for Declan to have found night work, Lily imagined Kenneth in his parents' bathroom, where he probably still was.

If he'd got a night job he'd have sent a p.c., Sylvie thought. He'd said he'd send a p.c. if ever he couldn't come. He probably had sent one. It was probably held up in the hospital somewhere, delivered to the wrong ward maybe. She imagined the postcard lying on a ward table or in a medicine room, with a bottle of medicine on it because the bottle was sticky and shouldn't be placed directly on a surface. She stayed awake, one moment thinking that he was working a night shift, and thinking the next that he didn't love her. Why should he love her, a girl who couldn't have children, a girl who'd been careless about handing herself out to other blokes? When it came to the point, men wanted girls like Lily, a virgin on their wedding night. Had it come to the point with Declan? Was that why he hadn't turned up? In the darkness she shook her head. However could it have come to that, with Declan whispering that there wasn't a girl like her in the entire world, with Declan laughing and joking and talking the whole night through?.

'The bloody young devil,' said Mr Maloney in the Cruskeen Bawn Lounge, having for the second night running waited in vain for his money.

'It's well past eleven, Kenneth,' Mrs Drucker said from the bathroom door. 'I've got your bed made up, dear.'

He was crouched on the linoleum, painting the skirting-board.

There was a spot of paint on his glasses, which blurred his vision slightly.

'You finish up, dear, and I'll get the Ovaltine going. You're chalk-white tonight, Kenneth.'

She rose from the chair she'd been sitting on and put the chair against the wall of the landing, where it belonged. He didn't say anything. He didn't say that he had finished anyway, that if she'd look closely she'd see that all the surfaces in the bathroom had been covered with green paint, eggshell or gloss. He rose from his cramped position and cleaned his brushes and wiped the paint from his glasses with Polyclens. He removed his father's slippers and the overalls, as he had done the night before, the repetition reminding him that in his parents' house repetition was the most familiar part of daily life: cloth being cut and stitched, pins in his parents' mouths, the whirring of the two sewing-machines, his mother's talk, his father's silence.

In the sitting-room it was the same, too. She gave him the Ovaltine and told him to sit down. She turned off the television his father was watching, said again that he was chalk-white, she offered him a Lincoln Cream. 'Come on, your favourite, dear,' she said. For a moment her large eyes and teeth were close to his face, before she went to sit down. She had once carried him about in her stomach, like Lily was carrying something now.

'I can't stay the night,' he said, not sitting down himself. 'There's Binks –'

'I was saying to Mrs Taggart – she has cats, too, you know – I was saying only this morning, Kenneth –'

He interrupted, shouting incomprehensibly. The noise came violently out of him. The mug of Ovaltine was in his right hand, the Lincoln Cream in the other. Their faces stared, amazed, at him.

'I've told you! I can't stay here.' His voice was high, quivering on an edge. 'I've told you before, I can't stay here because of the cat. Don't you understand?' he shouted. 'For God's sake, don't you understand?'

'Kenneth,' she said, crossing the small room to him. 'Kenneth dear, what's the trouble?'

He began to shout incomprehensibly again, and for a moment he thought he'd throw the Ovaltine over her, all over her face and her hair, or against one of the walls, or on to the floor, or at the television set. She put her arm around him and he told her in a whisper to go away.

'He's ill,' he heard her say. 'All strung up over that girl lying there. He's been chalk-white for weeks, poor thing.'

'Sit down a minute, Ken,' his father said.

He didn't sit down. He moved across the room and put the biscuit and the mug of Ovaltine on the mantelpiece. He intended simply to go, to put on his coat and scarf as he'd put them on last night, and leave the house. But she spoke again, referring to Mrs Taggart and to Lily's pregnancy.

'Oh, for God's sake!' he shouted at her.

'Kenneth,' his father reprimanded him.

He shook his head. He could feel the blood in his face and wondered what it looked like with the chalk-whiteness she was always on about. Somewhere on his forehead there was sweat.

'Leave us alone,' he said, still shouting noisily. 'Leave us, can't you?'

'Leave you, dear? But what harm have we ever done, Kenneth?'

'You've driven Lily to miscarriages, you've scared the living daylights out of her. And, my God,' he said more quietly, but with greater bitterness, 'look what you've done to me.'

'No one's driven her to miscarriages,' his mother said, cross herself. 'No one could, Kenneth. That's nonsense talk –'

'It isn't nonsense talk. People like you are always driving other people. Look where you've driven him,' he shouted, pointing at his father. 'You've killed him stone dead.'

His father's impassive face was jerking with a kind of life that Kenneth had never before seen in it. His mother's mouth was gawkishly open. The sight of them made him angrier. Why couldn't his father ever have protested? Why couldn't his father ever have told her to leave Lily alone? They deserved one another, they were awful people.

'I don't like either of you,' he shouted at them. 'I've never liked you,' he shouted. 'With your jam-rolls and your television and your bloody sewing-machines. I don't like Lincoln Creams, I don't like Ovaltine, I hate this house.'

'Kenneth –'

'I used to walk out at night and go in taxi-cabs with prostitutes.'

Their faces changed again. His mother whispered something and then, slowly, sat down. The flesh of his father's face was creased and puffed, bewilderment all over it. 'Prostitutes?' his mother whispered, looking up at him. 'Prostitutes?'

'Yes,' he said, emphatically nodding, wanting to hurt both of them.

'I used to go to prostitutes' rooms and sit there while they took their clothes off.'

His father shook his head.

'Yes,' Kenneth said.

'She's turned you into a monster,' his mother whispered. 'Saying stuff like that to your mum and dad. Who d'you think you are, Kenneth?' she cried, her voice suddenly shrill. 'Who d'you think you are, saying stuff like that?'

'It isn't true,' his father said.

'She put you up to it, Kenneth. She doesn't like us, never has. God knows where her blood comes from –'

'What kind of blood d'you think I've got, for God's sake? I'm a perverted person as soon as I spend ten minutes in your company. I'm as frightened of you as Lily is.' His hands and his lips were shaking. He could feel himself shaking all over his body. His head was shaking.

'Don't you ever come near the hospital again. Neither of you ever come near that hospital.'

'You've no right to talk like that, Kenneth,' his mother said.

His father shook his head in agreement.

'If you don't leave us alone, if you don't stop coming to that hospital and ringing me up at the library, I'll put the police on you. Leave us alone. D'you understand me? Leave us alone to have our baby.'

'Kenneth,' she said, softly, half rising from her chair.

'No,' he said.

As he opened the door, the door-knob rattled because of the shaking in his body. He closed the door behind him and in the hall he put on his gabardine coat and his gloves and his scarf. He could hear his mother weeping in the sitting-room, a sound to which his father did not respond. It had taken him thirty-five years, he said to himself, suddenly quite calm, to tell his parents he hated them.

cf Lorkin play
Young Irishwoman in Miss Gomez

16

It was Wednesday, 14 February, St Valentine's Day. At a quarter to
eight Henry replaced his telephone receiver, which had been off the
hook for fifteen hours. Almost at once the telephone rang and the
attendant at the swimming-baths said that he'd reached the end of
his tether. Henry laughed. He cut the man off in the middle of a
stream of abuse.

At eight o'clock Mrs Orvitski found a note from Joanna to the effect
that she had gone away and that her mother knew about it. Mrs
Orvitski didn't know what to do. She put the note aside and waited
until Mrs Singwell had come to take Jennifer and Alice to school in
her car. Then she telephoned her husband, who said she must go to
the hospital immediately, since she would otherwise be held responsible. He'd thought something like this would happen, he said.

'I'm sorry you've had this trouble,' Elizabeth said, and Mrs Orvitski
said it wasn't any trouble at all except that the porters in the hall
downstairs had been dubious about permitting her to visit a patient
outside the official hours. Sister O'Keeffe had been dubious also, and
had warned Mrs Orvitski that she wasn't to stay more than a minute
or two. Sister O'Keeffe didn't like it, a patient being upset just because
a girl had left home.

'Joanna did tell me,' Elizabeth said. She asked Mrs Orvitski to find
her her address book, which was in her bedside cupboard somewhere, and when Mrs Orvitski found it she wrote down the telephone number of Joanna's school and asked Mrs Orvitski if she'd
mind ringing it. 'Just say she'll be away for a while. Say I'm in hospital
and will be in touch when I get out. It'll be simplest like that.'

'You're better now, Mrs Aidallbery?'

'I'm getting better, thank you. Jennifer and Alice –'

'All the time lovely. Two good, lovely children, Mrs Aidallbery.
Tonight they come to you –'

'Hurry, please,' said Sister O'Keeffe.

*
159

On his bank's credit system Henry bought a grey flannel suit with a faint white pinstripe in it. 'Fits you like a glove, sir,' the assistant assured him. He bought two shirts, wide blue stripes on a white ground, and some socks. He changed into these clothes in the shop where he bought them, put on his Radley tie, and asked the assistant to wrap up his trousers and golfing jacket. 'And this, sir?' the assistant inquired, fingering the shirt Henry had been wearing when he entered the shop, a garment that had suffered during the days he'd spent clearing the rubbish out of his house and attending to his garden. It would all come out in the wash, Henry said with a laugh. The assistant placed the shirt in a bag with the other clothes.

Having completed this purchase, Henry made his way to the offices of the frozen foods firm, where he spent the day being briefed on the work he was to begin the following Monday. He was given a large-scale map, marked in red with the shops and supermarkets where he was to call. He received lists of profit margins and selling points, details of the firm's packaging programme, copies of national advertising that had been devised to create a demand for the four different products of the firm's fish division: haddock, plaice, cod in breadcrumbs, and kippers.

He was given point-of-sale material: stickers for supermarket deep-freezers, and cardboard display units with a woman holding up a packet of cod beneath words which stated, without reservation, that all the firm's fish was fresh. _Bed-of-the-Sea Fresh!_ the message noisily proclaimed. He was also given samples of the four different packets, colour-coded to assist the retailer, which would contain the four different fish products. He was briefed on the firm's delivery system and given notes to remind him about this, with details of delivery days in different areas. He was told about, and asked to remember carefully, weak points in other firms' fish programmes.

At five o'clock Mr Bastable and Mr Ring came briskly into the office where Henry was receiving all this information from three members of the sales organization team. They shook hands with him and invited him, when he'd finished, to step into Mr Bastable's office and have a drink.

'Well, a gin and tonic,' Henry said ten minutes later, feeling that after an afternoon like that a gin and tonic was a suitable stimulant. Two secretaries had packed the point-of-sale material and the sample packaging into one of the firm's special containers, a yellow case made of laminated plastic, with a stylized fish on it and the firm's name boldly reproduced in black.

'Here's,' Mr Bastable said, lifting his own gin and tonic in an executive salute. Mr Ring said and did the same.

They talked about the prospects for the fish division, and about another division that the board of directors was considering opening in the autumn. Henry asked what this other division would sell, but Mr Bastable said they couldn't reveal that at this juncture in time.

'Correct,' said Mr Ring.

Mr Bastable poured himself another drink, not appearing to notice that Henry had finished his. The point-of-sale material for the fish division was brilliant, Mr Ring said, and urged Henry to say so when he displayed it for the retailers. *Bed-of-the-Sea Fresh!* was a brilliant slogan, Mr Bastable said.

Mr Ring poured himself another drink, and Henry wondered if he was expected to help himself also, but decided he didn't know the two young men well enough to take this liberty.

'I think I'd best be going,' he said.

'Come and see us any time, Henry,' Mr Bastable said. 'Any problem at all, anything that worries you.'

'Correct,' Mr Ring said.

'Take the lift to the basement,' Mr Bastable said. 'You'll find a chap in a brown coat down there. He'll have your car for you.'

The two young men shook hands with him and wished him well on Monday. If there was anything at all, Mr Bastable repeated, they would be pleased to help.

In the basement Henry found a man in a brown overall emptying waste paper into a large sack. He stated his business and the man led him into a yard that contained several of the firm's delivery lorries and some parked cars. Henry spoke about the weather as they crossed this yard, but the man didn't seem much interested in the weather. 'How're you doing, George?' a lorry driver called out to him, but the man in the brown overall didn't reply to that either. He walked on and Henry walked beside him, carrying the laminated plastic case and the bag that contained his old clothes. The man eventually halted by a car, and handed Henry a set of keys. 'Been serviced,' he said, walking away.

The car was red, with the name of the firm in bold black lettering on either side of it. Attached to the roof was a large yellow fish.

Henry stared at the fish. It stretched the full length of the roof, its mouth slightly open, its eyes bulbous. It was the same stylized fish that appeared on the laminated plastic case and on the fish division's cartons and point-of-sale material. A fat herring it looked like, except for the colouring.

'Excuse me,' he called out, running after the man in the brown overall.

The man walked on. Henry overtook him, out of breath. 'Excuse me,' he said. 'Are you sure that's the car that's meant for me?

The man looked at him as though he hadn't seen him before.

'What car?'

'That car. The one you gave me the keys of.'

Henry pointed. The man didn't look. 'The car with the fish on it,' Henry said.

'They've all got fish on them. If it's a fish division car you've got a fish on it.'

'I know, but –'

'They said give the geezer a fish division car.'

'Geezer? Look, I think there's been a mistake, you know.'

The man walked on again. Henry walked with him.

'Listen, I'm an area sales executive.'

The man said nothing.

'Do area sales executives have to have fish on their cars?'

The man cleared catarrh in his throat and then spat the catarrh on to the ground.

'I'm an area sales executive,' Henry said again.

He walked with the man back to the building. He'd left the laminated case and the bag with his clothes in it on the bonnet of the car, but he didn't imagine anyone would be interested enough in these articles to take them. 'Is there a phone I can use?' he asked. The man said there was one near the lift, but when Henry asked what number he should ring to get Mr Bastable or Mr Ring the man didn't answer.

Pasted on to the wall by the telephone was a house telephone list. Mr Bastable's number was 85. Henry rang it and said he wondered if the car he'd been allocated was the right one. 'It's got a fish on the roof,' he said.

'Correct,' said Mr Bastable.

'But surely as an area sales executive –'

'All our cars carry their division symbol. The chicken leg, the pea-pod, et cetera. You've probably seen the pea-pod on our vegetable division cars? Green pea-pod, black-and-yellow lettering?'

Henry nodded and then said yes. The cars with the pea-pod were difficult to miss in London; they looked ridiculous.

'All right then?' Mr Bastable inquired.

162

'Yes,' he said.

He replaced the receiver and returned to the yard. In the distance he could see the yellow case on the bonnet of the car, and the black lettering on the side of the car, and the yellow fish on the roof. How could he drive a car like that into Meridian Close? How could he drive it over to Elizabeth Aidallbery's house and park it outside while he went to ring the bell, to collect her for dinner? How could he expect her to get into it?

He got into the car himself and threw the yellow case and the bag containing his old clothes on to the seat beside him. The woman next door would put another note under the windscreen wiper. Mrs Passes would halt her shopping basket and examine the details of the fish.

He started the engine and drove out of the yard, into the evening traffic. When he stopped at a red light he saw people in a car next to his pointing at the fish, showing it to a child.

He wondered if the fish could be removed. If it was bolted into position, or held there on the same principle as a roof-rack, it might be a simple enough matter to take it off and carry it inside the car on all occasions except when he was travelling about in his sales territory. It could be covered with a rug, and wrapped up in the rug if he had to carry it into the house in the evening or at the weekends.

He turned into a quiet street and drew up outside a public house called the Duke of Wellington. He got out of the car and examined the method by which the fish was attached to the roof. The fish itself was made of plastic, but metal bands, welded into the body of the animal, were also welded to the roof of the car.

Gloomily, he entered the public house. 'Large gin and tonic,' he said. Everything was going fine, everything was ready for turning over a whole new leaf, and suddenly you were a figure of ridicule, driving around London at forty-one years of age with a fish on top of your car. How could he sit by her bedside and say he was about to start a new job, with a new car, and not mention that the car had a yellow herring on its roof?

He sat in a corner of the Duke of Wellington, thinking about the problem. He bought another drink and carried it back to the corner. A spaniel came up to him and licked his shoes. He imagined the car parked outside the King of England, and Carstairs and D'arcy remarking on it. They'd think it amusing to be driven to Rosslyn Park on a Saturday afternoon in a car with a fish on top of it.

It was while still possessed by these melancholy thoughts, and just as he was finishing his second gin and tonic, that Henry discovered his problem was not without a solution. With sharp abruptness, he saw the red Viva standing in Meridian Close with a rectangular container, not unlike a coffin, hiding the fish from view. It would take a carpenter maybe an hour and a half to knock up such a thing, with four grips that could be screwed or unscrewed in less than a minute, like the grips on a roof-rack. It could be sprayed the same colour as the car itself, and there was no reason why rectangular pieces of hardboard shouldn't be sprayed the same colour also, and stuck with little suction-buttons to the sides of the car to cover the bold black lettering. In the same way as the fish-cover they could be quickly removed or replaced, according to the current usage of the car.

In some excitement Henry left the public house to make certain that all this was possible. He walked around the car. He couldn't see any snags, and was about to return to the Duke of Wellington for another drink when it occurred to him that if he had a rug or other large expanse of material he could cover the fish at once, so that it need never be seen outside the hospital in Cheltenham Street or outside the King of England when he went there later that evening, or in Meridian Close. He was considering the possibility of asking the barmaid in the Duke of Wellington if there was anything in the public house that wasn't wanted when he noticed that he was standing opposite a large building site. He crossed the street and entered the site through a gap in the wooden hoarding that had been erected on the pavement. The light was fading; it was difficult to see anything except scaffolding and stacks of concrete blocks, and foundation trenches in which walls were already being built. 'How do,' a voice said.

Henry turned round. A man with a limp had come out of a hut. He was wearing a black donkey jacket with pieces of leather on the shoulders. 'Gerry's gone home,' he said.

Henry said he wasn't looking for Gerry. He asked the man if he was the nightwatchman and the man agreed that he was. He was just going to get a fire going, he said, adding that he had two Alsatian dogs in his hut. As he spoke, the dogs ambled out, sniffing the air. They had muzzles on, which the man said he'd later remove. They'd eat you alive, he said. People were always stealing scaffolding these days.

Henry explained what he wanted: a large piece of plastic sheeting or canvas, anything at all, even strong paper would do. 'I'm parked across the way,' he said. 'I just wondered if you'd have anything.'

The nightwatchman inquired if Henry wished to purchase this

material. Henry said he did, and ten minutes later the fish was no longer visible. There was a bundle on top of the Viva, wrapped up in stiff brown canvas and tied with pieces of rope. No one would have guessed that this bundle was a fish.

Henry paid the nightwatchman a pound, which was what he had demanded, and brought him into the Duke of Wellington and bought him a pint of Guinness. He came from Lancashire, the nightwatchman told him, from a town called Guide, where he'd been a plasterer before he was crippled in his right leg. He found it hard to stand up now for any length of time, which made plastering impossible. Henry enjoyed his company and would have stayed with him longer if he hadn't had to go to Cheltenham Street. He was a pleasant man, he considered, not at all like the taciturn individual who'd led him to his car. 'Thanks a million,' he said to the nightwatchman, and the nightwatchman said it was a pleasure.

17

Jennifer and Alice came, with Mrs Orvitski. Kenneth came. Everyone from Number Nine came, including Arthur and the little Welsh girl: they waited in the corridor on the mahogany seat, visiting Miss Samson in twos.

They had brought her flowers, Mrs Orvitski said. 'Jennifer, you have your mother's flowers.'

'Jennifer left them on the bus,' Alice said. 'We wrote to you today, Mummy. We wrote to Dick Emery for his autograph.'

They were on her bed, restrained by Mrs Orvitski.

'Careful,' Elizabeth said, smiling at them.

'I took a tooth out.' Alice pulled down her lower lip.

'We miss you terribly, Mummy', Jennifer said.

She would go to a bus-station, Mrs Orvitski said. The flowers would be handed in. No one would take flowers that were for a sick person. Seventy-five pence they cost.

'Oh, please don't worry, Mrs Orvitski.'

'Stupid going to a bus-station,' Alice said.

'The bus-station have the flowers, child. No one take away flowers –'

'Are you feeling better, Mummy?' Jennifer asked.

'Much better now, Jenny. Thank you.'

'Are you coming out soon?'

'I don't quite know. Not long, I'm sure.'

'It'll be lovely. Oh, Mummy, it'll be lovely when you're home again.'

'You take it easy, Mrs Aidallbery, heh? I come when you want me, Mrs Aidallbery. Any times you want me I come to you.'

'You're very kind, Mrs Orvitski. I hope you two have been good girls.'

'Jennifer hasn't.'

'Oh, very good,' Mrs Orvitski cried. 'Lovely children, Mrs Aidallbery.'

'Alice is late for Mrs Singwell every single morning,' Jennifer said. 'Do tell Alice, Mummy. Mrs Singwell's *furious*.'

'Jennifer was rude to Henry.'

'I wasn't.'

'She said he was touched in the brainbox.'

'It was you, Alice –'

'Oh, Alice,' Elizabeth cried, 'you didn't tell Henry he was touched in the brainbox?'

'No, I didn't. I said it afterwards, after he'd phoned. You're upsetting Mummy, Jennifer.'

'Why did Henry phone?'

'He wanted us to play with someone called Timus.'

Mrs Orvitski didn't understand. Her gaze moved rapidly from one set of lips to another. She shook her head. She said:

'I explain to Mrs Singwell. I explain that tomorrow we all wait outside the house, ready for the car. I explain, Mrs Aidallbery, I understand.'

'When did he phone?' Elizabeth asked her children.

'On Sunday,' Alice said. 'Jennifer thought it was a heavy breather. D'you remember, Mrs Orvitski?'

'Heh?'

'The man on the phone.'

'My God!' cried Mrs Orvitski.

'D'you think Dick Emery'll send his autograph, Mummy?'

'I'm sure he will.'

'I say we have this rule, Mrs Aidallbery. Nobody answer the telephone except Mrs Orvitski. Sometime Leopold ring up, sometime some lady to ask to visit you, or flowers maybe. Never to answer the telephone,' she commanded the children. 'Never neither of you answer.'

'A man on the telephone asked Susie Purchase to the pictures,' Alice said. 'He said he'd meet her at two o'clock. D'you know what the film was called?'

Elizabeth shook her head.

'D'you know what it was called, Mrs Orvitski?'

'Heh?'

'You're not to say, Alice,' Jennifer cried, red in the face, glaring at her sister. 'You're not to, now.'

'*Naughty Knickers*,' Alice said.

Mrs Delve spoke of the Seaview Hotel, Bexhill. Carol Pidsley smiled.

Miss Samson said she still hadn't been given an official date for her release.

Carol looked different, just as Mrs Delve had said. There was lipstick on her lips. She'd powdered her cheeks and her nose, and definitely she'd been to a hairdresser or else had taken a great deal of care with her hair herself. Her eyes were different; before they'd been as dull as cardboard. Her long navy-blue skirt hid most of her legs, her lace-up shoes shone joyfully.

'The breakfasts are marvellous at the Seaview,' Carol said. 'I well remember my aunt saying that.'

Sylvie read Lily's *The House on the Strand*. She hadn't made herself up. She'd gone to the lavatory so as not to have to go when the other people's visitors came. She pushed herself lower down in the bed and read about Roger Kylnerth.

'Is it yourself there?' the voice said, and for a moment the Irish intonation made her think the voice belonged to Declan. The print ran about on the page. *Roger set his flare upon a bench, lighting the room.*

'Are you keeping fit, Miss Clapper?'

'Mr Maloney!'

'That old gurrier.'

'Is Declan with you? Is Declan here, Mr Maloney?' She spoke hastily, edging herself up in the bed, words stumbling over one another. 'Declan,' she said. 'Have you a message from Declan, Mr Maloney?' She peered around the large bulk of Mr Maloney's body in case Declan should be playfully hiding. But Declan wasn't there. Mr Maloney was wearing the familiar long black overcoat. So far he hadn't removed the hat from his head.

'It's about Declan I'd like a word,' Mr Maloney said. 'Is it in order to sit down, Miss Clapper?'

'Pull up one of those chairs. Is Declan all right, Mr Maloney?'

He moved heavily, seizing a chair from beside the fawn-topped table and carrying it back to the bedside. He sat down, still without taking his hat off. 'Declan's a great fellow,' he said. 'Declan'll make a great husband and father.'

'Mr Maloney –'

'Declan and myself had great gas on Sunday night, wait till you hear, Miss Clapper. We were over in the Cruskeen Bawn, taking it easy for an hour or two. Did you ever know I played hurley with Declan's father? A gas artist he was, he opened a fellow's skull one time. Did Declan ever tell you that? And how the judge said that no man had the right to have a skull that would open as easily as that? The judge was a great hurley man himself, and there was talk of Declan's father for the Wexford team –'

'Has Declan got night work, Mr Maloney?'

'Night work?' Mr Maloney laughed. He examined the fingers of his hands, splayed out on his knees. The fingers were large and of uniform thickness, like sausages. He shook his head.

'Have you seen him, Mr Maloney?' Her voice rose. She could feel it rising, like a distant shriek inside her. 'Where is he, for God's sake?'

'Take it easy. Don't hurt yourself now. Declan's not to be found, Miss Clapper. I went round to the digs he had. There was a big buck nigger sitting up in Declan's bed.'

'Mr Maloney, please –'

'I had a word with the black woman that runs the place. He stripped the room, she said. He took the curtaining off the window and the sheets off the bed. He left cleansing materials behind in replacement of rent. Six pounds fifty he owed the black woman.'

She didn't say anything; she didn't want to know. She gazed at the cover of *The House on the Strand*, a woman in medieval dress, a man without a face. She heard the rattle of matches. She looked up and saw that Mr Maloney was about to light a cigarette.

'Visitors aren't allowed smoking in the wards,' she said.

He nodded sagely, accepting the rule without protest. He removed the cigarette from his mouth and placed it behind an ear. He returned the match to the box.

'Declan's gone to a funeral,' he said.

Mrs Delve and Carol Pidsley gave up their places to the Tonsell brothers, who said that Miss Samson was looking well.

'I'm feeling fitter,' Miss Samson said.

Edward mentioned the Seaview Hotel, Bexhill. They both spoke of the printing-press they ran. It was their dark jowls that gave them their sombre look, she thought, and she remembered the fearsomeness of that look in her dream.

'We didn't take on the Jehovah's stuff,' Robert said.

'Mr Ibbs would be glad. He never liked the Jehovah's, you know.'

She looked away when she mentioned Mr Ibbs's name, feeling she shouldn't mention it. Silly, she thought, and looked again at the Tonsell brothers and smiled at them.

'We're too busy, anyway,' Edward said. 'We've a whole little book

169

to do by the end of March. For the nuns in the Mansion Street convent.'

'They're good people, those nuns. They came round to Number Nine once, collecting for down-and-outs. They take soup down to Waterloo Bridge every night, to the meths drinkers. Did you know that?'

The Tonsell brothers indicated that they didn't.

'They have big Thermos flasks,' Miss Samson said. 'Seven or eight of them go down and give out mugs of it. That's sometimes the only food the meths drinkers get.'

'We were surprised they asked us to do the book,' Robert said. 'Usually the Catholics like to do their own printing.'

'We think it's maybe evidence of the ecumenical movement,' Edward said. 'We were delighted when they came.'

He didn't look different, she thought. He hadn't changed like Carol Pidsley had changed. But then, of course, men didn't.

'You're managing the washing-machine, Mrs Orvitski?'

'Oh, yes. All fine, very nice.'

'She had a flood,' Alice said.

Mrs Orvitski shook her head. A little water had come out, she explained, but she'd telephoned Leopold and he'd come round and told her what she was doing wrong.

'Oh, dear.'

'The entire kitchen,' Alice reported, 'was covered in water. Unfortunately my geography book got dropped in it.'

'It wasn't the entire kitchen, Alice. It was just where the washing-machine is. Mrs Orvitski cleaned it up in a minute.'

'She didn't clean it up in a minute. She and Mr Orvitski were mopping it up for two and a half hours.'

'Oh, dear,' Elizabeth said again.

'A little water come out because I press in the wrong switch. It's all better now.'

'But your poor husband having to come all the way over –'

'Leopold come on nis bicycle. He enjoy the exercise, Mrs Aidallbery. Leopold enjoy to mend things –'

'He didn't enjoy it when he saw the flood. He said it was stupid.'

'He didn't, Alice.'

'Don't be rude, Alice. Please now.'

'He told me. I was standing there looking at him. He said it was

170

the most stupid thing he'd come across in his entire life, causing a flood when all you had to do was to read what it said on the switches.'

'Alice –'

'He was soaking wet. All his trousers and his jacket and his shirt and his tie. His underclothes were soaking, he said. His vest and his –'

'Alice, please apologize to Mrs Orvitski for being unkind.'

'Sorry, Mrs Orvitski.'

'Oh, lovely child,' Mrs Orvitski cried, endeavouring to embrace her.

'Tell me about school,' Elizabeth suggested.

'It's most unpleasant,' Alice said.

'We're doing *Noye's Fludde* at Easter.'

'Are you, Jenny? Are you going to be in it?'

'She's going to be a rat.'

'Oh look, you're not forgetting your hamsters, are you? You got my letter, Jenny? You're not forgetting to feed them?'

'Of course we're not,' Alice cried. 'We've never once forgotten them.' She bounced up and down on the bed. She told Elizabeth she loved her.

'We're not, Mummy,' Jennifer said. 'I promise we're not.' She paused and then she said: 'Joanna's gone, you know.'

'Yes, I know. Mrs Orvitski kindly came to tell me.'

'Oh, look, there's Henry,' Alice said.

He hung about by the door, with daffodils. Nurse Hampshire was restraining him, explaining that Elizabeth had her full quota of visitors at present.

'*Blockbuster*'s top of the pops,' Alice said, not wanting to go. 'Susie Purchase got The Sweet's autographs.'

'See you on Saturday,' Elizabeth said. She pushed herself up from the pillows again and kissed them both. She said goodbye to Mrs Orvitski and thanked her again.

The children ran from the ward. Mrs Orvitski followed them, tightly clothed and shiny, moving with dignity. She looked at none of the women in the other beds, nor at their visitors. She ignored Henry when he smiled at her, considering that he did not concern her. She was concerned only with the Aidallberys, whom two years ago she had taken to her heart.

'I brought you these,' Henry said.

He held out the daffodils. His clothes were different, she saw: he looked smart.

'How are you?' he asked.

'Much better.' She smiled at him, touched that he'd dressed himself up and brought flowers.

'Listen,' he said. 'I'm an area sales executive.'

'He went back to Enniscorthy because the mammy died. D'you know what I mean, Miss Clapper? Aren't the Irish always going to funerals? Isn't it a way they have with them, to be always burying the dead?'

'Has Declan's mother died, Mr Maloney?'

'I'd say she had, Miss Clapper. I'd say that definitely, without a shadow of an argument.'

'Did he say –'

'He didn't utter a word, the poor devil didn't have time. He received an urgent call from the Enniscorthy police, nothing bad at all, nothing criminal, only that the mammy had died with her boots on.'

'Do you know that, Mr Maloney? Did somebody tell you?' It wasn't unlikely. It would explain everything. 'Mr Maloney –'

'Amn't I telling you? Didn't I go round to the digs and find the black woman giving off like a steam-boat? Wasn't the curtaining taken off of the window, and money removed from a drawer? The poor devil had to raise a bob or two on the curtaining on account of having to make up the price of a ticket across the water. He hadn't a penny to play with and word comes in that the old mammy has hooked it. He sold that curtaining at a shop in Fishguard and maybe got thirty-five pence for it, enough to make up the difference and maybe buy him a bottle. He'd be all right in Rosslare, wouldn't the Gardai drive him on to Enniscorthy?'

She looked at him, sitting upright on the chair, with his eyes half closed, as though guarding them from cigarette smoke. Declan said he was incapable of telling the truth if there was a lie handy. Declan said he actually preferred telling lies, that he got pleasure out of it.

'So nobody mentioned a funeral?' she said. 'The woman you went to see, Mrs Vendericks at the lodgings –'

' "Give it a week," I said to that one. "Give it one week to sort itself out before you approach the police concerning the curtaining." You and I know where the curtaining is, Miss Clapper, in a shop in Fishguard –'

'Did Mrs Vendericks say he'd been called to a funeral?'

'She didn't say anything except she'd see him behind bars. "Was he called to a funeral?'' I remarked to her, trying to get to the base of the thing.'

'What did she say, Mr Maloney?'

'She said there'd be a funeral if she ever got her hands on to him. I didn't like that woman, to tell you the truth –'

'So the funeral's an invention of yours, Mr Maloney?'

'Sure, where else could the poor devil be?' "With the girlfriend in hospital," I said to the black woman, "would he run out on us without a reason?" To tell you the truth, I don't think she understood me, a lot of them are like that. But sure what did it matter when she agreed to give him a week? "I'll go and see Miss Clapper," I said to her, "and discover if she's had a line from him." Mary Tracy's giving him a week too.'

'Mary Tracy? Who's Mary Tracy?'

'Oh, there's nothing wrong there at all. He had a drink with Mary, I was present myself the entire time. The only thing was he must have put his hand in her handbag. Mary Tracy had to get work washing floors when he had it promised to her he could start her in the Goldhawk Hotel. The amount he owes myself is twenty-seven.'

His teeth were small, like fish's teeth in the large redness of his face. She looked away from him because she didn't like looking at him. She looked at the freckled man who was talking to Elizabeth, and then at the two blue-jowled men with Miss Samson and then at Lily's Kenneth.

'I have a feeling the typewriters is stolen property. D'you understand, Miss Clapper? It would go against Declan if the typewriters was shown to be thieved. You can't incur debts and then walk out on them, any more than you can thieve curtaining and typewriters, and money out of a young one's handbag. Did he have anything off you, Miss Clapper?'

She turned her head, wearily shaking it. She looked at him again.

'Declan didn't steal anything from me. I'm a bit tired, Mr Maloney –'

'Mary Tracy was all for approaching the police, only I cooled her down. I cooled her down for Declan's sake, in case they'd throw the book at the poor devil. All I'm thinking is, wouldn't it be better business to hush it up?'

She didn't reply to this suggestion, not understanding what he was talking about. She watched his small teeth moving again.

'All I was thinking, wouldn't it be better for Declan to have free access to come into the country when he'd finished his bit of business in Enniscorthy? I was thinking maybe if you had a pound or two by you we could tide the situation over with, you know what I mean? ''If Miss Clapper has a sum of money,'' I said to myself, ''we could share it out until Declan gets back.'' A few pounds for Mary Tracy and another few for the black woman. A few pounds on account, to show willing. I wouldn't take anything myself, in spite of being had over the typewriters. In fact,' Mr Maloney said, 'if I had anything to spare at this present moment I'd slip it into the kitty.'

'I've no money to spare, Mr Maloney. I'm sorry. And I don't think Declan's gone to a funeral. I've had an operation and I'm tired. I'd as soon you went now.'

'He has a great affection for you. He told me that. He told me he was mad to be a husband and a father.'

'I can't spare you any money.'

'I'm asking you for five pounds only, so's Declan can get a bit of time to take a breath in.'

'I'm sorry, Mr Maloney.'

'He hasn't a chance so. He'll never enter this country again. You'll never walk up the aisle with that fellow, Miss Clapper.'

'No, maybe I never will.'

'Even three pounds would help fix matters.'

She looked into the redness of his face, seeking his eyes. All around them the red flesh was screwed up. Two tiny points gleamed blackly in the midst of this. She stared at them. She said:

'We spent the last money I had the night before I came in here, on a meal we had and a few drinks. Declan was going to get money this week. He was going to start a new job on the understanding that in a few weeks' time he'd leave to go up to Liverpool. I've maybe thirty pence in my purse, Mr Maloney. You can have it if it's any use to you. It won't get me far.'

'Ah sure, I'd never take it off you. Listen to me, could you raise a collection?' While still looking at her, he moved his head backwards, indicating the other beds in the ward. 'Couldn't you put your predicament to them and maybe they'd come to your aid? I could look in tomorrow, no trouble whatsoever. If you could raise five, or maybe ten, on the grounds of destitution I'd fix those two females for you.'

'I've asked you to go away, Mr Maloney. I wish you would now.'

'He'll get him fourteen years by the time they've brought everything to the surface.'

'I'll have to call the nurse if you don't go away.'

'I only came to help the boyfriend, Miss Clapper, and to help yourself. I came out of the kindness of my heart. I came to see how you were –'

'You came looking for money. You came to get money out of me so's you could sit in the Cruskeen Bawn and drink whiskey.'

'I won't listen to lies, Miss Clapper –'

'You're a horrible man, Mr Maloney.'

He did not reply to this accusation. His eyes appeared now to be entirely closed. He drew a pair of leather gloves from one of the pockets of his overcoat and put them on. The cigarette remained behind his ear. He spoke slowly and quietly. He said:

'You wouldn't get a two-penny piece for him on the open market. As soon as your back is turned he's off with a female from Tralee that looks like a cow. He gets the contents of a distillery inside her and then he strips her in her bedroom. A fellow like that isn't fit to breathe the Queen's air. A fellow like that isn't fit to feed to diseased pigs. He hasn't the brains of a yo-yo or the morals of a sardine. You're the same type of performer yourself, sitting back in a bed for yourself, laughing at an old man because he can't get his money back. I could get you removed from that bed on account of decent women wouldn't share a room if they knew the type you are. I could get you removed like a flash, only I wouldn't demean my mouth with referring to you.' He nodded at her and rose. Moving slowly, he left the ward.

Kenneth told her because he couldn't prevent himself from telling her. He told her how he'd gone walking about the streets before he'd ever known her and how a woman had spoken to him, offering him companionship for three pounds, and how he'd gone in a taxi with her and had afterwards gone in taxis with other women. He'd had a quarrel with his mother, he said. He'd told his mother all that, too, because she'd driven him to it.

'Your mother?' she whispered. 'Your mother?'

'I feel ashamed of hating them.'

Arthur didn't say much, he never did. But the little Welsh girl talked and talked. Mrs Delve had shown her how to fillet fish. She'd found an old bell on a coiled spring, one of the ones that used to hang outside the kitchen in the old days. She'd taken off all the green paint with paint-remover, and underneath it was brass. She'd been shining it in the evenings. The Kleeneze man came on Monday. Mrs Delve hadn't known what to order except O'Cedar Oil, which they were low in.

'I think I'd like a little word now,' the Reverend Rawes said, coming in from the corridor.

'So kind of you to come,' Miss Samson said, which was her greeting for everyone. 'So kind,' she said to Arthur and the little Welsh girl, as they rose in deference to the clergyman.

'Well?' he asked. 'Less troubled, I hope?'

'I'm a nuisance.' She tried to give a little laugh, to make it all seem light and unimportant, because that was the treatment it deserved, it being absurd.

But he was serious, and her little laugh did not correctly materialize. 'You're not a nuisance,' he said.

'I am to you, Mr Rawes.'

'The nightmare has not returned?'

'No, it has not come back.'

'And how do you feel, Miss Samson?'

'I cannot forget it.'

'The doubt is there?'

'Yes.'

'You must pray. As often as the doubt afflicts you, you must pray.'

'I cannot pray.'

'God sends us doubts to test our faith.'

'I know.'

'To strengthen us in the end, Miss Samson.'

'I know.'

'Miss Samson –'

'I cannot pray, Mr Rawes. I cannot.'

She looked at him, gazing straight at him in the way she had taught herself to gaze at people. Her bad eye was dead and steady, her good one blinked in the silence that fell between them.

'What a time to choose for it,' she said, 'when you haven't the strength to fight it.'

'God has been your greatest comfort, Miss Samson. All you had was a bad dream.'

'When I pray I feel nothing. I feel nothing coming back.'

'But, Miss Samson, why –'

'Because I was taken from our house.'

'No, no, that couldn't be so. That couldn't be so in the very least, Miss Samson.'

'I feel it.'

'No, Miss Samson. You are walking in a wilderness because Our

176

Father for His own reasons desires that you should. Please believe that. Please hold on to it.'

'It's good of everyone to want to send me to Bexhill. I know you're behind it, Mr Rawes.'

'The sea air'll do you good, Miss Samson.'

'I love you, Lily.'

She wept, quietly, without making a fuss. She couldn't believe what he'd told her. She couldn't believe that he was sitting by her bed, white-faced and tense, telling her that he was a different kind of person from the person she'd always thought him to be. She couldn't imagine him talking to the women or staring at them in a room, while they took their clothes off. Or looking through a keyhole, or letting a woman in a cinema put a coat over his knees. She listened while he told her about the man who'd approached him on the street, who had made him feel disgusted because once he'd been like that man himself. She thought of Ally Glazier and Mr Hopegood, whom people had considered to be sick. She listened, still quietly weeping, while he spoke of his parents.

'I had to tell you,' he said, 'because I told them. I couldn't have a secret with them. Not a secret from you, Lily.'

'I'm really not up to marrying anyone, you know.'

'I mean when you're better, Elizabeth.'

'It's terribly sweet of you to ask me, Henry. Dear Henry,' she said, smiling at him. 'Dear Henry.'

She listened while he told her about his new job. She tried to visualize Mr Bastable and Mr Ring. He'd had a drink or two, she could see. He mentioned a nightwatchman, but she couldn't quite understand who this nightwatchman was. Everything was all right, he kept saying. He wanted her to see the house and garden in Meridian Close.

'I can't marry you, Henry,' she said. 'I'm terribly sorry, but I really can't.'

'Why not?'

'Because I don't love you, Henry. I'm sorry.'

He talked about the past, about his parents taking her on holiday with them and the day her mother had made magenta-coloured ice-cream. He talked about Budleigh Salterton and creeping up on people on the towpath, and creeping up on Mr Giltrap, and the clergyman on the beach. There were blackberries they'd picked one time, and

177

fudge they'd made in her mother's kitchen. There was a time they'd swung on the bathroom door and pulled it off its hinges. 'Please, Mr Giltrap,' they'd said in the garden. 'Oh, please, Mr Giltrap.' And in the end Mr Giltrap had found a screwdriver and repaired the damage before anyone found out. 'Let's buy him some cigarettes,' Henry had suggested, and they'd undone the catch at the bottom of her money-box and taken out a two-shilling piece and bought him some Woodbines in Mrs Stringer's.

'I'm sorry,' she said again.

'Look, it'll be all right, Elizabeth.'

In the past they were two different people: she tried to say that. She tried to explain that Henry was no longer the red-haired boy who was always running, nor was she still a girl with pale plaits. The friendship they'd had then was different from their friendship now. She was sorry for Henry now. No one could possibly have been sorry for the laughing, red-haired little boy.

'Joanna's gone to live in a commune,' she said to change the subject. 'In Somerset.'

'Commune?'

'She's gone off with her friend Samuel.'

Vaguely, he shook his head. He could take Jennifer and Alice out at the weekend, he said. He'd telephoned on Sunday actually, but Jennifer hadn't quite understood. He'd go down to Somerset, he suggested, and bring Joanna back. He loved her, he whispered, his freckled face doggy. He'd always love her.

'When we met that day outside the Gas Showrooms,' he said, 'I realized I loved you. When I came to your house that night I shouldn't have taken no for an answer.'

'I'm sorry, Henry.' She remembered roses growing in people's gardens the night he'd come to propose to her. She remembered the smell of them on the late-evening air, and Henry's voice saying she'd always been his best friend. She remembered saying herself that that wasn't so actually, that after he'd gone to Anstey Grange they'd ceased to be such friends. He hadn't seemed to listen, or to understand. He had been just like anyone else as they strolled about, not special like he'd once been.

He took her hand. For a moment she thought he might attempt to kiss her. Gently she pulled her hand away. She said it was nice of him to come to see her.

'I waited until everything was settled. I sold the Zephyr last night.'

'The poor old Zephyr. You won't be the same without it.'

'Elizabeth –'

'It's out of the question, Henry.'

He shook his head. He smiled, and she was reminded of the child he'd been, for the smile was the same.

'I'd better go,' he said.

'I'm sorry. Dear Henry.'

'Listen, Elizabeth –'

'Please come in again. Thank you for the daffodils.'

He smiled again. He went away, waving a hand at her.

Walking in Cheltenham Street with the others from Number Nine, the Reverend Rawes felt disturbed beyond measure. He felt it unfair on them that they should not know. He felt it unfair on them that they should not share because they would wish to share and to pray. He could not tell them because she'd asked him not to, and in any case he doubted that he would have had the courage. It would be like dropping a sudden bomb, when no one was at war.

The small procession passed the woman with the banner, who was resting for a moment, sitting on the low wall out of which the hospital railings sprouted. The little Welsh girl nudged Arthur, drawing his attention to the words on the piece of cardboard.

'Excuse me, sir,' Mr Maloney said. 'Only I seen you in the ward.'

The Reverend Rawes and Mrs Delve paused in their progression. Mrs Delve smiled at Mr Maloney, waiting for him to say something else. He said, addressing the Reverend Rawes:

'Did you notice that young girl I was with, sir? She hasn't a penny in the world, due to no fault of her own. I'm desperate to raise money for her. Mr Maloney the name is, sir.'

Mr Maloney held out a gloved hand, which the Reverend Rawes took, saying that his own name was Rawes, and introducing Mrs Delve. Mr Maloney shook hands with Mrs Delve.

'And Miss Pidsley,' Mrs Delve said. 'And Mr Edward Tonsell and Mr Robert Tonsell.'

Mr Maloney shook hands with all of them. Arthur and the little Welsh girl had walked ahead and so were not involved.

'She was doing a line with a tearaway,' Mr Maloney said, 'only he hooked it. As soon as the poor creature's inside the hospital your man hooks it.'

'Hooks it?' repeated Mrs Delve.

'Wouldn't it sicken you to your backbones, missus? He left that poor girl destitute. Did you mind me addressing you on the public

179

street? Only I represent the Society of St Vincent de Paul. I'm on hospital work mainly these days.'

The Reverend Rawes gave him fifty pence and Mrs Delve added thirty to that. Carol Pidsley and the Tonsell brothers gave ten pence each. It would certainly be a help, Mr Maloney said.

The Reverend Rawes nodded and passed on, his mind engaged with other thoughts. He did not speak again in Cheltenham Street, nor on the bus, nor in Balaclava Street when they reached it. In Number Nine he went immediately to his room.

When their visitors had gone, the women in the Marie Atkins Ward didn't speak much, either.

Lily had a feeling of wanting to be far away. She wanted to walk and to go on walking, until she couldn't see him in the taxi with a woman any more; until she couldn't see the woman smiling at him, her lips drawn far back, her teeth like animal's teeth; until she couldn't see the woman's two long hands holding on to him, finger-nails gleaming.

She got out of bed. She pulled her dressing-gown on and pushed her feet into her slippers. She walked through the dimness, into the softly lit corridor, down it to the left, and left again, to the lavatory. How could he have told her? How could he have sat beside her bed and told her that he had gone to prostitutes' rooms? How could he have told her now, when she was seven and a half months pregnant? She remembered him the day she'd borrowed *Dr Bradley Remembers*, coming up behind her as he'd probably come up behind the other kind of woman, only taking her to the Geranium Café instead of into a taxi. She remembered the faces of the waitresses, and the pineapple cup-cakes, and Kenneth so thin and young, awkward across the table. She wept in the lavatory. It was his mother's victory. She felt that in her bones.

There was no use being wet about it, Sylvie convinced herself. It wasn't the first time a man suddenly hadn't been there. Declan had been different, but in the end he hadn't been different at all. Good luck to him, she thought with only a trace of bitterness in her mind, good luck to him wherever he was. It was better to know that he had definitely gone than to go on wondering and making excuses: at least you knew where you were.

Miss Samson prayed with her eyes closed. She prayed in her mind, not moving her lips. 'O Lord,' she said, but it was all still meaningless. She was jealous of Carol Pidsley. Her birth injury was unfair. 'Ha, ha, ha,' said Mr Ibbs.

He didn't love her, Elizabeth thought, any more than she loved him. It was her help he wanted, and it was too late for that. 'A clown in a circus,' he'd said, laughing, as a child; how could she suddenly say in the Gay Tureen that that was right, that he should have been a clown in a circus? He was still a child, but that, too, was an impossible truth to reveal, too cruel and sorrowful, for no one could be a child at forty-one and properly survive.

'Poor Henry,' she murmured. And then, since he'd raised the subject, she found herself wondering what marriage with him would actually be like. Impossible, she estimated; but even so there were many men much worse than Henry. At least he wasn't desiccated. It had been hard of Joanna to say he slobbered about the place.

18

In the saloon bar of the Rose and Thorn Dr Pennance waited for Nurse Hampshire to come off duty. Other nurses from the nearby nurses' home were there. Dr Talkler came in and asked him if he'd seen Sarah Gillingham. Dr Pennance shook his head and was pleased when the other houseman didn't linger.

'Excuse me, sir,' Mr Maloney said to Henry. 'Only I seen you in the ward. Isn't it mild weather we're having?'

In the corner of the public bar the woman who paraded outside the hospital sat with a glass of Double Diamond, as she did at this time every evening. Her placard, attached to its sweeping-brush stick, was propped against an outside wall of the public house, by a side door. No one spoke to her, for it was known in the Rose and Thorn that she did not incline towards conversation.

'I went in to see that girl,' Mr Maloney said. 'I'm from the St Vincent de Paul.

Nurse Hampshire, having been back to the nurses' home to change out of her uniform, joined Dr Pennance. She wanted to go to a film, she said, *The Clockwork Orange*, which she'd heard was fantastic.

'Can you beat that, sir?' Mr Maloney said to Henry. 'Wouldn't it turn the heart inside in your ribs, sir, the creature stretched out there and your man laughing his head off? Maloney the name is. Delighted to meet you, sir.'

Henry nodded. As he consumed another glass of gin and tonic, it seemed to him that Elizabeth had not actually turned down his proposal in so many words. What she'd actually said was that she wasn't up to marrying anyone at the moment, which was a natural enough statement to come from anyone in a hospital bed. She'd also said that she didn't love him, but saying you loved a person or didn't love a person was neither here nor there. There was a time when his ex-wife had categorically stated that she loved him. She'd said it repeatedly, in a sports car particularly, a pre-war Morgan that he'd had at the time. Elizabeth must have repeatedly said it to her ex-husband also, and must have believed it. She must have looked into the man's face and said she loved him more than anyone in the world. 'I never did love you,' his own wife had said when he'd brought the matter up at the time of their divorce. 'I thought I did, but of course I couldn't have.'

'Is Azu married?' Nurse Hampshire asked Dr Pennance. 'That woman was in the hall again tonight. Aylard says she isn't his wife.'

Dr Pennance said that Mr Azu was having some kind of trouble with this woman, who was not, so he'd heard also, Mr Azu's wife.

'He makes mistakes. O'Keeffe says Alstrop-Smith's incapable of a mistake.'

'God in His firmament,' Dr Pennance said. 'O'Keeffe's the angel Gabriel.'

Nurse Hampshire laughed. The film started at eight twenty-two, she said. They'd easily walk it in a quarter of an hour, she could do with the air. Nurse Gillingham asked them if they'd seen Dr Talkler and they said he was there somewhere, looking for her.

'I have it fixed,' said Mr Maloney, 'that she'll stay with a niece of my own until such time as she's on her feet again. The poor creature's employed in a basement of Woolworth's and very good employers they are, but we couldn't expect them to bear the burden entirely. D'you follow me, sir? We couldn't expect them to equip the poor girl with clothing and a bit for spending, on account of your man hooked it. Are you with me, sir?'

Henry said he was. You couldn't have a silver lining without a cloud, he'd once heard someone saying on the radio. It was like the Passes' lawnmower and the disappointment over the price he'd got for the Zephyr and the fish on top of the Viva: everything looked gloomy until you'd had time to think matters over and get them into perspective. After that, everything was naturally more cheerful. 'Have a drink,' he said to Mr Maloney, and Mr Maloney said he would.

'I saw you there with your wife, sir, and I made a note to myself that I'd put the girl's case to you. I was down this morning, seeing the manager of the Woolworth's. I put the case to him and he naturally said the firm couldn't be dipping its hand into its pocket for every young creature that got caught with a fellow like that. It was the matter of the clothes I was after in particular, wondering if they'd have a few old garments there that maybe we could wrap her up in to make the journey out to my niece's. Well, they didn't have a stitch. "Wait till I ring up the bosses," the manager said, as decent a man as ever walked a pavement. He came back with a message that he could take two pounds out of the till to start a fund going for her. He put his hand in his pocket and added another ten p to it. So we have two pounds and ten pence to start the little fund with, and I'll maybe add ten pounds to it myself. Would you be able to let us have a few pounds yourself, sir?'

Dr Pennance and Nurse Hampshire passed behind Henry, arm-in-arm, about to leave the public house.

'Excuse me, miss,' Mr Maloney said. 'Only I noticed you in the hospital. Excuse me addressing you. I'm from the St Vincent de Paul.'

'Yes?' Nurse Hampshire said.

'The little girl I was visiting in the hospital has had her entire wardrobe of clothes lifted.'

'Miss Clapper?'

'This gentleman and myself is after starting up a little fund with the assistance of F. W. Woolworth. Maloney the name is.'

Mr Maloney held out his hand. Nurse Hampshire, not taking it, frowned. Dr Pennance regarded Mr Maloney coldly.

' A patient's personal misfortune,' Dr Pennance said, 'has nothing to do with the nursing staff.'

'Ah, I'm not saying it has, mister –'

'We're in a hurry,' Dr Pennance said.

Nurse Hampshire and Dr Pennance left the public house. 'Would you credit that?' said Mr Maloney. 'A well-dressed couple like that? There could be earthquakes and floods, and a fellow like that would say it didn't concern him. Isn't it a damn disgrace the way some people are constructed?'

The woman who paraded outside the hospital collected her placard from outside the side entrance of the public bar and carried it away. On a 30 bus she placed it under the stairs and when she left the bus she carried it again. People passing turned their heads sideways to read it, as they always did when she wasn't holding it the right way up.

Henry gave Mr Maloney a fifty-pence piece and said it was all he could manage.

'Well, it'll help matters certainly,' Mr Maloney admitted. 'Any donation, however small, will help matters.'

'Can I give you a lift at all?' Henry offered, explaining the direction he was taking. As he spoke, he was aware of a faint nausea and of a familiar floating sensation in his head. He hadn't had anything to eat since lunchtime, when he'd had a Scotch egg. Counting the gin and tonic he'd been given by Mr Bastable, he'd now had six glasses of

184

this mixture, the majority of them containing double measures of gin. He was drunk and he intended to get drunker, because when you were drunk you felt better. The nausea was temporary and would disappear after two more drinks. The floating in his head could not be described as unpleasant.

'D'you know the Cruskeen Bawn Lounge in Hammersmith?' Mr Maloney asked him. 'A lounge bar in the George public house, sir, bang up against Lloyds Bank? Only I'm due there on business.'

Outside the Rose and Thorn Henry paused on the pavement, waiting for Mr Maloney, who had gone to the lavatory. He noticed that the buildings around him were sharply etched in the fading evening light. He'd noticed before when he'd had a few drinks that buildings, and sometimes people, were sharply etched for the first ten minutes or so after you stepped out of a public house. He'd once remarked on the fact to D'arcy, seeking a medical explanation, but D'arcy had said that Henry was talking rubbish. He swayed slightly as he stood on the pavement reflecting on this matter, and was aware that he was swaying. He moved to a lamp-post and stood with his shoulder against it. 'The hard case,' said Mr Maloney, emerging from the alley by the side of the Rose and Thorn.

For a moment Henry couldn't remember where it was that he had met Mr Maloney, or what the circumstances of the meeting had been. Then it came back to him, and at the same time he recalled a man and a girl being unpleasant to Mr Maloney, the man saying that a patient's personal misfortune had nothing to do with nursing staff. Henry considered that an unpleasant remark. He said so as he stood with Mr Maloney on the pavement. He said that in his opinion it was an unpleasant remark to make to a person who was seeking to help someone else.

'Are you OK?' Mr Maloney inquired in reply. 'Are you fit to drive a car, mister?'

Henry gave a laugh. 'I drive a damn sight better when I'm drunk,' he said.

Mr Maloney did not, that night, attend to his business in the Cruskeen Bawn Lounge. On the way to Hammersmith in the Viva Henry said that he, too, was moving between one public house and another. He was on his way to the King of England off the Upper Richmond Road, he wondered if Mr Maloney knew it? Mr Maloney did not, but he sensed that it would be in his interests to remain with this obliging man as long as possible. 'I often heard of that place,' he said. 'I often thought I'd like to see it, sir.'

In the King of England the two car salesmen were at the bar. Other people, known to Henry, stood with drinks in their hands or sat at tables. In the usual way a few called out to him, and he waved back at them. He asked Mr Maloney what he'd have and Mr Maloney replied that he'd have Irish whiskey.

The car salesmen were again talking about the boxing match that was to take place in a matter of hours now, in Las Vegas. Mr Maloney spoke at length of a wrestler he'd known well, a man called Dano Mahoney. At twenty past nine, when Mr Maloney was in the lavatory, the smaller salesman asked Henry if his friend ever bought anyone a drink, but Henry didn't hear what he was saying.

'How's the beer going these days?' the larger salesman inquired, recalling the occasion when he and his colleague had been invited back to Meridian Close after the King of England had closed for the night. They'd sat in the sitting-room with the electric fire on. Henry had brought in a red plastic bucket full to the brim with beer, and three mugs.

'I'm moving the brewing kit out of the bathroom,' Henry said. 'to a cupboard under the stairs.' At the moment, he said, he didn't have any beer that was ready to drink.

'I never drink beer if I can help it.' said Mr Maloney returning from the lavatory.

Henry was feeling happy. He recalled again, with pleasant imprecision, that he'd sorted everything out, the lawnmower, the Zephyr, the rubbish in the house, the fish on top of the car. Elizabeth had definitely not turned down his proposal in so many words, in fact when you thought about it she hadn't turned it down at all. 'Great,' he said, and ordered a final round of drinks.

'Good luck to you, gentlemen,' Mr Maloney said, lifting his glass from the bar.

'D'you know what I'd like to do?' Henry said. 'I'd like to go up and get a drink off D'arcy. Dr D'arcy,' he said, 'of Kingston Hill. We were at school together,' he told Mr Maloney. 'Anstey Grange and Radley.'

'Tip-top schools,' said Mr Maloney.

Turning his back on Mr Maloney, the smaller salesman remarked to his colleague that Henry's friend appeared to be a species of idiot. The larger salesman agreed.

'Are you game to go out to D'arcy's place?' Henry asked the car salesmen, but after some discussion they decided that they could not pay a visit so late at night without a definite invitation.

'Sure, isn't our friend here inviting you?' Mr Maloney said, fearing

186

that if these two men didn't agree to make a journey to a house where there was further drink, the whole thing might be put off. It was very many years since Mr Maloney had fallen in with such good company.

'Don't let them move,' Henry commanded Mr Maloney, and went away to telephone D'arcy.

People were leaving the King of England. Some of the lights had been switched off. 'Hurry along now, please,' Felicity called out from behind the bar.

'Your man and myself met earlier over charitable business,' Mr Maloney said, inclining his head towards the corner where Henry was speaking on the phone. 'A young girl in the same ward as his wife, the poor creature's without a stitch to leave the hospital in. I'm from the St Vincent de Paul myself. If you was inclined to aid the poor creature, any donation would be a charity.'

'I'm not much inclined to aid anyone,' the smaller salesman said. He laughed loudly, and his companion laughed with him. Mr Maloney watched them. 'I'm a mean devil,' the smaller salesman said, and laughed again.

'Come along now, please,' Felicity urged.

'I had to ring through to Carstairs' place,' Henry said. 'The D'arcys are playing bridge there. Carstairs said come out for a drink.'

'You and three friends, did you say?' The larger salesman was sharply punctilious, his eyes expertly searching Henry's. He had no wish to be involved in any trouble with these two doctors, who had both, on separate occasions, made promises about remembering Putney Square-Deal Motors when next they were changing their cars. 'Are you sure it's all right, Henry?'

'Sure, why wouldn't it be all right?' Mr Maloney said. 'Sure, wouldn't doctors want company like anyone else, for God's sake?'

'Please now, gents,' Felicity said. 'The evening's over.'

'Are you doing anything, Felicity?' Henry asked. 'Would you like to come out to Kingston?'

Hearing this, the car salesmen exchanged glances. Felicity told Henry she was tired. 'I think we'll give it a miss,' the larger salesman said.

On the pavement outside, as Henry and Mr Maloney were saying good night to the salesmen, doubt was expressed by the salesmen about Henry's ability to drive. But Mr Maloney said the journey he'd made with Henry had been the most peaceful of his life. Both salesmen shook their heads. The smaller one pointed at the top of the car.

'What on earth's that?' he asked.

'Machine guns,' said Mr Maloney.

The larger of the salesmen drew Henry aside and asked him in a lowered voice if he thought it wise to bring Mr Maloney to Dr Carstairs' house.

'I was at school with Carstairs,' Henry said, 'Anstey and Radley. I've been a friend of Carstairs' for thirty-three years.' He placed a hand on the salesman's shoulder. The cigarette in his mouth had gone out. It was bent and beginning to disintegrate, because on the way out of the King of England he'd stumbled and knocked it against Mr Maloney. Henry smiled at the car salesman, but the car salesman shook his head.

'I'm not talking about Dr Carstairs, old chap. I'm talking about this fellow who says he runs a charity.'

'Which fellow's that?'

'That man there, Henry. He's not entirely sane, I'd say. I wouldn't think Dr Carstairs or Dr D'arcy would thank you –'

'D'arcy's wife's a bit strange, you know.'

He told the salesman about the time he'd arrived early at one of the D'arcys' parties and had sat with Peggy D'arcy in her coffee-coloured underclothes, while she dried her hair in front of a fire. Carstairs' wife was different, he said, a dumpy woman. Henry nodded at the larger salesman and then laughed because he felt like laughing. He'd be in the King of England tomorrow at lunchtime, he said. As likely as not he'd be there.

The salesmen watched while Henry started the engine. The smaller one knocked loudly on the window beside Mr Maloney just before the car began to move, to remind Henry to put his lights on.

'God, that frightened the life out of me,' Mr Maloney complained as they drove along Upper Richmond Road. 'Knocking on the glass like that. Thoughtless bloody man, I thought him.'

Henry laughed again. Mr Maloney continued to denigrate the smaller car salesman. He'd mentioned about the girl who was without clothes, he said, and all the smaller salesman had said was that he was a mean devil. In his opinion, Mr Maloney said, both salesmen were most peculiar men. 'Moustaches like fir trees,' he said. 'Look bloody ridiculous.'

Henry laughed. 'They thought you were insane,' he said.

The D'arcys and Mrs Carstairs were extremely angry. Carstairs was angry too, but in a different way. Carstairs was angry with his wife and his friends because they blamed him for agreeing to let Henry come and break up their bridge evening. He was angry, as they were, with Henry for making the suggestion at half past ten at night, but he didn't see that they had any cause to blame him for what had occurred. Any one of the three of them would have been obliged in the circumstances to have acted as he had. His wife disagreed with that assumption: had she answered the telephone she'd have told Henry that it was most inconvenient for him to come around for a drink, bringing another person with him. When Carstairs reminded his wife that he and D'arcy had known Henry for thirty-three years, she replied that in that case you'd imagine they'd have seen enough of him. 'I know *I* would,' Mrs Carstairs said, a woman who had been outspoken before on the subject of Henry.

'Steady on, Gillian,' Carstairs said.

The Carstairs' sitting-room had soft wall-to-wall carpeting in a shade of rust. There were chairs of polished tubular steel and four large, steel-framed pictures of abstract composition, one on each wall. There were polished steel standard-lamps and several matching tables, black leather surfaces and short steel legs. The sofa, four armchairs, and all the room's cushions were covered in a woven fabric that tastefully incorporated several shades of purple.

D'arcy and Mrs Carstairs were winning when the bell rang, a circumstance which naturally angered Mrs Carstairs further. 'Finish this hand,' she said, but after a moment the bell rang again, repeatedly and persistently.

'Evening all,' Henry said jollily, leading Mr Maloney into the Carstairs' sitting-room.

'He drove like a prince,' Mr Maloney said.

It had occasionally happened in the past that Henry had arrived at night in Carstairs' or D'arcy's house, with or without a companion or companions. Once he'd brought another vending-machine operator, a Major Tile, with whom he'd earlier spent five hours in the King of England exchanging abusive comment about Rammage and New-Way Vending Limited. On another occasion he'd arrived, unheralded, with two men whom he'd met in the Nog Inn in Wimbledon, who'd claimed to be old boys of Anstey Grange and Radley, but who'd turned out not to be.

'Maloney the name is,' Mr Maloney said, and Mrs Carstairs said to herself that this time Henry had gone too far.

'Won't you take off your coat?' Carstairs suggested to Mr Maloney, but Mr Maloney said he didn't think he would. The cigarette he'd put behind his ear four hours ago in the Marie Atkins Ward was still there. He sat down in a chair and remarked that it was the most comfortable chair he'd ever sat in in his life. He kept his hat on.

Mrs Carstairs said she'd better make some coffee, but Henry explained that what they were after was another drink.

'We had great gas down in the King of England,' Mr Maloney said. 'I never knew a better place than that.'

The Carstairs' sitting-room moved around Henry. Afterwards, he remembered the moving room and the faces that moved with it: the faces of his two school friends and the dumpy face of Mrs Carstairs and the gaunt, attractive face of Peggy D'arcy, and Mr Maloney's face, red beneath his hat. He remembered the Carstairs' dog, a German pointer, panting in front of the fire, and the glass of whisky that Carstairs placed in his hand, the wrong drink because he'd asked for gin and tonic.

Afterwards, he remembered Mr Maloney's voice saying that the whisky he was drinking was the best whisky he'd ever tasted in his life, and saying the Carstairs' house was a beautiful residence. He remembered his own voice whispering confidentially, telling Peggy D'arcy about the day she'd dried her hair in coffee-coloured underclothes. 'I kept thinking of them,' he said. 'When you came downstairs with a dress on I thought of the other things underneath it.'

'There's a girl stuck in a bed,' Mr Maloney said. 'I'm a man from the St Vincent de Paul.'

Henry laughed and patted Peggy D'arcy's knees. He picked up a small blue and white china bowl and went round everyone, insisting on contributions to the fund. As he was doing so, there was some kind of altercation. A table with cards and money on it was overturned, accidentally, by himself. He threw a cushion across the room, making a rugby pass to Carstairs. 'Andy Ripley,' he cried, laughing and clapping his hands, wanting Carstairs to pass it back to him. But Carstairs put the cushion on the arm of the sofa. 'I'm getting married,' Henry said.

'The top of the day to you,' said Mr Maloney, raising his glass in the air.

'Cheers,' Henry said, laughing again.

Mr Maloney said that some people were extraordinary. There'd been two different sets of people, he said, that he'd met that night in two different public houses: a man and a nurse, and later on two men with moustaches like fir trees. 'They'd sicken you to your backbones,' Mr Maloney said. 'Degenerate characters like that.'

The D'arcys said they'd better be going. D'arcy said something to

Henry but Henry couldn't understand it, something to do with the business, years ago, of Peggy D'arcy sitting in her underclothes. 'Don't worry about it,' Henry said. 'Water under the bridge.' But it seemed that D'arcy wasn't apologizing. He wagged his head in annoyance, and Henry smiled at him and wagged his head back.

'Elizabeth's going to marry me,' Henry said.

'Top of the day to you,' said Mr Maloney, raising his glass again.

He was an area sales executive, Henry said. He had a brand-new car standing outside the door at this very moment. He'd cleaned the house out from top to toe. He'd tidied the garden, back and front. He'd lopped an ash tree because the woman next door couldn't see in her hall.

'I'll drive you back,' Carstairs said. He asked Mr Maloney where he lived, but Mr Maloney said he was in no hurry.

The D'arcys had put their coats on and were standing uncertainly by the door, as though doubtful about leaving in case their help should be required.

'Elizabeth Orpen,' Henry said. 'Elizabeth Aidallbery.'

Mr Maloney rose and moved with careful deliberation across the room, to the whisky decanter. Watched by the Carstairs and the D'arcys, he filled his glass to the rim and returned to his chair. 'God save the Queen,' he said, raising the glass again. 'You're a decent man, sir,' he said to Carstairs.

The D'arcys looked worried by the door. Mrs Carstairs said loudly to her husband that Henry and Mr Maloney must leave the house. 'Come on,' Carstairs said, taking Henry's elbow.

Henry laughed. It was usually D'arcy who took your elbow. D'arcy had been laughing like a drain in the King of England a day or two ago, holding on to his elbow, giggling into his face.

D'arcy wasn't laughing now; no one was laughing except himself. The man he'd had a few drinks with was sitting with his hat on in the middle of the room, muttering to himself about the Queen. The others might have been standing at a funeral.

'Let's get you home, Henry,' Carstairs said, trying to drag him by the elbow.

Henry sat down on the sofa. Somewhere in the room there was a glass of whisky belonging to him. He looked around for it and saw it on a table. He laughed because they were all standing like that, as though someone had died. He put a cigarette between his lips but had difficulty in lighting it. He crossed the room to where his glass was. He drank some whisky and tried to light his cigarette again.

191

'Excuse me,' he said to Carstairs, 'would you mind lighting this cigarette for me?'

He was aware that Carstairs didn't do so. Carstairs just stared at him, like the others were staring. 'What's the matter with you?' he said to them all.

Nobody replied except the man he'd had a few drinks with. 'The hard case,' said Mr Maloney.

'Listen,' said Henry, 'have I done wrong or something?'

'We want to get you home, Henry. I'll drive you,' Carstairs said. 'You can pick up your car tomorrow.'

'Have I done wrong, Carstairs?'

'You're drunk, Henry.'

'I know I'm drunk. What's wrong with being drunk, for Christ's sake?'

'You need to pull yourself together, Henry.'

'I have pulled myself together. I'm going to marry Elizabeth. I've put my house in order. The whole caboodle's different now. I've put my house in order,' he said again, because he liked the expression.

Carstairs' wife said she'd like him to go now if he didn't mind. 'And kindly take him with you,' she said, pointing at Mr Maloney. 'Really, Henry!'

He'd been the best man at her wedding. She hadn't been so dumpy then, or so unpleasant. She'd been quite a good-looking little thing, he'd considered Carstairs quite lucky. He reached behind him for the cushion on the arm of the sofa, not wanting any of them to see what he was up to. He grasped the cushion with the tips of his fingers and threw it across the room at Mrs Carstairs, trying to cheer things up. 'Pass, pass, pass!' he cried, lurching forward, preparing himself for a rugby pass. He laughed and clapped his hands, but Mrs Carstairs didn't return the cushion to him.

'God, isn't it a great gas?' said Mr Maloney.

All of a sudden it seemed to Henry that Mr Maloney was the only civilized person in the room. He felt angry that he'd brought this man, a man he hardly knew, to the house of friends and that the friends had let him down. Someone had said, he couldn't remember who, that this inoffensive man wasn't entirely sane.

'Listen,' Henry said belligerently, 'what's up? Would you mind telling me,' he said to Mrs Carstairs, 'just what the trouble is?'

She didn't reply. He reminded her that he'd been the best man at her wedding. At Anstey Grange, he said, her husband had had no position at all. Her husband had been a cheat and a liar. D'arcy had knocked the front teeth out of a boy called Pinmack-Jones. Bodger Harrison had predicted that they'd end up in the gutters of Soho. 'That woman there,' Henry said, pointing to Peggy D'arcy, 'sat down on the floor as though I hadn't eyes in my head to see through her underclothes. I'm a human being,' he said to Peggy D'arcy, raising his voice. 'like anyone else.'

'You're a bloody fool, Henry,' D'arcy said.

'I'm actually not a bloody fool. I'm actually a human being –'

'Oh, for God's sake, Henry!' D'arcy shouted.

'Am I or am I not a human being?'

'Of course you're a human being.'

'Well then.'

'Stop shouting, Henry,' D'arcy said.

'Listen: I came out here tonight in a perfectly decent way to show you the car I've got. I came out here with that man there, who I had a few drinks with. I came out here specially and there isn't a civil word out of any of you. Listen,' he said, swaying forward so that his face was close to Carstairs' where he wanted it to be. 'Listen. Did a woman ever sit half-naked in a room with you, crouched down on the carpet so that you could see every bloody part of her body? Not enticing you, mind, but because she didn't think you mattered.'

'Will you kindly shut up,' D'arcy snapped at him. 'You've practically got the d.t.'s, Henry. You don't know what you're talking about.'

'Did Bodger Harrison know what he was talking about when he said you'd end up in the gutters of Soho?'

'Oh, for heaven's sake, give over about Bodger Harrison!'

'They were dodgy at school,' Henry said to Mr Maloney, 'and they've been dodgy ever since. As a matter of fact, they interfere with patients.'

There was a silence in the room when Henry said that, a silence he enjoyed. He enjoyed the feeling of having caused it, and the sight of Peggy D'arcy's flushed face. Carstairs' wife began to say something but Carstairs prevented her by placing a hand on her arm. Carstairs said something himself, but Henry didn't listen to him. He attempted to light his cigarette again and this time he succeeded.

'I am not a bloody fool,' he said, not bothering to raise his voice to say it.

Mr Maloney nodded and went on nodding. D'arcy, whose face was redder than his wife's, laughed unpleasantly. 'If you want to know the truth,' he said, 'you're pathologically hopeless.'

Henry ignored that remark. He said he did not intend, ever again, to enter the house he was in, or to enter the King of England on a Saturday at lunchtime or on a Sunday at lunchtime. He said he did not intend ever again, on a Saturday afternoon, to go to see Rosslyn Park playing rugby. 'In case by chance I run into people who cheat and knock other people's teeth out.' He was going now, he said to Mr Maloney, and would be able to give him a lift.

There was some confusion in the room then. There were protests and voices were raised in alarm, and then in some kind of agreement. Henry didn't listen. He spoke again to Mr Maloney, but Maloney didn't rise from his chair. 'Are you coming?' Henry said. 'D'you want a lift?'

'I don't know. Dare I trust myself to you? Are you fit?'

'As a matter of fact, I drive a damn sight better –'

'I think I'd rather the other man did the driving, mister.'

'You are not to drive, Henry,' Carstairs said.

Henry laughed. He was going to the lavatory, he said, falling against Peggy D'arcy as he left the room. He laughed again and said he'd had one or two drinks too many. 'Sorry,' he said.

There was a taste of whisky in his mouth and then he was sick, just before he reached the lavatory door. He held on to the wall and opened the door and was sick again. When he'd finished he washed his face. The suit he'd bought that morning was wet where something had been spilt on it. He didn't want to go into the sitting-room again. He wanted to go to bed.

He felt better with the wind in his face, with both front windows open and the cold air pulling across him as he drove. You could drive mechanically. It was like walking, after so many years of pulling the self-starter and turning the lights on and letting the choke in. Even in a car you weren't used to, it was just like walking. The secret was not to go fast.

The other car passed him and then slowed. An arm, protruding from a window, waved up and down. He eased the Viva towards the kerb and brought it to a halt.

'Morning, sir,' the policeman said.

'Good morning to you, sir.'

There was a second policeman behind the first one, reading the black lettering on the side of the car.

'Sorry to stop you, sir. Late-night check, sir. Can you tell us what you're carrying on top of your car?'

'What?'

'You have a wrapped object on the roof of your car, sir.'

Henry stepped out of the Viva. On the road he felt unsteady, due to having to stand upright and at the same time glance at the top of the car.

'Oh, that,' he said. 'It's a fish, actually.'

'Fish, sir?'

The second policeman drew the attention of his colleague to the black lettering. Henry undid one of the ropes that he'd bought from the night-watchman on the building site. He pulled aside part of the canvas, revealing the fish's tail. The fish was a business symbol, he said.

'You're a fishmonger, sir?'

'Actually, I'm an area sales executive.' He found it difficult to tie the two ends of the rope again. He wound them together, resolving to make a better job of it some other time.

'Executive, sir?'

'That's right.'

'Could we see your licence, sir? And your insurance?'

Henry leaned against the side of the car and took his wallet from the inside pocket of his new suit. He'd have preferred to have handed the wallet to the policeman so that the policeman could find the licence and insurance certificate himself, but he knew that this would be regarded suspiciously. He poked through the wallet and eventually found the required documents.

The policeman handed them back to him. 'Would you mind telling me the registration number of this vehicle, sir?'

Without thinking, Henry gave the registration number of the Zephyr.

Both policemen shook their heads.

'Oh, of course,' Henry said, and he explained that he'd been confusing this car with another car, an old Zephyr he'd just sold. He'd only taken delivery of this one this afternoon, he explained. He had no idea what the registration number was.

'It's a way we have of finding out if a vehicle's stolen, sir. An old dodge, sir.'

'Yes, well, it's not stolen, actually.'

'Oh, you're absolutely in the clear, sir. Just a late-night check, sir. We get a lot of stolen vehicles up and down this road in the small hours. And vehicles carrying stolen goods, all sorts of things, sir. Which is why we were curious about your fish. Sorry about that, sir.'

'That's quite all right.'

'You say you're a sales executive, sir?'

'That's right.'

'And tell me this, sir. Do you think it right and proper for a sales executive to be driving about in the small hours in the kind of condition you're in at present, sir?'

'Condition?'

'Would you mind just breathing into this little bag, sir?'

Carstairs drove Mr Maloney from Kingston Hill to Shepherd's Bush. In Roehampton Lane they passed Henry and the two policemen. The bag was being held up to Henry's mouth by one of them. The other waved Carstairs' car on.

'Will you look at your man?' said Mr Maloney. 'Isn't that fellow the hard case, sir?'

Carstairs did not reply. Mr Maloney had made other remarks to which he had not replied, either. He drove carefully, well within the speed limit. Ever since Henry had called him a cheat he'd felt anger, like a piece of ice, enlarging inside him somewhere. 'I never knew you cheated at school,' she'd say when he returned, on top of everything else.

'Excuse me,' Mr Maloney said. 'I'm feeling unwell.'

19

Henry kept struggling his way out of sleep and then thankfully slipping into it again. The nausea he'd experienced early the night before came at him in waves, the back of his neck and his right eye ached. In his mind there was a confusion which began with the assistant in the shop saying the new suit fitted him like a glove, and ended with a policeman asking him to breathe into a bag. Threads ran through the confusion, but the threads were confused themselves. He didn't want to unravel them.

Beneath the sheet and blankets, Henry still wore the suit he had bought, and the shirt and socks and his Radley tie. There were no shoes on his feet, but otherwise he was as he'd been in the Carstairs' sitting-room. He didn't want to remember the Carstairs' sitting-room, or the man in a hat who'd been there, a man he had a feeling of responsibility for in his mind, as though he'd brought him to the Carstairs' house. He couldn't remember the details of the man's face, only that the face had been red. He remembered being sick outside the Carstairs' lavatory, in the hall.

Every time he woke more of it came back to him. He heard his own voice in the Carstairs' sitting-room, talking about Peggy D'arcy in her underclothes, saying that Elizabeth had promised to marry him and that Carstairs had cheated at school. He remembered being in the King of England, and trying to persuade Felicity and the salesmen from Putney Square-Deal Motors to come with him to Carstairs' house.

It was dark, but outside his window, too faint yet to penetrate the room, a muzzy dawn was beginning. With an effort, he drew his left arm from beneath the bedclothes and felt on his wrist for his watch. The luminous hands suggested that the time was twelve thirty-five. Automatically he listened for the watch's tick, and didn't hear it. 'Oh, and he's on the ropes,' a distant, wavering voice cried, after he'd located and switched on the transistor radio on his bedside table. It was the night before in Las Vegas. He wished it was the night before in London.

197

In the darkness he moved a knob. A woman spoke in rapid French and then a man in German. The time, an English voice said, was six-thirty. Henry turned the radio off.

In this same bed he had lain, with his wife wide-eyed beside him, going through a series of events that had ended in some other disaster, trying to sort things out. Through calm, dead, headachy mornings he had tried to find reasons, he had waded backwards through cause and effect. In this same bed the day after he'd been sacked from his job in the tyre division of the rubber company, he'd tried to understand. 'I'm afraid you're not quite right for us,' Mr Dibbens had said. 'On a number of counts.' A year before, Mr Dibbens had been excessively enthusiastic. Like Mr Bastable and Mr Ring, he'd said that Henry was just the kind of material his firm was looking for. Things had just gone wrong. Things went wrong repetitively. Whenever they went right they turned round, like an army of some kind, and went wrong again. You couldn't fight them.

Reflecting on that and recalling in a jumble some of the bits and pieces of the day before, Henry wanted not, ever again, to have to get out of the bed he was in.

'My God Almighty,' he said, on his back staring into the gloom. 'My God Almighty.'

An hour later on that same day, Thursday, 15 February, George Trigol, in charge of the furnaces in Cheltenham Street Women's Hospital, awoke and rose immediately. Some streets away Nurse Hampshire awoke to find herself in the arms of Dr Pennance and hoped that no one had missed her in the nurses' home. Sister Kolulu stepped out of the hospital into the soft morning air, ready for her sleep. 'Morning, Sister,' Pengelly said in Cheltenham Street, hurrying to go on duty. In her small bed-sitting-room in Battersea the woman with the banner made herself cocoa on a gas ring.

On that day, too, in the institution called St Clare's Home for London's Girls, the illegitimate and the abandoned rose and washed themselves in a disciplined manner. And in the institution from which Miss Samson had taken Arthur, to do the rough work at Number Nine, the handicapped rose also. In the Sunset Home in Richmond the elderly slept on.

In the Caledonian Hotel in Aberdeen Mrs Vincent, in her bath, thought about Aidallbery. In the Morning Star Hotel in Liverpool Declan's uncle stood uniformed in the hall. In the Foxley Hotel in Bishop's Stortford a couple called Mr and Mrs Rulke, married for sixteen years, occupied the room that Elizabeth had once spent a weekend in, Number Eleven. Elsewhere in Aberdeen the face of Mrs Vincent was part of Aidallbery's first moment of consciousness. Elsewhere in Liverpool Declan's uncle who was in the priesthood celebrated mass. Elsewhere in Bishop's Stortford people yawned and got up.

In her commune in Somerset Mrs Geraldine Tabor-Ellis still slept, as did Joanna and Samuel. The girl who had played the harp the night before milked the goats.

Bugner Stays the Course the morning papers said everywhere, keen with the news from Las Vegas.

In the Marie Atkins Ward they talked, but still Miss Samson did not mention her trouble because her trouble was still a private matter. Nor did Lily repeat all that Kenneth had told her, but only said that Kenneth had for the first time in his life quarrelled with his mother. Sylvie, who had told the night before of Declan's defection, spoke about her clothes and said that the way things were at the moment it didn't look as if she'd have any to go home in, wherever home was. Elizabeth had not mentioned the night before anything about Henry's proposal and she did not mention it now. She'd said who Henry was, her childhood friend. She could lend Sylvie something to wear, she promised, but Sylvie said her friend, Sharon Timpson, probably would.

There was a picture of a church in Taunton on the postcard Elizabeth received from Joanna. *It's really good here*, the message on the other side said. *I'll write a letter soon.*

Dear Lily, Mrs Drucker had written. *We had a most unpleasant evening with Kenneth, who says we must not come and see you. He says we upset you, but Dad and me do not agree with Kenneth on this. It is all due to Kenneth worrying, and what I think is best to say is let bygones be bygones. Dad and me are trying best as we can to forget the things Kenneth said last night. I think you should ask Kenneth, Lily, why he said these things to his mother and father, bringing dirt into our home. Kenneth was always brought up as best we could. There was never anything like that, which seems to be something that has come since marriage. If Kenneth is going with other women it is his own affair, but there is no need to bring the details of it into our home. Dad joins me in what I say. Mr Caperdown's cavalry twill has come at last and Dad is busy with it, but very upset. As I am too and hoping for a reconciliation all round.*

Yours truly, Mavis Drucker.

P.S. Please reply and say if we are to come and see you, Lily. In the temper Kenneth's in there's no use Dad and me talking to him. M.D

Dear Mum and Dad, Mr and Mrs Drucker read. *As I said last night, there is no need to visit Lily in hospital because it upsets her. I will let you know when the baby is born. Yours, Kenneth.*

Joanna has joined a commune in Somerset, Aidallbery read, *run by a Mrs Geraldine Tabor-Ellis. I don't know the address. She went this morning, with a friend called Samuel. I was in no position to prevent her, as you can see. I simply thought you should know this. I am in here for a hysterectomy. Elizabeth.*

Dear Mummy, School dinner's worse than ever, Jennifer had written. *Fish fingers that were bad, Alice wouldn't eat them. Hope you are getting better. XX.*

Dear Mummy, Alice had written. *I made a pig out of bits of paper. Miss Bawden showed the class. Miss Bawden said to write this letter. I said we were coming to see you but she said write anyway.*

Sylvie tore an envelope open, realizing that she didn't know what his handwriting looked like. There was a card inside the envelope, a Get Well Soon card from the girls in the Woolworth's basement. *A little bird told us*, the message said, *you'll soon be out and about!*

There are mysteries everywhere, the Reverend Rawes had written. *We cannot understand. 'Behold, the bush burned with fire and the bush was not consumed.' The miracles are mysteries, too. The loaves, the fish, the water into wine, the healing of the sick, the walking on the water. Would we, meeting Him face to face, understand our Lord God? 'For the imagination of man's heart is evil from his youth' means only that evil is within us and must be struggled with. That was the import of my sermon in St Matthew's. God does not mean our worship to be an easy task. Nor has He made His world an easy place.*

In dreams and in reality there will always be evil within us. Pray with me, Miss Samson. I have told no one at Number Nine of this private matter.

He must have written the letter immediately after visiting her the evening before. He'd caught the eight forty-five post. It worried her that she'd made him so anxious.

'We got Dick Emery's autograph,' Alice shouted at Mrs Orvitski. 'Daddy's getting married.'

'*An American lady called Pamela Vincent*,' Jennifer read from the letter.

'So.' Mrs Orvitski was sniffish. 'So,' she said again, and made other

200

small noises of disapproval and distaste. She knew Aidallbery only by reputation and did not care for the sound of him.

'You'd think he'd have had enough of marriage,' Jennifer said.

'Ready for school, please,' Mrs Orvitski commanded.

'D'you think Mummy'll marry again?' Alice asked. 'That Henry fancies her.'

'Please for school now,' Mrs Orvitski cried. 'Please for school immediately.'

The horn of Mrs Singwell's Hillman Estate sounded outside. 'I've lost a gym shoe,' Alice said.

'Oh, for Jesus' sake!' shouted Jennifer from the hall.

'Go now,' cried Mrs Orvitski, pushing at Alice.

But Alice insisted on finding her gym shoe, which was in her bed, and then made her way at her own leisurely pace downstairs. Mrs Singwell had got out of her estate car and was at the hall door. She'd been ten minutes late at the school the day before, she said. Marks were taken off if the children were late, she told Mrs Orvitski, and her own child didn't consider it fair that marks should be taken off just because two other girls weren't ready in time. 'You can see her point,' Mrs Singwell said with an abrasive smile, and Mrs Orvitski, who had begun to feel tired, promised to do better in future.

In Aberdeen he was greatly vexed. It was not the time for a burden like this. Joanna was in her final year at school, she had A-levels to take. It was nonsense that she had been permitted to take off to a commune in Somerset, run by a Mrs Tabor-Ellis.

A hysterectomy: well, women had their operations, not many of them escaped with nothing at all. If she married again there could be no more children. There'd hardly have been anyway, at forty-one. It wasn't unlike her, that she didn't know the address of the place their daughter had gone to.

'I shall have to fly down,' he said later that morning to Mrs Vincent. 'Elizabeth's in hospital, having a hysterectomy. Extraordinary that she didn't send a wire.'

If he was flying anywhere, his bride-to-be announced, she intended to accompany him.

'So be it,' he agreed with a smile, amused at that way of putting it.

20

Henry boiled a kettle and made tea. He sat at the kitchen table drinking it, staring out at the long grass in his garden. Tea with milk and lots of sugar was good for a hangover, he'd once heard on a radio programme. He drank slowly, the pain remaining at the back of his neck and in his eye. He had pins and needles in both hands, and numbness in the joints of his legs. As part of a hangover, he had experienced these symptoms before.

Beside him on the table, the transistor radio which he'd carried downstairs from his bedroom murmured information that it had murmured already – on the hour and on the half hour, between music and the fighting of the flab. 'Defeat with honour,' the voice of a sports reporter said, a message recorded earlier in Las Vegas. 'Sir Alf's naturally jubilant,' another voice revealed, referring to the outcome of a different contest, a 5–0 victory for the English football team over the Scots.

He didn't know how he'd got to bed, and wondered if the police had put him there. He wouldn't be allowed to drive again for twelve months. Breathing into a breathalyzer bag when you were drunk was the same as hearing a magistrate saying that he intended to deprive you of your licence. The car with the fish on top of it would be in some pound with the cars of other early-morning drunks. It didn't really matter where it was.

On the stairs the telephone rang. He listened to the sound, and the pain in his right eye throbbed in rhythm with it. After five minutes the ringing ceased, but in his eye the throbbing persisted.

Nothing mattered, when you thought about it. It didn't matter that people let you down, that a wife let you down, not sticking to you, and Timus, not speaking in the car. It didn't matter about D'arcy and Carstairs, who should have been able to forgive a drunk. Or about Elizabeth, who could have changed everything. None of it could possibly matter in the long run.

In the model-railway club at Anstey they used to make coffee. D'arcy used to buy it somewhere, a quarter of a pound at a time in a brown paper bag tightly tied with string. They toasted bread they'd taken from the dining-hall, and once D'arcy had a tin of grape jam. 'For God's sake, of course I'm going to be a doctor,' Carstairs repeatedly insisted. D'arcy laughed, with grape jam all over his chin. D'arcy used to say that Carstairs would make a good builder's labourer.

For no particular reason Henry remembered a time when his knee had been caught between the bars of a chair-back. He had cried because he was frightened, but his father had laughed, saying they'd have to saw the leg off, sawing a bar off the chair instead. They laughed together while his father sawed, and afterwards his father stuck the chair with glue. 'Henry's chair,' his mother used to say.

Henry watched the minute hand of the electric clock on the wall. All over London, all over the world, hands were moving at precisely the same rate, uncompetitively. The clock had a pale blue surround. He remembered hanging it on the wall, four or five years ago, drilling a hole and putting a Rawlplug in and then a screw. She'd bought him the clock for his birthday; his thirty-eighth birthday, it probably had been. His watch had never been accurate, and people used to telephone the house to say he'd been due with supplies for their machines an hour ago. It was the watch that made him late, he explained, so she bought him an electric clock. He remembered her handing him the clock and then he remembered her on Sunday, waving from the window of the mock-Tudor block of flats. He remembered the grimness in her face towards the end of her time in Meridian Close. He remembered her saying she thought she was going mad.

He drank more tea and felt slightly better. There was a warmth in his stomach where the sickness had been before. He felt hungry. He'd go out at eleven o'clock and get a bottle of Bell's – or Haig, or Teacher's, it didn't matter, they were all the same – and he'd buy a Fray Bentos pie and a packet of frozen peas. There were potatoes in the vegetable rack under the sink, which he'd cut up and fry. He'd have a really good meal, whenever he felt like it, when he didn't want to drink any more.

He took his wallet from the inside pocket of his suit and discovered that it contained a single pound. In change, mainly in two-pence pieces, he counted out a pound and fifty-eight pence. It wasn't enough for a bottle of whisky, and on this particular occasion he didn't want to buy a half bottle.

He left the kitchen and went upstairs to his bedroom, carrying his cup of tea. The house was full of two-p pieces; he was always making little stacks of them when he came in from emptying a machine. He remembered that when he'd been clearing out the rubbish he'd collected all the coins and put them into some old handcream jars she'd left behind her. He found the jars on the bedroom window-sill. They contained two pounds and seventeen pence in assorted nickel and copper coins. He'd have plenty left over for the pie and the frozen peas.

The telephone rang again. He stood on the stairs looking at it. He found a crushed packet of cigarettes in his pocket and lit one. Sometimes when he smoked with a hangover it caused the sickness to return to his stomach, but the smoke he inhaled now seemed to have the opposite effect. The telephone ceased to ring. 'Anyone at home?' a voice was shouting through the letter-box.

Two youths were standing on his doorstep, tough-looking youths with closely-cut dark hair and pointed faces. At first he couldn't understand what they were saying: they appeared to be talking about the roof of his house. They gestured at him, indicating that he should step out into Meridian Close. They pointed at his roof. There were tiles missing, they said; they had ladders in the neighbourhood, they would replace the tiles cheaply. He shook his head. He offered the youths cigarettes from his crushed packet because he felt he'd wasted their time by not understanding what they were saying. They took one each. He'd soon find rain coming in, they warned him. It didn't matter, he said.

In the house he made more tea. He remembered one night about a year ago he'd tried to get Felicity in the King of England to come back with him to try his beer, because for some reason he didn't want to return to Meridian Close on his own. Felicity was only about twenty, but after all the conversations he'd had with her and all the drinks he'd bought her, her age didn't seem a deterrent to the formation of a deeper relationship between them. In the King of England she wore mini-skirts and sometimes dresses that dipped low across her tightly clasped breasts. He'd often found his eyes wandering over her body as he leaned on the bar, and long before the night he'd invited her back to Meridian Close he'd begun to think that he'd quite like to be married to her. As far as he could see, she was a girl who never became angry. She blew kisses to him when he came in at night, when the bar was too busy for her to greet him more formally. But on the night he'd invited her to Meridian Close she'd told him she had a boyfriend. After that, as soon as he began to take Elizabeth out he'd realized that Felicity would have been far too young.

As he drank his tea, Henry wondered what exactly had happened that night. He remembered waiting in the lavatory of the King of England until the whole place was quiet, and then coming out and finding Felicity and the landlord clearing up. He remembered beginning to collect the ashtrays from the tables, and when the landlord had gone down to the cellar he remembered making the suggestion to Felicity, putting his arm around her waist. He'd been drunk or he wouldn't have done it. He'd kissed her, and a tray of glasses had somehow been upset, but she hadn't been angry with him as far as he could recall. The next day he hadn't referred to the matter, nor had she.

With D'arcy and Carstairs, of course, that kind of not referring wouldn't be possible. Nor would it be advisable to pretend that something hadn't happened when dealing with Mr Bastable and Mr Ring. Twenty or so years ago he'd have attempted to perform the duties allocated to him without the assistance of the provided car, but experience in the meanwhile had taught him that after a month or less he would be apologizing to Mr Bastable and Mr Ring for attempting to deceive them. The truth of the matter was that his misfortunes of the night before were of a different nature from the misfortune of the lawnmower and the fish on top of the car, and the attempt to get Felicity back to sample his beer. There was no way of continuing as if nothing had happened.

He wanted to go and get the whisky but for some reason he didn't want to be seen in Meridian Close, and if he had to be seen he didn't want to be recognized. He found an old tweed hat that he hadn't worn for years, and a mackintosh coat that he didn't wear much now, either. His sunglasses were in a drawer in the kitchen.

He opened the hall door cautiously and went down the paved path with his head bent. But as he turned into the Close itself he saw the Passes coming towards him, with a dog. He crossed to the other pavement, hurrying, turning away from them like a criminal in a film. 'How's the lawnmower going?' Mrs Passes called across the road. He didn't look in their direction. He didn't answer.

On the way to the King of England, Henry called in at two other public houses and drank a pint of beer in each. He stayed for a short while in the second one, watching the barman scrubbing a draining-board. He could have purchased the bottle of whisky in either, but he wanted to get it in the King of England. He wanted to see Felicity in her mini-skirt, to hear her laugh in her nice, happy, relaxed way. He wanted to sit there and watch her serving her lunchtime customers.

The barman who was scrubbing the draining-board was a cheerless, uncommunicative person who reminded him of the man who'd given him the keys to the Viva the evening before. There was a smell of disinfectant coming from the draining-board, which had the effect of bringing on his nausea again.

He walked along the Upper Richmond Road, feeling better in the breezy air. The pain in his eye had lessened and if he didn't move his head too quickly the aching at the back of his head wasn't too bad. He bought a small tube of codeine in a chemist's, and in the Express Dairy next door he bought a Fray Bentos steak-and-kidney pie, Bird's Eye peas, and a packet of raspberry mousse.

'Good morning, Henry,' Felicity said in the King of England.

She was as fresh as a daisy in a tiny white dress with lace on it. Her nice legs emerged gracefully from beneath its skirt, the division between her breasts was tight under pressure. He could have married her tomorrow and been happy with her. He could have sat with her for ever in his kitchen, smoking cigarettes and listening to programmes on the transistor, *The Archers*, and sports reports, and Alan Dell with the big band music of the forties.

'I think I'll have a little Scotch,' he said.

Everyone had kept saying no to him last night. Even the man he'd brought to the Carstairs' house had seemed to say no in the end. Everyone had told him not to drive.

'I got drunk last night,' he said.

Felicity laughed. 'I know you did, Henry.'

'Have something yourself. And cigarettes, Felicity, and a bottle of Bell's or something.'

'Haig all right?'

'They're all the same.'

She laughed again in the same nice way. She'd have a lager, she said.

He paid her, and then the men from Putney Square-Deal Motors arrived and asked him how he was feeling. 'Where d'you end up, old chap?' the larger one inquired, sprawling over the bar.

'Whatever became of that extraordinary man?' the smaller one asked.

'God knows.' He smiled at them, lighting a cigarette. He didn't want to talk about going to the Carstairs' house, or his journey back from the Carstairs' house. 'I see Bugner stayed to the finish,' he said.

He remained in the King of England until three o'clock. When he emerged into the afternoon sunlight he was drunk.

In Meridian Close Henry sat in his kitchen again, drinking the whisky. At five o'clock he sliced the potatoes and lit the gas oven in readiness for the pie. He'd had a lot of the Haig, he noticed. It was surprising sometimes how much whisky you could drink if you mixed it with ordinary water, or how much gin if you mixed it with orange squash. There was nothing like drink, in a way. It got you up there, it dragged you there from nowhere. On a radio programme he'd once heard someone say that if he should ever be wrecked on a desert island he'd like to be allowed to take a distillery with him.

The telephone rang, but he didn't answer it. It would be the swimming-baths attendant or the woman at the Washthru Launderette, not anyone else, not anyone interesting. It wouldn't be Elizabeth to say it wasn't out of the question, she'd made a mistake. It wouldn't be D'arcy or Carstairs to ask him how he was, to ask him in the name of friendship if he'd got safely home and hadn't been killed in a drunken accident. It wouldn't be the Putney Square-Deal Motors men to say they thought he'd been a bit off-colour at lunchtime and were concerned. Or Felicity to say she loved him.

For the third time that day the ringing of the telephone continued unheeded and shrill in the otherwise silent house. He turned the gas low under the potatoes, not wanting them to be cooked for a little while longer because he didn't feel like eating until he'd had some more to drink. The noise from the telephone ceased. Outside, it had begun to drizzle.

For a long time he sat at the kitchen table, sipping at his whisky, pouring more and adding water to it. He walked about the house once, upstairs, into the room Timus had occupied, and into the bedroom he'd shared. He found it difficult to retain his balance on the stairs when he was coming down again. He had to hold the banister-rail tightly; he slipped and the whisky in his glass spilt over his trousers.

He stood for a moment in the doorway of the sitting-room, surveying the familiar contents, the stained grey carpet, the empty book-shelves on either side of the fireplace, the two armchairs, the television set, the sofa. In this room, it seemed to him now, all the trouble had been contained. In one of the armchairs she'd waited for him when he returned later than he'd said he would. On the sofa men he'd brought back from the King of England had spent the night, after the beer was finished. There had been quarrels here: her shrieking voice drilling out accusations, his mumbling in reply.

In the kitchen he turned the gas off altogether, thinking he'd heat the food up later on. He filled his glass again and took it to the garden, walking through the grass he hadn't managed to cut, careful with the movement of his legs in case people in other houses were looking out of their windows. He'd forgotten to put on his hat and the sunglasses, but it didn't matter because no one would be about in the drizzle, no one would want to talk to him.

207

He hadn't had his bonfire. The rubbish was all there, the cardboard cartons and the clothes she'd left behind, and the old copies of the *Radio Times*, and the letters they'd exchanged. The weeds he'd pulled up were still there, too. They might even burn if the fire became hot enough. He found paraffin in a drum outside the kitchen window, and began to pour some into an old Suncrush Orange bottle, but when the bottle was half full he decided that he'd really rather sit in the kitchen.

He sat with a third of the Haig bottle left. The last time anything had been any good was an afternoon at Radley when he'd scored ninety-three not out in the second innings. He remembered it abruptly, knowing for certain that that was the last occasion. After that, there was only the business of leaving Radley and the boredom of learning about how to buy and sell wine, and then the boredom of women's clothing and motor-car tyres and showers for hotels and the *Encyclopædia Britannica* and Rammage. If Bodger Harrison had been absurd, so were D'arcy and Carstairs. Better to end up in a Soho gutter than to end as they'd done, playing bridge on Kingston Hill. They weren't the same people who'd made coffee in the model-railway room, or the people who'd smoked in the shed in Carstairs' garden, or the people who'd roamed the golf course. 'We're not the same,' Elizabeth had said in her hospital bed. 'Don't you see, Henry?' At the time he hadn't.

From as far back as he could remember, right up until the day he'd made ninety-three not out in the second innings, everything had been happy. There'd been happiness with his parents, listening to his father's jokes, sleeping in the garden in a tent he and his father had put up, telling his mother all the things he one day intended to do. Even at Miss Henderson's and Miss Gamble's Kindergarten there'd been happiness, because Miss Henderson and Miss Gamble had liked him. He hadn't worked hard enough for them, sometimes he hadn't worked at all, but even so they'd liked him. *A happy disposition*, someone had written on a report at Anstey Grange.

You couldn't go back to that. You didn't have to at the moment because you were sitting in a kitchen with most of a bottle of Haig whisky inside you, almost as drunk as you could possibly be. You were forty-one years of age and ever since that last walk back to the pavilion you'd made a bog of every single thing. You'd made a bog of it because it wasn't worth making anything else of it. It was dreary and grey and full to the brim of Mrs Passes wanting two pounds for a lawnmower, and a tired woman waving from the window of the mock-Tudor flats, and Felicity thinking it amusing when a man of forty-one wanted to sit in his kitchen with her. It was full of four kinds of powdered soup in

New-Way's Mark-4, and salty-bacon crisps, and cheese-and-onion crisps, and Bovril-flavoured crisps, and Nutty Pops. All the way to the pavilion there'd been clapping, but when you were drunk in your kitchen you had to tell the truth: you couldn't cope with it because you didn't like it. There'd been clapping, and that had been that. From that day on, there had first and foremost been the business of getting drunk.

Henry laughed and poured more whisky. He felt as he'd felt that morning, when he'd woken up and hadn't ever wanted to get out of the bed he was in. He felt now that he never again wished to return to the ordinariness of sobriety, to people saying no to him, and people no longer liking him, as Miss Henderson and Miss Gamble had liked him. He turned on the transistor radio on the table beside him: Dan Archer was speaking, talking to his son Phil about a bull.

Aloud, Henry said he felt fine. It was good, he said, to be as drunk as he was at ten to seven on a Thursday evening, with nice people talking about a bull. You could go on like that for ever, with Dan and Phil and Doris and Walter Gabriel, Sid Perks and the Tregorrans and old Zebedee Tring, and Lillian, and Joby Woodford. 'You certainly made no mistake with this one,' Dan said.

Henry got up and turned on the oven to heat up the pie again. He looked for a match but couldn't find one, and then realized that he'd left his cigarettes and matches outside, on the windowsill beside the Suncrush Orange bottle. It didn't really matter because when he drank a lot he didn't smoke much. 'You're going back to Brookfield, Phil?' Dan said. Henry laughed affectionately, feeling for the edge of the table so that he wouldn't fall as he made his way back to his chair. You did occasionally fall, he'd done it before, you had to be careful. The other thing was, you had to be careful about driving because you thought you were soberer than you were and there'd been that trouble last night. The edge of the table had unfortunately eluded him, but as he lay on the floor it didn't seem all that unfortunate because in point of fact the floor was quite comfortable.

Henry smiled, lying on the floor. He was happy, he said to himself. He might have been just dropping off to sleep in the tent, or even slogging Tick Rowlands's bowling. He was laughing, thinking of poor old Tick Rowlands, and Wiltshire Minor dropping the Bodger's false teeth into a saucepan of porridge and the false teeth appearing at breakfast, on Greenshield Minor's spoon. The smell was sweet in the kitchen, reminding him of something, he couldn't remember what. He didn't want to remember, anyway. No point in lying there thinking of smells, for heaven's sake, no point in being silly. The voice of Dan Archer came and went, and the voice of his son Phil came and went also.

The telephone rang again, and Henry continued to laugh. The smell was a smell of gas, which was coming from the open oven of the gas-cooker. He laughed more, thinking about that: he was lying drunk on the floor of his kitchen, finding it hard to move, and all the time gas was pouring out of the oven.

He laughed loudly and delightedly. He heard from where he was lying his own laughter bouncing about the kitchen, bouncing off Rammage and D'arcy and Carstairs and Carstairs' dumpy wife and Peggy D'arcy in her coffee underclothes. It bounced off the cold eyes of the men who'd employed him, off Mr Rinsal's eyes and T. J. B. Antler's eyes, off the eyes of Z. Jacob Nirenstein. It bounced off Nutty Pops and the Washthru Launderette and the homebrew in the bathroom and mushrooms in plastic bags and a fish on top of a Vauxhall Viva. It wasn't a sound like the elbow-gripping cawing of D'arcy or the squel-chier giggle of Carstairs. It wasn't a sound he foggily recalled making himself while he threw a cushion, while a man in a hat sat in the Car-stairs' smart sitting-room. It was a sound he hadn't made for years and years, and it seemed to Henry that he could make it now because he knew for a fact that the whole bloody lot of them were more absurd than poor old Bodger Harrison who'd eaten his moustache. His laugh-ter spluttered and gurgled, becoming louder and louder the more he thought about everything. It was the merriest sound he'd ever heard in that kitchen, Henry said to himself. He used to laugh like this, he began to say, but he couldn't think when. He was feeling great, he said to himself.

21

A day went by.

'That you should attempt, sir,' Mrs Tabor-Ellis said on the morning of Friday, 16 February, 'to conduct your daughter back to a decayed world is naturally your own affair. That you imagined you would succeed displays gross ignorance of all we are attempting here.'

'We have travelled from Scotland,' Mrs Vincent said.

'It is only to be regretted in that case that you have travelled so far for so brief an interview. I cannot help either of you.'

Mrs Tabor-Ellis stood firm, preventing entry. In the hired car that Aidallbery and his fiancée had taken from the station the driver read a newspaper. Twice before he had witnessed a similar scene in the farmhouse yard. On both occasions Mrs Tabor-Ellis had been triumphant.

'Good-day,' Mrs Tabor-Ellis said.

'Now listen to me,' Aidallbery began.

'No, sir, I will not listen to you. I have no intention of listening to you. I know your kind, Mr Aidallbery. I have only to look at your daughter.'

'Mrs Tabor-Ellis –'

'You daughter is repressed and dehumanized, sir. But she is also young. It is not too late to release the shackles.'

'Joanna hasn't finished her A-levels.'

'What are A-levels, Mr Aidallbery?'

'For God's sake, woman, you must know what A-levels are.'

'Do not call me woman.'

'Mrs Tabor-Ellis –'

'Any time you wish to join your daughter here, Mr Aidallbery, I can assure you I would do my utmost to find accommodation for you – provided you sought, as we all here seek, liberation from a world that has failed. There are thirty-eight of us here, six are of middle age or older; you would not be overwhelmed. We share all we possess. Our only wealth is the cultivation of goats and the sale of their milk. Our wheat and our mead is for home consumption only.'

'I would ask you kindly to listen to me, Mrs Tabor-Ellis.'

'It is pointless talking to me about A-levels, sir. Do me the honour of reading my book before you come here creating a hullabaloo.'

Mrs Tabor-Ellis closed her farmhouse door.

Later that morning Aidallbery and Mrs Vincent returned to Mrs Tabor-Ellis's farmhouse and waited in their hired car, in the hope of catching a glimpse of Joanna and approaching her direct. But their second visit turned out to be as fruitless as their first. Noticing the car, Mrs Tabor-Ellis emerged from her farmhouse and said that Joanna, having done her share of tending the farm's goats, had now gone to the river with her friends. 'To play,' Mrs Tabor-Ellis said, without specifying the nature of the play.

When he inquired where the river was and which area of it Joanna and her friends were playing at, Mrs Tabor-Ellis refused to say, and then became abusive.

They took a lunchtime train back to London.

That same morning, Elizabeth read an account of Henry's death in a newspaper. Carstairs read the same report and telephoned D'arcy, unable to believe that the report could be true. 'My God!' exclaimed D'arcy.

The men from Putney Square-Deal Motors read it, and Rammage of New-Way Vending Limited, and the residents of Meridian Close. The Passes at once telephoned the police, to report that on the morning of the tragedy they had met the deceased as they were returning to their house, having taken the dog for a walk. He was wearing sunglasses, they stated, although the weather hardly warranted them, and a hat they had never seen him wearing before, and a soiled mackintosh coat. 'Did he seem depressed?' a desk-sergeant inquired, and Mr Passes replied that in his opinion the deceased had most definitely been depressed. He'd been walking in a strange manner, as though he had hurt himself, and when spoken to had not replied. Henry's immediate neighbours told the police, when the police called on them, that they'd observed him in the course of the afternoon, walking unsteadily around his garden with a glass in his hand.

Later that morning Mr Maloney extracted a newspaper from a wastebin attached to an electric-light pole. He folded it more neatly than its previous owner had done and tucked it under his arm. With his first drink of the day in front of him in the Cruskeen Bawn, he read the newspaper from cover to cover, including the item that concerned a death in Meridian Close. He shook his head over it, deploring the effects strong drink could have on a man, unaware that the man mentioned in the item was the one in whose company he had spent the previous Wednesday evening.

Some boys at the preparatory school called Anstey Grange read of the death and were unaffected by it and uninterested, not knowing that Henry had been an old boy of their school. But boys at Radley learnt with fascination that a man who had accidentally gassed himself while drunk had been wearing a Radley tie.

Felicity read the news in the King of England and cried over it. She remembered the lager he'd bought her on the afternoon of his death, and the way he'd once tried to get her to go home with him. 'Poor old Henry,' she said, crying more painfully.

'Dead?' Timus said.

'Oh, darling.'

Timus cried. His mother cuddled him to her, feeling miserable herself.

'Poor Henry,' she said, tears falling on to Timus's fair hair.

Mr Bastable interviewed Henry's successor at twelve o'clock that day. 'Ask Mr Ring if he'd mind stepping by,' he murmured into his mushroom-coloured telephone, and when Mr Ring arrived they both agreed that Henry's successor was just the kind of material they were after.

It was some time before Elizabeth could bring herself to tell the other women in the ward. She did so after lunch, when she and Sylvie and Miss Samson were still sitting around the Formica-topped table. Lily had already gone back to bed.

'Henry's dead,' she said 'Henry's dead, Lily,' she said more loudly.

Lily stared at her, seeing her muzzily through her reading-glasses. 'Dead?'

'It's in the papers. He got drunk and gassed himself. They say it was an accident.'

'God, I read it!' Sylvie cried. 'I read it and I didn't know, I didn't realize –'

'Your friend?' Miss Samson said. 'The man who came here?'

'Yes.'

'He looked so cheerful,' Lily said.

Miss Samson recalled him as a man in a grey suit with a faint white stripe running through it. He'd come into the ward with a bunch of daffodils and he'd knocked against the bottom of her bed in an effort to avoid the Reverend Rawes, who'd been moving across the ward with a chair to sit on. His reddish hair was going grey, his face was brown with freckles. She'd wondered who he was at the time.

She listened while Mrs Aidallbery spoke of him, but Mrs Aidallbery wasn't talking about a man with hair going grey. Listening, Miss Samson visualized this man and Mrs Aidallbery playing together in their childhood. In a children's pretence they had a shop which sold strawberries and cream. Once they'd swung on a door and damaged it.

It seemed that he might have deliberately taken his life. He had apparently sat down and drunk whisky and then turned on gas taps, confused by the whisky, or not confused, nobody quite knew. Food he'd prepared had gone cold, not touched, as though he'd had second thoughts about taking a last meal. *Death by misadventure*, the paper said. From being that child, he had become someone whom people had a way of looking down on, Mrs Aidallbery had said. Mrs Aidallbery was trying not to weep. She had wept already; the rims of her eyes were red, there were marks of tears on her cheeks.

Miss Samson left the table and returned to her bed. She lay in bed hearing the whispering of the other three, sensing the rawness of this recent, awful death. A week ago she would have prayed. 'O God, look after him,' she would have asked, and would have prayed that other people, lonely and distracted and looked down upon, should not be careless about death. A week ago she would have attempted to offer comfort to Mrs Aidallbery, even though none of it was her business.

'Well, we're looking glum today,' Sister O'Keeffe remarked, bustling into the ward, starched garments crackling as she walked.

'A friend of Elizabeth's died,' Lily said.

'Oh, my dear, I'm sorry.' The words came rapidly, without a trace of hesitation. The smile was slipped away, as one professional face replaced another. Yet the sympathy was genuine.

'The man who came on Wednesday,' Elizabeth said. 'I think you'd gone, Sister,' She looked away, not wanting to talk any more about it. She read the newspaper report again, as though it might say that the victim was recovering. But the print said what it had said before; there was no piece she'd overlooked, that contradicted everything.

'Heart?' Sister O'Keeffe said.

214

Sylvie told her it hadn't been heart, and then told her more. 'Oh no,' Sister O'Keeffe whispered.

There'd been alcoholic poisoning as well as the effect of gas, the report said. A police doctor had expressed the opinion that the deceased might have died anyway, even if there hadn't been an accident with gas. *Death by misadventure*, the report repeated.

A sound came from Miss Samson's bed. 'Oh dear, she's upset,' Sister O'Keeffe murmured. 'Come along now, Miss Samson,' she said more briskly, crossing to the bed.

Elizabeth closed her eyes to help her to concentrate on ridding herself of images she didn't want to see: Henry lying on his kitchen floor with his transistor radio still playing: Henry in Budleigh Salterton, pretending they had run away, talking to a woman in a dog-cart. No, she said to herself, I am not responsible for this death.

The hours of that afternoon went sluggishly by.

Elizabeth continued to be upset, and so in a different way did Miss Samson.

'I can't pray,' Miss Samson whispered, touching Elizabeth's hand. 'I can't pray any more. That poor man.' And then Miss Samson told Elizabeth about finding the diary. She told her because Elizabeth was an outsider, unconnected with Number Nine. She asked her not to tell anyone else. She repeated to Elizabeth the words Mr Ibbs had written and said they'd caused her to have a terrible nightmare. 'I'm so sorry,' she said, touching Elizabeth's hand again. 'I'm so sorry,' Mrs Aidallbery.'

Lily wrote to Mrs Drucker, saying she'd rather not be visited for a while at least, but her difficulties with her mother-in-law seemed slight compared with what had happened elsewhere. And to Sylvie the continued absence of Declan was slight in comparison also.

Mrs Orvitski opened the hall door and saw a tall, birdlike man standing on the step. He was wearing dark-rimmed spectacles and a dark-coloured overcoat over a darkish suit. There was a woman with him, tall also, with grey hair fashionably arranged.

'So?' Mrs Orvitski said.

'Good evening,' the man said.

'So?'

'We've come to see Jennifer and Alice. This is Mrs Vincent. I'm –'

'Mrs Aidallbery is in the hospital.'

'Yes, we know. I'm Mr Aidallbery.'

'Mr Aidallbery is in Aberdeen.'

'No, no. *I* am Mr Aidallbery.'

'So,' said Mrs Orvitski, opening the door a little more. 'You come in.'

He stood aside. Mrs Vincent, bearing a parcel wrapped in gold-coloured paper, stepped in first. So this was the house where they'd lived together for nineteen years, a house inherited from her father.

'What a charming house!' she said.

Mrs Orvitski led them through the hall. Still nothing had changed, he noticed. Nothing ever seemed to have changed in this house, from the first day he'd entered it.

'Oh, really!' cried Mrs Vincent, going to the french windows in the drawing-room, looking out at the narrow garden with its apple trees. 'Oh really, how charming!'

'I'll fetch the girls down,' Mrs Orvitski said.

So that was him. And that was the woman he was going to marry. *An American lady called Pamela Vincent.* She didn't like the look of either of them. He hadn't smiled and asked her if she was helping out, or said, as Mrs Aidallbery never stopped saying, that she was very kind. They hadn't been civil. She'd stood for a moment in the drawing-room, thinking they'd surely be civil then. But they'd turned straight away from her and looked out through the french windows. The woman hadn't the softness of Mrs Aidallbery.

She called the children on the stairs and again on the first-floor landing. They could have run out to the shop for sweets. They often went for sweets, where they got the money from she did not know. They'd slip through the garden and out of a door at the end of it, into the lane that ran to the nearby group of shops. 'Jennifer!' she called again. 'Alice child!'

They emerged from a room upstairs. She heard a door opening and closing, and then there was silence. They were playing a game with her. They were standing still on the upstairs landing, hoping to be a nuisance by not replying.

'Your daddy,' she said.

They came downstairs, half sliding on the banister in the way she'd told them not to, dragging their feet on the paint of the treads.

'Daddy?' Alice said. 'What about Daddy?'

'Please to wash hands and face in the bathroom. Please to comb hair.'

'Daddy's in Aberdeen,' Jennifer said.

'Your daddy is in this house now.'

They ran downstairs, taking no notice when she said again that they must wash themselves first.

'Hullo, Daddy,' Alice said in the drawing-room.

He kissed them both. He stood away from them and looked at them. He said they'd grown enormously.

'Hullo,' Mrs Vincent said.

He introduced them. He told them to shake hands with her. She smiled at them.

'Jennifer,' he said. 'And Alice.'

'Hullo,' Alice said.

'You're missing your mummy, I daresay,' Mrs Vincent said.

'Yes, we are,' Jennifer said.

'Is she the one you're going to marry, Daddy?'

'Alice!' Jennifer cried.

Mrs Vincent laughed. Aidallbery smiled a little. Mrs Vincent said: 'Yes, I'm the one, Alice. D'you think I'll do?'

'Do what?'

'Do as your father's wife.'

Alice stared at Mrs Vincent. She didn't say anything. Jennifer said: 'I hope you'll be very happy, Mrs Vincent. And Daddy.'

He nodded. Mrs Vincent said she was sure they would be happy. It was kind of Jennifer to hope that, she said. She handed her the gold-wrapped parcel and said it was for her and Alice.

'Chocolates?' Alice asked.

'Thank you very much,' Jennifer said.

'Oh, Lindt,' Alice cried when Jennifer had undone the wrapping paper. 'Very expensive.'

'Would you like one?' Jennifer offered the chocolates to Mrs Vincent and then to her father. Mrs Vincent said smilingly that she had to watch her figure. He shook his head.

'I'd like one,' Alice said.

They were all still standing. Mrs Vincent wondered if the stout woman who had let them in would perhaps arrive with coffee, but this did not occur.

'Well, let's sit down,' he said.

Jennifer and Alice sat on the sofa with the Lindt chocolates between them. Mrs Vincent and he occupied two armchairs near the french windows. He asked them about school.

'The dinners aren't eatable any more,' Alice said.

'Really?' murmured Mrs Vincent, interested in the garden.

'Shepherd's pie, you should smell it. Cold fish fingers, stew that hasn't even been *cooked*.'

'We're doing *Noye's Fludde*.'

He nodded, Mrs Vincent smiled again. She wondered what on earth *Noye's Fludde* was.

'I'm a rat.'

'Oh, how very sweet, Jennifer!' Mrs Vincent cried. 'A rat!'

'Are you an American?' Alice asked.

'Yes I am, Alice. From a place called Boston.'

'We've all heard of Boston, actually.'

'The Boston Tea Party,' Jennifer said quickly. 'We learnt about it at school.'

'Tea party?' Alice said. 'Boston's a town.'

Mrs Vincent laughed. 'Jennifer's quite right –'

'Miss Willoughby says she gets everything muddled up.'

'Well, we all get muddled now and –'

'*Muddled thinking*, Miss Willoughby put on her report.'

'Miss Willoughby didn't, Alice.'

'Miss Willoughby did. The end of the Easter term. And when Mummy saw her she said muddled, muddled. Even playing netball, she said.'

'Oh, Alice, for heaven's sake!'

The garden was looking bleak, he thought, and just a little neglected. The roses should have been pruned back in the autumn. There was canker in an apple tree.

'It really is a lovely garden,' Mrs Vincent said. 'Nice for playing in, I'm sure?'

'Mummy played there when she was little,' Alice said. 'She used to creep up on a man called Mr Giltrap.'

He remembered warm afternoons in the garden, sitting in a place he'd made for himself beyond the apple trees. She'd carry out tea to him; it was like being in the country.

'It's a nice old garden,' Alice said. 'It's nice when the snow comes.'

'It's lovely,' Jennifer murmured. 'I love it.'

Mrs Vincent said she liked gardens, too. When she was a child, she said, about Jennifer's age, she'd lived in Virginia, in a house with an old, grown-over garden, a most exciting place. There had been brambly roses, she said, with twisted branches as thick as your arm.

'*Branches*?' Alice said. '*Branches* on roses?'

'Really. Almost like trees the roses were, huge big bushes with gnarled branches.'

'We call them stems in England. You never saw a rose as big as a tree in England –'

'They were very old, Alice. They'd been there for generations.'

'If you saw a rose as big as a tree in England you'd think you'd gone mad in the night or something. Wouldn't you, Jennifer?'

'Mrs Vincent's trying to tell you, Alice.'

'They'd gone wild, you see. They'd just grown and grown, sucking up the good out of the soil, which was all going into the branches instead of the flowers. They had thorns an inch long.'

'A boy at school's got a banana tree.'

'Oh, Alice –'

'He has, Jennifer. Mikey Lasswell's got a banana tree in a pot. It's nearly as tall as his mum.'

'You can't grow banana trees in England.'

'I've seen it. I've actually touched it. It had little clutches of tiny, tiny –'

'Oh, don't tell lies, Alice.'

'I'm not telling lies.'

'Of course you are.'

'I tell you, I touched the blooming thing.'

He turned his head, reluctantly drawing his eyes from their survey of the garden. The chair he sat in had the same loose-cover on it, striped in two shades of blue. In nineteen years he must have sat in it several thousand times. To the right of the french windows, catching his glance as he swivelled it towards his children, were the two Persian miniatures that he had given her mother, that he'd bought in Isfahan and brought back specially for her.

'How's your granny?' he asked.

'In a home,' Alice said.

'Yes, I know. And do you still see her?'

They saw her once a month, Jennifer said, about once a month, sometimes more often. 'Mummy goes a lot,' she said. The last time they went, Alice said, Mrs Orpen had had a lapse of memory.

'I wonder if I could prevail on that good lady,' Mrs Vincent said, 'to bring us in a cup of coffee?'

She rose and moved towards the door. 'Who's going to show me the way?'

They both went with her, which surprised Mrs Vincent, because she'd imagined that Jennifer would probably have wished to have a quiet chat with her father. Alice she found a tiresome child, and hoped that a suggestion she'd made in the train, that both girls should in future spend some of their holiday time in Aberdeen, had not been rash.

He sat on, alone, in the drawing-room. The reminder that Mrs Orpen was in a home had distressed him. It distressed him more that he had lost her friendship. He felt cross and irritated suddenly, thinking of that. Why should the miniatures he'd bought her still hang in this room? They belonged now to no one in the house. He had chosen them for her specifically, two tiny paintings on ivory of a traditional polo scene, mounted on green velvet, framed in traditional mosaic. He had chosen them and then had gone away, walking about the evening streets of Isfahan, wondering if they were the right ones for her.

He rose from the blue-striped chair and crossed to the wall where the miniatures hung. He examined them for a moment, recalling again their selection and purchase. He lifted them from the wall and placed them on a table near the door, to take away when he and his fiancée left.

'Coffees?' Mrs Orvitski said. 'You want coffees, heh?'

'It would be lovely, if you wouldn't mind. You must be frightfully busy, of course –'

'So.'

Mrs Orvitski boiled a kettle. The girls went away with the box of chocolates they'd been given, which meant they wouldn't eat any of the supper she was preparing. The woman talked to her, telling her about some garden that was apparently like the garden here, with roses going wild. Mrs Orvitski didn't find it interesting. 'It must be no joke looking after two lively little girls,' the woman said. 'Mrs Aidallbery is awfully lucky to have you.'

Mrs Orvitski made the coffee, thinking that half past five was a peculiar time to ask for it. She heated milk and placed it, with sugar and the coffee-pot, on a red tray. She added a coffee-strainer, coffee-spoons, and two cups and saucers.

'I'll take it,' Mrs Vincent said, smiling helpfully, but Mrs Orvitski said she would carry the tray to the drawing-room herself.

'Aren't the children here?' Mrs Vincent said in surprise, as she entered the room behind Mrs Orvitski.

'The children?'

He looked like an old man, Mrs Orvitski thought, sitting there with his hands clasped. As soon as you laid eyes on him you could see that that marriage couldn't have been right.

'Jennifer!' she called in the hall. 'Alice child!'

They didn't come. She returned to the kitchen to prepare bacon and baked beans.

In the drawing-room Mrs Vincent poured coffee. They waited for it to cool, looking through the french windows at the bleakness of February in the garden. She spoke again of the garden in Virginia; he listened with interest. He pointed at a loganberry bush he'd planted, in place of one that had died.

'You miss it all a little?' she suggested, and he agreed that occasionally he did.

She smiled. She took a flat tin of Hermesetas from her handbag and dropped one into her coffee. She'd start tomorrow, she said, looking for a house near Aberdeen, a country house, as they'd agreed.

They drank their coffee. In the hall he shouted for his children, and they came to say goodbye.

'How very nice to meet you,' Mrs Vincent said, shaking hands with them but refraining from mentioning the prospect of visits in the future to Aberdeen. 'How very nice,' she said again, shaking hands with Mrs Orvitski, which Mrs Orvitski considered to be a peculiar thing to do.

'These are mine, actually,' he said to Mrs Orvitski, showing her the miniatures. 'I'm taking them away.'

22

He was there, with great abruptness, beside her. So suddenly did he arrive that she thought afterwards she must have dropped off to sleep for a moment over a letter she was writing to Di Troughton, who was now Di Acheson.

'Hullo, Elizabeth,' he said.

'Joanna,' she began. 'You came –'

'I came down to see Joanna.'

'Look, there are chairs there.' She pointed. He went to get a chair. Automatically, she reached for the plastic sachet she kept her lipstick and compact in. She wished she'd known; it wasn't like him not to warn her. She touched her lips with lipstick, glancing in the small round glass of her powder-compact. She hated looking frowsy when he came like this. Her hair seemed greyer than before. She touched it with her fingers, settling it a bit.

'I've been to Somerset,' he said. 'I've met this Mrs Tabor-Ellis.'

'Did you see Joanna?'

'She was attending to the goats.'

He made it sound comic because he didn't smile. It was that more than anything, she thought: he didn't smile naturally, it was always an effort for him. She wanted to smile herself, just fleetingly, but she knew he wouldn't understand. It wasn't a laughing matter, he'd think, and put up a black mark against her. Nor was it a laughing matter, Joanna tending goats.

'What did the woman say?'

He shook his head, slowly, several times. He tightened his lips, sucking them in so that his mouth became a lipless slit in his face. Mrs Tabor-Ellis wasn't a reasonable woman. He had arrived at the farmhouse in the early morning and had attempted to discuss the matter with her. He had later returned in the hope of finding Joanna on her own.

In relating all this, Aidallbery didn't mention Mrs Vincent. He spoke as though he'd visited the Tabor-Ellis farmhouse on his own, and as though the conversation with Mrs Tabor-Ellis had taken place without the moral support of the woman who had agreed to be his second wife. Nor did he reveal that at the end of his second visit to the farmhouse Mrs Tabor-Ellis had called him a piece of middle-class garbage and a fascist, statements that had brought a quick rebuke from Mrs Vincent. 'Who d'you think *you* are?' Mrs Tabor-Ellis had demanded. 'Who on earth's this frightful woman?' she'd asked Aidallbery.

'It wasn't a pleasant day,' he said.

'I'm sorry.'

'It must run its course, I'm afraid. It would be a mistake to force Joanna, or even to attempt to persuade her.'

Mrs Vincent had said that on the train on the way back, over lunch. 'You can't with children nowadays,' she'd said. 'It makes matters worse.'

Elizabeth said, yes, she supposed it must run its course. It was just that she didn't much care for Samuel.

'He couldn't be worse than Mrs Tabor-Ellis.'

'He's different, I think.'

'I'll write to her. All I wanted to do was to talk about her A-levels to her. If only she'd waited and done all this in the summer holidays!'

'Joanna's not having a holiday. She doesn't see it like that.'

'Yes, I know, Elizabeth.' He spoke with a hint of the irritation she remembered, and was aware again of the sensation she'd become used to, the feeling that his brain worked at twice the speed of hers.

'How are you, Elizabeth?' he said.

'Better now. I'm sorry about Joanna.'

'It's common nowadays.'

'I lost touch with her.'

'It can't be helped. A pity you did, Elizabeth, but still.'

'She sleeps with Samuel. Samuel takes LSD.'

He didn't reply. She could feel him continuing to blame her, saying to himself that the girl had been in her care, saying to himself that it wasn't exactly the time to have a hysterectomy, with someone like Samuel around. He sighed without making a noise. Sylvie and Lily would know who he was because she'd told them he had a look of an eagle. She couldn't remember if Miss Samson had been listening when she'd said it. They'd be interested that her divorced husband, whom they'd last heard of as being in Aberdeen, should have come to see her.

'We have to face things,' he said. There was a silence until he

223

continued. 'I wrote to the girls. Their letter was for you, really. I'm getting married again.'

'Oh.'

'I wanted you all to know at once.'

'I hope you'll be happy.'

'I think so.' He paused. He said: 'I saw the girls this evening. I just called in.'

'Are they all right? Mrs Orvitski had an upset with the washing-machine.'

'They seemed all right.'

A silence fell again between them. He cleared his throat, unembarrassed by the silence.

'Henry died,' she said. 'Yesterday.'

'Henry?'

It was like him not to remember. She'd told him all about Henry. He'd met Henry several times. She'd told him about Henry dressing up as a clown.

'Henry?' he said again.

'I played with him as a child.'

'Oh, yes.'

'He died yesterday. It was in the papers.'

'I see,' he said.

He wasn't curious. He absorbed the fact of Henry's death as a person without an interest in food might eat a meal.

'It was in the papers,' she said, 'because of the circumstances.'

'Hmm?' he said, smiling a little, his bony face seeming for a moment like a skeleton's.

'Henry got drunk and somehow managed to gas himself.'

'I see.' He paused. 'Suicide?'

'The verdict didn't say that.'

'Bit of a flop, wasn't he?'

'I suppose so.'

She hated him. She hated him sitting there so correct in every uninteresting detail, the fingernails at the end of his bony fingers filed and shaped. He used to spend ages shaping his fingernails.

'Henry wanted to marry me,' she said.

'Good Lord!'

'He proposed to me the night before it all happened.'

'I see.'

'I said it wasn't a good idea.'

'Well, one doesn't want to speak ill of the dead, but –'

'Speak ill of the dead if you want to. I never know why people say you shouldn't speak ill of the dead. The dead can't answer back and can't be hurt.'

'Now, now, Elizabeth. I was merely going to say that Henry wouldn't have been at all suitable for you.'

'I would have married him in the end. He'd have kept on asking me and I'd have married Henry in the end.'

'Well, it's your affair of course, my dear –'

'It's nobody's affair now.'

'No.'

He was more of a failure than Henry. Everything went wrong for people like Henry, while other people efficiently laid out their lives like maps in front of them, covering each mistake artistically up, employing guile. He'd married her and he'd hidden his shortcomings beneath hers. He'd drawn hers out, so that in their marriage her shortcomings gathered strength, and stood in the end as an element that was a daily stumbling block. Looking back on it now, she knew he couldn't have done without the irritation of her shortcomings. She was to blame, she had done wrong, it was her fault.

He had taught her all that in their marriage. He had made her the woman she was at forty-one. For ever she'd carry the influence he'd left with her: her own acceptance of the guilt that crept about her now like other blood. He'd carry, for his part, the greater confidence he'd gained.

'I'll let you know,' she said, 'if anything changes where Joanna's concerned.'

'Yes, please do.'

For six months in their marriage she had lived a life of her own, loving another wife's husband, free from shortcomings. But all that had happened far too late, and in the wrong way. She laughed, and saw that he was surprised by this.

'What a mess I've made of things!' she said, looking straight at him. 'Don't you think so? Just like poor Henry. Two of a kind.'

He didn't reply. He had to go, he said.

Sharon Timpson and another girl from the Woolworth's basement came to see Sylvie. Kenneth came, and the Reverend Rawes on his own.

The girls brought Sylvie Toblerone, Kit-Kat, Embassy Kings, and grapes. They both had curlers under their headscarves, because they were going out dancing later.

'Honestly, you're lucky, Sylvie,' Sharon said. 'We've been run off our feet this week.'

'The Jamaican creature's away with flu,' the other girl said. 'So's Marjie Thomas. Stella'd have come tonight only her mum got a broken rib or something.'

'Stella sent you the Kit-Kat.'

'It just takes time,' Lily said. 'I wrote back to your mother. I said what you'd said, that I didn't want them to come. But the other takes time.'

'I shouldn't have told you.'

'She wrote it in her letter. That's why you told me, Kenneth.'

She mentioned the death of Henry, finding it easier to talk of something else.

He was gone, Sylvie said, no doubt about it now. 'I should have known. You always know afterwards, with a fella.'

'I'd skin him if I saw him,' Sharon Timpson said.

Sylvie laughed. 'I should have known,' she said again. 'A girl should always know.'

'Our Father,' murmured the Reverend Rawes.

'Our Father,' murmured Miss Samson.

23

At half past one in the morning, Saturday 17 February, Elizabeth
Aidallbery developed acute abdominal pain. Its intensity increased
as she lay on her back with her eyes closed, hoping that it would go
away. She had woken up with it and had immediately thought about
Henry, whom she'd still been thinking about before she'd finally
managed to sleep, at twelve forty. The children would know of his
death now: Mrs Orvitski or Leopold would have read it in a newspaper. It would pass her mother by; but in Somerset she could hear
Mrs Tabor-Ellis commenting that the death of a middle-class man
didn't matter to women like Elizabeth because women like Elizabeth
strung such men along, going out with them and accepting flowers.
Restaurants and flowers were useful for raising a lone woman's self-
esteem, Mrs Tabor-Ellis would say, and Samuel would soundlessly
laugh. Joanna would find it true.

She rang the bell above her bed, but even while her hand was still
on it and while the pain intensely continued, some kind of uncon-
sciousness overcame her.

They asked her questions but she didn't want to answer. She was too
tired to answer any more. She'd told the truth, she didn't want to
take it back: she'd hated his hands the first time he'd touched her
body with them, she'd hated them ever since, those awful fingernails.
His voice wasn't beautiful; his voice was like dust.

She wanted to lie and let the sea flow over her. If the sea flowed
over her, seaweed would cling to her body and she would be washed
up on a coast somewhere, it wouldn't matter. She didn't want to
argue with anyone, not with Joanna, nor with the people who were
there, taking her clothes off because the sea had wet them so. There
was no point in people taking her nightdress off and putting something else on. Whatever was the use, since the sea would wet anything she wore?

'Mrs Aidallbery,' Dr Pennance said.

227

'Yes.' Her voice was faint, she could hardly hear it. 'Yes,' she said again, but it wasn't any better.

'Are you still in pain, Mrs Aidallbery?'

'Yes.'

'We've given you something to send it away. You'll sleep quite easily, but we'll have to wake you up now and again.'

'Wake?'

'Just to see how you're getting on. To take your blood pressure.'

She closed her eyes and the face went away. 'I'm very hot,' she said with her eyes closed.

'You're a little feverish.'

'I'm sweating all over.'

'Keep someone with her,' Dr Pennance said quietly to Sister Kolulu. 'Blood pressure on the hour. If you're alarmed, get me up immediately.'

She didn't sleep. It wasn't sleep, she said to herself, this thin covering they had induced. A long way away, they strapped something on to her arm. They pressed something beneath her skin, like the stem of a flower. Sweat ran in her hair. They cooled her forehead somehow.

'I was in the sea,' she explained, and they put the band around her arm again.

'Yes,' they murmured.

'Poor Sylvie,' she said. 'He didn't come.'

Sylvie was all right, they said. It didn't matter that he hadn't come.

'Oh God, it matters,' she said.

Darkness was like a fog. There were shadows in it, and a dim glimmer of gold. Her feet and her hands were still a long way away. Heaviness weighed down on her.

'We're changing your sheets, Mrs Aidallbery,' they said.

It was her mother who kept things going, she told them, her mother looking after Joanna when Joanna was a baby, her mother gossiping on the stairs.

'Of course,' they said.

Dr Pennance came again. They moved her and she didn't know it. The feet of the night nurses and of Sister Kolulu and Dr Pennance made hardly any noise, the rubber bed-wheels were soundless on the linoleum.

In the corridor Mrs Thring, on her way back to bed from the lavatory, stood aside to let them by. She smiled at Dr Pennance, but he didn't smile back.

228

'Mummy,' the woman in the bed said.

She was in the hospital she'd come to in a minicab, with Alice and Jennifer, with Mrs Orvitski carrying her white suitcase. *Liberation Now!* were words that were there, black on white. She woke up and faces were there, the faces of Nurse Aylard and Nurse Wibberley, and Dr Pennance's face, and the black face of Sister Kolulu. The dog had been run over. The dog was dead, she told them. Henry was dead, as well.

'Now, Mrs Aidallbery,' Mr Apple said. 'Let's just get to the root of all this.'

'I thought you were a joke,' she said. 'I paid you off.'

'Actually I'm not a joke, Mrs Aidallbery. I'm a psychiatrist, but please forget for the moment that I'm a psychiatrist. Think of me as a friend, Mrs Aidallbery.'

'Henry is dead. I'm guilty of that, too.'

'No, Mrs Aidallbery.'

'Everything I touch has that about it. My marriage was awful. I was just a bit of paper.'

'You were more than that, Mrs Aidallbery.'

'Two of a kind, I said to him, and he didn't bother to deny it.'

'Your husband is not in psychiatric medicine, Mrs Aidallbery. Let's talk about your personal happiness, shall we?'

'Mr Feuchtwanger says you'd go mad if you didn't believe in happiness.'

'Mr Feuchtwanger is not in psychiatric medicine. Mr Feuchtwanger is not qualified to speak. But Mr Feuchtwanger is right.'

'Poor Henry in that house. Poor Henry –'

'Henry has nothing to do with your happiness, Mrs Aidallbery.'

'Henry in his golfing jacket, Henry drunk and wanting things, Henry laughed at –'

'Henry is irrelevant, Mrs Aidallbery. Henry is dead in a kitchen. You are not responsible for Henry's death, Mrs Aidallbery.'

'When I think of Henry I only want to drown.'

'If you drown, Mrs Aidallbery, we cannot help you.'

'Please let me drown. I'd rather drown. Please.'

There were other people, too. They replied to her, one or two of them, but she couldn't hear what they said. Again they took her nightdress off and put another on.

'Please,' she said. 'I'm tired. The pain's still there. What on earth is the point of it all?'

In the room a man stood near to Elizabeth, a man she couldn't properly see. All she knew about him was that he wasn't the man she'd married, nor the one who'd made Harrods Depository seem beautiful for her, nor Henry. He was a man who loved her and smiled away her guilt. He listened, he forgave her, he did not cease to love her. It didn't matter in the least, he said, the keys dropped down a drain. He was a man like a ghost because she could not quite see him and was more aware of him with other senses. 'Mr Nobody,' her mother said, telling her to go to sleep now.

And then in her dream it happened that Lily's baby was not born alive, and that Miss Samson wandered the shore at Bexhill-on-Sea, seeking and not finding her God, and that Sylvie never again laid eyes on Declan. The world was a wilderness, her own voice said in her dream, in which these things happened to other people every day, in which a man might die in a drunken misadventure, in which she herself might wish herself dead also. No other voice spoke in her dream, not Mr Feuchtwanger's nor Mr Apple's nor her mother's. There was only silence then.

Five hours went by but she didn't know it. Mr Azu was there, but she didn't know the face was Mr Azu's. 'Have you pain still, Mrs Aidallbery?'

She moved her head, indicating that she had. The pains in her stomach, which had earlier gone away, had now returned. There was a soreness, which was nothing at all, around the area of the operation.

Mr Azu spoke to Sister Kolulu in a voice too low for Elizabeth to hear what he said. They'd moved away from the bed for this conversation. Mr Azu now returned to Elizabeth. Sister Kolulu left the room. Mr Azu said:

'We will recommence the treatment, Mrs Aidallbery. Shortly you will experience a benefit.'

She didn't know what treatment he was talking about. She moved her head, trying to indicate that she didn't mind what they did to her. 'What's the matter with me?' she asked. 'Am I dying or something?'

She opened her eyes because he was speaking. He said:

'You have a slight complication, Mrs Aidallbery. It's not unusual to have a slight complication after this operation. Recuperation will recommence once we have cleared up this slight condition.'

He smiled at her, as though seeking to comfort her in this way, as though aware that his words were inadequate. His hair was black and bushy, he had a bushy moustache and sideburns; his skin was the colour of coffee with very little milk in it.

'You will feel a great deal better, Mrs Aidallbery,' he said, 'once the treatment has been recommenced.'

Her mind was empty. Scenes from her life were not reenacted, people did not vividly appear when she closed her eyes.

The pains had receded, but she didn't trust the recession. She lay still and awake, concentrating on what remained of the pain, living only with it, as though in this way she might control it better. She fell asleep at five to eight.

Sister O'Keeffe listened while Mr Alstrop-Smith gave her instructions.

'She's been upset by this death,' Mr Alstrop-Smith said. 'It never helps. Did she say much?'

No, Sister O'Keeffe said, Mrs Aidallbery hadn't said very much; not to her. She seemed a nice woman. Divorced.

'Yes, I did know that.'

'She was quite happy about leaving her family. People were helping. She had a good charwoman, she said.'

'She has a tired look.'

'Yes, she's tired.'

He knew nothing about her. She was his patient, he'd suggested the hysterectomy after his examination, he'd told her he would be performing the operation himself: that had been their communication, that and her body on the table. Her doctor's notes showed that she hadn't been often ill. She'd had the same doctor all her life, a man whose handwriting he'd often read but whom he'd never met. It was rare enough these days for people to have the same doctor for a lifetime. He said:

'There's nothing the matter with the hysterectomy, you know. She's making a good recovery.'

'She's maybe allergic –'

He shook his head while Sister O'Keeffe spoke. She interrupted herself to ask him what he thought the condition was.

'Oh, just colic,' he said. 'Like that Thompson woman had. Nothing, really.' He nodded at Sister O'Keeffe and went away.

'He thinks Mrs Aidallbery's got colic,' she said to Nurse Hampshire when Nurse Hampshire came into the medicine room. 'Apparently she kept your friend Dr Pennance up half the night. Kolulu was dropping this morning.'

Nurse Hampshire, sensitive where Dr Pennance was concerned, ignored this reference to him by asking, with an edge of sarcasm in her voice, if Mr Alstrop-Smith believed that Mrs Thring had colic, too.

Sister O'Keeffe shook her head. 'Mr Alstrop-Smith,' she said, 'generally knows what he's talking about.'

The D'arcys were at the funeral, and the Carstairs. Other people who had known Henry in his lifetime filled a chapel in Putney Vale Crematorium, among them his son Timus and the woman who had had to divorce him, and a cousin who lived in Warwickshire.

They listened while a clergyman spoke of a man he had not known, or ever seen. The coffin was there for a while and then slid away.

In pale February sunshine wreaths were arrayed on grass outside the chapel. The people coming out stood by them, murmuring for a moment. The D'arcys and the Carstairs hurried away, to late-afternoon surgeries.

Ten days passed. The judge ordered the trial at which the army officer was accused of murdering his wife to be brought to an end, on grounds of insufficient evidence. Nurse Hampshire agreed to marry Dr Pennance, but they decided to keep the matter a secret for the time being. In some hospitals, ancillary staff went on strike. The managing director for whom Henry's ex-wife worked asked her to stay late one night and told her he loved her. Jennifer and Alice received the autograph of Cilla Black. In the Cruskeen Bawn Lounge Mr Maloney lent, against security, fourteen pounds to a man on the understanding that he'd receive back nineteen within one calendar month. In his prefabricated office Rammage warned a Mr Cox that all New-Way customers, including garage attendants, must be addressed as 'sir'. A New-Way engineer examined the drinks machine at the swimming-baths and informed the swimming-baths attendant that the machine had come to the end of its useful life. In the fish division sales were good.

In the Marie Atkins Ward Elizabeth recovered from her setback, and she and Miss Samson and Sylvie felt stronger day by day. Mr and Mrs Drucker did not visit Lily, and Lily took heart from that, saying to Kenneth that the things he'd told her didn't matter. She said she understood now, which wasn't true. Miss Samson's secret, revealed to Elizabeth, was not passed on by the Reverend Rawes to the other inmates of Number Nine. Elizabeth read the autobiography of Lady Augusta and was surprised to learn that Lady Augusta did not seem to have minded the fact that her husband hadn't loved her.

Elizabeth felt calm now. Because of her setback, she should go to the convalescent home in Eastbourne for ten days, Mr Alstrop-Smith told her. He could find a place for her, he said, even though she hadn't booked. She explained that it would be difficult. Mrs Orvitski would come in every day when she went home.

The girls from the Woolworth's basement brought clothes for Sylvie, a skirt and a jumper and a blouse, tights and underclothes. 'I'm lending you a pair of shoes,' Sharon Timpson said. There was a new assistant manager in the Woolworth's, the girls reported. Unmarried, they said, twenty-four or twenty-five. They described him to Sylvie. They said he was smashing. Ian his name was.

In Number Nine, Balaclava Avenue, Mrs Delve continued to worry about Miss Samson's holiday. Although, they still didn't know the date of her release from hospital, Mrs Delve insisted one evening in the sitting-room that they would have to do something about booking a room.

'Do?' Carol Pidsley repeated. 'But whatever can we do?'

'We can ring up the Seaview. We can put the situation to the manageress.'

'You mean –' Robert Tonsell began.

'I mean if we don't do something now we'll find the Seaview booked out. I've said it before. It'll be well into March by the look of things before she's ready for the room, and March is spring, you know. A lot of people take holidays in spring these days.' Mrs Delve's voice had risen as she spoke, a flush of agitation had spread across her face and neck.

The Tonsell brothers nodded and, noting their approval of Mrs Delve's line of thought, Carol Pidsley nodded also. The Reverend Rawes said nothing. He sat in the armchair that over the years had become his, with his library book face downwards on his knees. He'd been enjoying this library book, and for a moment had escaped from his concern over Miss Samson's doubt. He blamed himself for that now, for escaping irresponsibly into an historical novel when he should have been still racking his brain for some way to help her. It was really difficult, not being able to share any of it with the others.

Mrs Delve roused the Reverend Rawes from his reverie. Had he heard what had been said? Did he consider it a good idea to telephone the manageress of the Seaview Hotel?

'Oh, yes, of course,' he said.

Robert Tonsell offered to telephone, but Mrs Delve thought that since Carol's aunt had stayed at the Seaview it should be Carol.

'I'll do it, of course,' Carol said.

'Mention your aunt, dear. Ask for the manageress straight away.'

Carol Pidsley left the sitting-room. The telephone was in the hall. Mrs Delve stood beside her, and the Tonsell brothers stood in the sitting-room doorway. The Reverend Rawes remained in his arm-chair by the cosy-stove. Arthur entered the hall from the kitchen, with cups of tea on a tray. It was a duty of the little Welsh girl's, the preparation of tea in the evenings, but on Tuesdays she had the afternoon and evening off. Arthur wore a short white coat, his Tues-day coat he called it.

'Seaview, Bexhill,' a voice said in Carol Pidsley's ear.

'Oh, good evening,' she said.

'Yes?'

'Would it be possible to speak to the manageress, please?'

There was a series of clicks and then a voice said:

'Manageress, Seaview.'

'Oh, good evening. My name's Miss Pidsley –'

'Say about your aunt,' Mrs Delve said.

'My aunt, Miss Eccles, stayed with you two years ago. Miss Kitty Eccles, with her friend, Mrs Trump. We'd like to book a room –'

'A nice front room,' Mrs Delve said.

'A nice front room for a Miss Samson.'

'When was it you wanted the room, madam?'

'Well, we don't actually know, you see. If we could make an arrangement, a provisional arrangement, perhaps –'

'What is it you want, please, madam?'

'Well, a single room. For next month. We think it will be next month now.'

'A single room for March. Please confirm it in writing, madam. Your name, you said –'

'No, no. No, we want the room for one week only, please.'

'You just said for a month, madam.'

'No, no, I'm sorry. No, what we want –'

Mrs Delve took the receiver out of Carol Pidsley's hand. The hand was shaking, she noticed. The telephone was warm and damp.

'Good evening,' Mrs Delve said.

Aware that Edward Tonsell was looking at her, Carol tried to stand in a shadow cast by the coats on the hall-stand. She pressed herself against the wall, staring miserably at Mrs Delve's arm. The arm was in a green knitted cardigan that she remembered Mrs Delve working at in the autumn. He thinks I'm a fool, she thought.

'The point is,' Mrs Delve said, 'we have a friend who's in hospital, having a hysterectomy, actually –'

'Seaview reception here.'

'The point is, we expect her out in less than a week, but we cannot be precise –'

'What is it you want, please?'

'We want a nice front room.'

'For when, madam?'

'I'm trying to explain to you. We don't rightly know when it's for.'

'I'm sorry, madam, I cannot book you a room unless I know when it's for. We are extremely full –'

'Full?' cried Mrs Delve, the flush returning to her neck and face. 'Full?'

'Certainly we are full, madam. If you give me your dates I will ascertain what accommodation is available. I doubt that we have anything at the front, though.'

'Not anything?' cried Mrs Delve. 'Oh dear, I knew this. I knew it. I knew it.'

'Madam –'

'Excuse me.' Mrs Delve put her hand over the mouthpiece and whispered loudly at the Tonsell brothers, asking that the Reverend Rawes should come.

'Mr Rawes,' Edward Tonsell whispered, beckoning the Reverend Rawes.

'A clergyman is coming to speak to you,' Mrs Delve said to the manageress.

Pressed against the wall, between Mrs Delve and the hall-stand, Carol Pidsley felt better. Mrs Delve had taken the telephone from her, but after that Mrs Delve had failed also. She glanced through the dimness of the hall at Edward Tonsell, but he was whispering something to his brother, who was nodding.

'It's the manageress,' Mrs Delve whispered in agitation to the Reverend Rawes. 'They're extremely full, she says.'

'Hullo,' the Reverend Rawes said.

'Look, I cannot stand here,' the manageress testily began.

'Good evening. My name is Rawes. What we're concerned about is a room for our friend, Miss Samson.' He listened for a moment to the manageress and then said that he would like to make the booking for a week from March the seventh, provided the room was a good one, and at the front of the hotel, with a view of the sea. March the seventh, he repeated, Ash Wednesday. The manageress spoke again,

235

and the Reverend Rawes thanked her. 'You have been very kind,' he said, 'and very patient. We live at Number Nine, Balaclava Avenue, S.W.17. If you are ever in the area we should be extremely pleased to welcome you at any time. One of us is always here. No, no. Thank *you*.'

The Reverend Rawes replaced the receiver and the others in the hall stared at him in astonishment. One moment the Seaview Hotel was full and its manageress was being difficult, the next a good front room had been booked and the manageress invited to Number Nine.

'She should certainly be out by March the seventh,' the Reverend Rawes said, 'and if she has to wait here for a day or two it won't do her any harm.'

'Well, thank heaven for that,' Mrs Delve cried. 'I'll sleep better tonight, I can tell you.'

Edward Tonsell smiled across the hall at Carol Pidsley, implying that her failure with the manageress didn't matter, since all was well now. I would die for him, she whispered in her mind.

In the sitting-room the tea was cold. 'It can be heated,' Arthur said. He carried the tray of cups and saucers back to the kitchen. The Reverend Rawes accompanied him, wishing to take his own tea up to his room.

'Funny,' Mrs Delve said. 'He settles everything and yet he looks so sad these days.'

'I think he misses her more than any of us,' Carol said. 'He's been here longer, after all. He's known her longer.'

'He's getting on, of course,' Mrs Delve said.

24

On the Thursday of that week he came with a jaunty step, carrying a suitcase. People were waiting outside the hospital because it was not yet seven o'clock. No visitor was permitted to enter until the clock in the hall registered the hour precisely. The people explained all this to him when he asked what the hold-up was.

At seven, Pengelly removed a red velvet rope that stretched in front of the swing-doors at the top of the steps. He or Frowen stretched it there at twenty to seven every evening, before the first visitors arrived.

'Right you are,' Pengelly said, and the visitors entered the hospital in a bunch.

'I can't remember the name of the ward,' Declan said. 'It's a Miss Clapper I've come to see.'

'The Marie Atkins, sir. First floor, end of the corridor.'

'Thanks a lot.'

Still jauntily, he mounted the wide, linoleum-clad stairs. The smell that had offended when he'd first come with Sylvie was still there, but he felt better able to cope with it because of his sprightly mood. He wore a blue suit, and a shirt and tie that went nicely with it.

'Declan!' she said. 'My God, Declan!'

'How're you, Sylvie?' He was smiling. He leaned down and kissed her.

'Declan!' she said again.

'I had to go away. I had to sort things out.'

He sat close to her, holding her hands. She couldn't help crying. It was ridiculous, crying, when all she wanted to do was to laugh.

'I didn't know whether I was coming or going, Sylvie. I hadn't a penny of money. There was rent owing for a fortnight and the debt to Maloney and the other debt up in Liverpool.'

'Oh, Declan, why didn't you send me a p.c.? It's nearly three weeks.'

'Listen to me, Sylvie. I didn't write you a p.c. because I didn't know

237

what to put on it. I acquired a loan from a friend and went up to Liverpool to fix matters up.'

'Oh, Declan!'

'I saw you right, Sylvie. I wrote a letter to Mrs Vendericks, saying I was called away and would be back with the rental. I told her to come over with your stuff in the bag –'

'She never came, Declan.'

'She maybe didn't have time yet, Sylvie. I'll look in there tonight and pay her up what's owing and collect –'

'The girls from the basement came in with clothes for me.'

'God, I'm sorry they had to do that, Sylvie.'

'Who lent you the money to go back, Declan?'

'Oh, a friend, I wonder do you know him? Cathal Condon,' he said, recalling the name of a boy who'd sat in the next desk to his in the Christian Brothers in Enniscorthy, thirteen years ago. 'A decent skin, Sylvie.'

'I thought I'd never see you again, Declan.'

'Isn't that ridiculous, for God's sake? Sure, I had no option in the wide world. After I left you here that Sunday I considered the trouble I was in. The way it looked, Sylvie, we could never get married at all. I'd be chasing the bloody debts and the debts would be chasing the two of us. We'd be all over the place, Sylvie.'

'I was miserable without you. It'll be three weeks on Sunday –'

'I have a job fixed up in a bacon factory, Sylvie. I have the money borrowed and laid down on the bungalow.'

'Oh, Declan,' she cried. 'It's lovely to see you.'

She was sobbing again, and angry with herself because she'd given way. She asked him to find her some Kleenex tissues in her cupboard.

'Don't upset yourself,' he said, rummaging among her belongings. He comforted her, patting her arm, pulling tissues out of the Kleenex package for her.

She didn't want him to go away. She didn't want him to stop holding her hands and patting her. She didn't want to remember the things she had thought about him.

'I'm due out tomorrow,' she said. 'Tomorrow afternoon.'

He expressed surprise. He said he'd imagined she'd be stuck there for another week at least.

'God, I might have missed you,' he said.

'I'm going to share Sharon Timpson's room. She's borrowed a camp bed and a lilo. It'll all be ready.'

'We could go up to Liverpool on Sunday.'

She didn't say anything because she didn't know what to say. She'd said to Sharon Timpson that she'd probably be back in Woolworth's at the beginning of next week, although Mr Alstrop-Smith had told her that she should rest for two weeks at least and Sister O'Keeffe had said longer. But everything was different now that Declan was here, everything had changed back to what it had been.

'God, I'm sorry about your clothes, Sylvie. I'll go out there tonight –'

'It doesn't matter about the clothes.'

From an inside pocket Declan took one of the five-pound notes that he had removed from Mary Tracy's dressing-table drawer and placed it on Sylvie's bed-table. 'I owe you that, if not more,' he said.

'Oh, Declan, I couldn't.'

'I'll fix up with Mrs Vendericks. I had to borrow two typewriters for security for Maloney.'

'He told me about the typewriters, Declan.'

'They'll be returned tonight to where they came from.'

'Maloney said they were stolen property. He said the police –'

'Maloney wouldn't go within two thousand miles of a police station. When Maloney sees a policeman he crosses the road and goes into a shop.'

'He said about a girl called Mary Tracy from Tralee. He said she had money stolen from her – oh, Declan, I thought you might have! I thought maybe he was right.'

'Never in my life,' Declan said, 'did I hear of a girl called Mary Tracy.'

'He said other things, too, Declan. He said –'

'Maloney's pathological. Maloney says the first item that comes into his head.'

'He said you were in Mary Tracy's bedroom.'

Declan laughed. He wagged his head at the absurdity of that. Sylvie asked him if he was certain he'd never met a Mary Tracy from Tralee, and Declan said that the only person he knew from Tralee was a man called Carroll who was currently employed in the public conveniences in Hammersmith. He dismissed the subject of Mary Tracy, and spoke of other matters instead. He described the bungalows in Liverpool, telling her that they had cork floors. He tightened his grasp on her hands. He couldn't live without her, he said.

The visitors' bell sounded. He asked her what it was for, and she explained.

'Will you be able to come tomorrow, Declan? To help me out with

239

things? It doesn't matter if you can't. I wasn't expecting anyone anyway –'

'God, of course I'll be here, Sylvie. Half past seven in the morning.'

'Half past three in the afternoon actually.'

He kissed her. The thin lips that were always moving so rapidly in speech felt the same as they'd ever felt. There was a salty taste to them, which had been there before, too.

'I'll see you so,' he said. 'I'll be here on the dot, Sylvie.'

She watched him going, as jauntily as he'd come, smiling at the other visitors. At the door he turned round and looked at her. He winked and threw a cigarette into the air, catching it between his lips, a trick of his that always made her laugh. She waved at him.

'Declan,' she said when he'd gone. 'That was Declan.'

She told them what he'd told her, about the money borrowed from the uncle who was a priest and laid down on the bungalow, about the bacon factory where he'd found work.

In the Rose and Thorn Declan drank his Guinness slowly, savouring the bitter tang. The main thing was to keep out of everyone's way. Out of Maloney's for a start, and Mary Tracy's and Mrs Vendericks's. He'd give Hammersmith and Shepherd's Bush a wide berth, maybe find a room for a few days in the Wapping area. On Sunday or Monday they'd catch a train or a bus to Liverpool, and after that they could relax themselves.

It was great she was coming with him. If she hadn't agreed he'd have stayed where he was himself. As long as he was on the other side of London from Maloney, he wouldn't worry too much about it. There was no proof of any kind that the removal of the typewriters from the betting-shop's filing-cabinet was his responsibility; there was nothing to stop him denying on oath that he'd ever seen Mary Tracy before in his life.

It would be great walking about Liverpool with her, showing her off to his two uncles, noticing them admiring her London accent. How could he stick it, putting bacon into plastic packets, if he hadn't a girl like Sylvie to come home to? He'd never cared for Enniscorthy girls the same way, any more than he'd cared for Mary Tracy. You got used to girls from the town you were in, or Irish girls come to that, Catholic-minded girls that only opened up when they came to London. You could give ten to one that Mary Tracy wasn't in London four minutes before some fellow had the togs off her. They slept with their arms crossed, girls like that, in case they'd die in the night, before they could get to Confession. Sylvie'll go to mass in Liverpool out of being game-ball for anything. She'd gone with him once to the Oratory and said it was great. She'd take the uncles in her stride, and all the old carry-on that went with them. It was typical of her not to press charges, not to probe and poke over a delay of a few weeks, a thing that could happen to any man through no fault of his own.

Sylvie smoked in the lavatory, leaning against a washbasin. Why on earth had she fallen in love with him? Out of all the perfectly straightforward men in London, why had she had to pick this one as the special one, above all the others she'd known?

He'd been in gaol: the more she thought about it the more certain she was. Fifteen days he'd done, or more maybe, because he hadn't been able to keep his hands off property that wasn't his. On the train on the way to Liverpool he'd perhaps taken his chance with a man's wallet, or maybe he'd unscrewed something in the toilet, a mirror or a fitting. Or maybe he'd walked out of a shop in Liverpool with something he hadn't paid for, something small and ridiculous, the kind of stuff Nickie used to take, a roll of Sellotape or a pencil. Afterwards his uncles had dolled him up, pulling him together and getting him a job in a bacon factory, hoping against hope with their eyes closed.

'I don't know what to do,' she confessed later to Elizabeth. She'd run away from people with criminal tendencies, she said, and now she'd ended up with a person who was just the same. It was all very well saying that Mr Maloney said the first item that came into his head. It was all very well saying the only person he knew from the town of Tralee was a man called Carroll, employed in the Hammersmith conveniences. She told Elizabeth what Mr Maloney had said about Mary Tracy, and said she believed Mr Maloney and not Declan. Could you marry a man and forget about Mary Tracy and that he'd told you lies, covering up a gaol sentence or whatever it was? 'Oh God, I love him,' she said.

25

The next day Elizabeth gave Miss Samson her address because Miss Samson wanted to send her a postcard from Bexhill-on-Sea. Miss Samson also promised to send one to Lily, and one to Sylvie.

Declan shook Miss Samson's hand and shook hands with the Reverend Rawes and Mrs Delve. In a low, private voice the Reverend Rawes said he was glad that Declan had returned to look after Sylvie. There'd been concern about Miss Clapper in the ward, he said, but he understood now that all there'd been was a misunderstanding. He didn't mention to Declan that a man representing the Society of St Vincent de Paul had actually been collecting money in order to set Miss Clapper on her feet again. The Reverend Rawes wondered what would now become of this money. The Society of St Vincent de Paul was not a charity he would have supported in normal circumstances.

'Don't go lifting things about,' Sister O'Keeffe warned Miss Samson. 'Lie up and rest, like a good girl.'

'She's going to Bexhill,' Mrs Delve said. 'The Seaview Hotel for a week.'

'I'm talking to you too, Miss Clapper,' Sister O'Keeffe said. 'No hauling furniture now.'

'She'll not lift a finger,' Declan promised. He smiled at Sister O'Keeffe, but Sister O'Keeffe's face expressed her dismay at having to hand a patient into his care. As a girl in Kinsale, she'd known a youth with eyes that had the same light in them as Declan's had. Bad news, Sister O'Keeffe said to herself.

'I'll send you a postcard, Sister,' Miss Samson promised. 'You've been very kind to me.'

'You take it easy now,' Sister O'Keeffe said. She left the ward, nodding at the Reverend Rawes and Mrs Delve.

'I hope it'll be all right, Lily,' Sylvie said.

'We'll have to see.'

'I'm sure it will.'

'I hope it'll be all right for you too, Sylvie.'

'She'll get every care and attention,' Declan said. 'I can promise you that, Lily.'

Sylvie said goodbye to Miss Samson. She shook hands with her, and then she kissed Miss Samson's cheek because she suddenly wanted to. 'I'll write to you at Number Nine,' Sylvie said.

Elizabeth was up, dressed in the clothes Mrs Orvitski had brought her on Sunday afternoon, in the grey dress she'd worn to come to hospital.

'I hope they'll release you soon, Elizabeth,' Declan said, shaking hands with her.

'Goodbye, Elizabeth.'

'Goodbye, Sylvie. Please keep in touch.'

'Goodbye, Mrs Aidallbery,' Miss Samson said, and the Reverend Rawes said goodbye to her, too, and so did Mrs Delve. She wondered if she would ever see these people again, if she'd ever call in at Number Nine, Balaclava Avenue as she'd promised she would, or if Sylvie would ever come and see her. There'd always be a room, she'd promised, if Sylvie was stuck.

'You see you do,' Miss Samson said to Lily. 'There's always a cup of tea.'

'Miss Samson'd never forgive you,' Mrs Delve said, 'if you don't bring the baby to Number Nine.'

'Of course I will,' Lily murmured.

They went, and the ward seemed emptier than their absence made it. Automatically, Elizabeth crossed to one of the windows and looked down into Cheltenham Street. The hired car from Timms' Garage was waiting for Miss Samson. As Elizabeth watched, the driver left his seat and hurried along the pavement to take Miss Samson's suit-case from the Reverend Rawes. The driver smiled and spoke to her. She spoke herself, to the driver and to the woman with the banner, whom she appeared to wish to hold in conversation. But the woman moved on, and the people from Balaclava Avenue got into the car. The driver banged the doors. He got in himself and slowly drove away.

In Cheltenham Street Declan carried Sylvie's belongings in the carrier-bag that Sylvie's friends had brought her. Sylvie clung to his left arm. Both of them were laughing. 'Goodbye,' Sylvie said to the woman with the banner.

Elizabeth sat on the edge of Lily's bed and Lily told her what she hadn't told anyone else, about Kenneth. She looked away from Elizabeth and said that he'd allowed himself to be tempted by prostitutes.

243

She couldn't get it out of her mind, she said. 'Are all men like that, Elizabeth? Like Ally Glazier and Mr Hopegood and the one in Sylvie's basement?'

'Wandering Hands.' Elizabeth laughed, trying to cheer Lily up. 'My husband wasn't,' she said. She laughed again, at the thought of Aidallbery watching a prostitute taking her clothes off, or writing obscenities in the margins of library books.

'Pornography's for men,' Lily said. 'And strip shows and brothels. And writing on lavatory walls, and peeping Toms.'

'We're just as bad. We're silly.' She told her how she'd imagined a man, a charming, marvellous man, different from her father, how she'd romantically thought that Aidallbery was the man, the day he'd walked into the Pensione Bencistà.

'I imagined Montgomery Clift,' Lily said, looking away again, feeling warmth in her cheeks and her neck.

'Well, then,' Elizabeth said.

'It's not as brutish.'

'It's rubbishy.'

'I have to love him while he sits there watching a woman he's paid money to taking her clothes off. I have to love him creeping out of his parents' house in the middle of the night because he wants to be furtive.'

'It's years ago, Lily.'

'When I think of him he's suddenly ridiculous. He's gangling and awkward and silly, goggling in those spectacles, getting into taxi-cabs with women who think he's a fool.'

'Lily –'

'It's easier not to love people, Elizabeth. It's easier not to love at all.'

'Yes,' Elizabeth said. 'It is.'

The daffodils he'd brought were gone now, taken away and thrown away. The glass vase was empty, an ugly vase, heavy and inelegant.

'I'm sorry about Henry,' Lily said, noticing Elizabeth's glance on this vase.

'If he'd lived I'd probably have married him.'

'But Elizabeth, you didn't even love him. You couldn't have sacrificed yourself for a failure of a man.'

'I sacrificed myself for a success of a man.'

'But you loved him in the beginning.'

'In the end that didn't matter.'

'But why on earth would you have thrown yourself away again?'

244

'Because it's lonely when you're forty-one and your children are rowdily growing up, when Joanna's gone off with a Jesus freak, and your mother's packed away in a Sunset Home. I've never been much good at being alone.'

Nurse Hampshire and Nurse Summerbee took the sheets off the beds that Miss Samson and Sylvie had occupied. They folded the blankets and placed them on the beds, with the pillows in a row. The beds would be made up a little later, for new patients after their operations.

'I'll miss Miss Samson,' Nurse Hampshire said. 'Both of them, come to that.'

Elizabeth rose from where she'd been sitting on Lily's bed. She'd promised to help with the teas in the Olivia Hassals Ward, a task that recuperating patients were encouraged to undertake.

'It'll be all right,' she said, 'when your baby's born. It really will, Lily.'

'We were talking about you.'

Elizabeth smiled. She left the ward, walking a little stiffly but feeling that walking was getting easier all the time. In the Olivia Hassals Ward the old women were pleased to see her.

26

Mrs Orvitski fussed, and Jennifer and Alice fussed. Breakfast was brought to Elizabeth in bed and Mrs Orvitski prepared supper on a tray, which Jennifer and Alice carried to her room. During the day she listened to the wireless and ironed the children's clothes. Mrs Orvitski showed her how to make chlodnik. Every morning she read *The Times*, the foreign news and the home news, the letters and the business news, the advertisements in the Personal columns for pregnancy testing and overland trips to India, and colonic irrigation by State Registered Nurses in your own home. Joanna did not write the letter she'd promised.

The weather was dry and warm. After a week Elizabeth took to going into the garden every morning, to take the spring weeds out of her rose-beds. She sat on a stool with a faded pampas-grass seat, enjoying the sunshine when it came, turning the soil over with a small fork. She pruned the roses.

Mr Giltrap was long since dead, but one afternoon Mr Redborn, Mr Giltrap's successor, came to prepare the lawnmower for the summer's grass cutting. He took the pieces apart and left them to soak in paraffin. He took the blades away with him to have them sharpened. There was canker in one of the apple-trees, he said; it would be better if he cut the tree down. He was quite like Mr Giltrap in that he didn't say more than he had to. He was a man of about her own age, with a solemn face. Watching him once, she'd believed for a moment that he was Mr Giltrap's son because as well as his quietness he had the same slow way of moving as Mr Giltrap had had, and the same way of picking up a cup of tea. But afterwards she knew that this was all nonsense. Mr Giltrap had been a most respectable man, not at all the kind to go about having sons where he shouldn't.

One day the washing-machine went wrong again, and when she telephoned English Electric she was told that their engineer would arrive in a fortnight, 'Leopold can mend it,' Mrs Orvitski said and, although Elizabeth protested, Mr Orvitski was summoned by telephone and arrived within half an hour on his bicycle. Elizabeth had met him once before, a rather small, bald man with a black moustache. He shook hands with her and said it would be no trouble to him, he could easily effect a temporary repair until the English Electric engineer came. She stayed in the kitchen with him, making coffee while he dismantled the washing-machine. When Mrs Orvitski had been talking to him on the telephone she'd got the impression that he'd been protesting, probably saying he had no intention of getting on his bicycle and coming at once, as Mrs Orvitski was demanding. But in the kitchen he wasn't in the least like that. He said he'd always oblige her in any matter about which he had some knowledge, all she had to do was to ring him up. He told her about an ulcer that occasionally bothered him, and about his retirement and the work he'd done before that, driving a van. They had coffee at the kitchen table, and when Mrs Orvitski arrived to have hers she beamed with delight at the sight of them sitting there, getting on together.

One morning Elizabeth walked over to Meridian Close. It was a sunny morning but colder than it had been since she'd come out of hospital, with a brisk March wind. A wooden notice had been erected outside Henry's house announcing that it was for sale. *Apply H. A. Mawer*, the sign said. *322 Upr. Richmond Rd., 01-788 2881*. A white Saab was drawn up outside the house, and the hall door was open. 'Tremendous possibilities,' a woman in a red suit was saying, coming out of the house. The woman stood near the ash tree that Henry had cut down. She spoke loudly and excitedly, addressing a man who was still in the hall. The curtains of a window next door moved, and Elizabeth saw a woman's face looking out, and then a man's face.

Elizabeth went round the side of the house to the back garden. The woman in the red suit, imagining her to be a rival purchaser, glanced sharply at her. The grass in the back garden was still as long as it had been, but the flower beds were different, and at the bottom of the garden was a huge pile of cardboard cartons, and weeds and trimmings from the ash tree.

'Good morning,' Elizabeth said to the woman and the man, who were both now standing together on the paved area in the front of the house. 'Good morning,' the man said, smiling genially. The woman was still frosty. 'Quite nice, really,' the man remarked, inclining his head towards the house.

'Yes,' she said. She walked away from the house, not wishing to linger there, wondering why she'd come and yet glad that she'd seen the tidying up he'd spoken of. She felt he'd have liked her to see the tidying up he'd done in the house itself, but the house was different and she couldn't face it. She wondered if these people knew that a man had died in the kitchen a few weeks ago, and imagined they didn't. She walked by the other houses of Meridian Close. The people who were still alive in them probably considered it typical of Henry to have blotted his copybook, even in death. They'd be pleased to see another couple moving in.

That afternoon Mr Redborn returned to cut down the apple tree. It wasn't a big tree; it wouldn't be much trouble, he said. She watched him for a while, sawing very slowly, knowing just how to do it. She went away to make tea and when she returned to the garden the tree was on the ground and Mr Redborn was sawing at its branches. He stopped to drink his cup of tea, lifting the cup to his lips in a way that again reminded her of Mr Giltrap. The apple-wood wouldn't burn for a while yet, he said, but he'd stack it ready for a bonfire in the autumn.

Days went by that were not dissimilar to the days that had passed since her return from hospital. People rang up to ask her how she was, people came to see her. She thanked Mrs Singwell for taking her children to school all this time, and said that next week she'd be able to drive them herself and would take Mrs Singwell's child any time Mrs Singwell would like her to. She wrote cheques in payment of bills that came. She stopped her weekly order for vegetables and groceries, explaining that she'd now be able to go out and shop again. She sat with Alice to make sure she did her homework. She reminded both of them about their hamsters.

No mood possessed Elizabeth. She felt empty of emotion except for the gratitude she felt towards Mr and Mrs Orvitski and Mr Redborn, and the familiar affection she felt for Jennifer and Alice. Before her operation she'd sometimes found Alice's demands a source of irritation. 'Mummy! Mummy!' Alice had a way of calling out whenever she felt like it or was bored, whenever she came in from the garden or when she couldn't do her homework, or wished to discuss her piano practice. In reply, Elizabeth had developed a way of taking a cup of tea to the bathroom, where it never occurred to Alice to look. A dozen or so times she'd sat on the edge of the bath reading a book and drinking tea, while Alice called out and eventually desisted. But none of that was now necessary. She didn't feel the same irritation, nor did Alice call out so much. 'You're not to bother Mummy,' Jennifer repetitiously commanded, and Elizabeth guessed that in time that, too, would be a source of irritation. But for the moment it passed over her.

Often the telephone rang, and if Mrs Orvitski wasn't there she didn't answer it. She didn't much want to see people, or even to talk to them. She didn't anxiously wait for the post in case it contained a letter from Joanna. She wasn't up to thinking all over again about Samuel and Mrs Tabor-Ellis, any more than she'd been up to entering Henry's house, even though she knew he'd have wished her to. In *The Times* a correspondence raged about the damage laundries inflicted on shirt-buttons. She quite looked forward to that each day.

She went to the Sunset Home to see her mother. 'My dear,' her mother said. 'My dear.'

Elizabeth didn't say she'd been in hospital in case it was upsetting. She said instead that she'd been away. 'Fiesole?' her mother suggested, because she wanted to have a conversation about Fiesole. 'Well, yes,' Elizabeth said.

It was pleasant sitting in the conservatory, in a cane chair with cushions on it, with the sunshine warming her. Her mother talked of Mino da Fiesole and the Pensione Bencistà, not asking Elizabeth how the pensione was now, but recalling instead times she had spent there herself, with Elizabeth's father and on her own, and with Elizabeth. She talked about food, delicious spinach, and *dolce*, and the thimbleful of *grappa* she liked to have every night with her coffee. 'Breakfast on the terrace,' she murmured. 'The sun in those olive groves!'

Her mother talked also of Mr Skimpole and Mr Jarndyce and other people in *Bleak House*, in particular Mr Tulkinghorn and Mr Krook. She said the food in the Sunset Home with the present cook was excellent, especially the gravy. Someone had died, she said, but that was only to be expected, a woman whose name she'd never known, whose husband had once had a jackdaw called Snapper.

Afterwards, Elizabeth caught a 33 bus. She sat on the upper deck, looking down at cars and pedestrians. She felt happy, having seen her mother, and wondering if that feeling would last. Ever since she'd come out of hospital she'd noticed that she moved more slowly, treating herself as an invalid because she felt she was one. For quite a long time you could go on doing that. You could go on seeing to the children's clothes and making cups of tea for Mr Redborn and not always answering the telephone. The children would become more demanding, but you could cope with that if you didn't have anything else to cope with. She felt that she smiled now in a different way at the children, a lazy kind of smile, bland and placid. She wanted simply to be there to see to their needs, to get in food and

249

cook it, to wash and iron and make their beds. She felt grateful to be alive in order to perform these tasks and was once or twice aware that in hospital, when she'd had her setback, she'd wanted to die because she'd felt guilty about Henry's death. In retrospect, she regarded this desire as part of her fever, irrelevant to her life. And in her moodless condition guilt did not affect her.

A card with an address on it came from Joanna, and a letter from Sylvie. Sylvie and Declan were married; his uncle in the priesthood had conducted the service. The same uncle had suggested to Sylvie that, for Declan's sake and for her own too, it would be a good idea if she joined the Catholic Church, and she was now taking instruction. She'd never thought she'd end up in the Catholic Church, Sylvie wrote with a series of exclamation marks. They were living in the bungalow of the other uncle and his wife, Kitty – the uncle who was a hall-porter. October was the date given for the completion of the extra seventy-five bungalows. Liverpool wasn't bad. Declan was working in the bacon factory. She was working herself, in another Woolworth's basement.

Joanna wrote less. She didn't refer to herself, but asked if Elizabeth had recovered and hoped she had. Elizabeth replied at length, referring to Henry's death and saying that Jennifer was to be a rat in *Noye's Fludde*, and that Mr Orvitski had come to mend the washing-machine and that she liked him. She didn't reply to Sylvie's letter, although Sylvie had said she'd like to hear from her. She'd write later on, she decided, when she felt more up to it. She smiled over the letter, imagining Sylvie and Declan married, and imagining no more. She'd buy them something for a wedding present, she resolved, and eventually decided on an electric kettle. She bought one one morning on the way back from taking the children to school. She asked the man to send it to an address in Liverpool and wrote a short message to go with it, adding that she'd write a letter soon.

Often she found herself staring at the two rectangles on the drawing-room wall where the Persian miniatures had hung. She wished they were still there because they'd been there for so long. She didn't like the dark, blank spaces, and looked about the house for other pictures that would cover them. She couldn't find anything suitable.

She didn't walk by the river, although there were times, particularly on sunny days, when she'd have liked to. She felt she hadn't the strength yet to look at Harrods Depository, any more than she'd ever have the strength again to walk into the Casa Peppino at lunchtime. She told Mrs Orvitski that there was no need for her to continue coming every day, and was glad when this routine ceased because she quite liked it in the empty house when the children were at school. There was something pleasant about standing at the top of the stairs and looking down through the gloom, to the hall below. There was something pleasant about just walking about with a cup of coffee in your hand. It was to do with being an invalid. She didn't want to stop being an invalid; she didn't want anything to replace her moodlessness.

'Mrs Aidallbery?'

She hadn't meant to answer the telephone. She wouldn't have answered it if she hadn't been passing it when it rang. It had rung several times already that day and she hadn't bothered with it.

'Mrs Aidallbery, it's Miss Samson.'

'Hullo, Miss Samson.'

'Now, Mrs Aidallbery, I want you to come to tea. Remember, Mrs Aidallbery? Number Nine, Balaclava Avenue?'

Elizabeth didn't want to go to tea. She didn't want to sit in the sitting-room she'd heard so much about, with its cosy-stove and the Reverend Rawes's own special armchair. She didn't feel up to continuing the hospital conversations she'd had with Miss Samson, hearing about Mr Ibbs and the dreams that had upset Miss Samson, and the Seaview Hotel, Bexhill.

'Tea's difficult with the children,' she began. 'They're home from school at teatime.'

'Elevenses,' Miss Samson said. 'Come for coffee on Wednesday, Mrs Aidallbery.'

She still didn't want to, but she couldn't bring herself to think up another excuse.

'That's very kind of you, Miss Samson.'

For four days she worked, with sprigs of wood anemone in a jam-jar on the kitchen table. She drew the outlines of the leaves and the perianth segments so lightly that her pencil-marks were scarcely visible, an operation that reminded her of her need for spectacles. She bought new water-colours and mixed a pale mauveine pink. When she'd finished, she began all over again, putting the sprigs of wood anemone in a vase and replacing them with marsh marigolds. In her two pictures the flowers were suspended on the blankness of the paper; the jam-jar didn't show.

When the pictures were finished, she rolled them up and took them to be framed in a shop in Putney, opposite the police station.

Bach was playing in the shop, on a tape-recorder or a cassette. A paperbacked copy of *Crime and Punishment* was open on the glass-topped counter. A man from an artists' materials firm was taking orders for paintbrushes. Two students were buying paper and boxes of pastels. The framing would be ready in ten days.

In the kitchen she made pancakes. They were French pancakes, she told the children, *crêpes*, different from English, with crushed macaroons and cream and a tablespoonful of brandy. She remembered Mr Feuchtwanger telling her about a pancake shop in Paris, a tiny room where an elderly woman cooked *crêpes* in a most ceremonial manner, on a griddle over a round black stove. She told the children about this. The room was so small that only three people could fit in it. Other people, customers for *crêpes*, had to wait on the street.

Elizabeth couldn't remember where this pancake shop precisely was. 'Somewhere in St Germain des Prés,' she said. 'A nice part of Paris.' Jennifer said that one day she intended to go there, to St Germain des Prés and to the pancake shop. 'Remember, you have to let the pancake mixture stand for an hour,' Elizabeth said, 'and then add the brandy.'

'He sounds so nice, Mr Feuchtwanger,' Alice said, 'knowing about a pancake shop.'

Jennifer watched while Elizabeth added the eggs, one at a time. 'He's dead, isn't he?' she said.

Yes, Mr Feuchtwanger was dead. There'd been a Mrs Feuchtwanger, she remembered, a shadowy, faded figure in Mr Feuchtwanger's house. 'He was very thin and very tall,' she said, and then she described Miss Middlesmith with her plump moon face. At school Tricia Hatchett said that Miss Middlesmith had once had a romance, with a man who'd died the morning he was to marry her. But no one believed this except Tricia Hatchett. Di Troughton pretended to.

'Miss Middlesmith's dead, too,' Jennifer said.

'Yes.'

'Like poor old Henry,' Alice said.

'Yes.'

'Tell us about the time you and Jean Friar bathed without any clothes on.'

She told them how one hot July afternoon she and Jean Friar had bathed in a stream called the Uff, how Di Troughton had suddenly appeared in the undergrowth with her camera. She told them again about the wartime evacuation of her school to this part of Gloucester-

252

shire, to Swanning Court; about Miss Ponsonby, the headmistress, and the eventual return to London. She hadn't seen Henry during all those years. They must have been fourteen when they met again. 'A new and repellent habit,' Miss Ponsonby had said in the hall of Swanning Court. 'Please have nothing to do with it. Unhygienic and distasteful. Tampons, I understand, they're called.'

'No one'd mind now if you bathed without any clothes on,' Alice said. 'People are always stripping down.'

'Oh, don't be silly, Alice.' Jennifer went red, stirring the pancake mixture.

'Strip clubs, Jennifer. Pictures in the papers. Don't be silly yourself.'

'It was a little different then,' Elizabeth said.

'Tell us about the time Miss Ponsonby stopped everyone playing tennis. Don't touch that, Alice,' Jennifer said, putting the pancake mixture on the windowsill.

No one was allowed to play tennis, Miss Ponsonby said, until the girl who had been seen talking to an American soldier came forward and identified herself. 'I have repeatedly told you girls,' Miss Ponsonby said. 'On no account reply if an American soldier addresses you. On no account smile. Walk straight on, please.'

'It was a French girl, wasn't it?' Jennifer said.

'Joëlle. But she never owned up. I can't remember her other name.'

'She sounds a tartar, that Miss Ponsonby,' Alice said.

'I love the taste of brandy,' Jennifer said when they ate the pancakes. Afterwards, in her bath, Alice pretended to be drunk.

She collected her framed pictures and hung them over the dark rectangles where the miniatures had been. She was glad she'd gone to all that trouble because the dark rectangles had caught your eye every time you entered the drawing-room, and if you were sitting there your glance was drawn to them.

She went to see her mother again. Her mother had finished *Bleak House* and was now reading *The Mill on the Floss* again. She talked about Tom and Maggie and St Ogg's and Mrs Tulliver's curls and cap-strings. In moments of boredom, she reminded Elizabeth, Maggie read the dictionary.

Mr Redborn came to give the grass its first cutting. She turned down an invitation to go to dinner with people called the Coffeys. She found herself avoiding Mrs Orvitski, going into other rooms, going out sometimes when Mrs Orvitski came. She poured Mr Redborn's tea and called to him, and left it for him on the edge of the grass. One morning she found herself pulling the curtains in the house to keep the sunlight out.

'Can't wait,' Alice said. 'Five more days.'

'What happens in five days?'

'Oh, Mummy!'

She sat in the drawing-room in a state of panic. It was the first feeling to break her moodlessness, the first feeling she was aware of since she'd wished not to be alive at the time of her setback. It was one thing to exist for two children, to have all day to prepare for their return, to spend a few hours with them and then to be alone again in the dark house. It was entirely another thing to exist for two children who were there beside you all day long. In five days' time the Easter holidays would begin.

Elizabeth sat for an hour in one of the blue-striped armchairs, still wearing the coat she'd come into the house in after driving them to school. Children could be sent away to camps. Other parents often did that, at Easter or in the summer especially. But it would be too late now to arrange any of that. If she telephoned, she'd find that camp after camp was booked up, and that would be depressing. She wondered if Evie would have them. She could telephone Evie and say she'd only been out of hospital a few weeks and didn't feel at all up to the Easter holidays. Evie's children didn't get on with hers, but it wouldn't matter for a fortnight.

'Good morning, Mrs Aidallbery,' Mrs Orvitski called out in the hall, and when she heard her voice Elizabeth immediately thought what a much better idea it would be to ask Mrs Orvitski to live in again. There was no reason why Leopold shouldn't come, too. She'd have suggested that he should while she'd been in hospital, except that she'd never thought of it. It would make it easier for Mrs Orvitski having her husband in the house, and there were even things that Leopold could mend, like the clothes pulley over the bath and the garage doors. He was always happier, as Mrs Orvitski said, when he was mending things.

'Hullo, Mrs Orvitski,' she called out, still sitting in the blue-striped chair. 'I'll be with you in a minute.'

She didn't know where she'd go, some quiet hotel maybe. She thought about it, imagining it happening and not seeing any snags. She knew it would be all right because when she'd thought of a quiet hotel the feeling of panic had immediately left her. In a hotel she'd sit alone in her room. She'd go for a walk when the maid was doing

254

out the room, and when she returned she'd be alone until it was lunchtime and she could pull the curtains over. She'd save *The Times* up: the home news and the foreign news at breakfast, the letters about shirt-buttons at lunch, the Personal columns for dinner.

'Mrs Orvitski, d'you think you could possibly live in again for ten days or a fortnight? Your husband, too,' she hastily added, as Mrs Orvitski's face betrayed more than surprise.

'Leopold?'

'During the Easter holidays. I think I should maybe go away. Your husband could mend things. There really are quite a lot of things.'

'But the children in the holidays are in here all day long. The children are not at the school.' Mrs Orvitski's voice was excited; her fingers played uneasily with the apron she was wearing.

Elizabeth smiled reassuringly. She would leave the children lots to do, she said. Their friends would invite them to tea. She'd arrange that. They'd go out to tea almost every single day.

'Please, Mrs Orvitski,' she said, and smiled again and went away. It was the morning she was to visit Miss Samson.

'A very nice thing,' Miss Samson said. 'Edward Tonsell has proposed to Carol.'

It was the first thing she said after she'd greeted Elizabeth and shown her the framed embroidery in the hall and brought her upstairs to show her the other one, *Strength groweth from affliction*.

'The wedding's set for June the fourth,' Miss Samson said. 'It's really lovely.'

Mrs Delve was out. So was the Reverend Rawes, exercising someone's dog.

'A Monday,' Miss Samson continued, and added that Carol Pidsley didn't intend to go in for a slap-up wedding. An amber-coloured gown, and lilies of the valley.

Somewhere in Gloucestershire, she thought. She'd always liked Gloucestershire, ever since her schooldays, not that the schooldays themselves had been all that enjoyable. Even before she'd ever gone there she'd liked the sound of Gloucestershire, the word itself. 'The Gloucesters,' her mother used to say, speaking of the Duke and Duchess.

'Now do draw up,' Miss Samson insisted in the sitting-room, opening the doors of the cosy-stove. 'Excuse me, dear, a minute.'

She went away and returned with a tray that contained an electric kettle, milk, sugar and a tin of Nescafé. She went away again and returned with a plate of scones. The room was very warm.

'I hope you enjoyed Bexhill,' Elizabeth said. 'You're looking much better.'

'I feel better,' Miss Samson agreed, spooning Nescafé into Elizabeth's cup. 'Tell me when.'

'That's lovely, thanks.'

'Now please have butter on that scone.' She poured boiling water on to the coffee.

'Thank you very much.'

'And milk and sugar?'

'Thank you.'

'Well, this *is* nice.'

'It's very kind of you.'

'I had a card from Miss Clapper. She married her boyfriend. She's taking instruction. Isn't that lovely?'

'Yes, I heard all that, too. Yes, it is nice.'

'I sent her a word from Bexhill. And little Mrs Drucker. And Sister O'Keeffe, of course. I wrote you a card, too, Mrs Aidallbery, but I didn't post it. I have it here.'

Miss Samson handed her a stamped postcard with a brown and white reproduction of the esplanade at Bexhill-on-Sea on it. *Hope you're recovering*, a message said. *It's mild as summer here.* Elizabeth murmured appreciatively and handed the card back. Another ten minutes and then she'd get up and go.

'No, no. Keep it, please.'

Elizabeth smiled and murmured again. She wondered why she hadn't been sent this card. Miss Samson said:

'I didn't send it because I thought I'd rather invite you to tea, Mrs Aidallbery. Or elevenses, as it turns out. I found it hard to write what I wanted to say. Even in a letter.'

'Yes, it sometimes is –'

'I couldn't pray, you know.'

'You told me, Miss Samson.'

'That's why I wanted you to come to tea. No one here knows, Mrs Aidallbery, except Mr Rawes. I told no other person except yourself, the day you were troubled by your friend's death. I told you because I wanted to comfort you and couldn't. I couldn't offer you anything at all.'

'Oh no, no. You were kind to me that day.'

'I didn't tell Mr Rawes about Mr Ibbs's diary. I never will. I'll never tell anyone else.'

'It's best to forget these things.'

'You can't, of course.'

'No, I suppose you can't.'

'It was finding the diary and then the upset of leaving Number Nine. Every night since I was seventeen I've gone to bed in Number Nine. You get used to a place and all it means to you.' Miss Samson laughed. 'The churchiness of it.'

'Yes.'

'You get used to the feeling of prayer around you. It's hard to manage in a different atmosphere.'

'Your faith came back, Miss Samson?'

To Elizabeth's surprise, Miss Samson shook her head. She offered Elizabeth the plate of scones, shaking her head again. She said:

'It's not the same. It'll never be the same again. I was in love with Mr Ibbs, Mrs Aidallbery.'

Elizabeth took another scone because it was something to do. She cut it open and smeared butter on the two pieces.

'Mr Ibbs was everything to me, Mrs Aidallbery. Even in death that continued.'

'I see.'

'When I was a child I realized I was different from other people. I would not marry, I realized, because no man would want me. Until just recently, Mrs Aidallbery, I didn't realize that I'd fallen in love with Mr Ibbs all those years ago. I didn't know that that was what it had been.'

Elizabeth ate part of the scone. She drank some Nescafé.

'I thought it was something to do with God,' Miss Samson said. 'Mr Ibbs seemed to be God's chosen person in this house. Because I'm religious, I suppose I thought it had all to do with that. Do you understand me?'

'Yes, of course.'

'But now it's different. Now God is on one side and Mr Ibbs is on the other.'

Miss Samson smiled at her, but Elizabeth didn't want this conversation to continue. She felt it didn't concern her, all this detail about Mr Ibbs and God. She remarked on the weather.

'I suppose you think it's laughable,' Miss Samson said. 'People like us, all that churchiness. I daresay I'm laughable myself.'

'I don't think you're laughable, Miss Samson.'

257

' "Hell is confusion," Mr Ibbs once said in a sermon in St Matthew's, "where a father destroys his sons and the buds of spring wither as they bloom." Every twist of the garden worm, Mr Ibbs said, was part of God's desire. Look, Mrs Aidallbery.'

Miss Samson rose and took from a table in the window a small, black diary. 'It's an earlier one of his. Look.'

Elizabeth read an entry, for a Tuesday in September, 1931. *She has an artificial eye and is hideously marked on the left side of her face. Yet it is better that she has entered into life a good woman with one eye rather than sin and be cast into hellfire. God has greatly blessed her.*

'Yes,' Elizabeth said, returning the diary.

'He left the diaries for us to peruse, for me and for whatever inmates came afterwards to his house. But he hid the last one in the hat-box, maybe intending to burn it before he died. Death came on him quickly.'

The black diary was returned to the table in the window, and Elizabeth noticed that there were other diaries in a pile there, in different colours.

'The Tonsell brothers are going to print them one day.'

Miss Samson went on speaking. She referred to her own past, to the time she'd first come to work in the house, and what she'd thought of Mr Ibbs when he'd first interviewed her in the kitchen. She spoke of other people who had lived in the house, all of them regular in their attendance at St Matthew's. She told anecdotes that related to people Elizabeth had never heard of before.

Elizabeth nodded now and again, imagining herself walking about the Gloucestershire countryside. She remembered the names of the villages: Upper Quinton, Offenham, Pillerton Priors. She wondered what had become of Swanning Court. In April the meadow saxifrage would be out, and speedwell and henbell and Jerusalem sage. If she was near enough, she might go and look at Swanning Court.

'Sometimes He's there,' Miss Samson said, 'and sometimes He isn't. Sometimes I'm certain when I pray and sometimes I keep seeing Mr Ibbs instead. All the loveliness has gone.' Miss Samson smiled sorrowfully.

'I see,' Elizabeth said. She didn't know what Miss Samson was talking about. 'Loveliness?' she said, politely taking part.

'The wound of doubting is the worst thing of all for a Christian.' Miss Samson touched her face. 'This isn't a wound at all.'

She hadn't drunk her Nescafé, Elizabeth noticed. She hadn't had a scone. Her bad eye stared awkwardly from the crimson side of her

258

face, her good one was faintly troubled. Her grey hair was neat with hairpins.

'You must come and meet the children some time.' Elizabeth said. 'I'm going away for a little. When I get back I'll ring you up.'

'Mrs Aidallbery, have you ever thought about that woman with the banner? The woman outside the hospital?'

Elizabeth frowned. She hadn't thought much about the woman, she admitted, but added that of course she remembered her, a woman in red trousers. Miss Samson interrupted her.

'I spoke to her as I was leaving. If ever you're passing that hospital, Mrs Aidallbery, look into that woman's eyes: they're full of bitterness.'

'Bitterness?'

'Oh, they are. That woman has suffered once.'

'Well, yes, maybe she has –'

'A husband perhaps. A lover, Mrs Aidallbery? A father? Some casual man, which is why she walks outside a women's hospital. Men and women do tend to hurt each other.'

'Yes, they do.'

'I thought of her in Bexhill. I thought what a terrible thing it was that a woman should have been so much hurt that she decided to walk up and down a London street with a banner. Day after day, Mrs Aidallbery.'

'I really must be getting on, I think. I've shopping to do and –'

'Please don't go, Mrs Aidallbery.'

'It's just that shopping takes so long, I find. I seem to be still moving more slowly than before. D'you find that?'

'In Bexhill I thought of Lady Augusta, too. You remember Lady Augusta, Mrs Aidallbery?'

'Well, yes, I do, but –'

'Her husband didn't ever love her. She discovered that quite early in her marriage. You remember how she reveals it towards the end? How she lived with it?'

Elizabeth stood up, but Miss Samson did not. Miss Samson asked her not to go for another five minutes.

Elizabeth sat down again. An image of a hotel had come into her mind a moment ago, a warm building in Cotswold stone, low and snug beneath a hill. There was a large expanse of grass in front of it, and a pond. It was famous, she seemed to think, for its home-made soups and raspberry-sponge pudding. She must have read about it, or someone must have told her.

259

'If you read the autobiography carefully you'll see that she realized he didn't love her one day in June, about a year after their marriage. She was pregnant at the time.' Miss Samson paused. 'I didn't go alone to Bexhill.'

'You went with friends, Miss Samson?'

Miss Samson shook her head. 'I don't mean that,' she said. 'It was just that I couldn't stop thinking of the woman outside the hospital. And Lady Augusta, and you, and Miss Clapper, and little Mrs Drucker.'

Elizabeth stared at Miss Samson in astonishment. Miss Samson was different. She wasn't like she'd been in hospital, not even when she'd been upset. Her hands gripped one another, the left made tightly into a fist, the right clenched around it, the knuckles unnaturally white.

'I cried,' Miss Samson said. 'I used to walk along the promenade at Bexhill, Mrs Aidallbery, and I couldn't stop crying.'

Again Elizabeth was astonished. She was aware, as well, that the panic she'd felt when Alice had reminded her of the Easter holidays had returned. As though in a scene from a film, she saw herself moving silently from room to room in her house, pulling the curtains in the daytime. She saw herself putting Mr Redborn's tea on the edge of the grass in a careful invalid's way, and quietly calling out to him. All that was going to cease now. You went out to have coffee with someone and it began to cease almost immediately. You couldn't bring it back by hiding in a hotel.

'I really must go now,' she said again. Her voice was shaky. Her lips trembled in a way they used to when she was a child, when she was angry. She stood up and held out her hand, but Miss Samson did not take it. Miss Samson had still not drunk her Nescafé.

'Please sit down, Mrs Aidallbery.'

'I must go. I don't understand what you're talking about, Miss Samson –'

'Please.'

She sat down slowly. 'I'm trying to live quietly,' she said. 'I don't really want to talk like this. I just want to look after the children, to put things in the washing-machine and take them out again, to weed the garden –'

'Lady Augusta Haptree had a miserable life.'

'In her book she says she didn't.'

'I don't care what she says,' Miss Samson cried, with sudden vehemence. 'She founded that hospital because she had to make a

260

gesture from her misery, because she wanted other women to know they weren't forgotten. Just like the woman with the banner.'

'We neither of us know the woman with the banner, Miss Samson. She presumably belongs to the Women's Liberation movement. It's quite common nowadays for women to make protests –'

'Two people stopped me on the promenade at Bexhill to ask me if I knew where Sackville Road was. A man and a woman. It upset them to see that I was crying.' Her voice was agitated. She paused, controlling it, and then continued. 'They thought I was maybe crying because of my ugliness. I could see them thinking that it wasn't an ordinary ugliness. I'm used to seeing that thought in people's faces, Mrs Aidallbery.'

'Miss Samson –'

'They thought I'd become depressed, all by myself on a windy day at Bexhill-on-Sea. They were kind people, and it disturbed them. So I told them what it was.'

The panic settled, and in a quieter form remained with her: without fuss, the old feeling of guilt was there again. While Miss Samson talked crazily about the promenade at Bexhill-on-Sea, she felt guilty that she'd ever wanted to leave her children in the Easter holidays, and guilty that she'd ever crept to the bathroom with a cup of tea when Alice was calling her. She was a bad mother, she mechanically said to herself.

Miss Samson continued to talk with urgency, as though all she said was important. She leaned closer to Elizabeth, her good eye pressing into Elizabeth's face, her mouth rapidly opening and closing. Words flowed over Elizabeth. Sentences fell apart because Elizabeth didn't properly listen. Only names slipped through to her. 'Little Mrs Drucker,' Miss Samson said. 'Miss Clapper. Yourself, Mrs Aidallbery. I told two people on a promenade.'

'Yes, I see.'

'I described to them,' Miss Samson said, 'the woman with the banner, and the bitterness in her eyes. I told them how I couldn't forget Lady Augusta's loveless marriage and Lady Augusta making the best of things, founding a hospital. The wind blew rain into our faces as we stood there on the promenade. I felt it extraordinary that I should be talking like that to strangers, explaining my tears away, and yet of course it wasn't extraordinary at all. D'you understand, Mrs Aidallbery?'

'What?'

'The people who asked me where Sackville Road was: was it extraordinary to tell them all that?'

261

'I'm afraid I don't understand anything you're talking about, Miss Samson.'

'It's because you're not listening,' Miss Samson cried. She leaned closer still to Elizabeth, pushing herself foward to the edge of her chair. Unsuccessfully, she tried to calm herself. 'I want you to listen to me,' she cried. 'I've asked you here to tell you, Mrs Aidallbery. You're not listening to a word I say.'

'You talked to strangers about me and Lily Drucker and Sylvie, and Lady Augusta Haptree and a woman we none of us know. It's just that I don't understand why.' There was irritation in her voice, the first irritation that had been there for a long time now. Hearing it, she felt angry that her pleasant, invalid state was ending in this ridiculous manner. 'I think you're being morbid and gloomy, Miss Samson,' she said with greater irritation.

'Yes, yes, I know I am. It's what happens, don't you see, when your faith goes? Hell begins, Mrs Aidallbery. Don't you see?' She cried out loudly, as though in pain. Tears shone on her cheeks. 'That man who came to see Miss Clapper, that Mr Maloney. He took charity from Mr Rawes and other people here, pretending he was going to buy clothes. He said he was from the St Vincent de Paul.'

'He's a kind of crook, Miss Samson. Sylvie told us –'

'Why should he be a crook? Why should he take ten p from Carol? And where was Miss Clapper's boyfriend all that time?'

'In gaol,' Elizabeth said harshly. And since Miss Samson was going in for gloom, she began to say that Lily Drucker couldn't reconcile herself to her husband's habits in the past, and that she herself had hoped she might die. She opened her mouth to say all this, but noticed as she did so that there were further tears on Miss Samson's cheeks. She said instead:

'You're upsetting yourself, Miss Samson. There's no need –'

'Of course there's a need!' Miss Samson was suddenly shrieking, still sitting in her chair, her hands still gripping one another. She panted, and when she closed her mouth Elizabeth could hear her teeth chattering.

'It isn't fair!' Miss Samson shrieked, spitting the words out so violently that Elizabeth felt a soft spray of saliva on her cheek. 'Why does He make it so hard for people? Why create His silly world in the first place? What kind of a thing is He?'

'Miss Samson –'

'When people get old,' Miss Samson interrupted again, though in a slower, calmer voice, 'they often turn quite nasty. Did you know that,

Mrs Aidallbery? The nicest gentlest people become quite nasty. Or they become like babies, without much of a mind. Did you know, Mrs Aidallbery, that when people become very old they sometimes speak in a language of their own, inventing words just like a child of three? There's a medical word for it, actually.'

'Miss Samson, this has nothing to do with anything –'

'He plays that ugly little trick on us. He gives us human cruelty. And people throwing bombs about. Your friend drinking whisky and gassing himself. Little Mrs Drucker abandoned as an infant to a home. Miss Clapper's parents not caring a fig about her. Your own father, Mrs Aidallbery, whom you didn't like. And Arthur born backward and with multiple sclerosis.'

Miss Samson sat back in her chair with her eyes closed, and Elizabeth could see that she was trying to pray. When she spoke again, her voice was low and sad, as though the room they sat in was filled with some unbearable anguish.

'He permits all that. You remember it when your faith's in doubt. Floods and earthquakes. And marriages between two people He calls His children, in which everything goes wrong. Men murder their wives, and wives their husbands. Will it be like that for Carol? I wondered in Bexhill. Will Carol lie in a deep-freeze, undiscovered for four weeks?'

'Miss Samson, please –'

'Or will Carol end like Mrs Aidallbery? I wondered to myself. Divorced and alone, looking back on her mistakes? With a daughter gone on to drugs?'

'Miss Samson, I'm perfectly certain Carol will be all right. And I must tell you that I'm all right myself. We're all all right: Lily Drucker and Sylvie and myself. And I'm certain that the woman with the banner –'

'One day your children will grow up and you'll find yourself alone, with nothing to comfort you except faces on a television set. Your mother'll be long since dead, and there'll be no husband to help you on your way. One day little Mrs Drucker's father-in-law will die also, and her mother-in-law will come and live with them, because that's the way it always happens. She'll last to the healthy age that He in His mercy grants her, becoming more difficult with every passing minute. One day Miss Clapper's boyfriend won't return from his bacon factory, and not long afterwards Miss Clapper'll be a woman in a courtroom, crying out when she hears a sentence passed. In Bexhill-on-Sea I thought about all that.'

Elizabeth did not say anything. Miss Samson said:

263

'I wanted it to be all different, I wanted miracles to happen. I wanted you not to have married the man you did. I wanted you to be married to someone nice, not worrying on your own, not blaming yourself any more. I wanted Miss Clapper suddenly to be rich, and her husband to undergo a character change. I wanted time to turn backwards so that Lady Augusta wouldn't have had to make do with a loveless marriage. I wanted the woman to put away her banner and forget whatever it was. I wanted little Mrs Drucker's mother-in-law to kneel down and ask forgiveness of her. I wanted your friend to be still alive and somehow to find happiness.'

'But, Miss Samson –'

'That's why I cried, Mrs Aidallbery. On the windy promenade I told those two strangers about Mr Maloney, and people throwing bombs, and little Mrs Drucker, and Arthur born backward. "Mr Maloney's deprived," I said. "Maimed and deprived, like little Mrs Drucker's mother-in-law. Mr Maloney perhaps never knew love. Perhaps He in His infinite mercy again forgot one of His children." I went on talking, and the woman suddenly asked me who Mr Maloney was. Little Mrs Drucker did not concern them, the man said. Nor did you, Mrs Aidallbery, nor Miss Clapper, nor Lady Augusta, nor the other women. Those two people didn't want to understand. They'd been so kindly at first, but after a time they looked at me with hatred in their faces because I was speaking the truth. I told them about your friend lying dead on a kitchen floor. "I think she's mad," I heard the woman whisper, and then they walked away. Extremely crossly they walked away, Mrs Aidallbery, a man in a waterproof coat and a woman with a small umbrella.'

There was silence in the room.

'I'm sorry,' Elizabeth said.

'No, no.'

'I'm sorry you were upset.'

'All I wanted to tell you was that I felt better after I'd met those people on the promenade. Even though they walked away.'

'It often helps to blurt things out.'

'I went into a church and sat in a pew at the back. It was cold and silent there, quite late in the afternoon. I thought God spoke to me. I wasn't sure, Mrs Aidallbery, but I thought He did. I thought God tried to comfort me because I'd become so agitated.' She paused. 'I asked you to come here because I wanted to tell you that. I didn't want anyone to go on thinking of me as a faithless person.'

'I won't think of you as faithless.'

'I thought He was explaining to me, Mrs Aidallbery, but I couldn't quite hear Him. I don't know if I'll ever hear Him properly again.'

Miss Samson blew her nose. She stirred her cold Nescafé, and then lifted the cup to her lips and drank from it. Neither of them said anything for several minutes. Then Miss Samson plugged in the electric kettle.

'I make do,' she said. 'The doubt comes, and then it goes away again. At least it goes away. There's that to be cheerful about.'

Miss Samson smiled, forcing the smile on to her face. She insisted that Elizabeth should have another cup of Nescafé before she went. She told Elizabeth that there'd been a time in her life, long before she'd come to work in the kitchen of Number Nine, when she'd been given to depression and the kind of hysterical outburst that had taken place on the promenade at Bexhill, and again that morning.

'It's just that sometimes now I can't stop thinking about unhappy people. And I suppose the people I came across in hospital were nearest at hand to brood on.'

'But, Miss Samson, we're just ordinary women. We're not particularly unhappy.'

'Oh, I know it's stupid of me, my dear.' She gave a little laugh. 'Drink it while it's hot.'

Elizabeth drank more Nescafé. She said again that the women Miss Samson had come across in the Cheltenham Street Women's Hospital, including the one who was dead and the one who was a stranger, had lives that should not be wept over. The woman with the banner retained the spirit to make her eccentric protest, and in a spirited way also Lady Augusta Haptree had built a hospital with her husband's money. And Sylvie and Lily Drucker and she herself would manage. She wanted to add, but could not, that the lives of these five women contained no tragedy to compare with the comfort so savagely torn from Miss Samson's own life.

'I'll always feel for those women,' Miss Samson said, 'because I came across them at this particular time, I daresay. "Please help Miss Clapper," I'll always pray, as best I can. And for little Mrs Drucker I'll pray as well. I'll pray for you, Mrs Aidallbery, that maybe in the end you'll find yourself most happily married.'

Elizabeth tried to laugh, but found it difficult. Miss Samson was serious.

'Miracles do happen, you know,' Miss Samson said. 'And even shaky prayer might perhaps be answered. Please do have another scone.'

265

Elizabeth shook her head. In the warm sitting-room the compassion of Miss Samson affected her, and seemed extraordinary. She felt ashamed that she'd so rudely tried to leave after only ten minutes, and that she'd then become irritated and had spoken unpleasantly. The compassion of Miss Samson bewildered Elizabeth. It felt precious in the warm sitting-room, yet it also seemed unnatural, as if it were part of a miracle itself.

Wanting to say more, wanting to be dramatic and emotional in her response to Miss Samson, Elizabeth said she was sorry she hadn't listened properly at first to what Miss Samson had been saying. The words sounded flat and irrelevant. She said she was glad Miss Samson had invited her. She said she felt honoured to have seen the house they'd all heard so much about.

'Good heavens,' Miss Samson protested, 'I've been an awful bore.' She apologized for becoming so agitated. 'I'm grateful to you, Mrs Aidallbery,' she said. 'I had to tell someone. Thank you for listening.'

'Oh no, no.'

Miss Samson nodded and smiled her difficult smile. 'Thank you,' she said again, and in silence Elizabeth watched her finishing her second cup of Nescafé. In her hospital bed Miss Samson had not seemed extraordinary. She'd seemed a normal woman with a small misfortune, going on a bit about the house she lived in.

'You want to go now,' Miss Samson, said, and rose and led the way to the hall. 'Goodbye, Mrs Aidallbery.'

She stood with the door open, with her right hand on the Yale latch. Her bad eye stared, the other had the same troubled light in it.

'You did hear, I suppose,' she said, 'that little Mrs Drucker's child was born?'

'No. No, I hadn't heard.'

'There's that, too, to be cheerful about.' Miss Samson smiled at Elizabeth and shook her hand.

Elizabeth drove for fifteen minutes and then she parked the car and walked away from it. She walked through suburban roads, into busier streets. Other women were shopping, queuing at large greengrocers', coming out of butchers'. In the glass of a wine merchant's window she saw her face reflected, thinner even than it had been, still pale after her operation, a twitchy kind of face, she thought again. Bottles of V.P. Wine stood in a pyramid, Regency Cream, labels with *R.S.V.P.* on them.

She walked on, past a cinema and a Woolworth's, which made her think of Sylvie for a moment. She should go into a baby shop and buy something for Lily, except that she didn't know whether the baby was a boy or a girl, not that it mattered much. She walked by Mac Fisheries and Dolcis, and Marks and Spencer's, and the British Home Stores and Littlewoods. Girls came out of an employment bureau that promised to find them exciting positions as temporary secretaries. *Start Living!* a sign in the window said. Women read magazines in a launderette.

Elizabeth turned away from this morning busyness, on to the embankment, and on past boatyards, to the towpath. The sun was shining, but the river didn't gleam. On murky water a lone rower shot ahead in short bursts of speed; crowds pointed from a pleasure steamer. There was the sound of a circular saw and the smell of varnish. She walked on, past playing fields on her left. In the distance Harrods Depository looked bleak.

She sat on a seat. A golden retriever bounded up to her and was whistled at by a man. In Number Nine Miss Samson would continue in her deception that Mr Ibbs had died as he had lived. She'd go on smiling as best she could, polishing the glass of the embroideries, and the walking-stick that had once been owned by Mr Ibbs's great-grand-father. On 4 June Carol Pidsley would marry Edward Tonsell, and two other Church folk would take their places because there were always Church folk at Number Nine. Arthur wouldn't live long, Miss Samson once had said in the ward, which was why she tried to be kind to him. Struggling against depression and hysteria, she'd go on trying.

'For heaven's sake, come back, Larry!' the man shouted at his golden retriever. 'I'm sorry,' he said, for the dog was again bounding at her. 'Can't think what's got into him this morning.'

'It doesn't matter,' she said.

She'd thought a week ago, a day ago even, that she'd never bring herself to walk on the towpath again because of its scattered memories. But she walked now, past Harrods Depository, past the spot where Henry had once found a pound. She thought of Daphne, as she'd guessed she would on the towpath. She thought of Henry. The guilt she felt was the same as ever. If she went on thinking, she knew that other faces would slide about her mind, and the guilt that accompanied them would pointlessly slide about also. Yet for a reason she didn't understand, the unnatural compassion of Miss Samson made her feel happy, like Mr Feuchtwanger and Miss Middlesmith had made her feel happy because they'd been happy themselves, and Miss Digg because of her kindness, and her mother because of her gentleness, and Henry because he'd been jolly, and Di Troughton and Evie Faste because they thought everything was a party.

On her honeymoon in Crete she'd said she thought Mr Feuchtwanger had given her strength. She'd felt embarrassed, saying that, and had blushed. When he hadn't replied she'd assumed that he was thinking over what she'd said. They'd all given her strength, she'd continued in the same embarrassed way, all the people whom she thought of as special. She'd spoken timidly, wanting him to tell her if there could be any truth in what she was saying, or if it was all rubbish. He hadn't said anything, but after a moment he'd given a short, characteristic laugh and had patted her on the shoulder. 'Poor silly thing!' he'd have said if Miss Samson had come to tea one Sunday. 'What nonsense she talked!'

She turned and walked back to the street with the shops in it and then through the suburban roads, to where she'd parked her car. In her house she explained to Mrs Orvitski that she had changed her mind, that she wouldn't go away for the Easter holidays. When Mrs Orvitski had gone she sat alone in her kitchen, still thinking about Miss Samson, seeing her face, and the grey hair made neat with hairpins.

There was *Noye's Fludde* and then the holidays. One week was wet, the other fine. The holidays were just like other Easter holidays. Elizabeth and her children went to Chessington Zoo and the Safari Park at Windsor, and to a revival of *Snow White and the Seven Dwarfs*. The children had friends to tea and went to tea with the same friends. It wasn't possible to have Daphne's children to tea, which Jennifer understood about. One day, Elizabeth said when Alice asked her, it might be possible again.

A card arrived from Lily saying that the child which had been born to her and Kenneth was a son: Andrew James. Elizabeth bought a blue woollen suit and sent it. She wrote to Lily and she wrote to Sylvie, asking Lily that the baby should be brought to tea and reminding Sylvie that if ever she needed a bed all she had to do was to telephone. She did not mention her visit to Balaclava Avenue because so much of what had been said seemed a private matter between Miss Samson and herself.

Days and then weeks went by. Elizabeth could still see no pattern in her life, and was aware that being affected by the unnatural compassion of a woman she'd met in a hospital had in no way changed the circumstances of her existence. Charged with the spirit of Miss Samson, she did not herself seek an understanding with God, nor did she

268

herself become more compassionate towards distress in other people. But whenever she thought of Miss Samson crying on the promenade over the everyday lives of other women, Elizabeth continued to be moved. And when she thought of Miss Samson making do with so little in Balaclava Avenue she considered that Miss Samson's unnatural compassion was beautiful, like the *Dianthus carthusianorum*.

One night in her bedroom she looked at herself in the mahogany-framed looking-glass just before she put on her nightdress. She'd never understood her body and had never much cared for the sight of it. Yet she couldn't help wondering as she got into her large double-bed if ever again a man would embrace it, if Miss Samson's shaky prayers would perhaps be granted. She didn't mind one way or the other, she said to herself, except that it might be nice to have someone who wasn't boring to chat to before you went to sleep. She pushed herself down in the bed, on to her warm electric blanket, and just before she fell asleep it occurred to her that she'd have been just as embarrassed having to say in the Casa Peppino that other people could give you strength. And she'd have blushed and felt awkward if she'd had to admit that she thought Miss Samson's compassion was beautiful. In the Casa Peppino he wouldn't have laughed and patted her on the shoulder. He'd have listened without wanting to listen. 'Woman's talk,' he might lightly have murmured, dismissing it as he poured more wine. He might have been right: such talk was for Daphne maybe, or Mrs Pamela Vincent, come to that. 'Oh yes, of course,' her mother once had said. 'It's other people who make sense. You never do yourself.'

Elizabeth slept and dreamed of flowers, of cornflowers and poppies and wild succory and paper-bell flowers. She drew them and coloured them, and then drew and coloured the nodding heads of the Turk's cap lily and the *Dianthus carthusianorum*, the Carthusian pink. In her dream she picked cow-parsley on a hot afternoon, walking alone between hedges that were full of it.

On the morning of Wednesday 23 May, a wet day in London, Elizabeth shopped as usual. That morning also Mr Alstrop-Smith set off from Victoria Station for his early-summer holiday, thankful that for the next three weeks, in small Alpine villages, he would not be an important person. In Kensal Green Mr Maloney entered the lodgings of the man to whom, some weeks ago, he had made a loan of fourteen pounds. In the man's absence Mr Maloney removed from the lodgings a suitcase full of clothing, on the grounds that the man's security, a transistor radio, had parts missing.

While Elizabeth bought sausages and butter and biscuits and jellies and spring greens, the woman who had so upset Miss Samson still walked outside the hospital and the hospital itself continued its routine. In their cubbyhole in the hall Pengelly and Frowen discussed a news item in the morning newspapers, a scandal involving the association of a minister of the Crown with call-girls in Maida Vale. In the St Beatrice Ward and the Faith Rowan and the St Ida, women continued to recover from the operations that had been performed on them two days before. Some were moved to the Marie Atkins Ward and to the St Susanna. Still in the St Agnes, Mrs Thring read the facts about the minister and the call-girls and said that in her opinion sex would sicken you. 'Same kind of tricks as Kenneth,' Mrs Drucker remarked to her husband in their terraced house, and Mr Drucker did not reply. Later, however, they both took heart from the news, feeling that if a minister of the Crown consorted with the same kind of women as Kenneth had, they could afford to feel less ashamed.

At twelve o'clock Elizabeth returned to her house with two baskets full of groceries and vegetables. She let herself in and found Joanna in the hall.

'Hullo, Mummy,' Joanna said.

'Hullo, Joanna.'

Once she would have dropped her baskets and hugged her daughter, but now she didn't move. She looked at her and saw that Joanna had a cold and that her teeth had a yellowness about them which they hadn't had before. She listened while Joanna said that she had left Mrs Tabor-Ellis's commune, that she no longer loved Samuel, that she was sorry. 'It doesn't matter,' Elizabeth said.

Joanna cried in the kitchen, going on about the commune, although Elizabeth didn't want to hear about it. A goat had bitten her, she said. Local people had come and thrown bricks through Mrs Tabor-Ellis's windows. Samuel had thrown a chair at a policeman.

Elizabeth made tea and cut slices of bread. She beat up eggs in a bowl, and added butter and salt and pepper, and a little milk. She opened a tin of soup and scrambled the eggs. She reminded Joanna where the tissues were because Joanna kept sniffing.

'I'm sorry about Henry,' Joanna said when she had stopped crying.

'Poor Henry.'

'I'm sorry for what I said about him.'

'It doesn't matter now.'

As well as everything else, Mrs Tabor-Ellis had lesbian tendencies, Joanna said as they ate the soup and scrambled eggs. In this respect,

Mrs Tabor-Ellis had tried to promote the view that all experiment was liberating, but some of the girls in the commune had not wished to be liberated to that extent.

'Your father's married again,' Elizabeth said. 'A Mrs Pamela Vincent. An American person.'

'He came down.'

'I know.'

'Well, perhaps he'll make a go of it this time.' Joanna, whose spirits had risen during the eating of the scrambled eggs, bit a piece from an apple.

'I hope he does. I hope he'll be happy with her.'

When they'd finished, they walked about the garden. Elizabeth showed Joanna the pile Mr Redborn had made of the apple tree he'd sawn. Summer would come and in the autumn they'd have a bonfire, like Mr Giltrap used to have. Mr Redborn would put away the lawn-mower for the winter and wouldn't come back himself until spring. It was nice to think of everything going on, Mr Giltrap and then Mr Redborn, her mother reading *The Mill on the Floss* all over again. One day Jennifer would look for Mr Feuchtwanger's pancake shop in St Germain des Prés. One day Joanna might marry someone and live in this house, and perhaps the house still wouldn't change much. One day they'd all pack her off to a Sunset Home, and Lloyds and the Midland would still race on the Thames, and London would not be much different. The Cheltenham Street Women's Hospital would be there for a bit longer, and Nine Balaclava Avenue, and the room in Shepherd's Bush that Sylvie had illicitly shared with Declan, and the small terraced house where the Druckers' sewing-machines rattled, and Meridian Close. Other drama would develop in all those places. Other women would make do, with the dazzle gone out of their marriages, or on their own because they'd never been dazzled in the first place, or had never been asked, or because things had fallen apart. Other daughters would go away, and return to apologize and forgive, and no doubt go away again. In the King of England other men would drink their way into oblivion. Other lovers would love in the Casa Peppino. Other people would be burnt in the Putney Vale Crematorium.

'One of these days,' Joanna said, 'you should marry again yourself. You sometimes look sad, you know.'

Elizabeth laughed. She knelt to pick some dock from a rose-bed. She was happy enough alone, she said.